TIMEBOMB

Also by James Barrington

OVERKILL
PANDEMIC
FOXBAT

TIMEBOMB

JAMES BARRINGTON

MACMILLAN

First published 2008 by Macmillan
an imprint of Pan Macmillan Ltd
Pan Macmillan, 20 New Wharf Road, London N1 9RR
Basingstoke and Oxford
Associated companies throughout the world
www.panmacmillan.com

ISBN 978-0-230-01473-2 (HB)
ISBN 978-0-230-71449-6 (TPB)

1 3 5 7 9 8 6 4 2

A CIP catalogue record for this book is available from
the British Library.

Typeset by Intype Libra Ltd
Printed and bound in the UK by
CPI Mackays, Chatham ME5 8TD

Acknowledgements

Looking back over my previous books, I've noticed how the same three names have cropped up in the dedication of each one, and with very good reason.

As always, I must thank my friend and agent Luigi Bonomi, principal of LBA, for his constant enthusiasm and encouragement. I've said it before, and I mean it – without him I am nothing. Thanks are also due to the whole team working at Macmillan, and especially to Peter Lavery, one of the most talented and skilful editors working in publishing today, not to mention an excellent companion for a leisurely lunch!

And last but by no means least, Sally, my first and fiercest critic.

James Barrington
Principality of Andorra, 2008

Glossary

ARV   Armed Response Vehicle. Police vehicle carrying weapons in a locked case in the boot. Known within the force as a 'gunship'.

CINCFLEET   Commander-in-Chief Fleet. The most senior operational command in the Royal Navy, subordinate only to the First Sea Lord, with its operational headquarters based at Northwood in Middlesex.

The Company   Slang term for the American Central Intelligence Agency, based at Langley, Virginia.

Double-transposition cipher   A basic but very secure encryption technique involving no special equipment whatsoever, just two memorized key words, each usually containing ten or more letters. The result is a series of groups of four, five or six letters. Cracking this kind of cipher is possible, but extremely difficult without access to complex decryption algorithms running on a supercomputer.

The Doughnut   The new one-billion-pound electronic eavesdropping centre at Government Communications Headquarters (GCHQ) at Cheltenham in Gloucester. So named because that's what it looks like from the air, the building is almost as big as Wembley Stadium. At its core is an underground bomb-proof chamber the size of the Albert Hall that accommodates rows of supercomputers. Some 4,500 specialist staff work in the Doughnut, including linguists fluent in 67 languages.

Echelon   Echelon is a satellite and communications monitoring network jointly run by the USA, the United Kingdom, Australia, New Zealand and Canada, which monitors *all* communications – telephone calls, faxes and digital data streams – that begin, end or pass through these territories. Echelon searches for incriminating words or phrases, these being submitted by some 300 agencies from these five governments, which form the so-called 'Echelon Dictionary'. The Echelon programme is the biggest employer in the American state of Maryland, with over 20,000 people on the payroll, and has a budget that equates to almost one million pounds sterling per *hour*.

FOE Foreign Operations Executive. The organization which employs Paul Richter. Though FOE is fictitious, the concept is not: SIS has always relied heavily on ex-services personnel recruited to carry out deniable operations on its behalf. The generic term used for these recruits is 'The Increment'.

Fort Detrick Established in Maryland in 1943 as the site of the US Biological Laboratories, when it was known as Camp Detrick, during the Second World War, this facility became America's principal biological warfare establishment. It was renamed Fort Detrick in 1956 and continued its work until 1969, when the USA finally signed the 1925 Geneva Protocol banning the use of chemical and biological weapons. Since then, the Fort has been officially involved only in defensive research, but it's a fact that you can only defend against biological and chemical weapons if you either hold or can manufacture the weapons yourself. So Fort Detrick, by default and no matter what official line is taken, is still involved in the biowarfare business.

Four numbers An oblique reference to the Special Group, originally known as the 5412 Committee. See Author's Note.

GSG 9 Formerly known as Grenzschutzgruppe 9 – Border Guards Group 9 – GSG 9 is Germany's elite anti-terrorist organization.

IED Improvised explosive device.

Legoland Slang term for the British Secret Intelligence Service's headquarters at Vauxhall Cross on the bank of the Thames.

SCI Special Compartmentalized Intelligence. In addition to the normal security classifications, there is also a code word clearance system which applies to subjects classified at top secret level and above. The system is known as Special Compartmentalized Intelligence or SCI, and allows knowledge of specific subjects to be restricted to people on a 'need to know' basis, even if their normal security clearance would theoretically give them access. For example, a file classified 'top secret' could be viewed by anyone with a 'top secret' or higher clearance, but not if a specific code word was also applied to the file.

SM or Sierra Mike CIA operations are often given a geographical designator as part of their code name. For example, 'BE' refers to Poland, 'DB' to Iraq, 'DN' to South Korea and 'SM' to the United Kingdom.

UBL Usama bin Laden. Referred to in the UK as Osama bin Laden.

Vauxhall Cross The London headquarters of the British Secret Intelligence Service.

Prologue

Present day; early January; Wednesday
Washington DC

The sudden silence was as eloquent as anything Gregory Stevens could have said. For a few seconds he just stared at the immaculately dressed man sitting on the leather seat beside him, then turned his head to glance out of the heavily tinted side window.

The late-afternoon traffic was moving comparatively freely by Washington's rush-hour standards, and the black Lincoln was making good progress despite the light dusting of snow on the roads. But neither of the two men occupying the back seat behind the driver's partition had the slightest interest in where they were going or even how long it took them to get there.

'This isn't a request, Greg. We need to get this done, and you're the obvious choice.'

Stevens looked back at him and shook his head. 'It's madness. Who the fuck dreamt this one up? Langley's come up with some crackpot schemes before, but whatever idiot put this one together is in a class all to himself.'

'This hasn't come from the Company.'

'Then who? And if it's not from Langley, why are you even talking to me about it?'

'Think of four numbers,' Richard Kellerman said.

Stevens looked blank, then his face changed. 'Five four one two?' he asked, and Kellerman nodded. 'Oh, Jesus. Does the president know about this?'

'You know I can't tell you. That's the whole point. But you can assume that this has been sanctioned at the highest possible level.'

Stevens shook his head. 'I hear what you say, but I still don't believe it. This makes Iran–Contra look like a Little League baseball game.'

'Believe it, Greg. You know the situation we're in. If we don't do this, we could lose all the support we've enjoyed up to now.'

'And if word gets out, our asses will be kicked on a global scale.'

A slight smile crossed Kellerman's face. 'But word won't get out, will it? That's why we've picked you. You've got the languages, and you've got the training and the skills we need.' Then his expression hardened. 'But make no mistake, Greg, this is a wholly deniable operation. You'll have whatever logistical and financial support you need, but we'll drop you like a handful of hot shit if anything goes wrong.'

'Do I have a choice?'

'Not since the moment you agreed to step inside this vehicle.'

'OK,' Stevens gestured to the sheets of paper Kellerman had taken from his briefcase, 'get on with it.'

'Right. This operation is codenamed SM/VIPER, classified top secret and SCI code word clearance "Dingo". This is a verbal briefing, and you will take no notes. First, support. We've pre-briefed auxiliary agents for you in every country you're likely to visit in Western Europe. They're all clean, and none of them has been indoctrinated into VIPER. All they know is that they may be approached by a US asset and they're to extend all possible support and assistance short of compromising their own cover identities. These are the contact details, including challenge and response codes. It also contains your fall-back and emergency exfiltration procedures.' He passed Stevens a single sheet of paper on which were typed forty-eight five-letter groups, arranged in ten vertical columns. 'Encryption is by a standard double-transposition cipher. I presume you're familiar with the technique?'

Stevens looked at Kellerman as if he'd just asked him to add two and two together. 'Decryption keys?' he demanded, tucking the paper into his inside jacket pocket.

'Key word one is "NOTATIONAL" and key word two is "OVER-WHELMS". You need me to spell those?'

'No. What's the timescale?'

'As soon as possible, but the longstop date is June.'

'That's real tight.'

Kellerman nodded and looked down at his notes. 'I know.'

'Who's in my team? From Langley, I mean?'

'Nobody. It's just you. This is far too sensitive for anything but a solo operation.'

'This just gets better and better,' Stevens muttered, as Kellerman then began the formal briefing.

The car they were sitting in belonged to the Central Intelligence Agency, which meant it was not only armoured, with bulletproof glass, multiple layers of Kevlar panels in the doors and bodywork and run-flat tyres, but also checked for bugs at least once every day. The driver – Roy Craven – was a senior CIA agent, one of a pool of men selected for their ability behind the wheel and skill with weapons. Craven also had other qualities which wouldn't have appeared on his CV, should he ever have chosen to write one, and which was why he'd been selected for this particular tasking.

In a padded box beside him were four loaded Uzi 9-millimetre sub-machine guns and spare magazines, and in the door pocket a Browning semi-automatic pistol fitted with a small but effective suppressor. The vehicle was equipped with a GPS satellite navigation system, plus a beacon which, when activated, enabled it to be tracked by satellite and its position relayed to a designated control suite at Langley.

The vehicle itself – known to CIA insiders as 'The Triple B', which stood for 'Big Black Bastard' – was normally used for transporting the DCI and Langley supergrades to and from meetings in DC. When it wasn't fulfilling this function, it also provided a secure environment in which could be addressed matters perhaps too sensitive to be discussed inside any building.

Craven was isolated in his driving compartment, unable to hear anything said by the two men sitting behind him, and also unable to see them, as the raised divider was heavily tinted. Neither factor bothered him because, just like the man on the back seat, he was following very specific orders.

As Kellerman wrapped up the briefing, he reached into his pocket, pulled out a small photograph and handed it to Stevens. 'You recognize him?'

'No. Should I?'

'Probably not. We only found out about him around six months ago, and you've been out of the loop for a lot longer than that. We believe he's probably the principal European liaison officer for UBL, and that he might be receptive to the right kind of approach. We suggest you target him first.'

Kellerman took a folded sheet of paper from another pocket and passed it over.

'This is pretty much everything we know about him. Now, the final point is most important. Whether you deal with this man or not, any subsequent investigations have to reach the conclusion that we want.'

'Yeah, I get it,' Stevens muttered. 'Payment?'

'I was just getting to that. We've got your offshore bank details. There'll be half a million dollars transferred to your account there by the close of business today. There'll be a further million available for you in Europe, split equally between five separate banks, for your expenses. They're listed here' – Kellerman handed over another sheet of paper – 'and there'll be another half a million due to you as a bonus on successful completion of the operation.'

'Two million dollars? Somebody wants this done real bad.'

'You'd better believe it.'

Ten minutes later the divider slid downwards, and Kellerman leant forward. 'Take us to Union Station to drop off our passenger, then head back to Langley.'

'No problem, sir.'

The divider hissed upwards again as Craven took the next available left turn and began increasing speed. At the corner of F Street and Second he pulled the car into the kerb and stopped. He watched in the door mirror as the bulky and untidy man climbed out. They'd picked him up just over an hour earlier outside a small hotel in the north DC area. Craven had no idea who he was or why he'd been meeting with the junior Company agent still in the back seat, nor had he the slightest interest in finding out.

Stevens held the heavy door open for a few moments, looking back down at Kellerman, then closed it and walked away down F Street without a backward glance. In every respect bar one, Gregory Stevens *was* the right man for the job. As Kellerman had said, he had the skills and the languages, but he also had something else that the CIA hierarchy wasn't aware of, because it wasn't listed on any of his reports or analyses. Stevens had a conscience.

The moment the door closed, Craven indicated, pulled out and moved the car back into the traffic flow, heading north up Second Street. He made the turn onto H Street, and a couple of minutes later was heading north-west on Massachusetts Avenue out towards Bethesda. It wasn't the most direct route to CIA headquarters at Langley, but he knew the traffic around Foggy Bottom and on both the Memorial Parkway and Canal Road would be a bitch. And he had another reason for choosing this particular route.

A couple of minutes later he flicked a switch mounted just below the dashboard. It was a recent addition to the vehicle, fitted just days earlier. The only apparent result of this action was a faint clunk, virtually inaudible against the background traffic and the engine noise.

In the rear compartment, Kellerman was again scanning his briefing notes, checking he'd covered everything, though if he hadn't it was now far too late, so he heard nothing. Satisfied, he opened his briefcase and slid the papers inside. He gazed incuriously out through the window, mentally rehearsing the report he'd deliver to Johnson once he got back to Langley.

He first realized the Lincoln was driving a somewhat circuitous route when the driver turned left off Massachusetts Avenue onto Goldsboro Road, just east of Glen Echo. Kellerman knew the area reasonably well and guessed that the driver – Kellerman thought his name was Craven, but he wasn't sure – had chosen to go this way because of traffic conditions in west DC. The obvious route was to make a right turn onto Seven Locks Road and pick up the southbound freeway at the cloverleaf just north of Cabin John. But the driver didn't make the expected turn in Cabin John. Instead, he continued straight ahead, along MacArthur towards the Naval Surface Warfare Center.

Kellerman frowned, leant forward and depressed the switch to lower the partition. The glass stayed exactly where it was. He tried again, then rapped on it, but it was as if the driver couldn't hear him, and Kellerman began to feel concerned. The Lincoln was maintaining a steady speed along the road, but that didn't mean anything. Craven could have passed out at the wheel, leaving the car running on cruise control.

Then Kellerman sat back, relaxing again in his seat. The car was pulling off the road onto a section of rough ground just north of Vaso Island. Obviously Craven had simply missed the earlier junction, difficult though that was to believe, and was now going to head back towards Langley.

But the Lincoln didn't continue through the U-turn. Instead, it stopped suddenly, the suspension almost bottoming. Kellerman looked out and saw only trees and bushes, grass and shrubs. No other cars were in view in either direction. Then the door beside him opened with a jerk and he looked up to see the driver staring down at him.

'What the—?' he started to say, then fell silent as he saw the Browning.

'Sorry about this,' Craven said. 'Orders,' he added, as he pulled the trigger.

Kellerman opened his mouth to say something, anything, but the 9-millimetre slug smashed into his chest before the words could form.

The pistol was clean and stock, straight off the shelf, purchased in Florida three weeks earlier, and the bullet was standard lead with a copper jacket. But the powder load was special, a much reduced amount, designed to generate sufficient muzzle velocity to kill the target after passing through the suppressor, but not enough to travel all the way through his body.

Kellerman slumped backwards, sprawling half across the seat, his legs twitching as his muscles began to spasm.

Craven took a half-step closer, wondering if he'd need a second round, then decided he wouldn't. He left the door open, stepped round to the back of the vehicle and opened the trunk. Inside was a grey tarpaulin, already spread across the floor. He walked back, paused for a brief moment to check that he was still unobserved, then reached down and dragged out Kellerman's body. Craven was a big man, powerfully built, and dropping the dead man into the trunk took him only seconds. Before closing the lid, he reached inside, pulled off the CIA officer's watch and ring and removed the wallet from his inside jacket pocket. Then he thoroughly inspected the back-seat area of the Lincoln, picked up the ejected cartridge case, ensured there were no bloodstains on the leather seats or carpet and checked his own clothes. He picked up Kellerman's briefcase, opened it and pulled out the VIPER briefing notes. On the front seat of the Lincoln was a portable shredder that could be powered from the car's cigar lighter. Craven separated the pages and fed each one individually through it, then tipped the contents of the shredder's basket onto the ground beside the car. Taking a cigarette lighter from his pocket, he ignited the confetti of paper. It immediately flared into oblivion and he trod the ashes into dust.

Craven checked all around the car one last time, then got back in the driver's seat, replaced the Browning in the door pocket and started the engine. He swung the wheel hard over, powering the heavy car across the road to head back the way he'd come, and then picked up speed.

Just under an hour later Craven accelerated the Lincoln away from a vacant lot in the north Chinatown area of Washington. Dumped in one corner, behind a parked Ford, was Kellerman's body, his open briefcase beside him, papers scattered about, the apparent victim of a mugging that had turned into homicide. The Browning, minus the custom-built suppressor and the magazine holding the special rounds, he tossed into a garbage bin a few blocks away from the lot. When he spotted a public phone, he pulled the Lincoln to a stop beside it, climbed out and made a four-second call to a Virginia number.

VIPER was now up and running, and its first phase had been completed exactly as planned and precisely on schedule. Including now Gregory Stevens, only six men in America knew anything about it. The briefing officer, Kellerman, had been the seventh, and, in the opinion of the architect of this plan, that had been one too many.

Chapter One

Present day; early May; Sunday morning
Autoroute A20, south of Limoges, France

Paul Richter had just pulled out to overtake a line of three lorries when his mobile rang. The cockpit of the Westfield was no place to hold a telephone conversation, at least while the car was moving, so he ignored it, and after half a dozen rings the phone fell silent as the voice-messaging system cut in.

Ten minutes later, Richter pulled the Westfield – the indecently rapid sports car he'd recently bought as a toy to play with when he was away from London – to a halt in an autoroute service area, parked well away from any occupied vehicles, and took the phone out of his pocket. He checked the 'missed calls' list and saw, not to his entire surprise, that the caller had been his boss, Richard Simpson. Or at least, someone using Simpson's private line.

He had thought it too good to be true. Despite a recent outbreak of minor terrorist incidents in Europe, everything had seemed quiet at FOE, and Richter had decided to use some of his accumulated leave to visit friends in southern Spain. He'd left London only the previous afternoon, and had been hoping to get as far as the Toulouse area before stopping for the night.

Whatever Simpson wanted, it probably wouldn't be good news, and, as Richter dialled the Hammersmith number, he could already see his holiday evaporating.

'Richter,' he announced as his call was answered.

'Where are you?'

'In the middle of France. In case you've forgotten, I'm supposed to be on leave.'

'I know that,' Simpson replied. 'I signed your chitty. Where are you exactly?'

Richter glanced at the screen of his Navman 750 before replying. 'Right now, I'm between Limoges and Brive-la-Gaillarde, just south of a place called Pierre-Buffière on the A20 autoroute. Why? What's happened now?'

'Nothing much. Are you in a secure area?'

'Not really. I'm in the car park of a service station, but there's currently no one within fifty yards of me.'

'That'll have to do. Right, Vauxhall Cross has had a request from FedPol – the Swiss Federal Police – for a Six officer to travel to Geneva as soon as possible. Nobody over at Legoland was very enthusiastic about the job, so it got shoved onto us. You're more or less on the spot, so I've offered your services.'

'Thanks a lot for asking me first. What's it about, anyway?'

Simpson's tone was dismissive. 'Nothing too exciting. FedPol's been tipped off about some suspected terrorist activity in the Geneva Canton, and they seem to think there might be a British connection. A possible target over here – something like that. All you have to do is get yourself over to cuckoo-clock land and check it out, then let us know why the gnomes have got their knickers in such a twist. It should take you two days, tops, then you can climb back into that rather vulgar sports car of yours and bash on down to Puerto Bañus.'

'Your Mercedes is vulgar, Simpson. My Westfield is a modern classic.'

'What frightens me is that I think you really believe that. Anyway, as a sweetener, you can consider your leave as starting again once this is over.'

'Wonderful,' Richter said, pulling a notebook and ballpoint out of the pocket of his leather jacket. 'OK, who do I contact?'

Simpson rattled off a name, address and telephone number. 'He speaks better English than you do, or so I'm told, so you needn't bother buying a German phrase book.'

'Right. You want me to report back to you?'

'Not unless you find something you think I ought to know about. Just give the duty officer a quick résumé and then push off down to Spain.'

'I'd better get moving, then,' Richter said and ended the call.

Before he started the engine of the Westfield, he made a call to the Playas del Duque complex in Puerto Bañus and left a message on his friends' answerphone to explain that he had been unavoidably delayed, but hoped to be there in about three days.

Then he programmed the Navman with the Swiss address Simpson had given him and waited while the computer calculated the fastest route. As he'd expected, the satnav instructed him to continue along on the A20 as far as Junction 45, just south of Uzerche, and then take the N120 towards Tulle before picking up the eastbound A89 autoroute. He checked the distance he had to cover, making mental calculations, then started the car and pulled out of the parking area and back onto the road.

He would, he expected, reach Geneva early that evening. Then, if he could sort out whatever FedPol wanted tomorrow, he might still be able to make southern Spain by late Wednesday night.

Stuttgart, Germany

Fritz Stiebling had been a police officer for almost twenty years and prided himself that he knew his city as well as anyone could. He sometimes said to friends that he could feel Stuttgart's pulse, a somewhat flowery statement from a man who was about as down-to-earth as it was possible to be. He worked shifts, like most policemen, but he never really clocked off, always keeping his eyes and ears open, checking for any irregularity in the well-ordered routine of the city that he knew so well.

So when he spotted two workmen, carrying a large and apparently heavy box between them, entering a building on the east side of the city his interest was aroused. The building itself consisted of an empty shop with storerooms above it, so men shifting boxes of equipment, fittings or stock was not in itself remarkable. What puzzled Stiebling was the fact that this was early on a Sunday evening. Furthermore, the building stood right next to the local branch of a large bank.

It could all be entirely innocent, just new business tenants working over the weekend to get their enterprise open as quickly as possible. Or it could be something else entirely. Stiebling decided to park his car a little way up the road and watch.

There was a café about a hundred metres away, on the opposite side of the street. The four tables outside were all occupied by diners, but that wouldn't be a problem. Stiebling marched inside and showed his identification to the manager. Within four minutes he was sitting at one of the outside tables and studiously contemplating the menu, while the two couples who had occupied it previously were being reseated inside, amid profuse apologies from the maître d'.

Stiebling ordered himself a half-bottle of red wine and a bowl of pasta, took out a notebook and pen and settled down to watch and record whatever might be happening at the far end of the street.

During the next hour he watched four other 'workmen' enter the same premises, all carrying boxes or bulky bags. Stiebling was too far away to be able to identify the men, or see exactly what they were carrying, but what he had observed was sufficiently unusual for him to decide to raise the matter officially. With his wine finished and an empty plate in front of him, he took out his mobile and called the duty inspector at his police station.

'Stiebling,' he announced, and gave his exact location. 'I think I might be witnessing preparations for a bank robbery.'

Within two hours, the building was under surveillance by teams of watchers using cameras fitted with powerful telephoto lenses, and Stiebling himself was sitting in an interview room back at the station, describing exactly what he'd witnessed.

Onex commune, Canton of Geneva, Switzerland

Richter had changed his mind just before he entered Switzerland. It was already almost eight thirty in the evening, and it made better sense to find a hotel for the night before visiting the police station. From past experience, he knew that continental hotels had a tendency to bar the doors to all comers the moment night fell, and sleeping in the Westfield wasn't an option he was prepared to consider.

With a room booked and his two small leather bags deposited on the bed, Richter climbed back into the car and drove less than a mile to the address Simpson had given him. The police building was large and square, and it exuded an almost palpable air of efficiency. There were dozens of free spaces in the public car park opposite, and two minutes later he was standing at the reception desk in front of a slightly belligerent police officer – probably a sergeant – asking if he could see Wilhelm Schneider. And, yes, he was expected.

Schneider appeared almost before Richter had sat down in the waiting area. He strode across to greet him, extending his hand.

'Mr Richter?' he asked.

'Yes.' Richter was immediately aware of the contrast between his own casual attire – trainers, faded blue jeans and black leather jacket – and the Swiss police officer's immaculate dark grey suit.

'Just a formality, but could I see some identification?'

'It'll have to be my passport,' Richter reached into his jacket pocket, 'because I don't have anything else with me.'

'No, that's fine.' The Swiss inspector opened the document and compared the tiny photograph there with Richter's unshaven countenance. 'I gather you've postponed some leave to assist us here, and we really appreciate that. Come on through.'

Richter followed him to a door secured with a combination lock, and along a cream-painted corridor to a mid-sized briefing room, where about half a dozen men, all wearing smart civilian clothes, were already waiting. The buzz of conversation ceased as they walked in. The Swiss police officer strode to the head of a long table and looked round the room.

'This is Mr Richter,' he began, 'from the British Secret Intelligence Service' – which wasn't strictly true, though Richter had no intention of explaining exactly who he worked for – 'who's here to help us clarify this situation.'

Schneider then turned to Richter. 'Let me explain what we've found. Two days ago, a middle-aged Swiss businessman walked into the local police station here in Onex and asked to speak to the counter-terrorism section. We don't often get requests like that, and when we do they're as likely as not made by people who are mentally disturbed or else reading far too much into an innocent sequence of events. But after listening to what the man had to say, the commune officers decided he should be taken seriously. Our local police force obviously doesn't have its own counter-terrorism unit, so they contacted the Federal Police, and details of the report were passed on to me. I myself am a senior inspector in the Terrorism Investigations Unit, and when we'd analysed what the man had said, I travelled down from Geneva with most of the team you see gathered here.'

Schneider waved a hand to indicate the others in the room, and Richter nodded.

'This businessman, whose name is Rolf Hermann, owns several apartments in a certain building here in Onex, which he rents out. Onex is very close to Geneva, almost a suburb, but rental costs here are a lot less than they are in the city itself, and many of his tenants are working in Geneva on short- or medium-term contracts. Two weeks ago, he agreed to rent one of his apartments for just a month to a German national, supposedly living here on his own. That wasn't particularly unusual in itself, since quite a lot of people take a property for a similar short period while they look around for more permanent accommodation, but he became concerned on learning that this man might be sub-letting the flat. If he was, it was a clear breach of the terms of the lease, so he decided to enter the property at a time when it was unoccupied and check how many of the bedrooms were being used.'

Schneider turned to a map of the commune on the wall behind him and picked up a pointer.

'We're here,' he said, indicating a square shape marked more or less in the centre of the map. 'The apartment building is precisely here, on the edge of Onex, and about a mile away from where we are now. The landlord waited until the German tenant had left the property – accompanied, he noted, by three other men – and then used his master key to enter the apartment. Inside, everything was clean and tidy, but he noted that four of the five beds – one double and three singles – were obviously being slept in.

'The other thing he noted was a laptop sitting on the table in the dining area. It was still switched on, though the screen was blank. Out of curiosity, he touched the space bar. When the screen illuminated, what he saw there prompted him to contact us. It was like a shopping list, composed in German, but none of the items mentioned on it would be found in your local supermarket – at least, not here in Switzerland. The list included plastic explosive and detonators, timing devices, grenades, and weapons including pistols, assault rifles and shotguns, and ammunition.'

Richter shook his head. 'I'm not sure I'm buying this,' he said. 'It's just as likely to be some hack novelist preparing a list of details to research, or maybe a journalist writing up a story about the black-market arms trade. If these people really are terrorists, you have to ask two questions. First, would they really be prepared to leave their safe house so conveniently unoccupied that somebody could just wander in and take a look around? Second, assuming they were stupid enough to do that, would they leave details of what they were planning on a laptop computer that they hadn't even protected with a password?'

Schneider nodded agreement. 'Exactly what we thought at first,' he said patiently, 'and if that was all the landlord had seen, we wouldn't be here. But he also spotted a Kalashnikov AK47 assault rifle, with a fully loaded magazine, behind the living-room door. As you probably know, Swiss citizens are required to possess assault rifles and ammunition – our government policy has always relied on our nationals being able to function as a militia – so the landlord was perfectly familiar with this type of weapon, but here we normally use the SiG 550. He took a note of the serial number of the AK47, and we ran a trace. It turned out to be part of a consignment of 200 Kalashnikovs stolen from an army depot in Hungary about three years ago.

'The fact that we could identify the origin of the weapon the landlord saw lent credence to his story, even if it also suggested we were dealing with a particularly stupid – or careless – group of terrorists.'

'Agreed,' Richter nodded. 'So what's the British connection?'

'The "shopping list" the landlord saw included an entry for "FRB London". That could have meant the city, or was perhaps just someone's surname, but it looked significant enough for us to pass on the information to your SIS. Do you yourself have any idea what it means?'

Richter thought for a moment. 'No, frankly. If you'd given me just the initials "FRB", I'd have suggested "Federal Reserve Bank", but that makes no sense in terms of the word "London". Sorry, right now I can't think of anything, but there's one simple and obvious way to find out.'

'Which is what?' Schneider looked interested.

'We kick down the door of that apartment and ask these bastards exactly what they've got in mind.'

'We seem to think the same way, Mr Richter. We've got the building under surveillance, and we're planning on going in tomorrow morning, once we're certain all four men are there in residence. If you'd like to come back here no later than nine, I'd be happy for you to tag along – strictly as an observer, of course.'

Chapter Two

Monday
Sheerness, Isle of Sheppey, Kent

For a few moments, Barney wasn't sure just what had awakened him, but he reacted the way he always did, by doing nothing. He lay absolutely still, eyes closed, listening intently to the voices and trying to make sense of what he was hearing. He'd had many years of sleeping rough, and the biggest single problem he'd ever faced was teenagers – youths emboldened by drink and the support of their friends, eager to show their courage by attacking a target that couldn't retaliate – and he knew that his best defence was to do nothing to attract their attention. So he just lay still, hoping they hadn't yet seen him, but listening carefully.

His given name was Edward Holmes, but he'd been known as Barney for more years than he could remember, the origins of the nickname lost forever in the alcohol-clouded obscurity of his memory. Few people who saw him, a battered trilby topping his lined, weather-beaten, unshaven face, his body wrapped in a faded brown overcoat secured with string at the waist, would have guessed that he'd once been employed in a reasonably responsible position. His problem, predictably enough, had been the burgeoning alcoholism, which had eventually proved too great an impediment for any employer to ignore. When his money finally ran out and he could no longer pay his rent, Barney had been driven into that twilight world of the non-people: the beggars with their dogs, the tramps ever on the move and the other unfortunate derelicts of society.

In a community that possessed neither pride nor respect, Barney had no trouble at all fitting in. He had acquired a handful of acquaintances and still fewer friends, but in the past fifteen years he'd become a familiar figure around the coast of south-east England, trudging along the country roads, sitting outside shopping centres or lying on a bed of cardboard and newspapers in some shop doorway, almost always with a comforting bottle to hand.

His favoured location was the Isle of Sheppey, the low-lying island about ten miles long and four wide located just off the north coast of Kent with a bridge link over the narrow channel that separates it from the mainland. Barney felt as much at home there as he did anywhere, perhaps because his birthplace, Ramsgate, was close by. He'd also found the people, and perhaps more importantly the police, a little more relaxed and generous on the island than in many other locations. And when on Sheppey he was most often to be found in or around Sheerness, the only town of any size.

By Barney's somewhat modest standards, it had been a good day. He'd positioned himself in Bridge Road, not far from the old red and green painted clock-tower, and close to one of the cheaper cafés. He'd upturned his stained and tattered old hat on the pavement in front of him, seeded it with some coins from an inside pocket of his coat, then leant back against the wall and waited with the patience of a man with nowhere to go and all day to get there. He moved only three times, twice when he saw a police constable approaching and finally when the café closed at four thirty. The money arrived in dribs and drabs: mainly copper and low-denomination silver coins, but occasionally a twenty- or fifty-pence piece, which earned the generous donor a nod of thanks. By six, when the last of the shops had closed, he'd accumulated almost eight pounds, more than enough to buy a bottle of cheap wine and something hot to eat.

Just after midnight, his stomach pleasantly full of pie and chips and with still almost half a bottle of very average red wine tucked into his coat pocket, Barney had settled down for the night on the beach.

To be accurate, he wasn't actually *on* a beach as such, because the coastline at Sheerness is less conducive to shoreline activities than most English seaside resorts. The town is separated from the choppy waters of the Thames Estuary by a low sea wall that extends a considerable distance along the north coast of Sheppey. What beach there is tends to be steeply sloping and largely gravel, while large sections of the coastline are confined behind bare concrete.

But to the north-west of the Tesco superstore that abuts the sea wall in Blue Town, at the edge of Sheerness, is an L-shaped body of water known as The Moat. It is intermittently occupied by resting seabirds, clusters of partially submerged shopping trolleys and other less savoury debris. The sloping banks of this miniature lake lie below the level of the sea wall itself, and so offer some shelter from the wind. That night, the ground was damp because of the nearby water, but Barney's ragged tarpaulin held most of it at bay, and he was prepared to suffer that minor discomfort in exchange for some protection from the biting wind. Besides, it was far enough away from the town itself that he doubted anyone would disturb him. But that assumption had clearly been wrong.

Now, after a few seconds of listening quietly, he realized that these people didn't sound like teenagers. The soft, muffled voices had an unmistakably adult timbre, and then he registered something else: they weren't speaking English but some language he didn't recognize. That surprised him, and he opened his eyes to look.

Barney had no watch, but it was clearly the early hours of the morning. The moon by now was low in the sky, but provided sufficient light for him to see reasonably well. Directly in front of him, four or five metres away, three dark-clad male figures stood huddled close together on the concrete path that ran along the top of the sea wall. They were all peering intently out at the dark waters of the Thames Estuary.

Unfortunately for Barney, curiosity got the better of him. He shifted position to sit upright, wondering what had attracted their attention. But the sea wall rose too high for him to see the water's edge, so he stood up, allowing himself a clearer view down the sloping concrete towards the breaking waves. He still saw nothing, but there had to be some object, some reason the men were there. Barney shuffled slightly to one side and then he saw it: a dark, roundish object bobbing in the water close up to the sea wall. For a moment, he thought it was maybe a large seal, but then, as he recognized it, he let out an involuntary gasp of surprise.

Immediately he realized he should have kept silent, because one of the men turned round and looked in his direction. He then said something, and the other two stopped talking and all just stared at their uninvited audience.

Something about them, some indescribable sense of menace, sent a chill through the old man, and he decided immediately that his best option was to get himself somewhere else, somewhere less isolated, and quickly. He turned and started to run, heading for the path that led past the superstore, but this was always going to be a one-sided race. He was over seventy years old, stiff and arthritic, while each of his pursuers was half his age, strong and fit.

Within seconds, Barney heard the first of them directly behind him, his shoes loud on the concrete. He stopped and spun round to face his pursuer, right hand already raising his old hawthorn stick. It did him no good. The other brushed aside the old man's pitiful weapon, then smashed a fist into his stomach. Barney gasped and folded forward, as if hinged at the waist. He collapsed onto the path, his breath rasping painfully.

His assailant stopped and glanced down, as his two companions stepped up beside him. All three looked down at Barney, who stared defiantly back up at them. He was still expecting nothing more than a beating. It had happened before, so probably would again. But he sadly underestimated the situation. Two of the men exchanged nods, and one reached into his pocket for a knife, clicking open the switchblade. Barney immediately began trying to scramble to his feet, determined not to give up without a fight. He'd just made it back onto his knees when one of his attackers grabbed the hawthorn stick and, with all his strength, swung the knurled end at the back of the old man's head. This time, as Barney fell face-forward, he didn't move again, which turned out to be a blessing because he didn't feel them drag his body back up onto the grass bank of The Moat, or the blade of the knife stab into the left side of his throat just below his ear and rip its way through his windpipe and carotid artery. Barney took little over a minute to die.

His killer carefully wiped off the blood from the switchblade on a fold of Barney's overcoat, then closed the knife and slid it back into his pocket. Without speaking, the other two men grabbed the old man's wrists and ankles, picked up his corpse and carried it to the top of the sea wall. There they swung it backwards and forwards between them, to build up momentum, then tossed the corpse as far out as they could. The body landed with a splash in the dark water, limbs splaying out grotesquely, then the ebbing tide swirled it rapidly out of view.

One of the men then spotted Barney's tattered old haversack, picked it up and tossed it into the water, well clear of the shore. It quickly filled with water and sank, unlike the body of its owner.

Onex commune, Canton of Geneva, Switzerland

Richter didn't bother checking himself out of the hotel that morning. In his experience, almost every such operation he became involved in took far longer to complete than anyone expected, and this one was probably not going to be any different. So he just left his bags in the room, grabbed a quick coffee, then climbed into the Westfield and headed back to the police station.

In contrast to the previous evening, the whole station was buzzing. Six police cars and three unmarked vans – Volkswagen T5s – were parked outside, with their rear doors open, while officers in all-black combat clothing and carrying automatic weapons milled about.

Inside the station itself, Schneider was issuing final orders to his team before they moved off to their assigned locations to start the operation. He broke off as Richter walked in, and gestured towards a table on which lay a fabric bag containing an unusual-looking brown waistcoat, as well as an outer jacket and a helmet, on both of which the word 'POLICE' was boldly stencilled in white. Richter felt the fabric of the waistcoat and immediately recognized it as made from Dragon's Skin, a revolutionary – and very expensive – new type of body armour. Unlike Kevlar, which is basically a rigid fibre capable of blocking the penetration of most bullets, Dragon's Skin is flexible and moulds itself to the body of the wearer, offering greater comfort and therefore arguably better protection during action. He took a seat at the same table while Schneider completed his briefing.

'This could be a long day,' the Swiss police officer said finally, walking over to him. 'Our surveillance team reports that three of the four inmates have now left the building, so there's nothing much we can do until they return. The last thing we want is to challenge them on the street, in case they're carrying weapons and civilians get hurt.'

'Or wearing Semtex waistcoats?' Richter suggested.

'Exactly, though I reckon that's less likely. This lot look to me like white-collar terrorists, not Arab fanatics. I've got some plain-clothes officers going through the entire apartment building now, getting all the other residents out of the place – discreetly, of course. They should have finished in about half an hour. We've commandeered an apartment right on the other side of the street to use as our local command post. If you're ready, we'll drive over there now. But then all we can do is wait.'

Richter nodded. Waiting around for the action to start was one of the things he'd always been good at.

Sheerness, Isle of Sheppey, Kent

Jasper was a long-haired Jack Russell terrier with a firm view on taking regular walks, which fortunately coincided with the views of his owner, Walter Keane. At precisely seven thirty in the morning, three in the afternoon, and eight in the evening, no matter what the weather, Jasper could be seen secured on his long lead, pulling his master at a brisk pace down Beach Street, then up onto the sea wall and north-west to the end of The Moat, before returning home by the same route.

This morning was no exception, and just for a change it wasn't raining. Jasper led the way unerringly along the top of the sea wall, pausing briefly to inspect sites visited recently by other canine adventurers, and barking at any seagulls that had the temerity to alight in front of him. These pauses gave his elderly owner, grey raincoat now flapping in the wind, a bit of a chance to catch up, and also to catch his breath.

As they reached the rear of the Tesco superstore, and were about to take the path alongside The Moat, Jasper's barking reached a new crescendo, but this time it wasn't seagulls that aroused him. It was a handful of crows and a couple of magpies scrabbling about on the grass near the edge of the water. Probably a dead rabbit or maybe just a rat, Walter assumed, as he drew near, reeling in the terrier and trying to quieten him. The birds flapped off as the pair approached, and Walter looked down curiously to see what carrion they'd been feasting on.

But instead of the ripped and torn small furry body he had expected, all that was visible was a large discoloured patch of grass, stained dark brown. Puzzled, he peered more closely, then he noticed several other things that shouldn't have been there. He bent down, his old bones protesting painfully.

A few seconds later he straightened up slowly and looked around. There was nobody else in sight – though at that hour he would have been surprised if there had been – and for the first time in his life he wished he had a mobile telephone. Jasper was beginning to sniff eagerly at the stain on the grass, and Walter had to tug him away urgently. He looked over towards the superstore. Perhaps there was a public phone there he could use? Shortening the lead to keep Jasper out of further trouble, he walked away, taking the path that led across the superstore car park.

In the event, he didn't need a phone, because just then he saw a Kent Police patrol car drive into the parking area on a routine check. Walter Keane waved an arm vigorously till the vehicle stopped, and a couple of minutes later he was excitedly showing the two patrol officers what he'd found.

'This looks like blood to me, Colin,' the driver muttered, touching the edge of the stain with a cautious finger, 'but we'll need forensics down here to make sure.'

His partner looked less convinced, but he couldn't dispute that *something* questionable seemed to have happened here, where they were standing. The rucked-up tarpaulin, stained old trilby, and the walking stick they'd found a few yards away, one end smeared with what looked suspiciously like blood, confirmed it.

'I'll call it in, Dave,' the other officer announced, decision made. He pressed the transmit button on his personal radio and then described to the control room what they'd been shown by Walter Keane near the sea wall.

Ten minutes later, Jasper and his owner were able to continue their interrupted walk, the pensioner having given a brief statement and provided his contact details. Forty minutes after that, a white police van appeared and drove over to the side of the car park where the two police officers were still standing on the nearby sea wall. Four men climbed out, opened the back doors and plucked aluminium cases from inside, then headed up the slope towards them.

'James Monroe, SOCO,' the newcomer announced to the two constables. 'What is it and where is it?'

'We think it's blood, and possibly evidence of a serious assault.'

'Who's the victim?'

'No idea. All we've found so far is an area of stained grass and a walking stick that looks as if it might have been used in the attack. There's also a discarded hat and a tarpaulin that might have belonged to the victim.'

James Monroe, the senior Scene Of Crime Officer, didn't look over-impressed at such evidence, and even less so when he stood over the disturbed area of grass.

'Is that all?' he demanded.

'Yes.'

'Christ on a bike. This could have been caused by anything. Kids larking around, dogs fucking, a cat killing a bird, anything.'

The two police officers exchanged glances.

'Look, we reckon that's blood on the grass, and there's blood and loose hairs on the end of the walking stick. Unless the local cats have started beating the crows to death with cudgels, something else happened here, and we were right to call it in.'

'Don't try and get smart with me, constable,' Monroe grunted, then knelt down to open his case. After ordering a batch of photographs to be taken of the scene, he selected several samples of the discoloured grass, delicately picked up and bagged the battered trilby, and then the tarpaulin. For a couple of minutes he bent over the walking stick, carefully studying the discoloured end, then picked it up too and wrapped a plastic bag over its head. After handing the stick to one of the other SOCOs, he instructed them to cover the area in clear plastic sheeting and to erect stakes with crime scene tape around the perimeter.

'Probably a complete waste of our time and resources, this,' Monroe muttered irritably, after ordering his men back to their van. 'This was your bright idea,' he turned to the constables, 'so you two can stay here and guard the scene, just in case.'

'Just in case what?'

'Fucked if I know, but it'll do you good.' Monroe glanced up at the sky. 'Looks like it might rain,' he added hopefully, and trudged off back to the car park.

Onex commune, Canton of Geneva, Switzerland

The apartment building looked pretty much as Richter had expected: five floors with, probably, four flats on each, the whole building looking clean and smart. He and Schneider were currently watching the main door from a virtually identical building across the street, while two black-clad officers did the same from the other window in the same room. Net curtains covered both, and no room lights were on, so they knew they were effectively invisible from the outside.

The secure radio beside them crackled to life, then a voice said something in high-speed German, to which Schneider replied briefly in the same language.

'Right,' he said to Richter, raising a pair of binoculars to his eyes as an elderly couple, accompanied by a fit-looking young man wearing a jacket and tie, emerged from the entrance and began walking slowly down the street. 'That's my colleague Jean-Paul bringing out the last of the other occupants, so now the building's totally empty and we just have to wait for these three suspects to come back.' He replaced the binoculars on a side table, picked up the radio and crossed the room to a pair of armchairs. Richter followed him dutifully.

Empty mugs, soft-drink cans and half-consumed packets of crisps and sandwiches littered the low coffee table in front of the chairs. The provisions were ample because they were prepared for a long wait. Richter had skipped breakfast at his hotel, so he pulled a tattered novel out of his jacket pocket, selected a sandwich that looked as if it might have chicken in it, and popped open a can of Coke.

'I warn you, surveillance can make you fat,' Schneider remarked, eyeing him.

Richter grinned. 'Only if you do it for a living,' he said, and took another bite. 'How are you planning to do the entry?' he asked, dusting breadcrumbs off his trousers.

'This is still essentially an unconfirmed report,' Schneider reminded him, 'so we don't want to kick down the apartment door and go in with all guns blazing. We've decided to send one of our men to knock on the door and try to gain entrance without the use of force. If he manages that, our armed officers will be right behind him. If he doesn't, we'll have to use a ram. Either way, we'll get inside.'

Richter nodded. 'Personally, I'd use the ram and take advantage of the element of surprise.'

Schneider waggled his hand from side to side, indicating the fine line to be decided between the two opposing strategies. 'That might well be the right decision, but we'd prefer to avoid bloodshed if possible. My superiors have already decided that this approach is preferable.'

'But they're not here, in the firing line,' Richter pointed out.

'Agreed,' Schneider sighed, 'but they're still in charge.'

A few minutes later, the radio crackled again. Schneider held a short conversation in German, then issued brief orders to the other two men, who turned and left the room.

'They're coming,' he informed Richter. 'It seems the three of them went out to a local restaurant for breakfast, and they've just paid the bill. Our watchers report that they're heading this way, so we'd better get suited up.'

'Right.' Richter took off his leather jacket and donned the Dragon's Skin waistcoat, making sure it was securely fastened.

Schneider had already decided that they would approach the building in one of the vans, driving it around to the back entrance. The target apartment was situated on the third floor, on the street side, with windows that offered an unobstructed view up and down the thoroughfare, so they would have to approach from the other side of the building to remain undetected.

'Here they come,' Schneider murmured, involuntarily moving back slightly from the window. Richter stepped up beside him and peered out. Three young men were walking along the pavement on the other side of the street. About fifty yards behind them, an elderly woman, wheezing and bent with arthritis, was making heavy weather of pushing a bicycle along the kerb.

'Is she one of yours?' Richter asked, pointing at her.

Schneider nodded. 'Marjit Nielsen,' he said proudly. 'She's twenty-seven, got a figure like an hourglass, holds three marksman qualifications and can run a kilometre in a whisker under three minutes. But she's *really* good at impersonating old ladies.'

'Impressive. I'd like to meet her, maybe.'

Schneider glanced at him and grinned. 'Forget it. She'd eat you alive.'

'You're probably right.'

Down in the street, the three men turned left and entered the building. The 'old woman' continued past them and disappeared into a side street, giving no sign of glancing left or right, though Richter guessed she'd missed nothing.

'Show time,' Richter announced, picking up the helmet he'd been provided with.

They left the stake-out and walked down the stairs to ground-floor level, then out through the rear entrance into the courtyard, where one of the Volkswagen vans was waiting, engine running and the rear door wide open. Two of Schneider's men were already sitting in the back, weapons ready in their laps.

'The rest of the team will meet us behind the target building,' Schneider explained. 'I didn't want all three vans parked together, just in case one of the targets happened to walk this way and wonder what they were doing here.'

Schneider pulled the van door closed behind him and rapped on the side panel. The driver nodded, then engaged first gear. The vehicle drove slowly out of the courtyard and then turned immediately right, the opposite direction to the building that was their objective, so as to circle round and approach it from the rear.

Four minutes later the driver braked the van to a halt and switched off the engine. Schneider opened the door and climbed out, followed by Richter and the two armed officers. The other Volkswagen vans were already there, and now he counted ten officers in all, including Schneider, who once more reviewed the plan of attack with his men.

'There are two exits from this building,' he explained to Richter, after he'd finished, 'plus the door leading to the underground garage. I've got nine men here to do the job, and I'm leaving two of them in the lobby to cover the street entrance, the rear door and the lift, and one down in the garage. The plain-clothes officer will go up first, wearing a vest, to try to get the door of the apartment open without this degenerating into a shooting match. He'll claim he's carrying out a spot check on behalf of the landlord. If he does get inside, there'll be five armed men right behind him.'

'What about me? Where do you want me to be?'

Schneider considered for a few moments. 'You can come up to the third floor with us, but stay out of the way until we've secured the apartment.'

That suited Richter fine. Armed, he would have been happy to kick down the door, but without a weapon there was no way he was going to walk into the middle of a shoot-out.

Schneider and Richter headed across to the lift, accompanied by the plain-clothes detective, who was apparently a volunteer for this job, according to the Swiss officer, and they ascended to the third floor. Once the doors opened, they stepped out into a small lobby, with a corridor leading off to their right. Five armed police officers, wearing all-black combat outfits, were already standing waiting for them, weapons at the ready.

Schneider looked them over and then issued his final orders. Each officer carried either a SiG 550 assault rifle or a Remington 870 multi-purpose pump-action shotgun, which would have been Richter's own choice as a close-quarter combat weapon, plus a 9-millimetre SiG P220 semi-automatic pistol in a belt holster.

The plain-clothes officer checked that his body armour remained invisible under his civilian jacket, nodded to Schneider and walked off down the corridor. The armed officers moved back into the small lobby, out of sight, leaving only Schneider and Richter visible in the corridor. As they were both wearing civilian clothes, the suspects shouldn't be alerted if they noticed them.

But just before the plain-clothes officer reached the door, they could hear the sound of a telephone ringing. It stopped in mid-ring and, seconds later, they heard shouts from inside the flat. It could mean only one thing.

'Somebody's tipped them off,' Richter hissed urgently. 'Stop him now. They'll open fire as soon as he knocks on the door.'

Schneider nodded grimly and stepped forward but, even as he did so, the other officer rapped sharply on the door of the apartment. The result was immediate. A three-round burst from an automatic weapon tore right through the thin wooden door and hit him full in the chest, smashing him back against the opposite wall, where he collapsed in a crumpled heap.

Chapter Three

Monday
Onex commune, Canton of Geneva, Switzerland

The five officers thundered along the corridor, Richter and Schneider a few paces behind them. The first one grabbed the door handle, twisted it and pushed, but the door wouldn't budge. Half a dozen further holes were immediately punched through the wood at chest height, as an automatic weapon was fired from within the apartment, but the policeman was standing well to one side, so the bullets buried themselves harmlessly in the wall opposite.

Richter and Schneider seized the recumbent plain-clothes man by each shoulder and started to drag him to safety down the corridor towards the lobby. One officer followed, walking backwards to cover them, his SiG 550 held ready.

The locked door was never going to be a long-term obstacle. Even as they dragged the wounded officer into the lobby, one of Schneider's men fired two rounds from his Remington 870 directly at the top and bottom of the door on the hinge side. Gaping holes appeared in the wood, and a sharp kick did the rest. The door toppled inwards, and the police swarmed inside.

Shouts and a barrage of shots rang out – two from a shotgun, the others from automatic weapons or pistols – followed by cries of pain. Despite his instructions, Richter ran forwards, but then stopped at the door and peered round it cautiously.

It was an open-plan apartment, as he already knew from the architectural plans they'd shown him at the police station, the main door opening straight into the living room. A coffee table had been overturned, and pieces of broken china lay on the carpet. But Richter wasn't interested in crockery or furniture, only in the tactical situation. And what he now took in with a single glance was not encouraging.

One police officer was lying just inside the door, bleeding profusely from two bullet wounds, one to the shoulder and the other in his thigh. The armour only covered so much of his body, and he'd been unlucky enough to get hit by two rounds that had missed the jacket. The officer lying next to him had been even more unlucky: his throat had been torn open by a bullet, and not even immediate medical attention would save his life.

Beside a door that Richter knew led to the bedrooms, an unidentified man lay flat on his back, his chest splattered red by multiple wounds, and in the far corner one of the other occupants slumped against the wall, badly wounded.

Near the centre of the room, the two remaining officers were standing, almost back-to-back, their weapons covering all three doors that led off the living room.

As Richter took in this scene, the further door in the left wall opened for a brief second, just long enough for an unseen hand to lob a black object into the room and towards the standing officers.

'Grenade!' Richter yelled a warning, his voice echoed by the same word being shouted from somewhere inside the apartment. Having witnessed the effects of grenade explosions in confined spaces a couple of times before, Richter didn't hesitate. He stood up from a crouch, turned and sprinted off down the corridor, but he'd barely made ten feet before the entire building was rocked by the explosion.

Richter glanced behind him, to see that the corridor was empty, and he knew exactly what that meant. The four police officers in the apartment were almost certainly now all dead. He looked back towards the lobby, where Schneider was shaking his head, in an effort to recover from the effect of the blast. The remaining armed officer was still in the lobby, probably at least ten seconds away from the stricken apartment, and Richter didn't think they had ten seconds. Now that the grenade had neutralized everyone in the living room, the remaining two terrorists would likely appear any moment, guns blazing as they tried to fight their way out of the building.

Richter darted back to the apartment door and risked a quick glance inside before stepping into the chaos of the living room. Just as he'd feared, all six occupants – four police officers and two terrorists – looked as if they were dead, but that still left two bad guys unaccounted for.

He grabbed a Remington shotgun from the floor and then hurried over to stand at one side of the room. His eyes kept flicking between the three doors, but two were set in the left-hand wall and the third in the wall opposite, which meant covering two threat axes simultaneously. But, having seen the grenade thrown, he knew for sure where at least one of the terrorists was hiding.

The Remington possessed a full-length magazine, which Richter knew meant a maximum load of nine 12-bore shells – one in the breach and eight in the tube under the barrel – and the calculation was easy. Two shotgun rounds had been fired into the door of the flat to gain entry. Then he'd heard two blasts as the police officers went into the apartment, and three of them had been carrying shotguns. That meant that – even if all four of those shots had been fired from the weapon in his hands – he still had at least five rounds left. That should be enough to see this through.

In the corridor outside he could now hear heavy footsteps, and guessed the last remaining police officer, or maybe Schneider himself, was running towards the door.

Then the internal door to his right opened and someone peered out, a pistol clutched in his outstretched hand. Richter reacted instantly, dropping into a crouch as the man fired, then pumped two rounds from the 870 straight towards him. The first smashed into the wall, but the second took the terrorist full in the chest, catapulting him backwards. One down, one to go.

He heard a door open on his blind side, and instantly the room filled with the staccato hammering of a Kalashnikov on full auto. Richter span round, dropped flat, and then rolled over onto his back as the assault rifle's bullets ploughed a furrow into the wall behind him. He pulled the trigger of his own weapon, snapping off a barely aimed round, then pumped another shell into the chamber. He rolled further sideways, moving away from the stream of bullets, and fired again. The deep boom of the Remington was at that moment joined by a rattle of fire from the apartment door as the police officer opened up with his SiG 550. The last terrorist dropped backwards, the combined shots killing him instantly.

As silence fell, Richter climbed cautiously to his feet, racking another shell into the chamber of the 870, just in case. He nodded silently to the police officer, and together they went over and kicked open each door in the apartment in turn, checking that nobody else was there. Only then did they turn their attention to the bodies littering the floor.

'Dear God, what a fucking disaster,' Schneider muttered, now standing at the door of the apartment, staring at the carnage in front of him.

All four suspected terrorists were dead, the shotgun blasts having been instantly lethal at such short range, but as Richter looked around he noticed one of the wounded police officers move slightly.

'This one's alive,' he shouted, and crouched down beside the fallen man, who was lying closest to the main door of the apartment. He had been shot in the leg and shoulder, and the blast from the grenade had ripped open wounds all over him, but he was still just about breathing.

While Schneider pulled out a radio and issued urgent instructions, Richter hurried into the bathroom to collect some towels that he could press against the worst of the man's wounds. That wasn't going to be much help, but it was all he could do. He glanced at his watch and noticed that, bizarrely, it was less than three minutes since the plain-clothes man had first knocked on the apartment door. It had felt more like ten.

The other three officers were all clearly beyond medical help, though that fact would have to be confirmed by the doctor when he arrived. Two of the paramedics, summoned by Schneider, appeared at the door and stepped inside the apartment. Working with brisk efficiency, they strapped compresses on to the injured officer's wounds, then lifted him onto a stretcher and carried him out. A couple of minutes later Richter heard the wailing siren of an ambulance as it headed away from the target building.

He unloaded the Remington and rested it against the wall in one corner of the room, then looked around carefully, checking for the laptop computer that had been the trigger for this entire operation.

The dining table was lying on its side, probably blown over by the blast from the grenade, and Richter walked over to check there. The laptop, an expensive model with a built-in webcam at the top of the screen, was lying on the floor behind it, but one glance was enough to tell him that they weren't likely to get much information out of it. The screen had been almost completely ripped off and the base itself had taken at least three bullets. Even worse, Richter could see what looked like fragments of the hard disk's platters scattered over the carpet beside it. But forensic science could occasionally work miracles, so it was at least worth trying to recover something.

'I've found the laptop,' he called out to Schneider, 'but it's very badly damaged. You'll need to bag all the bits and see if your specialists can get anything out of it.'

The senior Swiss officer walked over and studied the wrecked machine. 'This fucking mess just gets worse and worse,' he said. 'I've got three officers dead and another who probably won't last the day, four very dead terrorists and the computer that might have given us information about whatever they were up to is a write-off.'

'Your plain-clothes guy?' Richter asked.

'That's about the only good news. It looks like he's uninjured, just badly winded. Thanks, by the way. If you hadn't gone in when you did, the last two of these bastards might have got out of the apartment with their Kalashnikovs, and then it would have been an even bigger blood-bath out on the street.'

'And you and I might both have been on our way to the mortuary in a couple of body-bags,' Richter added.

'Exactly.'

Behind Schneider, other medical personnel had been stopped at the door by a newly arrived police officer, and only a single doctor had been allowed into the apartment to confirm that all the blood-soaked bodies sprawled on the floor were dead. At that moment he crouched beside one of the downed cops, feeling vainly for a pulse.

Twenty minutes later, Richter sat in a police van heading back towards the station, preparing to write his report on what had happened.

Back at the apartment, the Swiss forensic team, having carefully photo-graphed the scene before the removal of the bodies, were now beginning a painstaking examination of the entire premises, looking for any clues that might indicate what the four terrorists had been planning. As a priority, Schneider had ordered the smashed laptop to be boxed, and that was already on its way to a specialist laboratory.

TIMEBOMB

Reculver, Kent

Just over three hours after Jasper's nose had led Walter Keane to the patch of blood-stained grass at Sheerness, another man walking his dog encountered more tangible evidence that a crime had been committed.

He spotted a dark shape lying awkwardly among the grey boulders that formed the estuary side of the footpath running between the car park and Reculver Towers, the remains of a medieval church that still dominated the hamlet. After peering at the object uncertainly for a few seconds, he came to a decision. He looped the animal's lead over one of the vertical stanchions of the fence running alongside the footpath and climbed nimbly over the rocks leading down to the water's edge. What he'd seen looked to him increasingly like a bale of some dark material, as he clambered over boulders made slippery with seaweed exposed by the retreating tide. It wouldn't be the first time he'd plucked something of value from the sea but, as he got within just a few feet of it, a breaking wave disturbed the mysterious object and he unexpectedly found himself staring into a pair of lifeless gaping eyes and an open, toothless mouth.

He jumped back involuntarily, slipped and lost his footing, landing painfully on his back amongst the boulders.

'Fuck,' he muttered, gritting his teeth in pain as he clambered to his feet again. 'Fuck, fuck, fuck.'

He scrambled awkwardly back over the rocks to the footpath and, in the absence of anything else upon which to vent his spleen, he kicked out clumsily at his dog, which dodged to one side with the ease born of long practice.

Unlike Walter Keane, this dog-walker had no particular wish to assist the police with their enquiries, having himself seen the inside of the local station's interview room on more than one occasion, but he did walk across to the pub opposite the car park, where he dialled '999' and left a brief anonymous message before returning home.

Forty minutes later, two constables were standing over the body, one of them speaking urgently into his personal radio.

About an hour later still, the Reculver Towers car park was choked

33

with police vehicles, and the whole area around the corpse had been marked out by crime-scene tape as the SOCOs began their work, with one eye warily on the tide, which was about to turn.

Detective Inspector Paul Mason stood by the head of the corpse, looking down at it. The pathologist – a lean and cadaverous elderly man with an unhealthy grey complexion that suggested he himself wasn't long for this world, and who was known as 'The Ghoul' – had already been and gone. He'd confirmed that the victim was dead, a fact blindingly obvious to everyone present, and that, although there was a severe contusion to the back of the corpse's head, the most likely cause of his demise was the knife-slash across his throat that had cut almost as deep as his vertebrae. Nor, the pathologist added, had he died where he'd been found. He'd been killed elsewhere and his body dumped in the sea. These conclusions, again, had come as no surprise. Now the police work could start in earnest, beginning with trying to identify the body and, just as important, finding out where it had come from.

There were no documents on the corpse that would assist with identification, and though there were numerous bits of paper stuffed in various pockets of the voluminous overcoat, none was in any way helpful. There was also around fifteen pounds, mainly in low-denomination coins, in one inside pocket, but it was clear from even a cursory examination that this man had been a tramp or derelict. That would ultimately have no bearing on the thoroughness of their search for his killer, but it would obviously make it more difficult to find out who he was, since there was little likelihood of a wife or lover somewhere waiting for him to come home.

'Not much of a life,' Mason muttered to DS Clark, his usual partner in such cases.

'Not even much of a death,' Dick Clark grunted, staring at the corpse's face with grim attention. It was doubtful if even the dead man's mother would have recognized this sad detritus of a wasted life. The heavily bloated face had a greenish tinge, and its features looked strangely distorted, partly caused by some of the soft tissues having been nibbled off by various forms of marine life.

'It's going to be a bitch finding out who he was.'

Clark nodded. 'I'll get one of the artists to try and knock up an image of his face before the crabs and whatever got at it. We can ask the local papers to print it and pass it on to the neighbouring forces.'

'Send some copies to the Sally Army as well. He might have been a regular customer at some of their soup kitchens. But if nobody local recognizes him, I don't know where we'll go from there.'

'About the only useful thing The Ghoul was able to tell us was that the corpse hadn't been in the water long. I've got a couple of constables studying the tide tables and an OS map of the neighbouring coast to try to work out approximately where Mr X might have been shoved in.'

'It's more likely they'll end up with a list of places where he *couldn't* have been killed, but that'd be a start, certainly.' Mason turned his gaze away from the corpse and looked west towards the mouth of the Thames Estuary, shielding his eyes against the driving rain. 'This wasn't a local crime, I'm sure of that. The answer lies somewhere up that way.'

'Then there's the problem of motive,' Clark said. 'Kids might have fun beating up a tramp, but they very rarely end up committing a murder, unless by accident. But there's clearly nothing accidental about this death. Whoever dragged a knife or razor across this man's throat knew exactly what they were doing. So what could this derelict have done that made his death a necessity?'

'If we ever find that out,' Paul Mason replied gloomily, 'we'll be a lot closer to finding his killers.'

Onex commune, Canton of Geneva, Switzerland

The only person in the briefing room, as Richter and Schneider walked in, was the same plain-clothes man, who stood up painfully to greet his superior officer. As Schneider had explained, he was just badly winded, but Richter knew from personal experience what the impact of a bullet from a Kalashnikov felt like at close range. Though the body-armour vest had saved the man's life, he was going to be aching for days or weeks still to come.

Richter walked across to the coffee percolator in one corner, where he poured out two cups and handed them to the other men. Then he made one for himself and slumped down in a chair right at the back of the room. Although he had become involved in the assault, he had really been there just as an observer. It was Schneider who had run the operation, and his team that had implemented it.

Richter always believed in keeping things simple, so the statement he now prepared filled barely half of the available space on a standard report form. Most of the other sections were not applicable to him, since he wasn't a member of the Swiss – or indeed any other – police force.

Fifteen minutes after it was completed and he'd handed it to Schneider, three grim-faced men strode into the room, and the way the Swiss officer immediately stood up to greet them signalled that these were senior officers. Richter spoke fairly fluent Russian, and had a smattering of phrases in French, Spanish and German, but he didn't need to be a linguist to realize that Schneider was on the receiving end of a comprehensive bollocking – though the Swiss officer was giving back pretty much as good as he was getting. He wasn't accepting the criticism now being levelled at him and kept snapping back a single phrase in German that Richter finally deciphered as 'You weren't there.'

After five minutes, Richter stood up and walked over to the briefing table. Schneider glanced at him briefly, but the other three ignored him completely.

'This isn't achieving anything,' Richter said quietly in English.

His calm voice, speaking in a different language, had the effect of immediately silencing the tirade. One of the senior officers asked Schneider a question, to which he replied in rapid-fire German, presumably explaining Richter's presence, then he switched to English.

'My senior colleagues believe we mishandled this operation. They reckon we should have been able to arrest the terrorists without it ending in a shooting match.'

'Yes,' Richter said firmly, 'and with hindsight we could all win the lottery. I don't think we ever had a chance of taking them down peacefully, for one very simple reason.'

'The phone call?'

'Exactly. Somebody rang that apartment just before we went in and obviously warned the terrorists that we were waiting outside. So when your man here' – he gestured to the officer sitting a few feet away, still nursing his chest – 'knocked on the door, they already knew exactly who he was, and that's why they blasted three rounds right through the door. Somebody knew our plans precisely and he timed his call to the second. I think you might have a mole here, Wilhelm.'

Schneider immediately shook his head. 'I can't believe that. I don't believe any Swiss police officer – and certainly no member of my team – would get involved with a gang of terrorists.'

One of the senior officers asked something, and Schneider answered him briefly in German before turning back to Richter.

'But money talks, Wilhelm, and *someone* made that call,' Richter argued.

'I know, and we're checking its origin through Swiss Telecom right now.'

'That might help, at least by a process of elimination. And there's something else I'd like an answer to. When the landlord – Rolf Hermann, I think you said his name was – did his snooping about in the apartment earlier, he told the local police he'd spotted one Kalashnikov. But I saw four AK47s and six pistols, and we know they had at least one grenade. That's a serious arsenal, and it presumably wasn't tucked away in a cupboard somewhere, simply because of the speed with which the terrorists reacted to us. So how come Hermann saw only one weapon?'

'That had occurred to me as well,' Schneider admitted. 'I've asked the local officers to locate Hermann and fetch him here for further questioning. As his precious apartment now resembles a battleground, I'm slightly surprised he hasn't turned up already.'

Another of the senior officers opened his mouth to speak, but at that moment there was a knock on the door, and a junior officer entered. He walked straight across to Schneider and handed him a slip of paper. After a cursory glance, Schneider then passed it to the senior officer closest to him.

'We've lost Werner,' he explained to Richter. 'The hospital just called to say he died on the operating table. So that's four of my officers in one day. If there *has* been a leak here,' he threatened, his voice heavy with menace, 'I won't rest until I've uncovered it, but I still think it's more likely there was a fifth member of the cell we knew nothing about – a man on the outside who witnessed our preparations and made the phone call.'

*

Precisely as Wilhelm Schneider resumed his acrimonious discussion with the three senior police officers, a door opened in a rental-apartment complex about a mile away, and a man looked out cautiously.

He was middle-aged, solidly built and unremarkable in appearance, wearing an overcoat that was perhaps a little too heavy for the prevailing weather, but which served to conceal the fact that he was wearing not one but two shoulder holsters. Under his left arm he had a Heckler & Koch MP5KA4 machine-pistol fitted with a fifteen-round box magazine: this is the variant of the MP5K equipped with a three-round burst trigger group. As it was much bulkier than a semi-automatic pistol, the overcoat was essential to disguise it, while concealed on the other side of his body was his back-up weapon, a Glock 17.

The name typed in his professionally forged German passport was Helmut Kleber, but this man had actually been born on another continent. He stepped into the corridor pulling a small suitcase on wheels, a leather laptop computer case strapped to the handle, with his left hand. He invariably kept his right arm free and unencumbered, just in case he had to draw one of his weapons. Having glanced round to check that nobody else was visible on the same floor of the building, he closed the door quietly behind him and began heading along the corridor towards the lifts.

Emerging a few minutes later at the rear of the building, he now made his way unhurriedly across the car park towards a hired Ford saloon over on the far side. He used the remote control to open the boot, but glanced around carefully before lifting the suitcase into it, because that would need both hands. The area was deserted, and moments later he strapped himself in, started the engine and turned the car towards the road heading for the French border.

He had a long drive ahead of him, and knew he wouldn't reach his objective for a couple of days, but that would still leave time enough.

Early that same evening, Richter was on his way out of the hotel to find a restaurant for dinner – he was planning to leave for Spain the next morning – when his mobile rang.

'We've another puzzle,' Schneider announced, when he answered it. 'Can you get back here?'

A few minutes later Richter re-entered the police station and was directed straight through to the briefing room. Sitting at the table, reading through a sheaf of papers, Schneider looked up as he entered. He waved his hand to the seat opposite and waited until Richter sat down, then slid an A4-size photograph across the table towards him. It showed an elderly man – about seventy years old – wearing spectacles and scowling at the camera.

'And this is?' Richter asked, looking up.

'Rolf Hermann, the owner of that apartment block.'

'So?'

'Hermann is seventy-three years old, not in the best of health, and currently in a very aggressive mood. He arrived here at the station late this afternoon in a wheelchair pushed by his daughter and was extremely displeased about what had happened to his property. He warned us that he would be seeking substantial compensation for the damage caused and for future loss of rental earnings. Quite apart from the repairs and redecoration now necessary, not everyone, as he pointed out, would want to live in a flat where eight men had been recently killed in a serious shoot-out.'

'Will he get anything?'

'I've no idea. That's not my department.'

'And your point is?'

'My point is that the first Rolf Hermann knew about the assault we mounted today was when he saw his own property appear as the lead feature on this afternoon's television news. Unfortunately, that was shortly *before* we phoned him, which might explain his somewhat hostile attitude. He hadn't previously contacted the police about the person who had leased his apartment – he always uses a rental agency – and had absolutely no idea what we were talking about when we began to question him about his tenants.'

'He's a doppelgänger?'

'Exactly. We've no idea of the identity of man who contacted the local police about these terrorists, but we do know he certainly wasn't Rolf Hermann.'

Chapter Four

Tuesday
Onex commune, Canton of Geneva, Switzerland

The ringing of his mobile woke Richter at just after four thirty.

'Richter,' he said groggily.

'What the bloody hell happened yesterday?'

'Simpson?' Richter was astounded. His boss was not known as an early bird. He preferred, he often said, to wait until the streets were properly aired before he ventured onto them. And as four thirty in Switzerland equated to three thirty in London, Richter was even more amazed.

'You were *supposed* to be liaising with the gnomes in Geneva, not staging your own version of the *Gunfight at the OK Corral*. What's the latest score, anyway? Four terrorists and three policemen dead?'

'Four cops, actually. The wounded officer died in hospital yesterday.'

'Four police officers,' Simpson echoed. 'And, just to remind you, we don't have any mediums on the staff, so dead terrorists are no fucking good to us. Why the hell did you get involved?'

'You weren't there, Simpson,' Richter explained, unconsciously echoing Wilhelm Schneider's remark to his superiors of the previous evening. 'These guys were definitely not prepared to surrender. It was either them or us.'

'And how come *you* ended up shooting two of them? You weren't even supposed to be armed, and you were there strictly as an observer.'

'I wasn't carrying and I didn't plan any of it, but four policemen were taken out by a grenade, and if I hadn't grabbed a gun and stepped in when I did, the result might have been even worse. And anyway I only shot one and a half terrorists.'

'What the fuck does that mean?'

'I hit the last bad guy with a round from a shotgun, but a Swiss police officer got him at the same time, so we're claiming half each.'

'Don't be flippant, Richter. I was called in here at two fifteen this morning, and I've had the Six duty officer bending my ear about you for the last half-hour. The Swiss authorities are extremely unhappy about what happened and they've communicated their feelings to Vauxhall Cross. Geneva is looking for someone to blame and, according to Six, the wheels in FedPol are considering issuing a warrant for your arrest – for either murder or manslaughter.'

'That's ridiculous.'

'It may be, but that's the way it's panning out. My guess is that they'll jump one way or the other sometime today, so my advice is you get dressed, forget about breakfast and get the hell out of Switzerland as soon as you can. I don't want the hassle of trying to spring you from some continental slammer, because there's too much else going on right now.'

'And what if the Swiss then ask the French to arrest me? I can't hope to outrun *all* of the European police forces, you know.'

'No problem. I'll make the appropriate noises to the FCO as soon as there's some chance of raising anyone there who possesses a brain, and then get them to liaise with Paris. If you do happen to get picked up in France, make sure you notify me about where and when. Oh, by the way, your leave is cancelled. Get yourself back here as soon as you can.'

'Right,' Richter said and ended the call. Just ten minutes later he was walking across the car park towards his Westfield, overnight bag in his hand, his room key left at the deserted reception desk in an envelope with a bundle of euro notes to cover the hotel bill.

Richard Simpson's assurance that the Swiss authorities hadn't yet decided whether or not to charge him was one thing. But if Richter had been employed by FedPol, and there was any possibility of an arrest warrant being issued, he would have soon placed a watch on the borders. Or at least on the border crossings immediately south of Geneva, so he wasn't going to take that route.

Before driving out of the hotel car park, he pulled out a road book of Europe and spent a few minutes working out what looked like a better option. Then he programmed his Navman, fired up the engine on the

Westfield – though regretting for the first time that his car wasn't just a *little* less conspicuous – and headed north-east out of Onex.

He had gone less than a quarter of a mile when he noticed two sets of headlights in his mirror, which were then switched off as the vehicles came to a stop. He pulled in to the side of the road to check what was happening, fishing a pair of compact binoculars out of his bag. Two police cars had parked outside the hotel and, even as he watched, four men climbed out of them and approached the main building.

They would now have to rouse the receptionist to gain entrance, but Richter guessed that within ten minutes they'd be inside the room he himself had just vacated. He slipped the binoculars back inside his overnight bag, put the Westfield into first gear and drove away.

Minutes later, as he approached the outskirts of Geneva, he saw flashing lights in his mirror. It could have been a routine patrol, or it could be the local plods responding to an emergency call from some respectable citizen. Or it could be something else.

Richter decided not to wait around to find out. He dropped two gears, swung the Westfield into a right-hand turn down a side street and floored the accelerator pedal.

Stuttgart, Germany

The relays of watchers had done what they could to establish what might be happening inside the vacant shop and storerooms, but the results of the surveillance effort placed on the building following the observations by Fritz Stiebling had been disappointing, to say the least. Getting any useful result was proving difficult, as the terraced building on the left of their target premises was deserted, which meant they couldn't use it for fear of alerting the suspects. They set up powerful cameras, and parabolic microphones linked to laptop computers, in whatever vantage points they could access on the opposite side of the road, but these were proving of limited use because few of the people under observation ever spoke outside the building, and they seemed to come and go fairly infrequently.

The primary concern for the police was the bank next door. The manager had already been visited by two senior officers who had explained their concern that the occupants of the adjacent building might be planning to tunnel into his vault. That, the bank official had insisted, would be almost impossible, because it was lined with steel plate and fitted with sensors that would instantly detect any attempted intrusion. But he was happy enough to let the police install additional microphones on the party wall abutting that of the other building. These were linked to another laptop computer and to a wireless router, while an further laptop housed in a building across the street was set up to access the wifi network and to burn the 'take' onto audio CDs.

That exercise had produced results, but they were confusing. Noises that could have been interpreted as tunnelling work had been detected but, in the opinion of the team monitoring the system, they originated nowhere near the wall of the bank. That didn't make much sense, but it was sufficiently interesting for the inspector in charge to keep the surveillance in place for the moment, despite the misgivings of his superior officer. But the operation, the chief inspector also warned, had a finite life. If they got nothing positive from the surveillance after another forty-eight hours, he was going to pull the plug on it.

But that was before he was called in during the early hours of that morning to listen to the last recording from one of the two parabolic microphones aimed at the target building. The conversation it had picked up late the previous evening, between two of the suspects, lasted for less than ten seconds but what one of them said was enough for the chief inspector to instantly alert not only his superior but also contact the BGS – the Bundesgrenzschutz or Federal Border Police.

Switzerland

Richter knew that outrunning a single police car was comparatively easy if the escaping driver knew the area, was competent behind the wheel and was in a car at least as powerful as the pursuing vehicle. Outrunning a police force, on the other hand, was almost impossible if the pursuit was conducted properly. The police could divert traffic, close roads, set up road blocks, deploy stop sticks or spikes, use multiple vehicles on the ground and get helicopters into the air, and against that kind of organization no solo driver could hope to evade capture for very long. Richter knew his Westfield could out-turn and out-accelerate any car the Swiss could send after him, but he'd never visited the country before and certainly didn't know the terrain or the local roads. He would have to rely on his Navman to keep him from driving down any dead ends and just hope he could get out of Switzerland before a comprehensive pursuit could be organized.

The only possible edge Richter had was that, if he could avoid the single pursuing car, there would be no way they could know which route he might plan to take out of the country, since the Swiss border can be crossed in literally dozens of places. The problem was that every crossing, even on the most minor roads, has a customs post located either directly on the border itself or on one of the roads leading to it, and he presumed that FedPol could initiate some kind of general alert procedure with just a couple of phone calls. He doubted if every minor customs post would be manned twenty-four hours a day, but his worry was that they might instead have barriers across the road, to prevent vehicles from driving through.

He kept checking his mirrors and already, less than a minute after he'd cleared the side street and got onto an eastbound road leading towards Annemasse, the flashing lights reappeared behind him. A couple of hundred yards behind, true, but far too close for comfort, so now it was time for evasive action.

The escape route he'd more or less decided on lay due east of Geneva, in the vicinity of Juvigny. According to his map there were a couple of customs posts there, but he reckoned his best chance of getting clear would be to use a minor road. Meanwhile, to ensure he had a clear run for the border, he needed to convince his pursuers that he was intending to head in a completely different direction.

The streets of Geneva were almost deserted as he ignored a red light and swung the Westfield into another side street, this time heading north, and suddenly accelerated. He crossed the Rhône where it entered Lake Geneva and immediately picked up Route 1, the road that runs along the western shore of the lake. The pursuit car followed, its flashing roof-bar lights now supplemented by a siren and pulsing headlamps. Richter pushed the Westfield as fast as he could and quickly increased the distance between himself and the pursuing police car to about a mile. Then he started looking out for the next junction.

As he spotted the sign on the right-hand side of the road, he immediately switched off the lights and also the ignition, since he couldn't risk the flare of his brake lights revealing what he was doing, and steered the Westfield off Route 1. The junction fortunately included an underpass and, as soon Richter knew he was out of sight of the main road, he restarted the engine. He powered through the underpass to rejoin the road he'd just left, but this time heading south. Even over the roar of the Ford Zetec engine, he could hear the howl of the pursuing car's siren as it sped past the junction, still heading north. He switched on his lights again as he was approaching Geneva and, as soon as he was back across the river, turned north-east on Route 3 to follow the east shore of Lake Geneva. Checking behind, he saw no sign of pursuit, but that could just mean they were waiting for him somewhere ahead. Yet he had neither seen nor heard a helicopter, and only just the single police car since he'd left the hotel, so perhaps he was going to get away with it.

But that wasn't the way he planned to get out of Switzerland, and after about six kilometres he turned off, taking the minor road that ran east through Corsinge and then on to Sionnet. The moment Richter pointed the Westfield away from the main highway he felt better: on these country roads the car was in its element. There he swung left, drove as quickly as possible to Jussy, and turned south-east again in the middle of the village, taking the white road that led to Les Curtines. Somewhere just ahead of him, he knew, there was a customs post on the road that crossed the border.

At the crossroads in the middle of the village – the point where he was going to physically leave Switzerland – there was nothing to be seen. No police, no customs post. But the moment he crossed the road towards Cabouet and turned the corner, Richter saw flashing lights again. This time they were in front of him.

Hammersmith, London

Richard Simpson was in a foul mood, for several reasons. He was annoyed with Richter for getting involved in the shoot-out at Onex, though accepting his subordinate's claim that he'd had little option in the circumstances. He was irritated at being summoned to the office in what he considered the middle of the night, but what had really pissed him off was FedPol.

Richter may have been sent to Switzerland simply as an observer on behalf of the SIS, and his involvement in the assault at the apartment building might have been not only unauthorized but technically illegal. And, in addition, he had killed at least one terrorist, perhaps two. But, as Simpson understood it, the reality was that, if Richter hadn't picked up a shotgun and done what he did best, the Swiss would probably now be looking at up to seven body-bags with policemen stuffed inside them, at least one of them a senior officer. That, he thought, was the important point and, now he was up and working, he decided to ensure that the most senior FedPol officer he could rouse in Geneva was made fully aware of his views on the matter.

Switzerland

There was no way Richter was going to stop. The single police car was parked partially sideways across the road, but the vehicle itself was no-where near big enough to block it completely. Beside the car, and clearly not anticipating that this particular tasking was anything more than a waste of their time, two cops stood smoking and chatting, not even glancing in his direction. But the moment they heard the sound of the Westfield's engine, they turned their attention directly towards the approaching vehicle. In the pre-dawn gloom, all they would see yet were two headlights. Both officers stepped forward, raising their hands for him to stop. Richter complied by dropping the Westfield down two gears and touched the brake pedal. He next reached over, undid the quick-release catch on the left side of the windscreen, did the same on the right, and then folded the screen down flat. The tallest thing in the car was now Richter himself. As the cops gestured that he should pull over to the side of the road, Richter ensured he was in first gear, which would give him electric acceleration, coasted towards the grass verge and waited for his opportunity.

The Swiss police officers were probably bored, and certainly careless.

As soon as the car slowed down, they obviously assumed the driver was going to stop like any good law-abiding citizen. But Richter was neither law-abiding nor a citizen.

One cop strode over to the kerb and began heading towards him, while the other remained where he was, on the right-hand side of the road with his arm held up, directly in front of the vehicle. The left-hand side of the road was thus completely empty, and, as the first officer approached the Westfield, Richter dropped the clutch, hit the accelerator and twitched the steering wheel to the left, aiming for the gap between the police vehicle and the opposite grass verge. His car instantly surged forward, its rear tyres leaving two black streaks on the tarmac.

Behind him he heard shouts, which he ignored, and just concentrated on driving. He swung the Westfield around the patrol car, then steered it immediately right and straightened up. Both the police officers were armed, but he heard no shots and guessed why. He looked ahead and there was the reason, just as he had anticipated. The map book had been right: there was no customs post on this road, but there *was* a barrier. Spanning the entire width of the tarmac were two red-and-white striped poles, counterweighted at the pivot end, and with a kind of dangling trellis below them, designed to stop any conventional car. But the Westfield was far from conventional. Inspired by the original Lotus 7, it was small, sleek and blisteringly fast. More than that, it was low – very much lower than almost any other car on the road, and, now that he'd folded the windscreen, Richter hoped he could simply drive under the barrier.

He hit the brakes as he reached it, slowing slightly as he confirmed the height of the cross bar, then ducked sideways down into the passenger side of the car as its long nose passed underneath.

The trellis passed no more than an inch above his head as he drove under the steel bar and accelerated away. He was safely out of the land of the gnomes, and, more importantly, the police car was still stuck on the other side and would remain so until they found the key that unlocked the barrier in order to raise it. And even then they would surely face the usual jurisdictional problems about armed police from one nation pursuing a fugitive into another country.

As far as Richter could tell, he was more or less clear. All he had to do now was avoid the French gendarmes until Simpson got the fix in place, because he had no more desire to sample the delights of a French jail than its Swiss equivalent.

At Cabouet he turned right, but stopped a short way down the road to raise the windscreen back into position, reprogram the Navman for Calais and check the map again. The E21 passed far too close to the Swiss border for his liking, so he decided to head south towards Bonneville, then route via Annecy, Bellegarde-sur-Valserine and Bourg-en-Bresse, sticking to the country roads as far as possible. Hopefully, even if the French *were* looking for him, they'd only have the manpower to cover the main roads and the autoroutes, and the further away he got himself from Switzerland, the wider the search area would become.

Driving on the minor roads would suit him down to the ground, because the Westfield wasn't a high-speed motorway cruiser. It was far more at home on twisting country roads, where its excellent handling and startling acceleration made it virtually impossible to catch.

As dawn broke, he was powering the Westfield through the silent streets of Mâcon and heading for Digoin and Moulins. And, up to that point, he hadn't even *seen* a single gendarme.

Canterbury, Kent

Detective Sergeant Dick Clark replaced the telephone in its cradle and looked up at DI Mason, who'd just walked in clutching a mug of black coffee.

'We might have a result,' the DS said. 'Sort of, anyway.'

'Yes?' Mason muttered encouragingly.

'Early this morning a man walking his dog at Sheerness reported finding what he thought was a patch of blood close to the estuary. He alerted a couple of patrolling constables, who thought it was worth calling in. They also found an old tarpaulin and other bits and pieces lying around, so it looks like Sheppey might be where our gentleman of the road met his end.'

DI Mason put the mug down on his desk, walked over to the area map on the wall and traced a line along the north coast of Kent, moving his finger west from Reculver to the Isle of Sheppey.

'Sounds about right,' he said. 'If the murder took place sometime last night, the timing probably works, too. The tide could have dropped him here this morning. But even if the two events *are* linked, we're not much further forward. We still don't know why somebody decided to kill this man, but we'll drive over to Sheerness anyway and see what they've got.'

Clark nodded. 'The artist's finished a facial reconstruction, so I'll collect a few copies before we go. Meanwhile, I'll see if The Ghoul's finished blood-typing or found other evidence that might give us a definite link.'

Central France

By late morning, Richter was approaching Chartres on the N154. He was going to avoid Paris, simply because he hated driving round the Périphérique, especially in a car like the Westfield, which most French drivers were apparently completely unable to see, and so he intended to route via Rouen instead.

His highly illegal but very efficient radar detector, which he'd fitted to a hidden bracket behind the dashboard, and equipped with a kill switch that was equally invisible, had screamed at him more than a dozen times that morning, warning him of fixed radar guns on the road – though the French authorities had helpfully provided a visual warning of each one as well, so the detector was almost superfluous. On each occasion, he'd hauled his speed down to the legal maximum before he went through the speed trap.

The Navman estimated that he should reach Boulogne by mid-afternoon, and he'd already booked his return trip on the high-speed catamaran operating between there and Dover. So, if nothing went wrong, he ought to be back in London by early evening.

Sheerness, Isle of Sheppey, Kent

The tentative identification of the corpse didn't take anything like as long as Mason had feared. The moment Clark showed the desk sergeant the artist's reconstruction of the dead man's face, he showed a spark of recognition.

'It's Barney, I think,' he said, then called out to a passing constable. 'Here, Derek, come and take a look at this. You reckon that's Barney?'

The police officer took the drawing and studied it. 'Could be,' he replied. 'I'm not certain. Some of the features look a bit odd.'

'Not entirely surprising under the circumstances,' Clark said, but didn't elaborate. 'So who's this Barney?'

'I think his real name is Edward Holmes, and we've picked him up a few times for drunk and disorderly, especially during the winter months. We give him a bed for the night and a couple of meals and then send him on his way. He's harmless enough.'

'He certainly is now,' Mason said. 'We found his body on the sea front at Reculver yesterday morning. The reason you're looking at a drawing rather than a photograph is because he'd been in the estuary for a few hours and some of the beasties out there had used him for lunch.'

'Poor old sod,' the desk sergeant remarked. 'Drowned, I suppose?'

'Nope,' Clark said. 'He got a back-street face-lift.'

'A what?'

'You read too much spy fiction,' Mason muttered. 'What my colleague is trying to explain, in a rather clumsy fashion, is that somebody cut Barney's throat. And then they tossed his body into the sea, so this is a murder inquiry.'

'Barney? Murdered? But he was just a harmless old tramp. Are you sure?'

'No, but this is the only lead we've got at the moment. We've already got the corpse's blood group, so if you've got any samples from the crime scene here, maybe your forensic people can do a match and see if there's a link. Then we can look at DNA and all the rest of it.'

The desk sergeant looked doubtful. 'Ah, well, we don't really have a *crime scene* as such. Some bloke out walking his dog found what he thought looked like a patch of bloodstained grass near the sea wall. We sent out a SOCO, and he came back with a walking stick and a couple of other bits. That's about it.'

Mason and Clark exchanged glances.

'A walking stick?' the DI asked.

'Yes. It looked as if the end of it might be smeared with blood, and there were a few grey hairs stuck to it.'

'And was it blood?'

'Yes, we've already established that much from the lab, but we're still waiting for the grouping and anything else they can tell us.'

Hammersmith, London

While he was waiting to board the catamaran at Boulogne, Richter had called the duty officer on his mobile and had been told to head straight to Hammersmith, where his boss, Simpson, would be waiting for him.

He parked the car in the secure garage underneath the building and took the lift up to the seventh floor. After knocking on the dark green door that bore the word 'Director' in faded gold leaf, he walked in to find Richard Simpson sitting behind his desk, the perimeter of which was guarded by a whole flock of cacti. At a quick glance, Richter thought he spotted a few new models among their prickly green ranks.

'They didn't catch you, then,' Simpson began, by way of greeting, as Richter sat himself down in front of the desk.

'Thanks to your call, no. A couple of plod-mobiles pitched up at my hotel in Onex just after I'd driven away from it, and I picked up a tail very soon afterwards in Geneva. Then I had to kind of dodge around the barriers when I crossed the border into France.'

Simpson grunted. 'And no problems with the French?'

Richter shook his head. 'I don't think I saw a single gendarme all the way back, and there wasn't even a reception committee waiting for me at the ferry port.'

'Right, good. Now, there've been some developments since we last talked, but first brief me on exactly what happened.'

Richter explained the sequence of events that led up to the raid on the apartment.

'You're sure about the phone call?' Simpson interrupted. 'Somebody definitely rang and tipped these guys off?'

'That's the only thing that makes sense. Up till then they seemed to have no clue they were even under surveillance. As soon as they received the call, somebody inside the flat started shouting.'

'So who made the call, do you think?'

'That's the big question, of course. I suggested to Schneider that he might have a mole in his Terrorism Investigations Unit, but—'

'Tactful as ever, Richter.'

'We had four dead terrorists, four dead police officers, and an apartment so totally trashed that retrieving any useful intelligence from it is pretty damned unlikely. So being tactful wasn't high on my list of priorities right then. Anyway, he absolutely rejected the possibility, and now it seems as if he was right.'

Simpson looked interested. 'Explain that.'

'I got a call from Schneider yesterday evening and went back to the police station in Onex. He'd just had a fairly acrimonious conversation with the owner of the apartment, an irritating old fart called Rolf Hermann, who was basically blaming the Swiss police for all the damage and was threatening to sue everyone from the head of the government down to the guy who sweeps the streets.'

'But I thought it was this Hermann who had contacted the local plods and tipped them off about the terrorists in the first place?'

'So did Schneider, but he was wrong. Hermann is over seventy and virtually wheelchair-bound. The man who delivered the tip-off was a well-built middle-aged man with dark hair who spoke fluent German.'

'Jesus Christ,' Simpson muttered, 'didn't they even check who he was?'

'They did, or at least they tried to. That particular "Rolf Hermann" claimed not to have either a passport or identity card with him, but he did provide the station staff with his address. After he'd gone they routinely checked that it matched the phone-book entry for Rolf Hermann, and even tried to call him, but his phone was out of order, which is also what the man told them when they interviewed him. But the bottom line is that they were far more interested in what he had to say to them than in confirming exactly who he was.'

'It's still seems pretty sloppy police work, mounting a major assault with armed officers based on a tip-off from some guy who's just walked in off the street.'

'Agreed, but what swung it for them was the serial number he supplied for the AK47 he claimed he'd seen. Schneider checked and confirmed that the weapon had been reported stolen and where from, which gave the tip immediate credibility. What's interesting is that the Swiss police recovered four Kalashnikovs from what's left of the apartment, but none of their numbers match the one this Hermann gave them.'

'So you mean there's either a fifth assault rifle out there somewhere or, more likely, this man just fed the police a piece of information he knew they could check and verify, just to get their attention?'

'That's what Schneider believes.'

'So who was the doppelgänger?' Simpson asked. 'And, perhaps more to the point, what was his motive in blowing the whistle on these people?'

'That's where it gets really interesting. We're quite certain it wasn't just a neighbour or anyone who'd seen something suspicious in the building. Quite apart from anything else, if that were the case, there'd be no need for the man to hide his identity. It also looks as if Rolf Hermann was chosen deliberately. Immediately after the real landlord called at the police station, Schneider ran some checks on him. The man's phone line had been deliberately cut, but Hermann probably wouldn't even have known that, since now he virtually lives with his daughter because of his poor health.'

'So even if the police had gone round to his house, they wouldn't have found him at home?'

'Exactly. Whoever impersonated Hermann knew quite a lot about him and took some care to ensure the police wouldn't discover the deception. He clearly wanted their assault on the place to go ahead. But the two facts that stand out are that the doppelgänger knew those men in the building were terrorists – or at least sitting on a small arsenal – and that he had the telephone number of the apartment. That has to mean he was somehow involved with them. And another check by the police seemed to confirm that.'

'The rental agency?' Simpson guessed.

'Yes. As far as the agency staff can remember, the person who rented that apartment fitted the description of the doppelgänger reasonably well, but there were no CCTV cameras in the rental office, and none close enough to the building itself to be worth checking. According to the agency's records, he gave his name as Heinrich Grunewald and he paid the rental and the security deposit in cash.'

'So it looks as if the fake Hermann – let's call him "Hermann II" – rented the place, moved his accomplices, or whoever they were, into it, and then blew the whistle on them.'

'Yes, and finally he tipped them off that the police were right outside the door, to more or less ensure that the result was a serious fire-fight with multiple casualties.'

'Is it just me or does that make no sense at all?'

'It's not just you, Simpson. Schneider has no clue what's going on either.'

'And have *you*? Has your devious mind come up with some half-way plausible explanation?'

'Not really.' Richter shook his head. 'When you look at that sequence of events, it really doesn't make sense. But if you forget *how* it happened and just look at *what* happened, perhaps there is a kind of twisted logic to it.'

'Like what?'

'Three days ago, neither of us had even heard of Onex. Now, we have four heavily armed terrorists lying dead – and unfortunately the same number of police officers killed – but with no civilian casualties, and with whatever atrocity the gang was planning in Switzerland presumably stopped in its tracks. Then there's Hermann II's statement about seeing the so-called "shopping list" and the reference to "FRB London" on the same terrorists' laptop, which was the reason you sent me there in the first place.'

'So?' Simpson prompted.

'So as a result of this operation, a genuine terrorist cell has been eliminated and Britain has been warned about a possible attack over here. I think somebody's trying to send us a message, a message that we would take seriously precisely because of what happened in Onex.'

Simpson mulled that over for a few seconds. 'Yes, I suppose that does make some sense. Do you think the Swiss will be able to get any useful intelligence out of that apartment?'

'Probably not much. The living room was really badly shot up, not to mention having a grenade explode right in the middle of it. I saw the laptop – or what was left of it – and that was pretty much wrecked, too. They might find some other stuff in the bedrooms, I suppose, but I wouldn't hold your breath waiting.'

'Right. I hope you haven't unpacked.'

'Unpacked? What do you mean "unpacked"? You know I've driven straight here from Dover.'

'That's good, because you're going on another little trip. Something rather like the incident at Onex seems to be going on in Germany as well, only this time there hasn't been a tip-off from some phantom phone-caller. Instead, an off-duty police officer spotted what looked like possible preparations for a bank robbery, but the surveillance now seems to suggest it could be terrorist-related.'

Simpson then briefly outlined what had happened in Stuttgart.

'So what's the terrorist link?' Richter asked.

'Only a snatch of conversation they recorded on their parabolic mikes. Two of the suspects stood talking outside the building, and one of them mentioned the "big one in London". The other one laughed and muttered something like "biggest bang since the war". The problem was the Germans can't be sure of the exact words, because of the distance of the mikes from the subjects, and there was a stiff wind blowing, and noisy traffic driving along the street. A whole bunch of fuck-factors, in short, but the BGS was still concerned enough to inform Five and Six.'

'If the German police have called in the Bundesgrenzschutz they *must* be taking it seriously.'

'And so is Vauxhall Cross. They want us to liaise with the BGS and, as you've already done such a wonderful job in Switzerland' – Simpson gave Richter a withering look – 'I've decided you can hop on a BA flight to Stuttgart tomorrow morning and give the Germans a hand.'

He passed an envelope across the desk. 'Your ticket and contact details for the plods in Stuttgart are in there. Don't even think about asking to take a weapon. You're going over there for *liaison* only, just in case this German thing is anything at all to do with what happened in Switzerland. This time, if possible, try very hard not to kill anyone.'

Chapter Five

Wednesday
Stuttgart, Germany

The moment Richter stepped into the arrivals hall just after eleven that morning, he saw a broad-shouldered man with very fair, almost white, hair and wearing a dark suit, holding up a piece of A4 paper with the name 'RICHTER' on it and, below that, 'BGS'. Richter walked over and showed his passport.

'My name is Franz.' The man spoke fluent English, but with the kind of accent that inescapably reminded Richter of all the caricature Germans he'd seen in old films. 'Did you have a good flight?' he asked.

'Not really,' Richter replied. 'I flew British Airways,' he added, as if that explained everything, which in many ways it did.

'OK. The car is outside,' Franz said. 'You have any other luggage?'

'No,' Richter replied, his computer bag slung over his shoulder and an overnight case in one hand. 'This is it.'

The car was a dark grey Opel, a driver waiting behind the wheel. Richter stowed his bags in the boot and climbed into the back seat, Franz sat beside the driver in the front. The extra equipment fitted to the dash, including a two-way radio and a data-entry keyboard with a small screen above, immediately told him the car was an unmarked police vehicle.

'Where are we going?' Richter asked.

'First to your hotel.' Franz turned round in his seat. 'You've been booked into the Holiday Inn, because it's fairly close to the focus of the operation. Once you've checked in, we'll head over to the police station, where we've arranged a briefing for you. I believe you were involved in that recent terrorist incident just outside Geneva?'

'I was only there as an observer,' Richter said. 'And how did you know about that anyway?'

Franz grinned at him. 'The world of counter-terrorism is really quite small,' he said. 'The BGS has good connections with all the other European units, and I have several friends in the Swiss TIU. Wilhelm Schneider, by the way, sends his regards, and an apology for the misunderstanding that marred the end of your visit to Switzerland. He asked me to tell you that he'd managed to stop any further proceedings and he assured me you'd know what he was talking about.'

Richter nodded. 'I know exactly what he means, and please thank him next time you talk with him.'

Forty minutes later, with his overnight case and computer bag locked away in his room at the Holiday Inn, Richter entered a briefing room in a police station on the east side of Stuttgart, where the BGS had set up their local command post.

'This is Mr Richter,' Franz announced in German.

At one end of the room were several pin-boards with maps and other graphics attached, with a couple of people standing staring at them. About half a dozen other men were sitting at computers which lined the side walls. The two men at the front of the room turned and moved towards the door. One of them, a short dark-haired man with a swarthy complexion, stopped in front of Richter, his hand out stretched. 'Welcome,' he said with a smile, in English almost devoid of any accent. 'My name is Karl Wolff, and I'm the local Bundesgrenzschutz commander.'

'Paul Richter. I'm a sort of rep for the British SIS.'

'You're rather more than that, I think.' Wolff's smile broadened. 'We heard about what happened in Onex.'

Richter was beginning to wonder if there was anyone who *didn't* know about the shoot-out near Geneva.

'It was only supposed to be a liaison visit,' he explained, 'but things got rather out of hand.'

'From what I'm told, if you hadn't stepped in, the result might have been a lot worse. Wilhelm Schneider speaks very highly of you.'

'I'm pleased to hear it.'

Wolff quickly introduced him to the other members of his team, finally gesturing to Franz.

'And you've already met Franz Kelle. Now, what exactly have you been told about our operation here?' Wolff said, waving Richter to a seat at the front of the room.

'Only that the local police believed they might have detected preparations for a bank robbery, but then a few words recorded during their surveillance made them decide to call in the BGS. Those remarks seemed to refer to a terrorist operation involving London, which is why I'm here.'

'That's a fair summary.' Wolff picked up an extendable pointer and turned to face the map of east Stuttgart pinned up behind him. 'We're here,' he indicated, 'and this building over here is the bank in question. Now,' he said, and shifted the pointer to an aerial photograph of a large square building, 'this is an overhead view of the bank itself, and this long oblong structure attached to it is a row of empty shops with storerooms above.'

'They're all empty?' Richter asked. 'Why's that?'

'The area is scheduled for redevelopment and, apart from the bank, the whole lot will be pulled down in about four months. With the end-date getting closer, leases on the shops are obviously much less attractive. The last property was vacated about a month ago, and they've all remained empty since. Then a local police officer spotted men carrying boxes into this shop here' – he indicated the property immediately adjoining the bank – 'and that made him wonder. The police checked with the landlords, and they confirmed that they hadn't leased the property to anybody, so they knew that at the very least these people were trespassing.'

'Anyway, after warning the bank manager, our men fitted microphones against that wall of the vault and began their surveillance operation. That didn't yield anything interesting until they caught that brief snatch of conversation.'

'The "biggest bang since the war",' Richter quoted.

'Exactly, that and something to do with London. Now,' Wolff continued briskly, 'we'll obviously be taking these men down, but not immediately. We decided to keep watching them for a while longer to see if we can glean any other intelligence that might help identify their actual target. The other concern,' he added, 'is that if we strike too soon we might not get all of them.'

'How many of them are there in the building?' Richter asked.

'We've spotted nine different individuals in all, but they keep on coming and going, and usually there are only three or four on the premises at any one time. When we do eventually go in, we might have to run two operations in parallel: one to take down the group inside the building and the other to arrest those still out on the streets somewhere.'

'And of course they could have external links as well,' Richter suggested. 'These people normally set up multiple cells, and the last thing we'd want to do is take out a single cell without having established any idea where the other ones are located.'

'Quite. Now, you've probably not heard, but the Swiss technical experts today finished their examination of the laptop found in the apartment at Onex. They got nothing from it, unfortunately, as the damage to the hard disk was too severe. In fact it had virtually disintegrated.'

'What about the rest of the apartment?'

'According to Schneider, they found very little inside the flat. It looked as if those men were just using it as a doss-house, because there was almost no personal information to be found in it anywhere. Three of the dead men were of European appearance, but the fourth was dark-skinned with Arabic features, which might indicate some kind of an Islamic link, and they all carried false Dutch passports. About the only thing the Swiss could do was send off their fingerprints to Interpol for checking, but there's no guarantee they'll already be on file anywhere.'

Canterbury, Kent

'That was the DS at Sheerness,' Dick Clark put down the phone and turned to look at Mason, 'with an update on Barney.'

The incident room at Canterbury had been set up only the day before, and the paucity of information on the boards so far was worrying both Mason and Clark. They had pictures of the dead man and the spot where he was found at Reculver, others of the sea front at Sheerness, and also a large-scale map of the area with these two locations marked on it. And that was pretty much it, because it was virtually all they knew about the victim. They had no clue about his family, even if he had one, or any acquaintances. One of the most bizarre aspects of the case was that the people who probably knew Barney best were the Sheerness police, and even they had almost no information about him.

'What have they got for us?' Mason asked.

'Not a lot. The lab's now confirmed that the blood and hairs found on the walking stick at Sheerness did come from the same body we found at Reculver. Yesterday afternoon they dragged The Ghoul himself over to the crime scene on Sheppey. He hummed and hawed a bit, but they finally got him to agree that the killing probably took place there, and he put that in writing earlier today.'

'So we know what happened, and where it happened,' Mason replied, 'so the only two questions that need answering now are who killed him and why.'

'They've run the victim's fingerprints through the system, and they found a match,' Clark added. 'That isn't too surprising, as we know the Sheerness plods had picked him up for disorderly conduct a few times, but there's almost nothing else known about him.' Clark scanned the notes he'd made during his telephone conversation. 'His name was Edward Holmes, aka Barney, age about seventy-two.'

'What do you mean, "About seventy-two"?' Mason queried.

'He's given the Sheerness boys three different dates of birth at various times, and that's the average figure. He's been arrested in the past by several officers in Kent, and also a few in Essex, but only for the usual drunk and disorderly. There's nothing that suggests he wasn't just a harmless old tramp.'

'Anything else?'

'They've organized a door-to-door, as you requested, but they're not very hopeful. The area where Barney was killed is almost entirely a commercial district, so unless there was another late-night dog-walker or courting couple or something like that, we're not going to find out much that way. They'll also check all the late-night shops and takeaways. We know he ate pie and chips that evening, about three or four hours before he died, so we presume he bought them somewhere in Sheerness. That might give us a fairly accurate time and confirm a location. But that's about it.'

'This case really bugs me,' Mason said thoughtfully, staring at the boards. 'I mean, that poor old sod's entire possessions added up to fifteen quid and change, and by all accounts he was just a completely harmless old drunk, not really bothering anyone. Nobody benefits from his death, and I just can't see any motive that makes sense. So why did somebody decide to almost cut his head off?'

'Maybe it *was* gang of teenagers after all,' Clark suggested. 'I know we discounted that possibility earlier, but perhaps some of the local thugs decided to elevate their game a step above merely beating him up. I mean, they're an odd lot on Sheppey.'

'They may be,' Mason shook his head, 'but I don't think that's the answer. If it was just a teenage prank that went a long way too far, you'd expect a different kind of injury on the body.' He picked up the report of the autopsy faxed to them from Maidstone that morning. 'Briefly, what we have here is three separate injuries inflicted at about the time of his death. These are a single large bruise on his lower abdomen, consistent with a hard kick or a punch, and a severe blow to the left side rear of the head, which we now know was administered with his own walking stick. Finally, his throat was slashed with a sharp, long-bladed knife, most likely single-edged. The Ghoul thinks it might have been a large pocket-knife, and his killer probably administered a single cut, from side to side.

'Every other mark on the body was either the result of Barney habitually sleeping rough, or was received post-mortem. If this was genuinely some kind of "tramp-bashing" incident, you'd be more likely to encounter multiple bruises and perhaps even the odd broken bone. And if they had then decided to cut his throat, there would probably be multiple jabs, not just a single stroke.

'To me these injuries suggest a deliberate and efficient method of killing. A kick to drive the breath out of him, the blow to the head to knock him unconscious, and to finish him off they slit his throat.'

'Can you be sure he was unconscious when they used the knife?' Clark asked.

'The Ghoul's pretty certain, yes. There were no signs of defensive wounds on his hands, and no apparent movement of his head or neck while the cut was made. So he was either out like a light, or several people must have held him very still while the killer did his work, and there's none of the bruising on his arms that you'd expect if that had been done.'

'OK,' Clark said, 'you've convinced me. But who did it, and why?'

'As I said before, I'm buggered if I know.' Mason glanced up at the clock. 'Get your jacket,' he said. 'We'll go and take another look at the crime scene at Sheerness.'

'We only went there yesterday,' Clark reminded him.

'I know, but maybe we missed something. Unless you've got a better idea?'

'Nope,' Clark said, checking the car keys were in his pocket.

Stuttgart, Germany

'Have you any idea at all who these people are?' Richter asked, standing in front of a pin-board that displayed a couple of dozen photographs of the men occupying the empty shop premises beside the bank.

Their pictures weren't particularly clear, having been taken from some distance away and in generally poor light. In only a couple of cases were the subjects facing towards the camera: in most they were caught in profile, and Richter knew that identifying them from such poor images would be very difficult.

Wolff shook his head. 'Not so far.' He tapped one photograph. 'We thought we'd identified this one, but it turns out the man we mistook him for is currently in an Austrian prison serving ten years for bank robbery. As for the others, we've no idea. We need better pictures, but the trouble is that, whenever they leave the building, they're usually wearing hats pulled low over their faces, and with collars turned up. They're clearly making a determined effort not to be recognized.'

'That could be good news,' Richter mused, 'because if they're that careful it might mean their mug-shots are on a database somewhere. Have you tried following any of them?'

'Yes, but as soon as they're out of the immediate area they always start running very competent anti-surveillance routines. We've decided it's safer to let them go than to risk any of our own people being spotted. At this stage we obviously don't want to show our hand because as far as we can tell they still don't realize we're watching them.'

'Apart from the brief exchange you recorded about some kind of an attack on London, have you picked up anything else useful?'

'We've got a few problems in that area,' Wolff admitted. 'The target premises are never empty, so we can't even use the deserted shop next door without it becoming obvious. That would be our preferred location for inserting spike microphones through the wall. The party wall shared with the bank is a considerable problem. It's actually a double wall, one section forming the end wall of the row of shops, and the other the structure of the bank itself. There's a lining of welded steel plates, two centimetres thick, embedded in the bank's wall, plus a network of vibration sensors. The sensors aren't a problem – obviously we can switch them off – but the plates are another story, because there's no way we can drill through them silently. We've attached microphones to the wall itself, and they did, oddly enough, record sounds of hammering that might be interpreted as tunnelling activities, but certainly not on the bank wall, so we discounted it. For picking up conversations, the mikes are almost useless.'

'I can see that. Two brick walls and a steel plate would certainly provide pretty good sound insulation. I suppose you can't get up on the roof and drop something down between the adjoining walls?'

'No. We thought of that, but there isn't a gap: the shop wall was built actually contiguous with the wall of the bank. And there are no cellars or sewers or any other route we can use to approach the target premises and then attach listening devices.'

'So all you have are the parabolic mikes, and obviously they're only of any use when the targets are outside the building.'

'Exactly,' Wolff agreed. 'Most of what they've said to each other is either meaningless or unimportant – one man telling another he's going out for half a hour, that kind of thing – but we have picked up a few names.'

'Yes?' Richter looked interested, but Wolff shook his head.

'They're not much help.' He pointed to a sheet of paper fixed on another pin-board. 'So far, we have "Helmut", "Dieter", "Max", "Konrad" and "Kleber". The first three are probably first names, and the last one most likely a surname, but "Konrad" could be either. We've run all possible combinations of these names through our databases here in Germany, and also through those of the police, security services and counter-terrorism forces of every other Western European nation. We've had hundreds of hits, as you might expect, because none of those names are that uncommon. But what we didn't get were any identifications with a proven link with any terrorist organization.'

'And, of course, they could easily be using aliases as well,' Richter said. 'Giving cell members randomly chosen names is a fairly common technique employed by terror groups.'

At that moment, one of the officers manning the computer workstations called out something, and the BGS commander walked over to join him. The two men conversed briefly in German, then Wolff translated for Richter.

'Things might be coming to a head,' he said. 'That was a report from the surveillance team. Two of the targets were standing outside the building a few minutes ago, and the parabolic mikes managed to catch bits of their conversation. One began, "When will—" and then a truck drove past and they lost the rest of his question. The other replied, "Tonight. About ten thirty." The first one said, "Good. Then we can get out of—" but the rest of that sentence was lost as well.

'That might suggest that whatever they're planning will take place this evening, or maybe they're expecting fresh orders from their controller. Or maybe even their boss is arriving. It could be almost anything, really, but if they're expecting to leave the building soon, that's obviously a significant development.'

'What will you do now?' Richter asked.

'We'll plan for the worst and assume they're intending to plant an IED somewhere here in Stuttgart. We'll ring the entire area, and if any of them leave the building carrying bags or driving vehicles, we'll take them down.'

TIMEBOMB

Sheerness, Isle of Sheppey, Kent

Dick Clark drove the Vauxhall into the Tesco car park and picked a vacant slot on the opposite side of it, near the sea wall.

He and Paul Mason walked along the narrow path and stopped beside the grassy area at one end of The Moat. It was the spot where forensic evidence was now telling them that Barney, aka Edward Holmes, had met his violent end. The patch of grass was still discoloured, but the birds and the insects had almost finished their clean-up operation.

'So why are we here?' Clark asked, as the two men climbed up onto the flat concrete walkway that topped the sea wall.

'If you want the truth,' Mason replied, 'it's because right now I don't have any better ideas. What bugs me about this is the motive. Why did somebody decide to slit that old man's throat? I don't believe it was kids. I reckon it was a deliberate act of murder, not just some fooling around that went too far.'

'So?'

'So I wonder if he saw something here that he shouldn't have done.'

Clark looked out at the choppy grey waters of the Thames Estuary. Out on the horizon he could see the southern coast of Essex, mainly flat and low-lying, a section of it – chalk cliffs, he guessed – gleaming white in the hazy sunlight. Closer to Sheppey, a couple of cargo ships butted their way west, heading for the Port of London, or maybe to the docks near the Queen Elizabeth Bridge.

'This is a pretty fucking desolate bit of coastline,' Clark remarked. 'What the hell could he have seen here, especially at one or two in the morning?'

'I don't know. That's why I wanted to come back here, just in case anything else struck me.'

'And has it? Struck you, I mean?'

Mason grinned and shook his head. 'No, not really. About the only thing that makes any sense is smuggling, and that's pretty bloody unlikely.'

'You got that right. The days when gangs of bad guys used small boats to land contraband fags in these parts have long gone. Now they ship the stuff here in containers, and it's more likely to be heroin or coke than anything else. So I don't think smuggling's the answer.'

'So what, then?' Mason raised his hand to shield his eyes and scanned the entire panorama in front of them, from the rooftops of Sheerness, sheltering behind the protective barrier of the sea wall, to the chimneys, towers and cranes of the industrial site that lay due west of their position.

'Buggered if I know. I mean, there's really nothing here. What about in the town itself? Could he have witnessed a robbery, or something?'

'I doubt it,' Mason said. 'About the only building you can see from here is the Tesco superstore, and if that had been hit, obviously we'd have known about it. And robbers don't normally kill witnesses, not even these days. No, I think the answer lies out there somewhere' – he waved his arm to indicate the estuary – 'but I've no clue what it could be.'

Clark glanced at him and shrugged. 'We should be getting back,' he suggested.

'Yeah, you're right,' Mason said, turning away. 'We'll grab a bite to eat somewhere here, then drive back.'

Stuttgart, Germany

Karl Wolff gave Richter directions to a cheap all-day restaurant fairly close to the police station, suggesting he grab a late lunch there rather than risk the police canteen. He located the establishment easily enough, and was pleased to see that it provided pictures of the meals it served, so all he had to do was point to what he wanted – which was a lot easier than trying to wrap his tongue around some of the names listed on the menu. When the plate arrived, the reality of it bore only the most tenuous resemblance to the full-colour rendition on the menu, but the food was hot and quite tasty. He finished his meal with a coffee, then headed back to the police station.

Immediately he entered the briefing room he was aware of a change in the atmosphere. There were more people present, and their mood seemed somehow elevated. As soon as Wolff saw him, he beckoned Richter forward.

'There's been another development,' he explained, pointing to a fresh picture pinned to the board.

Richter examined it closely. The photograph, taken almost full-face, showed a thin-featured man with a straggly moustache and beard.

'That's not a bad image,' Richter said. 'Have you got an ID on him?'

Wolff nodded. 'We think so,' he said, 'and if we're right, he's bad news. Have you ever heard of "Stammheim"?'

'I don't think so, no. Is it a town somewhere?'

'Not exactly. It's the name of a district here in Stuttgart, and also of the prison where some of the Baader–Meinhof Group were held in the seventies. You've heard of the gang?'

'Yes,' Richter replied, 'though I don't know very much about them. The ringleader was Andreas Baader, and I think they were anarchists rather than terrorists, and that's about all I do know. But Baader–Meinhof is now ancient history, surely?'

'You're right, it is, but there remain unpleasant echoes even today. Stammheim is a prison, but it's also rather more than that.'

Wolff glanced round the room to check that nobody needed his input for the moment and then led the way to a seating area over to one side.

'Let me explain something,' he began, as they sat down. 'The members of the Baader–Meinhof Group thought of themselves as freedom fighters battling against the rampant capitalism and imperialist tendencies of West Germany. But you're right. Most people probably did think of them as anarchists. The gang was formed in the late 1960s and carved a bloody swathe through German society, killing a total of thirty-four people and causing enormous damage to commercial property in a series of arson and bomb attacks. The group eventually became known as the Red Army Faction.

'In June 1972, Andreas Baader, Ulrike Meinhof, Gudrun Ensslin, Holger Meins and Jan-Carl Raspe were arrested and charged with murder, attempted murder and forming a terrorist organization. Meins died after a hunger strike on 9 November 1974 and the others were sent to trial, but this didn't start until May 1975. One year later, Meinhof was found dead in her cell. She'd apparently hanged herself using a rope made from towels.

'The three remaining defendants were found guilty in April 1977 and all sentenced to life imprisonment. But the Red Army Faction wasn't prepared to leave it there. On the 30th of July that year, a man named Jürgen Ponto, the head of the Dresdner Bank, was shot and killed in a kidnap attempt that went badly wrong. In September, they tried again and successfully abducted Hanns Martin Schleyer in a violent kidnap that left his driver and three police officers dead. Schleyer was a former SS officer and the president of the German Employers' Association. His kidnapping threw the German government into crisis, especially when a demand was received from the gang to release eleven prisoners, including the three Red Army Faction members held in Stammheim. That period became known as the German Autumn.

'Schleyer's kidnapping was the first step, if you like. The second was about a month later when a Lufthansa flight out of Palma was hijacked by four Arabs. The plane landed in Rome, and the hijackers issued exactly the same demands as Schleyer's kidnappers, plus demanding the release of a couple of Palestinians from jail in Turkey and a fifteen-million-dollar ransom. The government refused to play ball, and so the aircraft took off again, landing at Larnaca, then at Dubai and finally Aden. There the plane's captain was "tried" by the hijackers for failing to cooperate fully and was executed. From there, now flown solely by the co-pilot, the aircraft landed at Mogadishu in Somalia.'

'That I do know about,' Richter said. 'You sent in GSG 9, didn't you?'

'Exactly. Grenzschutzgruppe 9 stormed the plane just after midnight on the 18th of October. The action took just seven minutes. Three of the hijackers were shot dead, and the fourth badly wounded, but none of the passengers on the aircraft was seriously hurt. German radio stations broadcast details of the successful rescue later that night. In the morning Baader and Ensslin were found dead in their cells, and Raspe died in hospital later. On the same day, Hanns Martin Schleyer was shot dead by his kidnappers.

'Now,' Wolff continued, 'the official verdict was that the three prisoners died as a result of a suicide pact after the Red Army Faction's attempt to intimidate the government had failed. But there were obvious questions that people began asking. It's not that well known outside Germany how the three of them died. Ensslin, like Meinhof, hanged herself, and that's at least believable. But Baader had somehow managed to shoot himself *in the back of the head* with a pistol, and Raspe had also suffered a serious gunshot wound to the head, from which he died shortly afterwards.'

'They had guns in the prison?' Richter asked, disbelief in his voice.

Wolff nodded. 'Yes, and that served to start the inevitable conspiracy theory. Stammheim was the highest-security jail in the whole of Germany, precisely because of the identity of its prisoners, so how did they manage to obtain those weapons? Also, how did Andreas Baader manage to shoot himself in the back of the head? In almost every suicide by pistol that I've ever heard of, the weapon is fired either through the temple or the mouth. And there were no identifiable fingerprints on either of the pistols. The result was that virtually nobody, then or now, believes that those three almost simultaneous deaths were suicides. Instead, most people seem to believe they were extrajudicial executions performed by the German government.'

'I don't know any more about this than you've just told me,' Richter observed, 'but frankly that does seem a more likely scenario.'

'Predictably enough, the government inquiry decided that suicide was the most likely explanation and even suggested that the prisoners' defence lawyers had smuggled the weapons into the jail. But they couldn't prove it, and nobody was ever charged over the three deaths. The government's case was seriously weakened by a fourth prisoner, Irmgard Möller, who was another Red Army Faction terrorist. She apparently managed to stab herself *four times* in the chest near the heart but still survived. She was released from prison in 1994 and has since consistently maintained that she and the other three inmates were the victims of extrajudicial killing.

'Whatever the truth of the matter, the word "Stammheim" came to symbolize the abuse of power by the federal government.' Wolff paused. 'You might begin to wonder why I'm sitting here giving you this lecture on German history.'

'You obviously have a good reason,' Richter replied.

'I have,' Wolff nodded. 'Over the last few years, that word has acquired yet another meaning. There have been a number of small but very destructive terrorist attacks throughout Europe that we've linked to a shadowy group that seems to be calling itself "Stammheim". We've learnt very little about it so far, apart from the probable identity of one of the leaders, a man called Hans Morschel.'

Wolff pointed at the new photograph on the pin-board. 'That's his picture there,' he said. 'And just over an hour ago he walked into the target premises.'

Canterbury, Kent

Mason and Clark got back to the station to find a new interview report waiting for them in the incident room. The two constables assigned to check on all the takeaway food shops in Sheerness had discovered where Barney purchased his last meal and, more importantly, when.

DS Clark picked it up and read through it quickly, then walked across to inspect the town map of Sheerness. His fingers traced streets, and in a few seconds found what he was looking for.

'Here we are, sir,' he announced. 'Barney bought his supper right here, at a fish and chip shop. It's only about five hundred yards from where he was killed.'

Paul Mason moved across to join him. 'That's definite, is it?'

'Yes. They knew him in the shop because every time he bought a meal there he would wait until they were on the point of closing so that he could ask for a discount and take whatever they had left. He was the last to be served that night: a chicken and mushroom pie and chips at half the normal price.'

'And what time was that?'

'They closed at about eleven fifty that night, which puts the time of his death a bit later than we originally estimated, probably between three and four in the morning. Apart from that, though, we're no further forward. The door-to-door enquiries didn't come up with anything very interesting either, so the only other information we have comes from a handful of people who saw Barney at various times that evening, when he was sitting begging on the street or in the shop doorways in Blue

Town. As far as we can tell, the last people to see him alive that night were the staff of the chippie, at almost midnight.'

'Surely he must have bought some alcohol somewhere that evening?'

'Yes,' Clark nodded. 'He bought a bottle of cheap red at this off-licence here' – pointing at another street in Sheerness – 'at about seven thirty. We didn't find a bottle at the crime scene, so I assume he drank it all and chucked away the empty.'

'So,' Mason mused, 'we more or less know how he spent his last evening, but we still have no idea who killed him or why. I have a feeling,' the DI added, 'this will either be one of those cases that will get solved one day by somebody walking into a police station to confess, or else it'll stay open for years.'

Stuttgart, Germany

Richter stood up and stared at the photograph. As with the others, the quality wasn't particularly good, but the image was clear enough.

'It's almost full-face,' Richter said. 'How did you manage it?'

'Our cameramen were given orders to photograph literally everyone who approaches the building along the pavement. If they just walk on past, the image is marked for deletion later, but if they enter the building the picture is enlarged and sent over here by email.'

'Are you absolutely certain it's Morschel?'

Wolff nodded decisively. 'We got one good confirmed shot of him from a CCTV camera about three years ago, and a couple of our technicians have run a facial analysis program on the new image. That compares the bits of the face that can't change – the distance between the pupils of the eyes, the triangulation between the eyes and the nostrils, that kind of feature – and then checks for a match in the database. That man,' he tapped the photograph, 'is Hans Morschel, no question.'

'What's his MO?' Richter asked. 'I mean, what kind of attacks does he carry out?'

'We don't know too much about him, and what information we have is fragmentary because our intelligence is derived from third-party and often unreliable sources. We don't even know if "Hans Morschel" is his real name, but it does seem to be what he regularly calls himself. We think he's either Austrian or German by birth, he's about forty years old, and with some kind of military background, because all his activities are planned and executed meticulously.

'As far as we're aware, he's a linear descendant of Andreas Baader in terms of his philosophy, meaning he's a pure terrorist, and absolutely ruthless. The bigger the bang, the greater the destruction, the better he seems to like it. He's suspected of having links to radical Islamic groups, but so far we've never been able to prove that. One oddity is that he usually tries to make his operations self-financing. On several occasions there have been bomb attacks in major European cities linked to bank raids at about the same time.'

'Maybe in this case as well,' Richter suggested. 'Perhaps these guys aren't planning a tunnel through the wall of the bank. Morschel might be intending to blow a hole into the vault instead.'

Wolff didn't look convinced. 'That's not his usual routine. Normally, he arranges a big bang somewhere, which attracts a lot of attention from the authorities, and while they're busy picking through the rubble, a gang of robbers hits a bank fairly close by and cleans out the tills.'

'Divide and conquer?' Richter suggested.

'Yes, that's what it looks like. And Morschel doesn't normally seem to bother about vaults, perhaps because getting them open takes time, and he likes to get in and out quickly. If his men can just get a few tens of thousands of euros, that seems to satisfy him, so that's why we think the two events are linked.'

'How many times has he done this?'

'It's difficult to say. We know of at least five occasions, but there could have been others.'

'So what's your prediction for Stuttgart?' Richter asked. 'Is he going to blow the bank?'

'I doubt it. I think they're just using this building as a safe house and it's simply a coincidence that it also stands next door to a bank. My guess is that they've already identified some other target bank and where they're going to leave the IED and pretty soon they'll be leaving this property for the last time. If that snippet of conversation we heard earlier is accurate, they're probably intending to position the bomb somewhere late this evening, detonate it tomorrow during the morning rush hour and hit a bank at about the same time.'

'So what's your plan?'

'It's obvious. We hit them first. I've got a squad from GSG 9 already on the way here. We'll take these guys down this evening and try to seize Morschel alive. There are a lot of questions I'd like the answers to.'

Chapter Six

Wednesday
Stuttgart, Germany

'Where are they coming from?' Richter asked. 'The GSG 9 unit, I mean.'
He knew the unit had dropped the 'Grenzschutzgruppe 9' – 'Border
Guards Group 9' – back in 2005 as part of a renaming exercise.

'Group headquarters,' Karl Wolff replied. 'That's at Sankt Augustin-
Hangelar, near Bonn. They're flying to the city airport here by helicopter,
and we've sent a couple of vans to collect them. One of the standing
requirements is that GSG 9 must be able to reach any part of Germany
within a maximum of two hours, so they have a fleet of fast cars and
Bolko 105 all-weather helicopters permanently available to them.'

'Our SAS have a similar arrangement,' Richter said, 'only they use a
dedicated section of the Royal Air Force – the Special Forces' Flight of 47
Squadron – and they've got souped-up cars as well. How many men are
coming?'

'I've asked for two SETs' – the acronym translated as 'Special Service
Section' – 'which is ten men in all, plus their two officers, so a total of
twelve. With only nine identified targets, and with the police officers we
already have standing by here, that should be more than enough.'

Richter nodded in agreement. 'The target building's a fairly confined
space, and the last thing you need is too many of our guys milling about
in there getting in each other's way.'

A little over an hour later, two unmarked vans pulled into the courtyard
of the police station and a dozen casually dressed men climbed out of
them, each carrying a large kitbag. Wolff went down to meet them and
a few minutes later re-entered the briefing room with the GSG 9 per-

sonnel all following behind him. He introduced the rest of his team, and then came to Richter, whose identity caused several eyebrows to be raised. This resulted in a brief exchange in German between Wolff and one of the newcomers.

'This is Rolf Altmann,' Wolff explained. 'He's the senior GSG 9 officer, and somewhat concerned about you being here.'

A tall, fair-haired man with unusually broad shoulders, Altmann switched to English and addressed Richter directly. 'We're used to working with the German police,' he said coldly, 'but this is not the kind of operation where we can permit outsiders.'

'I hadn't planned on joining in the operation,' Richter snapped. 'I've been sent here by my own section purely for liaison, in case there's some link between this and a terrorist operation aimed at London.'

'I understand, you were only *supposed* to be acting as a liaison officer in Onex, too,' Altmann pointed out.

Richter was getting a bit tired of everyone complaining about what had happened in Switzerland. 'That was totally unexpected,' he pointed out, 'and I only got involved because the terrorists took out half their police officers in the first few seconds. If you check with Schneider, he'll explain exactly what happened.'

'I already have,' Altmann replied, 'which is why I raised the matter. This is our operation, and I expect you to take no part in it until we've secured the premises and restrained the occupants. Is that clearly understood?'

'That's fine with me. I'm not paid enough to get involved in something like this.'

Altmann sneered slightly, before turning his attention back to Wolff. 'Right, let's see what you have,' he said and sat down while the Bundesgrenzschutz commander ran through the sequence of events they'd observed and the layout of the building.

'So there are just the two entrances.' Altmann stood up to study the aerial photographs. 'One door at the front, which used to be the main entrance to the shop, and a single door at the rear. That makes things easier. You said there were ten occupants, including Morschel, but they're rarely all inside the building at the same time. Presumably you want to grab all of them?'

'Definitely, but if need be we can follow any still outside the premises and take them down on the street somewhere. The one we really want is Hans Morschel, and he's still in the building, according to our last report from the surveillance team. A group of plain-clothes officers is on standby waiting to follow him, if he does leave.

'Remember,' Wolff added, 'our main concern is Morschel. Nobody knows very much about him, but the mere fact of him turning up suggests that this plot of theirs is approaching its culmination. Our conjecture is that these terrorists have been working to his orders and have now completed whatever preparations he wanted. Since Morschel is known to be a planner and bomb-maker, his presence in the building presupposes he's here to supervise the final assembly of their IED.'

'That makes sense,' Altmann acknowledged and returned his attention to the photographs.

'Don't forget that I want them alive if possible,' Wolff reminded him.

'We'll do our best,' the GSG 9 officer replied grimly, 'but I can't promise anything. The problem is there's no obvious way we can mount a covert assault. To reach either door there are open spaces we would have to cross, and we must assume they'll have lookouts posted on both sides of the building.' He turned his attention to the architectural drawing. 'There are no cellars,' he said, 'but I was wondering about the attics.'

'I don't think that will work,' Wolff said, 'because each shop unit is separated from its neighbour by a solid wall. Obviously we could dig our way through them, but we'd make so much noise that we'd be heard long before we were half-way there. I even vetoed the idea of inserting a spike microphone through the wall. It's a quiet street, and the row of shops is set well back behind a wide expanse of pavement, so I think any unusual noise inside the property would become very obvious to the targets.'

Altmann nodded slowly. 'I think you're right. It looks like we'll have to do a classic two-door simultaneous entry, with lots of noise, stun grenades and maybe gas to disorient the targets. Right, I'll work with my men and prepare an assault plan, then we'll brief you and the other police officers who'll be involved. Subject to any outside considerations, like local traffic conditions, we'll aim to hit the building either early or mid-evening.'

'You'll close off the street?' Wolff asked.

'Yes, or rather the urban police will have to, but we won't do that until we're just about to go in. We mustn't do anything that might alert the suspects. Right,' Altmann finished, gesturing to his second-in-command, 'let's get busy.'

Wolff nodded, then approached Richter. 'Despite what you said earlier, I assume you *would* like to be present on the scene when the assault starts?'

'Yes, of course, unless it's going to be unacceptable to you, or cause problems with GSG 9.'

'I don't take my orders from them,' Wolff growled. 'They're a bunch of primadonnas, and sometimes they act just like it. Unfortunately,' he added, with a wry smile, 'they're a very effective and highly efficient bunch of primadonnas, so we have to allow them a certain amount of latitude. But as far as I'm concerned, you've been sent over here specially, and that means you ought to be present at the assault.'

Wolff eyed at him appraisingly. 'As long as you're there, you should be properly equipped. Before we leave the station, I'll make sure you're issued with body armour, a two-way radio and a personal weapon. Obviously I'd prefer it if you didn't end up shooting anyone,' he said, in an unconscious echo of Simpson's parting remark in Hammersmith, 'but I certainly don't want to leave you unable to defend yourself.'

'Thanks,' Richter said sincerely, 'and I promise to keep out of the way.'

Canterbury, Kent

Detective Chief Inspector Dave Richardson didn't seem perturbed by Mason's lack of progress. In fact, he was slightly surprised that the DI and his team had managed to positively identify the body washed up at Reculver as quickly as they had. Many of the 'floaters' – as the bodies found bobbing around in the Thames Estuary were irreverently referred to – remained unidentified for weeks or even months, and some were never given a name at all.

The longer the corpses remained in the sea, the less chance there was of a successful identification, simply because of the natural decomposition, greatly exacerbated by the bloating and abrading effects of salt water in constant motion and, not least, the inevitable depredations of marine creatures. Certain species of fish, and crabs in particular, were notably non-specialized in their diets: they'd eat pretty much anything they could find. After about a week or ten days in the water, most bodies would be so appallingly disfigured that a pathologist would need to examine the shape of the pelvis just to determine even the sex of the victim.

Their chances of identifying the dead tramp had been good because his face and body were still largely undamaged, but poor simply because he *was* a tramp. So Richardson was pleased that at least they had a name. It was just a pity that the name was pretty much all they *did* have.

'So what else have you done, Paul?' he asked, as Mason finished explaining what they'd found out on Sheppey.

'We've had the local plods doing house-to-house enquiries,' he said, 'but I'm not very hopeful, just because of where the killing took place. It's really isolated out there, at least after the shops close. We've also put up boards asking for anyone who saw or heard anything unusual that night to contact us. That might generate something.'

'It might,' Richardson agreed but he didn't sound convinced either.

'Apart from that,' Mason finished, 'I don't think there's a lot more we can do. We've still no idea about motive, unless Barney witnessed something he shouldn't have.'

'Like what?'

'The DI thinks it might involve smugglers,' Clark chimed in.

'Really?' Richardson asked, puzzled.

'No, not really,' Mason countered. 'It's just that nothing much else makes sense. Our victim was a penniless tramp in his seventies, so all the usual motives go straight out of the window. He wasn't murdered for his money, since he hadn't got any, or by his wife, because as far as we know he hadn't got one of those either, and I think we can probably rule out a sex killing. So what's left? The way he was murdered looked pretty professional to me, which means I don't think we're after a gang of teenage tearaways. So about the only other possible motive is that he saw or heard something that made him dangerous to someone, and they decided to remove that risk permanently.'

'So you mean he might have witnessed something, some other crime, that we don't know about yet?' Richardson suggested.

'Exactly. And my guess is that it's something serious. We're not looking at a burglary or anything like that. But if Barney happened to see maybe a couple of men disposing of a body, or a gang-rape, something like that, it would begin to provide a motive that makes sense.'

'Nothing's been reported?'

'Nothing yet,' Mason agreed, 'but if we receive any reports of a missing person in north Kent, I suggest we look at them very carefully.'

'Nothing from forensics, I suppose?'

'Nothing useful.' Mason shook his head. 'We've got a tarpaulin, an old hat and a heavy walking stick, all of them probably belonging to Barney. He was definitely hit on the head with the stick, and DNA traces on the hat and tarp also suggest that he'd owned them for some time. The only other thing worth mentioning is what we *didn't* find there.'

Richardson looked interested. 'What's that?' he asked.

'Almost every reported sighting of Barney, being a fairly frequent visitor to Sheerness, mentions him carrying a haversack around with him. We've got various descriptions of it: dark grey or brown, and it might have been ex-army. He always had it slung over his shoulder if he was walking about, and he used it to lean back against when he was begging in a doorway.'

'You think the fact that it's missing is significant?'

'No, not really. I certainly don't believe somebody killed him just to steal it. No, I think whoever murdered him there just threw it into the sea, or else tossed it into a skip. If it turns up, we'll look at it, obviously, but otherwise I don't think it's worth searching for.'

'What about forensic evidence of his attackers? Footprints or anything like that?' Richardson pressed.

'Nothing at all, for several reasons. If you wanted to kill someone that night, the location would have been a pretty good choice. The sea wall there is constructed entirely of reinforced concrete, with only a tiny gravel beach on the seaward side. The Moat, as they call the bit of water just inside the sea wall, is edged with rough grass where Barney was killed. None of that terrain will retain footprints or any trace evidence. As if that wasn't enough, it rained during that night, so anything that might have been left there was probably washed away. And, finally, the witness who alerted the police had trampled all over the crime scene, and his dog had even pissed on it.'

Richardson grinned. 'That's what they call crime-scene contamination, right enough.' He stood up. 'OK, I don't think we're likely to get anywhere with this case, or at least not any time soon. Let me know if you make any progress at all, and in the meantime leave it posted on the information boards at Sheerness. It might be worth doing another round of house-to-house enquiries, and maybe thinking about a TV appeal just to jog people's memories, but I'll leave that to you. We'll keep the file open, of course, but must give it a fairly low priority. There's no point in tying up too many resources on a case that's probably never going to be solved.'

Stuttgart, Germany

A little after seven that evening, Rolf Altmann opened the briefing room door and crossed over to Wolff.

'We've checked the architect's drawings,' he began, 'and three of us have been to have a good look at the premises from the buildings occupied by the surveillance teams. You're right: we can't do anything clever here, with that bank on one side and those disused shops on the other. The short version is I'll split my team in two. Half will hit the building from the front, with no warning, and hopefully we'll be able to get inside before they even realize we're there. The second group will be positioned in the street behind, so can assault the rear of the premises simultaneously. We'll have them neatly sandwiched between us, and then we'll simply clear the building floor by floor.'

He paused and looked at Wolff. 'I know you want them alive, and we'll do our best to comply with that, but the reality is that our target is a very enclosed space with little room to manoeuvre. Obviously we'll invite them to surrender, but if they don't, we'll just have to blow them away.'

'Understood,' Wolff replied.

'Now,' Altmann said, with a glance at Richter, 'because the property itself is so confined, I don't want any of the local police officers involved, or anyone else either. That would just make it too crowded in there, and I really don't want the risk of any blue-on-blue action. But if any of the suspects are still outside the building when we're about to hit it, I want them taken down. The police can handle that.'

'Agreed,' Wolff nodded. 'What time do you want the assault to start, so I can warn everyone else involved?'

Altmann looked at his watch. 'It's seven ten now. We'll need an hour for the tactical briefing, half an hour to get kitted up and about ten minutes to reach the target, so the go-time will be nine ten. That's exactly two hours from now, and well over an hour before whatever these men have planned for ten thirty.'

'OK. I'll tell the surveillance teams to ensure they know exactly how many people are inside. If any of them leave the building, I'll have them followed and arrested out on the street.'

'Good,' Altmann said, 'but make sure you instruct the police not to grab any of them before nine fifteen at the earliest. The last thing I want is one of them failing to make a regular phone call to base because he's sitting in the back of a police van. If these guys are well organized, which they probably are, they'll have a system of ops-normal checks to carry out whenever they're away from the building.'

'That's understood,' Wolff said, 'and I'll pass it on.'

Ninety minutes later, as night fell and the street lights began to flare into life, Richter peered through a broken pane of the attic window directly opposite the target premises and looked across the road at the building for the first time.

The property being used by the front-side surveillance team was, like many other buildings in the street, due for demolition as part of an extensive redevelopment in that part of the city. He was on the top floor of a warehouse that looked as if it had been abandoned months earlier. Scattered about the open space around him were camp-beds, folding chairs, blankets, coats, soft drink cans, empty sandwich packets and all the other detritus invariably accumulated during any prolonged surveillance operation. What there weren't, anywhere, were lights, and for obvious reasons.

Positioned in front of the windows were the tools of the watchers' trade: two professional-quality tripods, one holding a high-specification digital camera and telephoto lens, and the other supporting a video camera, this equipment mounted far enough back so that it would be invisible from the building opposite, but with a clear view of the target through the glass-less windows. Against one wall stood two other cameras that Richter guessed were designed for night vision, using infra-red sensitive media.

In front of another window further along were two parabolic mikes, their leads snaking across the floor to a pair of laptops running audio-capture programs. Their power leads were connected to a twelve-volt inverter that was keeping the computers' internal batteries fully charged, and was itself hitched to a heavy-duty car battery, with another standing beside it as a spare. On a low shelf made from a short length of wood resting on a few bricks stood spare batteries for the mikes and cameras, plus a pile of blank CDs so that recordings could be burnt onto portable media, plus an electrician's tool kit and a number of boxes presumably holding additional spares for the surveillance equipment. A good example, Richter thought, of belt-and-braces, simple German efficiency.

As well as Richter and Wolff, four other men were present in the attic, all members of the surveillance team. Every one of them looked bored, which wasn't entirely surprising, since long-term surveillance is one of the most tedious occupations known to man, but at least this particular operation was now entering its final phase.

Richter turned his attention back to the building opposite and studied it for a couple of minutes, figuring out the angles and approach paths. What he saw made him glad he wasn't going to have to take part in the assault.

In one respect, the terrorists had chosen their base well. One side of their building was protected by the solid square structure of the bank, while on the other the row of derelict shops ensured nobody could approach from that direction without being easily spotted. The wide pavement meant that anyone walking towards the property would be clearly visible from the upper floors, and the watchers confirmed that they'd seen frequent movement behind a second-floor window, indicating that a sentry was regularly posted there. A metal grille covered both the front display window and the original entrance to the shop, and the residential door beside it was solid wood, possibly even steel-lined. Nobody could get close enough to confirm that. From the architects' plans, they knew that the same door opened onto a narrow hallway, and an equally narrow staircase that gave access to the original living quarters situated on the first floor, and then to the storerooms above. This restricted access meant that a group of well-armed defenders could probably hold off an attacking force for some time.

But the corollary was that the occupants themselves were effectively trapped in a building with only two entrances, which was hardly ideal from a defensive point of view.

'It won't be easy,' Wolff muttered.

'No,' Richter agreed. 'If I were Altmann, I'd be worried about booby-traps on that staircase, and probably attached to the front door as well, not to mention the clear field of fire these bastards will have from the upper floors.'

'He is. He's discussed all those problems with me, but the reality is that there's no other way in. Except through the back door, which they'll be hitting simultaneously.'

'How many are inside the premises right now?'

Wolff conferred briefly with the leader of the surveillance team. 'Eight at the moment,' he said, 'including Morschel. Two of the players left together about two hours ago, but I've got other surveillance teams following them.'

Richter glanced at his watch. 'About fifteen minutes to go,' he said. 'I'll put that stuff on,' he gestured at a large bag on the floor behind him, 'then I'll find somewhere at the end of the street close enough to see what's going on, but far enough away so I won't irritate Rolf Altmann.'

'You could just watch what happens from here,' Wolff suggested.

Richter shook his head. 'Thanks, but I'd rather be down there on the street, just in case.'

He opened the bag and pulled out a Kevlar waistcoat, shrugged off his jacket, and put on the body armour, making sure that the straps were tight. Then he donned a shoulder holster and replaced his jacket. From inside the bag, he extracted a small plastic carry-case with 'SiG' stencilled on it in white paint. He opened this and took out a P226 semi-automatic pistol. Having first checked that there was no magazine in the butt, he racked the slide back to clear the breech as a final safety check. There were also two magazines in the case, and he took both out and methodically loaded them to capacity with shells from a box of fifty 9-millimetre Parabellum rounds. One magazine he slid into a pouch on the shoulder holster and the other he inserted in the P226. He pulled back the slide again and let it run forward to strip the top cartridge from the magazine and chamber it. Then he holstered the fully loaded pistol.

'You don't speak German,' Wolff pointed out, as he handed Richter the two-way radio to attach to his belt, watching as he slipped the speaker into his ear and clipped the microphone to his lapel, 'but Altmann and several of his men do speak English, so if you see anything you think they need to know about just press this' – he indicated a red button on the side of the unit – 'and then speak.'

'Right, got it.'

'There'll be quite a lot of chatter on that net,' Wolff warned. 'You'll hear the GSG 9 personnel talking, but both surveillance teams will be on it too, plus the output from the parabolic mikes as well. Now, where exactly are you going to be?'

Richter gestured to his left. 'Down there, I think, at the opposite end of the street from the bank. There are plenty of cars parked along the kerb, so I'll be able to keep out of sight, but I'll still only be about seventy yards from the target premises.'

Wolff pointed in the opposite direction, towards a group of shadowy figures now moving cautiously towards the bank. Behind them, Richter could see barriers being positioned at the side of the road as the police prepared to close off all vehicular and pedestrian access.

'You'd better go now,' Wolff said. 'Altmann and his men are almost in position.'

'Right.' Richter turned away and headed for the staircase.

Four minutes later, having worked his way around to the location he'd earlier selected, via a parallel street, he was watching the drama unfolding in front of him and listening to crisp commands and acknowledgements in his earpiece. Altmann had assembled his group alongside the bank, and was obviously waiting for the other team to report they were ready to begin their assault from the rear.

Richter studied the empty buildings to his left, checking angles, then switched his gaze to the area immediately beside the bank. Then he glanced back to his left. Something about the layout of the joint structure was bothering him and he was also trying to remember something that Wolff, or maybe somebody else, had said. Something that might have seemed unimportant at the time, but which now seemed relevant.

Then his attention was distracted by a sudden silence on the net. The flow of commands and acknowledgements had suddenly ceased after a single word in German, which Richter guessed meant 'Wait'. That didn't make sense until he heard, in the background, the faint sound of a telephone, possibly a mobile judging from its tone. He assumed he was now hearing the output from one of the parabolic mikes. With a sudden overwhelming feeling of déjà vu, he thought about Onex and the assault on the apartment by the Swiss counter-terror specialists.

'Christ on a bike, not again,' he muttered, listening intently, just as everyone else on the net must be doing.

Then he heard distant shouts – the mikes picking up these noises through the open windows of the target building – and then the unmistakable sounds of running feet and the cocking of weapons. The conclusion to be drawn was as inevitable as it was illogical. Yet again, at the precise moment the assault was due to begin, somebody had tipped off the terrorists. What Richter didn't know was whether the occupants of the building had posted a watcher somewhere nearby, perhaps in a building close to the one Wolff's surveillance team was occupying, or whether one of the two missing members of the cell had guessed they were being followed and had telephoned a warning.

But whatever the truth regarding the tip-off, nothing could be done about it at that moment. The assault was already going ahead, although the element of surprise – perhaps the most important element in the GSG 9 plan – had obviously been lost. Even as Richter stared down the street, it began. He heard further shouts over the net, this time from Altmann's men, and then watched as half a dozen black-clad troopers ran out, weapons held ready, from behind the side wall of the bank towards the front door of the derelict shop.

They'd barely left the cover of the bank wall when Richter heard the sound of breaking glass from the target premises, a faint noise that was immediately followed by the clamour of an assault rifle on full auto, as somebody fired down at the advancing troops from one of the second-floor windows. He was too far away to identify the weapon, but it sounded like an AK47 or one of its multifarious variants. Richter had heard Kalashnikovs often enough to recognize the type. The effect was immediate and dramatic. Two of the black-clad figures staggered and then tumbled to the ground, the weapons falling from their grasp, but a third paused briefly and fired his weapon up towards the window. Compared to the noisy rattle of the Kalashnikov, the sound of it was oddly muted, but a moment later the night was ripped apart as a grenade detonated inside the second-floor storeroom. The AK47 was instantly silenced, and the four remaining troops continued their rapid, weaving approach towards the front of the abandoned shop.

As one of them crouched by the entrance, Richter realized he was setting small charges to blow the door off its hinges, while the other three stepped back, weapons aimed at the windows above and in front of them, looking for targets. Then the door charges blew, and seconds later all four men vanished inside the building.

The moment they entered, the vacant property echoed with the sound of automatic weapons fire, long bursts interspersed with shorter, three-round groups that Richter guessed were fired by the GSG 9 specialists. It sounded to him as if Wolff's original instruction for Altmann to take the bad guys alive had just been superseded. All he could hope was that, once the shooting stopped, they'd still find something in the building to help them identify whatever target these terrorists had in mind for London.

Even that possibility began to look somewhat slim as a colossal explosion rocked the entire street, while smoke and flames erupted from the burst-open door and the first- and second-floor windows of the building. Richter knew immediately this was far too big a blast to be a grenade, or even several grenades, and he guessed that the terrorists had booby-trapped either an internal door or, more likely, the narrow stairwell. Anyway, someone had just triggered it – he hoped one of the terrorists, but realized it had more probably been a GSG 9 trooper. Even the most inept of terrorists would surely remember behind which door they'd placed a lethal bomb.

Richter's impulse was to run along the street and give what assistance he could, but he knew that would be counter-productive. The GSG 9 personnel were professionally trained for this kind of operation, while he wasn't, and the most likely result of him blundering in now would be to collect a stray bullet for his trouble.

So he stood his ground and watched and listened, staring at the stricken building, with the P226 cocked and ready in his right hand. The sound of gunfire continued loud but sporadic, and was interspersed with the deeper barks of grenades exploding as, he presumed, the GSG 9 men cleared the premises room by room. Smoke still billowed from the windows on the upper floors, and Richter guessed that the detonation of the booby-trap had started one or more fires inside the property.

Then Richter realized what had been bugging him, and it was something Wolff had told him while giving his initial briefing. The German had explained that their mikes had detected sounds that could easily have been tunnelling, but this noise hadn't been coming from the party wall adjoining the bank, as they might have expected. The row of empty shops, each with living accommodation on the first floor and storerooms above that, were all virtually identical in layout to the one currently under attack. From his own experience, Richter believed you had a better chance of surviving if you always knew more than one way out, and from the start it had puzzled him that the suspects had chosen a safe house with only two entrances. It was simply too restricting. But if you considered the layout of the building in conjunction with the sounds Wolff's men had detected, there was an obvious answer: the terrorists *did* have another escape route. The hammering noises had been made as they knocked holes through the dividing walls between the other terraced properties, either passing through the living areas or the storerooms.

Even as this realization dawned, Richter was suddenly aware of indistinct movements behind the dusty plate-glass window of the deserted shop immediately to his left, the last in the entire row. He could just make out faint shadows behind the glass, figures moving quickly and with obvious purpose.

The radio net was again alive with shouted orders and acknowledgements, all in German, so he was unsure if anyone would react to what he was about to say. The GSG 9 men obviously had their hands full, but he tried anyway, pressing the transmit button even as he ducked down behind a parked car, his whole attention now fixed on the last shop in the row.

'All callsigns, this is Richter,' he announced. 'There's movement in the shop at the very end. It's a possible escape route. Request assistance. Urgent.'

There was a brief silence on the net as he released the transmit key, then the commands and reports in German began again. Somebody, he thought, might have heard his call, but whether they understood what he said and, more importantly, could do anything about it, was quite a different matter.

Richter switched his gaze to the other end of the street, where a cluster of flashing lights showed that numerous police cars and vans, and even a couple of ambulances, had now arrived, though all were keeping well back from the target property. He looked back to his left, to see the shop door opening quietly. As he watched, a single figure stepped out, followed immediately by two others. They glanced along the street towards the activity at the northern end, then began to walk unhurriedly away, heading directly towards the Cherokee Jeep that Richter was using as cover.

He knew there was a police cordon all around the area, but if the terrorists had prepared an escape route from their safe house, Richter was quite certain they would also have worked out a way of getting clear, maybe by passing through other deserted buildings.

But they couldn't afford to have these guys walk away. He was now going to have to stop them himself.

Chapter Seven

Richter watched the approaching men carefully. None appeared to be carrying a weapon – or at least not an assault rifle or anything of that sort – though he guessed they probably had pistols and maybe even grenades in their pockets. But he couldn't just shoot them, in case they really were unarmed. The events in Onex still fresh in his mind, he didn't want to find himself under arrest in Germany, so he would at least have to go through the motions.

When the three terrorists were only about thirty feet away, Richter stood up from behind the Jeep and levelled the SiG at them.

'Halt,' he yelled, hoping the word meant more or less the same in German as it did in English.

The instant he showed himself, the three pulled out pistols and loosed off poorly aimed shots at him. Richter ducked back into what little cover there was as 9-millimetre bullets screamed over his head. The three terrorists moved apart, separating so as to create multiple targets, and Richter realized he was both outnumbered and outgunned.

Moving right, he dodged round the back of the Cherokee, where he risked raising his head for a quick glance. Only one terrorist was in sight but, even as Richter raised his weapon, the man caught sight of him and spun round, bringing his pistol to bear. Richter snapped off two rapid shots. The first of them missed, but his second caught his target in the left shoulder, and the man fell backwards onto the pavement, screaming with pain and letting the pistol tumble from his grasp.

One was down, but there were still two left, and Richter had no illusions about his chances of survival. He didn't know exactly where the other two were, but guessed they were probably using darkness and the cover of other cars parked on the street to close in from opposite directions, just waiting to get a clear shot at him. If he stood up, he would immediately become visible to them and a split-second later he'd probably be dead.

His only way out was down. The Cherokee Jeep right beside him had good ground clearance, so Richter dropped down and rolled under it, now well out of sight. It wouldn't fool the two remaining terrorists for more than a few seconds, but it might give him an edge, and sometimes that was all that mattered. He crawled right under the midpoint of the vehicle, then eased his way over to the pavement side. Sticking his head out for the briefest of instants, he glanced in both directions but saw nothing. After checking again, he hauled himself out from underneath and stayed in a crouch beside the Jeep, trying to watch in two directions at the same time and keeping the bulk of the vehicle between himself and where he expected the men to be. He then flattened himself on the ground and peered back under the Cherokee, trying desperately to spot a shoe or anything else that might indicate where his opponents were now positioned. Nothing was visible, so they had to be further away.

Slowly and carefully he eased himself up sufficiently to look through the windows of the stationary vehicle, but ducked again immediately as a figure standing out in the road a few feet beyond the Jeep aimed a pistol and pulled the trigger. The bullet struck the pavement right behind him, ricocheted off the surface and smashed through the window of one of the derelict premises.

So much for his attempt at gaining an edge. Now they knew exactly where he was.

Within seconds, Richter guessed, the two men would be coming at him, probably from both sides of the car simultaneously, and then his temporary refuge would become a killing zone. Somehow, he had to get out of there, quickly.

He checked the SiG, and then ran forward in a crouch, trying to outflank his two opponents.

It almost worked.

As he ran, Richter spotted one of them on his left, standing almost in the middle of the road with a pistol in his right hand. He dodged and dived, and snapped off a couple of quick and barely aimed shots in the man's general direction. The terrorist returned fire straight away, but Richter was too fast for him. Now he had reached the cover of the next parked vehicle, but ultimately that didn't help him.

As he paused beside the car, a quick glance back immediately registered another bulky figure standing on the pavement a mere twenty feet or so behind him. Richter instantly swung round to face him fully, but, before he could pull the trigger, three rapid shots rang out, and he felt a sudden searing pain in his left thigh, followed almost immediately by a massive blow to his chest.

He crashed heavily to the ground and involuntarily clutched at his leg, losing his grip on the P226, which fell uselessly onto the pavement. For a couple of seconds Richter lay still, the breath knocked from his body, but then he forced himself to move. At all costs he knew he had to ignore the pain in his leg and recover his weapon. He twisted his head from side to side, looking for it desperately. The SiG lay only about three feet away, and he dragged himself towards it, grimacing with pain. As he stretched out his hand to grab it, another bullet smacked into the pavement right beside his extended arm.

He twisted round to look, and saw a figure approaching, only a few feet away, walking slowly towards him, right arm outstretched and pistol held steady. Richter noticed it was unmistakably a Glock, his senses acutely sharpened by the trauma.

The terrorist smiled slightly, and Richter could actually see his finger taking up the pressure on the trigger.

Richter knew he had no chance, but he'd never believed in giving up without a fight. He lunged forward again, grabbing for the SiG, his body tensing in anticipation of the bullet he was sure was coming.

But the shot, when it sounded, was from further away. Richter twisted round, bringing the P226 up to the aim, but he realized his personal battle was over.

His assailant was still standing, but the smile on his face had been replaced by an expression of shocked surprise. The light-coloured shirt he was wearing was suddenly turning a deep red. As Richter watched, the man's right arm dropped and, almost in slow motion, he collapsed to the ground. Twenty yards behind him, a GSG 9 trooper was holding an assault rifle to his shoulder.

'Over there,' Richter shouted, pointing to where he'd last seen the other one. He doubted if the German would understand what he was saying, but his gesture was unambiguous. As the trooper nodded and turned away, Richter saw two other black-clad men running towards him.

From the road, too, he heard the sound of running feet, then half a dozen more shots, a sudden sharp cry, and then there was silence broken only by the terrorist Richter himself had shot a couple of minutes earlier, as he lay a few yards away, moaning in pain.

Richter collapsed back on the pavement and waited, the SiG still clutched in his right hand. A few seconds later a GSG 9 trooper jogged across and knelt beside him, firing a sentence at him in high-speed German. It sounded like a question, but Richter had no idea what he was asking.

'English . . . I'm English,' he said, still trying to catch his breath.

'OK. How many men came out of the building?' The GSG 9 man's English was heavily accented.

'Three,' Richter gasped. 'I shot one . . . he's over there.'

'Good. We have them all, then. Lie still now. The ambulance is on its way.'

'I think I need a tourniquet. I took a bullet in the thigh.'

The German trooper produced a small but powerful torch and by the light of it examined Richter's leg. 'Yes,' he muttered, 'you do.' Whereupon he pulled a small first-aid kit from a pocket and took out a bandage. Working quickly, he wrapped it around Richter's upper thigh and knotted the ends, then looked around for something to apply tension to it.

'Here,' Richter said, and pressed the magazine release on his SiG. The metal object dropped onto his chest.

'That will do,' the German said with a slight smile, expertly ejecting the remaining rounds onto the pavement. He slid the empty magazine into the loop he'd formed from the bandage and began twisting it.

Richter felt the makeshift tourniquet begin to bite around his thigh.

'Hold this,' the GSG 9 man instructed and guided the magazine, now slippery with blood, into Richter's left hand. 'It needs to be as tight as possible.'

'Right.'

The German picked up the SiG, pulled back the slide to eject the round still in the chamber, and tucked the weapon into his belt. 'You won't need this any more?' he enquired.

'Christ, I hope not,' Richter muttered. 'I only came along to watch.'

A couple of minutes later an ambulance pulled to a stop beside him, and five minutes after that the same vehicle was on its way to the hospital, Richter lying on a stretcher in the rear. His trouser leg had been cut off, and he now had two compresses strapped to his thigh, one covering each wound, both entrance and exit – the bullet, he was pleased to note, had passed straight through his limb and had obviously missed his femur – and a proper medical tourniquet was now in place. The pain had subsided to a dull ache as long as he kept his leg still, but every bump in the road would send a jolt of agony lancing through him.

The ride to the hospital took only a few minutes, and there Richter was wheeled straight into an examination room, where an alarmingly young-looking doctor cut off the compresses and peered with interest at his bloody thigh, while murmuring in German to the attending nurse. He asked Richter a couple of questions, neither of which meant anything to the Englishman.

When the door of the room opened, the doctor looked up sharply with an instruction to the nurse.

Richter glanced round and saw a familiar figure enter the room, his heavy build immediately making it seem too small to accommodate all four of them. 'Franz,' he said. 'I'm glad to see you. I think we need a translator here.'

Kelle nodded to him and waved a leather folder in the doctor's face, asking him several rapid questions. Then he looked down at Richter. 'You've been lucky,' he said. 'The bullet went straight through your leg and didn't hit anything vital – neither a bone nor an artery. They'll X-ray your thigh just to make sure there aren't any foreign bodies in the wound, then they'll just pump you full of painkillers, plug the holes and send you home. The medical explanation's a little more complex, but that's more or less what the doctor here is saying.'

He paused and gazed down at Richter. 'You look like shit,' he said, 'but how do you feel?'

'Thanks for that, Franz. My leg aches, and I guess it's going to be painful for the next few weeks. Otherwise I suppose I'm OK.'

'Good, because Wolff wants you urgently at the debrief back in the police station.' He glanced up at the wall clock at one end of the room. 'You've got just over ninety minutes.'

Franz then switched back to German as he spoke to the doctor again. Returning his attention to Richter, he explained, 'I've told him to get a move on. I'll be waiting just outside while they patch you up. Yell if you need anything.' Then he turned and left the room.

The street facing the row of shops was now ablaze with light. About a dozen police cars were parked haphazardly in front of the target premises, headlights on and roof bars flashing. Unmarked white vans stood close to the scene, most with their rear and side doors open. Portable floodlights had been assembled to illuminate both front and rear sides of the property. Meanwhile, police officers and white-coated forensic specialists walked briskly in and out of the building, carrying equipment or items so far recovered from the premises.

At each end of the street itself, barriers had been erected to block the roadway, and the cordons were reinforced by police officers tasked with keeping unauthorized personnel away from the scene. Despite the lateness of the hour, sizeable crowds had already gathered at both sets of barriers. Most were just interested passers-by on their way home from local bars or restaurants, but here and there long lenses pointed towards the constant activity as newspaper photographers and freelancers tried to get decent pictures of the scene. Reporters and stringers kept shouting questions at the police officers, but such requests for information were being ignored on Karl Wolff's specific orders.

In the darkened bedroom of a top-floor apartment located in a building a little over 300 yards away, enjoying an uninterrupted view of the unfolding scene, a bulky middle-aged man who called himself Helmut Kleber sat comfortably in a leather armchair. He was watching the activity through a pair of tripod-mounted binoculars, as he'd been doing for the last three hours, ever since he'd noticed the first of the police vehicles arrive, a now-empty bottle of decent red and a wine glass sitting on the occasional table beside him. He'd worked his way through both the wine and an assortment of cold snacks as he'd watched the preparations for the assault, and then the attack itself. As in Onex, where he had enjoyed a similar vantage point, he'd timed his call more or less perfectly.

The assault by the black-clad troops had looked every bit as professional as he'd expected, and the violent and uncompromising response by the men inside the besieged building was entirely predictable. He regretted any deaths or injuries among the law-enforcement officers, but his overriding concern was that this terrorist cell should be eliminated and, just as important, all its members killed. He couldn't afford to have any of them captured and questioned.

And that was now a problem, because he'd seen three men leave via the empty building at the far end, where they'd subsequently been challenged by a lone police officer. He'd carefully watched the outcome of the fire-fight and realized that one of the terrorists must have only been wounded, because the same man had been driven away from the scene in an ambulance.

Well, Kleber was going to have to do something about that, and quickly, before the injured terrorist could be interrogated.

He got up from his seat and walked across the room to a table on which sat a large briefcase. He opened it and took out just three items. One was a small 10 cc syringe with a fine needle protected by a plastic sheath, the second a vial of straw-coloured liquid, and the third a very well-faked Bundesgrenzschutz wallet that purported to identify him as a senior BGS officer.

But there was something else he needed too, something that would give him a plausible excuse for what he now intended. For a couple of minutes he stood pondering his options, then nodded to himself. That should do it. Taking a mobile phone from his pocket he proceeded to dial a number from memory. The call was answered in seconds, as he knew it would be.

'*Ja?*'

'It's Kleber here,' the man replied in fluent German carrying a slight trace of a Rhineland accent. 'I need just two more things.'

'What, exactly?'

Kleber told him briefly, then rang off.

Thirty minutes later there was a knock on the apartment door. Kleber approached it silently, a Glock 17 held loosely in his right hand, and peered through the spyhole. Only when he was sure that his visitor was alone did he open the door and usher him inside.

'Any problems?' Kleber began.

'No, but this must be returned to the office before the next shift starts, so that means I need to have it back no later than six thirty tomorrow morning.'

'Don't worry, it will be,' Kleber said, taking the large dark-blue ring binder held out to him. 'I only need it for a couple of hours. And the other matter?'

'You were right,' his visitor handed over a slip of paper. 'That's where you'll find him.'

Moments later, the apartment door closed and again Kleber was alone. He began making preparations for the job he had to do.

As Richter sat up on the stretcher and gingerly lowered both feet to the floor, he was pleasantly surprised that he didn't instantly fall over, his left thigh having been pumped full of anaesthetic. A wide bandage, secured with strips of plaster, covered almost all of his leg from the knee to the groin, but the good news was he could no longer feel any pain from the wound. His whole thigh seemed to be throbbing, but he could live with that. In fact, he was going to have to, because Franz was waiting outside the door of the examination room with a wheelchair.

'Do I really have to get into that thing?' Richter demanded. 'I'm hardly an invalid.'

'I've had a word with the doctor,' Franz replied, 'and he seemed fairly certain you'd be a difficult patient. You have two choices, he told me. You can insist on walking, in which case your leg will take at least twice as long to heal, or you can take his advice and just sit down in this, shut up and let me push you. I really don't care one way or the other, so you can decide.'

'OK,' Richter muttered, and sat down in the wheelchair. 'You win.'

Fifteen minutes later their unmarked car pulled to a stop outside the police station. Franz bustled round to the boot and pulled out the collapsible wheelchair, before opening the passenger door.

'You're enjoying this, aren't you?' Richter demanded, as the German solicitously helped him into the wheelchair and began pushing it up a gentle ramp into the main entrance of the police station.

'Actually, I *can* recall times when I've had rather more fun than this,' Franz replied.

In the briefing room itself, the mood was both hectic and subdued. Karl Wolff and Rolf Altmann sat opposite each other at a desk positioned at the front of the room, both studying papers and reports, while it seemed that almost all the telephones in the building were ringing simultaneously. Every other seat was occupied by police and BGS officers, either talking urgently on phones or working at the computers.

Wolff stood up as Franz pushed the wheelchair over to the table. 'How are you?' he asked. 'I'm pleased to hear it's just a flesh wound.'

'Fortunately, it is,' Richter replied. 'A 9-millimetre in the thigh that went straight through but missed everything vital. I'll be walking again – or at least limping – tomorrow, I hope. So what's the news?'

'Not good,' the BGS officer said. 'Four of Altmann's men are dead, and three more of them in hospital. Fortunately, they should all fully recover.'

'Was it a booby-trap, that explosion just after your men went in?' Richter enquired, as Altmann climbed wearily to his feet and walked round the table towards them.

The German first shook his hand, then nodded in confirmation. 'About ten kilos of plastic. We guessed the door at the top of the stairwell might have a charge attached to it, so before our guys went up they fired a grenade at it. That took the door off its hinges, and fired a small anti-personnel charge. But these bastards had second-guessed us and, as far as we can deduce, they'd placed a second, much bigger, device on the ceiling directly above the foot of the staircase, right where my men were standing, and linked that charge to the first one. The two devices went off simultaneously, killing three of the four men who'd rushed in through the front door. The fourth one who died took a couple of rounds in the head from an AK47 before he even reached the building.'

'I'm truly sorry.' There wasn't much else Richter could say.

'The terrorists fared rather worse, though,' Wolff continued. 'There were six of them and—'

'Six?' Richter interrupted, turning to Wolff. 'I thought your surveillance guys counted eight inside the building?'

'They did,' Wolff nodded, 'but that was before we knew about the escape route they had devised. We now think at least some of them were regularly using that as well. Anyway, Altmann's men accounted for three men in the building itself, and then there were the three you spotted coming out of the other end of the row of buildings. You yourself shot one, and the GSG 9 guys took out the other two. So we've now ended up with five dead terrorists, and one who's in the operating theatre right now having your bullet dug out of what's left of his shoulder.'

'He'll survive, then?' Richter asked.

'Unless something goes badly wrong at the hospital, yes. With any luck we should be able to question him tomorrow. The other bad news is that we didn't get Hans Morschel himself. It looks as if he probably only paid one brief visit to the safe house and left it through the escape route, which ran along the first-floor level of the entire row of buildings. How did you guess that was what they'd arranged there? Or did you just notice the three men escaping?'

'Both, really,' Richter said. 'I suddenly remembered how the mikes you positioned inside the bank had detected hammering and banging noises that could have indicated tunnelling activities. Then I recalled the design of the building as a whole, and put two and two together. But at almost the same moment I saw movement in the end shop. That pretty much confirmed my guess.'

'Right,' Wolff nodded, 'it was our mistake not to cover the whole row of buildings, but it's too late to do anything about that now. Hindsight is such a wonderful thing. Anyway, the result is that Morschel and at least three other members of the cell are still at large here in Stuttgart. I regret the surveillance teams lost contact with the two they were following just a few minutes before the assault went down. We've cleared the entire terrace and are quite satisfied there are no other hiding places inside the property, so now our forensic people are going through everything we've found.'

'Anything interesting so far?'

'It's too early to tell, but we've recovered pretty much what you'd expect: a lot of explosives, most of it Semtex, plus weapons and ammunition. More interestingly, we've found a couple of laptops, one intact and the other damaged, but not too badly. We should be able to extract some useful data from their hard drives.'

'That's good news, at least.'

'We also recovered six mobile phones, and the tech staff have already started analysing all the numbers dialled, messages received and so on. That, too, should provide plenty of leads we can follow up.'

'Have you identified which of the mobiles received the call that tipped off these terrorists, and the number it was made from?' Richter asked.

'Based on the exact time the assault began, we already know which phone took the call, but the originator concealed his number so it showed up on the receiving mobile as "private". But that shouldn't be a problem and we've got the network provider looking at it right now. We ought to have an answer shortly.'

Richter was silent for a few seconds, his gaze wandering around the room. Then he looked back at Wolff. 'Who do you think tipped them off?' he asked. 'I mean, are we looking for Morschel himself or another member of the cell who just happened to notice that the street was filling up with police vehicles and immediately rang his comrades to warn them? Or is there something else going on?'

'Like what?' Altmann demanded.

'That's the trouble. I don't know,' Richter admitted. 'But just look at what's happened over the last couple of days. We've found out about two terrorist cells operating in two different countries which, as far as I know, had no connection with each other. One was discovered because of a peculiar tip-off, the other by an alert police officer.'

'What do you mean, "peculiar"?' Wolff interrupted. 'I thought the man who alerted the Onex police was the owner of the apartment.'

'So did the Swiss police, at first,' Richter replied, 'but they were wrong.' He then explained about Rolf Hermann and his as yet unidentified doppelgänger.

'We hadn't heard about that,' Altmann admitted, 'but I don't think it's particularly significant. Maybe the man discovering the cell simply decided to alert the authorities but didn't want to use his real name.

Perhaps he was a criminal, or even a cell member who'd fallen out with the others.'

'You might be right, and we may never find out who he was or why he did it. But what I was going to say was that both events – the police assaults on terrorist cells here and in Switzerland – are linked in one way. In both cases, somebody telephoned the bad guys literally a few moments before the police moved in.'

'That could just be a coincidence,' Wolff suggested.

'It could be,' Richter said, 'but I'm not a big fan of coincidence. And it's also possible that in both cases there was another cell member located somewhere nearby who tipped them off. But there could be another explanation.'

'Which is?'

'I'm wondering if what we're seeing here is some kind of vigilante action. Maybe someone's infiltrating these terrorist cells, making sure that the police find out about them, and then giving a warning at the last minute, just as the good guys move in.'

'But why? And, more important, how?'

'Yes,' Altmann said, 'don't forget that the whole reason terrorist groups operate in cells is precisely because they don't trust any outsiders. Unless your hypothetical vigilante is vouched for by one of the other cell members, there would be no way he could infiltrate it. To do that once would be difficult enough, but doing it twice, with two different terrorist organizations in two different countries, *in the same week*, would be impossible. But,' Altmann went on, 'your idea that just one man is behind this does make some kind of sense. What we have to do is work out how. And, obviously, who and why.'

'If you're right,' Wolff said, the tone of his voice clearly suggesting he was unconvinced, 'why is he warning the terrorists? Surely he could serve his purposes better by letting the police, or whoever else carries out the assault, take them alive? By issuing a warning to them, he's almost guaranteeing that there'll be a shoot-out and a high death toll on both sides.'

'Unless he *is* some kind of vigilante, and wants the terrorists killed rather than just captured,' Richter said. 'But I have to agree with Rolf that the infiltration argument doesn't really work. I don't know who he is or why he's doing it, but I do think we're probably looking at just one man here. And there's something else. If I am right, and he intends that all the terrorists get themselves killed, he might now make an attempt to finish off the wounded survivor in hospital.'

'Relax, Paul,' Wolff said. 'We have armed police officers waiting outside the theatre suite, and there'll be at least one man with him at all times once he's back in the ward.'

At the very moment Karl Wolff issued this assurance, Helmut Kleber was pushing his way through the double doors of a hospital building not too far from the police station. Carrying a black briefcase, he walked briskly across to the reception desk, produced a leather identification wallet and asked a couple of questions. The receptionist didn't know the answer to one of them, but a short telephone call soon produced the required information.

Kleber thanked her and strode away towards the lifts. As one arrived he stepped inside and pressed the button for the fifth floor. Once the doors had closed behind him, he put down the briefcase and pulled a small bottle of yellowish liquid and a tiny syringe from his pocket. He removed the sheath from the needle and, with the deftness born of long practice, slid the point through the rubberized cap of the bottle, inverted it and extracted about a quarter of its contents. Then he replaced the sheath on the syringe and slid it and the bottle back into his pocket.

When the doors opened on the fifth floor, he picked up his briefcase and walked down the corridor, looking for a particular room. It didn't take too long to find, since the uniformed policeman stationed outside the door immediately identified it.

As Kleber headed towards it, the policeman turned to face him, his right hand automatically dropping to his holstered pistol.

'Relax,' Kleber snapped as he halted a few feet away. 'I'm Superintendent Schröder of the Bundesgrenzschutz.' He reached into his pocket and pulled out the identification wallet. 'I just want to take a look at the prisoner. How is he?'

'He came out of theatre about thirty minutes ago, sir, so he's still unconscious.'

'Obviously,' Kleber said. 'How many guards are there?'

'Two, sir. Myself and another officer stationed inside the room.'

'Only two? Don't your superiors realize how important this man could be? Who's your reporting officer?'

'Sergeant Brandt, sir. He should be here in about an hour.'

'Well, when he comes, I suggest you tell him I've recommended a minimum of four officers should be stationed on this floor. Now, open the door.'

The policeman stepped forward, turned the key in the lock and pushed the door open for the visitor. Inside was a single bed on which lay the almost naked body of a man in his late thirties, his left shoulder swathed in bandages, and with various drips and monitoring leads attached to an array of machines behind the head of the bed. Beside the bed were positioned a couple of steel and plastic chairs, and on one of them sat another police officer, a novel open on his lap. As Kleber entered the room, he stood up sharply.

'Superintendent Schröder, Bundesgrenzschutz,' Kleber snapped and walked over to a side table. He put down the briefcase, clicked the catches and extracted a blue ring-binder from inside it. He opened it, strode over to the end of the bed and began flicking through the binder, comparing what he could see of the face of the unconscious man with the police mugshots, as if looking for a match.

He'd glanced through about twenty when he found one that, oddly enough, was a fairly close match – he hadn't expected to get that lucky – and spent a couple of minutes alternating his gaze between the photograph and the man lying in front of him. Then he motioned the police officer out of the way and moved to the side of the bed so he could look more closely at the recumbent figure.

Then he shook his head and turned to the officer. 'Your eyes are younger than mine,' he said. 'Take a look at this picture and see how it compares with him.' He handed the binder to the officer.

Inevitably, the policeman accepted the binder in both hands, and so for a few seconds Kleber's right arm was shielded from the officer's gaze. But that was all the time he needed. His fingers closed around the tiny syringe in his jacket pocket, but, before taking it out, he slipped the sheath off the needle with his thumb.

'Well?' he asked, turning slightly towards the police officer, an action that served to further conceal what he was doing. 'What do you think? Is that Fritz Gras?'

As the policeman studied the black-and-white photograph in the ring binder, Kleber's fingers found the unconscious man's flaccid left arm, lying outside the covers, and slid the tiny needle into his biceps muscle. In less than a second he'd depressed the plunger and withdrawn the syringe, dropping it back into his pocket.

'I don't know, sir. There's certainly a resemblance.'

'I think so too,' Kleber said, taking back the binder, 'but that's not enough. It doesn't matter. I just thought we could save ourselves some time. We'll have to wait for the fingerprint results to come back from Interpol and the other databases.'

He returned the binder to his briefcase and closed it, then nodded to the officer, walked over to the door and stepped out into the corridor. There, he exchanged a few further words with the policeman on duty outside, then moved away towards the lifts.

Twenty-three minutes after Kleber had let the outer double doors of the hospital swing closed behind him, the unconscious man in the bed in the private ward on the fifth floor began to experience difficulty in breathing. This alarmed the police officer guarding him, and he immediately rang the bell to summon a nurse.

A few moment later, the patient convulsed just once, and then his body went into spasm. Alarms shrilled as his heart stopped, and the regular pattern undulating on the monitoring instruments was replaced by a flat line.

The first medical staff arrived at the ward with the crash-cart within ninety seconds, and they worked on him for nearly a quarter of an hour before finally giving up.

Chapter Eight

Thursday
Stuttgart, Germany

The pathologist was not best pleased to be called in early that same morning to perform an autopsy on a dead terrorist, which he considered the worst kind of criminal. In his experience, the deceased were not usually in any particular hurry and could normally await his convenience. But the senior BGS officer had been most insistent.

Ninety-five minutes after beginning his external examination of the body, the pathologist stepped away from the table, a frown clouding his face. The injury to the man's shoulder had been severe, but certainly not life-threatening, and the operation to repair the damage seemed to have been performed very competently by the surgeons at the local hospital. Apart from the bullet-wound, the man had appeared to be in good health, with no indications of any underlying cause that might have contributed to his sudden demise. In fact, despite his best efforts, he could find no obvious reason for the man's sudden relapse and death. The only cause that seemed even faintly plausible was shock caused by the massive trauma the terrorist had suffered, and that wasn't a diagnosis the pathologist felt at all comfortable with, particularly in view of the information he'd received about the circumstances of the man's death.

He extracted a number of tissue samples, including several from the heart and liver, and specimens of blood and other fluids, and placed them in plastic containers known as 'tox jars'. These contained no preservative, because that would destroy any toxins that might be present. The jars were prominently marked 'TOXICOLOGY', and the pathologist attached a self-adhesive label to each one, the label listing the case number of the deceased. Normally it would bear the patient's name, but at that stage they still had no idea of his actual identity.

Leaving his assistant to close up the body, the pathologist discarded his gloves, mask and gown and retreated to his office in order to phone Karl Wolff.

'I've really no idea what killed him,' he admitted once he was connected. 'The shoulder wound was serious, but he was basically a fit man and therefore should have had no trouble in making a full recovery.'

'So we're looking at some kind of drug or poison being administered?' Wolff asked.

'Yes, there's really nothing else it could be. I've sent samples off for toxicological examination, but that will take time.'

'Thanks.' Wolff didn't sound as unhappy as the pathologist was expecting. 'Let me know the results as soon as you have them, please.'

In fact, the tests would reveal nothing unusual when the results were returned within a few days. A small and extremely covert unit based at Fort Detrick in Maryland, USA, had already seen to that.

Hammersmith, London

Richter caught the 1125 British Airways flight out of Terminal One at Stuttgart Airport, gained or lost an hour during the flight – he was never quite certain which was the correct expression – and landed at Heathrow, in the rain, at ten past midday. He'd exaggerated his limp and tried out his best smile on the grim-looking BA check-in girl and thus, surprisingly, had been able to persuade her that he needed a seat with rather more legroom than the cattle-class offering he was used to. He'd ended up with an aisle seat next to an emergency exit and had enjoyed a marginally more comfortable flight than he might have expected.

His leg was stiff and sore, though the heavy-duty painkillers the German hospital had given him were taking the edge off it. At Heathrow he'd looked around hopefully, just in case Simpson might have sent a car to meet him, and then climbed into a taxi for the fairly short ride to Hammersmith.

'I thought you'd been shot,' Richard Simpson began as Richter limped into his office and sat down in one of the leather chairs in front of the desk.

'I *was* shot, thank you very much, but luckily the bullet went straight through my leg so it was only a flesh wound. You'll no doubt be pleased to hear that it's bloody painful, but I'm almost fully mobile.'

'It certainly doesn't seem to have slowed you down. We expected you to go home and lie in front of the TV for a couple of weeks.' Simpson sounded slightly disappointed. 'You could take your leave now, I suppose.'

'No thanks. Sending me off to Switzerland cocked that up nicely. I'll take a holiday when I feel a bit more like it.'

'So what are you doing back here, anyway? You talked to the duty officer last night, so all we need is your written report, and you could have prepared that at home.'

'I know, and you'll get the report this afternoon. I came back here because there are some aspects of what's happened this week that I want to run past both you and the Intelligence Director.'

'Like what?' Simpson asked.

'To save me saying everything twice, how about dragging the ID out of whatever hole he's crawled into and getting him up here?'

For a few seconds Simpson stared at him across the desk. 'Are you reading more into all this than the situation merits?' he asked finally. 'I mean, neither operation was what you might call big-league, and they were both isolated incidents.'

'Actually, I'm not sure they were isolated. But whether they were or not, there are at least two things I don't understand about what happened in Germany and Switzerland, and I'd like to flag them up. If you decide not to do anything about them, fine, but I want it on record that I've told you, just in case the shit hits the fan later. OK?'

'Very well.' Simpson leant forward and depressed a key on the intercom system. 'ID?' he demanded, and listened to the answering squawk. 'My office, immediate.'

'Can you actually hear what anyone says on that thing?' Richter asked.

'Not usually,' Simpson admitted with a rare smile. 'I just press the buttons and hope for the best. Normally I get the right person, and with the ID that's a much better bet than using the phone.'

A couple of minutes later the Intelligence Director knocked on the door and entered.

'You called, Director?' he asked. 'I must say this is not a particularly convenient time. I have several urgent reports to collate and—'

'I'm not interested in your convenience or otherwise,' Simpson snapped, cutting off the ID in mid-waffle. 'Richter's just got back from Stuttgart and he's apparently got a few things to tell us, so come in, sit down and shut up.'

The Intelligence Director peered at Richter as if seeing him for the first time. 'Oh,' he muttered, and took a seat in the second chair.

'Right,' Simpson continued, 'over to you, Richter.'

'Well, the good news,' Richter began, 'is that both groups of terrorists – in Onex and in Stuttgart – were killed, but there's actually quite a lot of bad news, too. We still don't know exactly what either group had planned to do, or whether there was or still is any threat to London. A known terrorist named Hans Morschel was sighted briefly at the target premises in Stuttgart, but wasn't in the building when the assault took place, so he's clearly now at large somewhere in Germany.'

'With respect,' the ID interrupted, 'I don't see the significance of either point. If the terrorists have been eliminated' – he was generally averse to using shorter and more accurate words like 'killed' – 'then whatever they planned to do has presumably ceased to exist along with them. And we know that Hans Morschel has been around for years, so the fact that he was sighted at or near a terrorist safe house in Stuttgart doesn't seem to me to be of any particular importance.'

'I don't dispute either argument,' Richter conceded, 'but that wasn't what was bothering me. It's more the overall picture that doesn't make sense, not the individual events. Forget the details and look at what's happened in broad terms. In less than a week we've identified and elim- inated two terrorist groups. But we've still no idea what their targets were, unless the BGS turn up something from the laptops they recovered, and in both cases all the terrorists are dead.'

'I thought the one you shot had survived the attack in Stuttgart,' Simp- son pointed out.

'Yes,' Richter agreed, 'but I had a call from Karl Wolff this morning. His surgery was successful, but late last night the patient went into cardiac arrest and died a few minutes later. Interestingly, shortly before he died, a Bundesgrenzschutz superintendent named Schröder had visited the hospital and tentatively identified the terrorist as one Fritz Gras.'

Richter stopped and looked at Simpson.

'So?'

'So Fritz Gras is essentially a mid-level crook who's never been known to associate with any terrorist organization, far less be a member of a cell.'

The Intelligence Director stirred slightly. 'It's not unknown for professional criminals to make what might be described as a career change. Perhaps Gras had decided to throw in his lot with these men for political or personal reasons.'

'That's not it,' Simpson said, his eyes never leaving Richter's face. 'There's more to it than that, I think. What else is there?'

'Fritz Gras is currently in prison in Munich, and has been for the last four years. He's about half-way through an eight-stretch for a bank robbery that went wrong.'

'Obviously that's just a simple case of mistaken identity,' the ID suggested.

Simpson ignored the Intelligence Director and gazed steadily at Richter. 'A BGS officer would know that fact, right?'

'I'd have thought so,' Richter replied.

'And there really is a Bundesgrenszchutz superintendent named Schröder?'

'Oddly enough, yes, but he's stationed in Hamburg and hasn't visited Stuttgart for the last year or so. Actually, the choice of name might just have been a lucky guess. "Schröder" isn't that uncommon in Germany.'

'And his ID was good, obviously?'

'Good enough to get him past two police officers, yes. Karl Wolff said he distracted the policeman in the ward by asking him to look at a mugshot in a binder, and for a few seconds the officer wasn't watching either "Schröder" – whoever he was – or the man in the hospital bed.'

'That would have been long enough?'

'If he knew what he was doing, yes. And he obviously did. Wolff has ordered extensive tests on the body to try to find out what agent the intruder used, but he's not particularly hopeful. It was obviously some kind of delayed-action drug, because the patient didn't die until about half an hour later.'

'What about "Schröder" himself? Description? Fingerprints?'

'Both police officers confirm he was a heavily built, middle-aged man with no obvious distinguishing marks. He spoke fluent German with a slight Rhine accent. He didn't leave a single fingerprint, as far as Wolff can discover. The cop on duty opened the door of the ward to let him in and out, and once inside the room the only things he touched were those items he'd brought with him: his briefcase and the ring-binder inside it. We must also assume that he's got a sense of humour.'

'Meaning?'

'He emphasized to the policeman standing outside the ward just how important the injured man's knowledge might be and suggested they double the number of guards there to protect him. Then he went into the room and killed him.'

'This does raise a number of issues,' the ID suggested, in a remarkably short and apposite sentence, for him.

'Exactly,' Richter concurred. 'My concern is that there's somebody in the background orchestrating what's been happening over in Europe, and we have no idea who or why.'

'OK,' Simpson said, 'give us your reasons.'

'First, in Switzerland the authorities were alerted to the presence of the terrorist cell by somebody looking very like the man who later impersonated "Schröder". I don't think that's just a coincidence, either. Second, in both Onex and Stuttgart the terrorists received warnings from somebody outside at the very moment the police assaults were starting. That meant that, on both occasions, when the plods kicked down the doors, they were met with a bunch of Kalashnikovs on full auto, resulting in heavy casualties on both sides. Third, the surveillance people watching the Stuttgart cell heard a definite reference to an attack being planned in Britain. According to the Onex tip-off, there was similar information on a laptop left lying in the apartment, but because of the damage to it, that couldn't subsequently be confirmed. Now, if I'm right, and the Swiss pseudo-landlord and "Schröder" are one and the same person, that's a very clear link between those two cells.'

Neither of the other men spoke, so Richter ploughed on.

'I raised this possibility with Karl Wolff and the GSG 9 squad commander, a guy named Rolf Altmann. Altmann pointed out that there's almost no chance that one man could manage to infiltrate two separate terrorist cells simultaneously, which was the line I was following. Realistically, it would be difficult enough for an outsider to penetrate even one group. But if the two cells were linked, then somehow that man must be involved with both of them.'

'That makes sense,' Simpson said. 'But how? If he's not a member of these cells, how come he seems to know so much about them – their location, phone numbers and stuff? Could we be looking at an undercover operation being run by some secret squirrel outfit?'

'I don't think so, for several reasons,' Richter said, 'not least the sheer number of police officers who've been killed this week during those raids. That, I hope, would be totally unacceptable to *any* law-enforcement or security service. I don't think this guy – let's call him "Schröder" for convenience – is anything to do with some government organization, and I also don't think he's actually joining these cells, or getting directly involved with them. No, I think it's a lot simpler than that. I think he's employing them.'

'What?'

'Look,' Richter said, 'apart from al Qaeda, most terrorist organizations are pretty short of cash. We know that a lot of them have carried out bank raids, kidnappings, that kind of thing, to raise funds to enable them to hit their real targets. Suppose somebody like Schröder comes along and offers to fund their causes by providing money so long as they act against a target of his choice.'

'It would have to be a target they were happy enough to attack from their own ideological point of view,' the Intelligence Director pointed out. 'I mean, something that conformed to whatever twisted philosophy their group follows.'

'Not necessarily,' Richter argued, 'and for one very simple reason.'

'Because he was going to blow the whistle on them before the attack could even be carried out?' Simpson suggested.

'Exactly.'

'OK,' Simpson said, 'what you say explains some of the more obvious anomalies, but what I still don't see is any motive that makes sense. Who is this Schröder and why is he getting closely involved with terrorist groups and then blowing the whistle on them? And why would he risk going into the hospital in Stuttgart just to kill that last surviving bad guy?'

'The answer to your second question's easy. He killed that man to prevent him revealing anything about the arrangement he had made with the cell, or maybe disclosing who Schröder really is. But as for Schröder's identity, or his ultimate motive, I haven't got the faintest idea.'

Stuttgart, Germany

'So what happened?'

In view of the events of the previous evening, the voice in the earpiece of the mobile sounded cold and almost unnaturally calm, and it was accompanied by a faint echo.

'I've no idea,' Helmut Kleber replied, though in truth he knew precisely what had taken place over the last twelve hours and had watched the entire assault itself from the comfort of his rented apartment. 'I didn't even know the building was being watched. Did any of your men report that, or being followed, or anything?'

'No.'

'Maybe the police simply received a tip-off?' Kleber still didn't know who had alerted the German authorities to the cell in the first place, so that statement was basically true.

'I doubt it.'

'Do you want to postpone the operation?' Kleber asked.

'Do *you* think we should?'

Kleber paused for a second or two before replying. He was well used to dealing with people who operated on the fringes of society, and on both sides of the law, but Hans Morschel was something else. For the first time, Kleber realized he was slightly frightened of the man.

'Not necessarily,' he replied.

'Good. Then I'll see you on the other side of the Channel.'

Kleber pressed the red button to end the call, and put down the mobile with a slight feeling of foreboding. Then he turned off the phone completely and put it down on the café table at which he was having breakfast. He'd pull out the chip and drop it in a trash bin somewhere down the street, and from then on use one of the other pay-as-you-go chips he'd already bought.

The operation was going exactly as he'd planned but, not for the first time, he had to wonder if recruiting Morschel had been such a good idea. The problem he'd faced was that the man was the only person he'd been able to identify who had proven links to al Qaeda. And that, as Kellerman had emphasized at the briefing, was an essential component of the overall plan.

On the other side of Stuttgart, Hans Morschel stared thoughtfully at his mobile, then dropped it into his pocket and glanced up at the man sitting opposite him.

'What do *you* think?' he asked, switching to English, as his companion struggled with German.

For a few moments, the other man didn't reply, just sat back in his chair, his fingers steepled. His appearance was a marked contrast to Morschel. The German was comparatively short and slight, with fair hair and a pale complexion, and he wore casual, even scruffy, clothes. The other man, however, was over six feet tall and strongly built, with black hair, dark eyes and deeply tanned skin, and dressed in an immaculate light-grey suit. He looked the epitome of a British-educated Arab, which was not surprising, since his wealthy sheikh father had sent him to Harrow, which had been followed by Cambridge and a stint at Sandhurst. Ahmed bin Salalah was clearly rich, urbane and sophisticated. In one of his pockets was a genuine British passport, and in his wallet a couple of platinum credit cards. Until the invasion of Iraq, he'd led the life of a typical Arab playboy – fast cars, fast boats, fast planes, wild parties and inexhaustible supplies of both alcohol and women. He'd deplored the 9/11 atrocity, like many other Saudis, but when the Americans decided the best response to al Qaeda was to invade Iraq and attempt to bring democracy to the country, he'd realized that not only was Osama bin Laden right in his actions, but the course the renegade Saudi was proposing was quite literally the only way forward.

By definition, you couldn't argue or debate with a country that tried to foist democracy on what had become a defeated and subject nation, a country led by men who were apparently too stupid or too ignorant, or perhaps both, to realize that democracy and the Koran were mutually exclusive. It was impossible to achieve a democratic Islamic state: it was an oxymoron, a contradiction in terms, and in the long run the Koran would prevail. It always had and it always would, because faith was stronger than mere political manoeuvring. And he knew that the American claims and justifications for their illegal invasion of Iraq were built wholly on lies. There never were any weapons of mass destruction in the country. There never had been, and the Americans had known it right from the start. And Saddam Hussein, far from sheltering and supporting al Qaeda as part of the so-called 'Axis of Evil', was in reality the only leader of an Arab nation who wouldn't tolerate the presence of Osama bin Laden's fighters in his territory. And their real reason for toppling Saddam didn't even occupy the moral high ground. It wasn't a desire to rid the country of a hated and brutal dictator so as to liberate his people. No, it was much, much simpler than that, and was blindingly obvious to anyone who looked behind the rhetoric. The real reason Bush had invaded Iraq was simply to seize control of the country's vast oilfields. That had been his objective from the start, and everything else was just a smokescreen.

But bin Salalah's biggest regret was that Britain, the nation that he knew almost as well as his own Saudi Arabia, had been suckered into tagging along behind the Americans and supporting their illegal actions. The blame for that, he knew well, lay with Tony Blair, a weak and gullible prime minister so enthralled by the 'Special Relationship' and apparently overawed by the Americans that he almost immediately acquired the nickname 'Bush's Poodle' and spent the rest of his political career trotting along obediently behind his master and barking when told to.

And by now, bin Salalah knew that the only message both the Americans and the British really understood was force and violence. And that was why he himself had joined al Qaeda. Not as a *shahid*, a martyr, though he would have been prepared to become one if called upon, but instead as a facilitator and planner. Al Qaeda had need of people like him, men who could travel openly to any country in the world and mix there in the most sophisticated company.

The Arab had been associated with Morschel for almost five years, but this was the biggest operation they'd undertaken together, and it had been, at least in part, at Kleber's instigation. Kleber was the one who'd come up with the idea of a coordinated campaign, with almost simultaneous bombing attacks in Europe to be followed by what he'd described as a 'main event' in Britain – some kind of major attack, though at that stage Morschel himself had been unable to suggest a suitable target.

When Morschel had relayed Kleber's suggestion to bin Salalah, the Arab had embraced it eagerly. And, more crucially, he'd suddenly recalled something he'd heard at Sandhurst, something he'd found almost unbelievable at the time. He'd then done sufficient research to confirm that his recollection was correct, and within a couple of days he'd met again with Morschel and laid a detailed plan in front of him. The German had instantly grasped both its brilliance and its simplicity, and since then both men had simply refined it. If it worked as they hoped, it would prove even more destructive than 9/11 but would be infinitely easier to carry out, and also technically undemanding, because the target was essentially undefended.

As to what he thought about the current situation, bin Salalah finally looked at Morschel directly and shook his head. 'Remind me about this man Kleber,' he said. 'Where did he come from?'

'I've already told you,' Morschel said.

'Humour me, Hans, and tell me again.'

'He approached Stammheim through a sympathizer about three months ago. He had a plan to hit a bank in a small town in southern Germany and he claimed he knew exactly when there would be an unusually large quantity of cash in the building. We looked it over, decided we'd got nothing to lose by mounting a raid, so we hit it on the day he suggested. And he was right. The take was about four times what we would normally have expected from a bank of that size.'

'So that gave him immediate credibility?'

'Yes, obviously. When I met him, he told me he was ex-military. He purportedly had a real grudge against the Americans because he claimed he'd lost a close relative in the invasion of Iraq, during a blue-on-blue incident.'

'And had he?' Ahmed bin Salalah asked.

'Maybe. The incident he told me about never really made the news, but a couple of my people checked what they could. The action was just as he'd described it, and one of the dead men was named "Kleber", so it's possible.'

'Or he could have identified the dead man, realized that the incident would be shrouded in military secrecy, and so decided to call himself "Kleber".'

'That's possible too.'

Ahmed bin Salalah leant back in the chair and clasped his hands behind his head. 'And what's he done since that bank raid?'

'Almost nothing directly. He's used his ex-military contacts to source weapons, ammunition and explosives whenever we've needed them, and he was also involved in the planning stages of the Stuttgart operation.'

'And Onex? What did he do there?'

'As you know, those men weren't part of Stammheim. We'd just recruited them to carry out the operation and supplied them with weapons and other stuff. Kleber was acting as a kind of liaison officer, so he went down there in order to make sure they had everything they needed.'

'Why did he go there in person?'

'Because, thanks to Echelon, you can't talk about that sort of thing on a telephone any more and because, if they needed other equipment, he'd be on the spot to sort it out.'

'OK,' Ahmed bin Salalah observed, 'that all sounds perfectly reasonable, but now you've got doubts about him, yes?'

'Yes,' Morschel nodded. 'Just because of what happened at Onex and then here last night.'

'How much does he know about the London operation?'

'Only that we're planning a spectacular assault. Nothing more. I've had no reason to involve or consult him.'

'Good,' bin Salalah said, standing up. 'Let's keep it that way. And once we get to Britain, I'll make sure we find out for sure what Kleber's agenda really is.'

Canterbury, Kent

'What's that?' Dick Clark asked, as he passed Paul Mason's desk.

Mason glanced up at the sergeant. 'It's an Admiralty chart of the mouth of the Thames. I was looking at the shipping routes, just wondering if maybe Barney was close enough to have seen something illegal going on out there in the estuary.'

'Like what? You back to thinking about smugglers again?'

'I don't know. It was just an idea.'

'Yes,' Clark said, 'but nobody could use that section of the sea wall to come alongside, so even if he did see a boat landing a few tons of hashish or something, it would have to have been some distance away. And that still leaves one other question you've got to answer.'

'I know. Who else was right there at the water's edge, waiting to cut the old man's throat? No, it really doesn't make sense. Whatever Barney saw had to have happened very close to where he was killed.'

Clark headed over to his own desk, and Mason began rolling up the chart ready to replace it in the cardboard tube it had arrived in. But as he did so a small symbol just off the north coast of Sheppey caught his eye.

'What's that mean?' he murmured and paused to refer to the legend. A few seconds later he sat back with a puzzled expression on his face. 'Dick,' he called. 'Come and take a look at this.'

DS Clark wandered over without much enthusiasm, certain his superior was barking up the wrong tree. He himself still thought Barney had been the victim of some teenage prank that had gone much too far.

'What is it?' he asked.

'This,' Mason said, pointing at the chart. 'There's an area designated as a "permanent no-entry exclusion zone" right here, pretty close to where Barney died. What's that mean?'

Clark had a little more experience of charts than the detective inspector, and had been known to occasionally hire small craft from various boatyards in the area for the odd afternoon afloat.

'It's probably a wreck,' he said, 'or maybe a dangerous shoal or sand-bank, something like that.' He looked more closely at the chart. 'Yes, here you are. It's just a wreck, obviously a danger to navigation because of where it is, right in the mouth of the River Medway.'

Mason stared at the chart for a few seconds. 'But why is there an *exclusion* zone around it?' he asked. 'If you look over here' – he pointed at another symbol on the chart – 'and here, there are other sunken ships, and they're just marked as wrecks. Why is this one ship given greater protection?'

'Probably just because of where it is,' Clark suggested. 'If a ship hit that wreck and got stuck it would partially block the Medway, and that could cause havoc to local river traffic. That's my guess, anyway.'

'Maybe you're right.' Mason sounded unconvinced.

'I don't see what this has to do with Barney,' Clark commented. 'He was killed in the early hours of the morning, when you certainly couldn't even see as far as that wreck. And I personally still think he was killed by a bunch of drunken teenagers out looking for kicks.'

Mason rolled up the chart and replaced it in the tube. 'You might be right,' he said, 'but I still reckon the killing was a professional job. Not that it matters, I suppose, because I doubt if we're ever going to solve it. But this whole case still bugs me. There's nothing new in, I suppose?' he asked hopefully. 'Nothing else from forensics?'

'No, absolutely nothing.'

Mason slid the cardboard tube into the capacious bottom drawer of his desk. 'Give the Sheerness DS a ring and see if the house-to-house generated anything else. If it didn't, we'll file this whole thing under "Pending" and let it gather dust for a while.'

As Clark sat down and picked up the phone to ring Sheerness, Mason once more pulled out the Admiralty chart and looked again at the site of the wreck marked within the exclusion zone, checking the distance between it and the spot beside The Moat where Barney had died. Then he replaced the chart in his drawer and input a search string into Google. The result surprised him, and he began hurriedly reading the text on some of the websites he'd found.

After about ten minutes, he sat back in his chair and laced his fingers behind his head, thinking deeply. There was, he thought, just a faint possibility that he might have found a link, but it was so tenuous that he certainly wasn't yet prepared to suggest it to Richardson. The DCI was unlikely to be impressed by a purely hypothetical solution to a murder case. But he could certainly run it by Clark. And if the DS thought it had any merit, maybe they could *both* take it to Richardson.

'Dick,' Mason called out. 'When you've finished doing that, come over here. There's something I want you to take a look at.'

Hammersmith, London

'Right,' Simpson said, as the Intelligence Director left the room. 'Despite the ID's reservations, I think you've established at least the possibility that the two terrorist cells in Onex and Stuttgart were linked in some way. What I'm not clear about is what we should do about it – or even if there's anything we *can* do, bearing in mind that all the bad guys are now dead.'

Richter shrugged. 'We'll just have to wait and see what the BGS techies find on the laptops and mobiles they pulled out of the safe house in Stuttgart. My guess is that there won't be much of any use to us. These people were far too cautious to write anything down, either on paper or onto a laptop's hard drive. The mobiles might be more of a help, but they've probably been using pay-as-you-go chips and dumping them once they've used up the initial credit.'

'And it would take a miracle to find Schröder, obviously, as we don't have a decent description or even a fingerprint. So what's your recommendation?'

Richter thought for a few moments. 'This is probably an overreaction, but my own inclination is to accept the information that we've been fed by this man, such as it is. Both cells were apparently involved in preparations for a major terrorist attack in London, so let's proceed on the assumption that something *is* being planned. We'll need to bring Five and the plods into the loop, and start checking for any signs of activity over here.

'That means all the usual stuff – increased surveillance at ports of entry, checking on known terrorists and sympathizers already here in Britain, that kind of thing – but if a big bang is imminent, that's probably too late because it's likely that the personnel and the materials they'll be using are already here. But we also need to be alert for anything out of the ordinary that might give us a clue as to what their target might be.'

'Like what?'

'Anything, really. Large numbers of suspects gathered in particular locations, people watching significant buildings for no apparent reason, unusual orders for equipment or chemicals that could be used to make explosives, thefts of dynamite from quarries, all that sort of thing.'

'But presumably this time we're not looking for Arabs?'

'We could be,' Richter said, 'because the world of terrorism isn't that big, and different groups have been known to work together. It's always possible that those two European cells were only involved in a supporting role, maybe just getting explosives into Britain or providing safe houses. The actual attack could be a major suicide bombing, and that almost certainly would involve Islamic terrorists. We need to look at everyone and everything.

'And we need to keep a particularly sharp eye out for Hans Morschel. If Wolff was right, he's a thoroughly nasty piece of work, and if there is going to be a terror campaign here in Britain, Morschel is very likely to come over here personally to supervise it.'

Canterbury, Kent

'What do you think?' Mason asked, as he finished explaining his theory.

Clark rubbed a large hand over the slight stubble on his chin. 'I don't know. It does make sense, but it just seems a bit far-fetched. I mean, there must be easier ways of getting the stuff than doing that.'

'Yes, but if this *is* happening, it would explain why Barney died.' He paused briefly, then made up his mind. 'I'm taking it to Richardson, see what he thinks.'

A few moments later Mason knocked on DCI Richardson's door, dutifully waited for the summons, then walked in.

'Afternoon, Paul. What have you got?'

'A possible explanation for what happened to Barney Holmes, sir,' Mason said and he began unrolling the Admiralty chart. 'I was looking at this, to check the positions of shipping lanes and then I noticed something.' He laid the chart flat on the desk and pointed at the clearly designated exclusion zone.

Richardson looked quizzical. Like Mason himself, he was no sailor. 'What is it, exactly?'

'It's a permanent exclusion zone around the wreck of a ship named the *Richard Montgomery*, which sank during the Second World War. Most wrecks are just marked with buoys so that people can identify where they are, but it seems this wreck is rather special.'

'In what way?'

'Let me explain what I found on the Internet.' Mason rolled up the chart and opened a slim green folder containing several sheets of paper. 'The *Richard Montgomery* was a Liberty ship built in 1943 in Jacksonville, Florida. In August 1944 she was loaded with over 7,000 tons of bombs, fuses and other munitions in Philadelphia and managed to get her cargo across the Atlantic safely.'

'And was then sunk by German aircraft off Sheppey?' Richardson suggested.

Mason shook his head. 'No, she was sunk by us – by a right catalogue of incompetence, in fact. Against the vociferous advice of his deputy, the King's Harbour Master decided that the best mooring for this ship, which drew a minimum of thirty-one feet, and probably rather more considering its heavy cargo, would be off the north edge of Sheerness Middle Sand, even though it was known that the depth there at high water was a mere thirty feet. On the 20th of September the inevitable happened, and the vessel grounded.

'The Liberty ships were very simply constructed, made up of welded steel sections that were then themselves welded together. This meant they could be built quickly: construction of each ship took an average of only about forty days from start to finish. It also meant they weren't quite as strong as other designs but, as they only had a design life of five years, this didn't matter. Because of the construction method used, once she'd grounded, the *Richard Montgomery* broke her back within a matter of days. Salvage operations were immediately started, and the contents of numbers four and five holds were removed, but once the hull split the other three holds were flooded and almost nothing else was recovered.'

Richardson was gazing at Mason with an obvious question forming on his lips and, as the DI finally paused, he asked it. 'So a Liberty ship sank off Sheppey sixty-odd years ago. So what? And what, exactly, has that got to do with the murder of an old tramp in Sheerness?'

'The fact is that the wreck contains an absolute minimum of 1,400 tons of explosives, and maybe as much as 3,500 tons. That's why there's an exclusion zone around the site, to stop any other ships ploughing into the wreck and setting them off.'

'Is that likely?'

'No, though most of the submerged munitions contain TNT, and that's basically unaffected by immersion in water. What worries me is that just off Sheerness is this huge repository of high-quality explosives. I wonder if what Barney saw that night was a group of divers going out to the wreck to recover a few of the smaller munitions so that they could extract the TNT from them. Maybe the *Richard Montgomery* is being used as a kind of explosives supermarket by a terrorist group, and they're planning a bombing campaign here in Britain. If Barney was a witness to their activities, killing him might make good sense. It probably would have been the easiest option they had to keep him quiet.'

'Can you actually prove any of this?' Richardson asked.

'About the *Richard Montgomery*, yes. It's well documented,' Mason replied. 'But everything else is pure conjecture. It just seems to me to make some sort of sense, that's all.'

Richardson nodded. 'You might even be right but, whether you are or not, this gets passed up the line. Look, I've just received this.'

He slid a single sheet of paper across the desk. The DI picked it up and read the three paragraphs it contained.

'That watch order has a nationwide distribution,' Richardson said, 'and was issued by the Security Service this afternoon. MI5 specifically asks for any information about possible terrorist activity, and I reckon what you've worked out so far just about meets that criterion. You'd better press your suit and polish your shoes, and I'll make an appointment for you tomorrow morning at Thames House. You can go and tell the men at Spook Central what you've just told me.'

Chapter Nine

Friday
Hammersmith, London

Richter had just got back from a brief lunch in the pub round the corner – he didn't drink alcohol but he did enjoy their food – when the direct phone buzzed from Simpson's office.

'Come up,' the Director ordered curtly and rang off.

When Richter reached the seventh floor, he found Simpson reading a report, with his feet up on the desk.

'How's the leg?' he asked, as Richter sat down.

'It's stiff and sore. Walking's not a real problem, but that's maybe because I'm mainlining some tablets the German hospital gave me. When they run out I might find it a lot more difficult and I'll probably need something stronger than aspirin to cope. But you didn't drag me all the way up here for a medical report?'

'No, of course not,' Simpson said. 'I've just had something interesting in from Five. Does the name *Richard Montgomery* mean anything to you?'

'The golfing idiot?' Richter suggested.

'That's Colin Montgomery. Think bigger, much bigger, and made of steel.'

'No idea.'

'It is, or rather was, a ship. This was news to me too, but I'm now informed that there are about three thousand tons of probably perfectly viable explosives, mainly TNT, sitting in the wreck of a Liberty ship just a mile and a half off the sea front at Sheerness. And this very morning a senior plod from Canterbury walked into Thames House with an interesting theory.'

Briefly, Simpson outlined what the interviewing officer at the Security Service headquarters had learned from DI Paul Mason.

Richter wasn't particularly impressed. 'It's a good story, OK, but what's he got in the way of actual facts? Has anyone spotted illegal divers at the scene? Or boats getting suspiciously close to the site of the wreck?'

'No to all of those, as far as I'm aware. So you're dismissing this lead?' Simpson asked.

'Not necessarily, but I would like to see a bit more evidence before we go chasing off to the wilds of the Isle of Sheppey looking for bad guys who might not be there at all. And I'm not even sure that what he's suggesting is viable.'

Richter paused for a few moments to marshal his thoughts. 'As you know, I spent some time in the Navy, although a lot of it was in the air, but I do know something about tides and currents, and quite a bit about diving. From what you've told me, the wreck's lying at the southern edge of the Thames Estuary, near the mouth of the River Medway. There's bound to be a reasonably strong current there most of the time, which would make working on the wreck difficult without a diving tender moored above it, and if there ever had been, presumably somebody would have noticed it.'

He paused again.

'Despite the circumstances of the sinking, I doubt if the holds are open, so trying to get inside the hull would mean cutting through steel plate, which needs expensive and sophisticated gear, or a diver risking his life by swimming down passageways. Getting inside would be a problem, but an absolutely doddle compared to the difficulty of getting out again, especially if the diver was trying to recover a Second World War bomb. He would definitely need flotation bags to lift it to the surface, and trying to manoeuvre those through passageways or even a hole cut in the side of the hull would be a nightmare.

'According to what you've read in that report' – Richter pointed to the buff folder lying on Simpson's desk – 'most of the munitions were thousand-pound bombs. No surprise, the reason they were called that was because they weighed a thousand pounds. That's half a ton, so lifting one out of the water would need a crane. Moving it away from the water's edge would need a powerful van or preferably a lorry.'

He smiled. 'After that, there's the difficulty of cutting open the bomb casing in order to extract the TNT. You don't just hack your way in with a Black and Decker and hope for the best. It needs specialist equipment and expertise. The whole operation would be a logistical nightmare, perhaps nearly impossible, and certainly very difficult to achieve without anyone noticing. And by that I don't just mean an old tramp who spots a man in a wetsuit, or whatever else Mason thinks this man Barney might have witnessed at Sheerness.'

Simpson nodded encouragingly, so Richter continued.

'On the other hand, plastic explosive is freely available throughout most of Europe, as long as you know where to look. So why would any terrorist group go to all the trouble of trying to extract TNT from a wreck in one of the busiest tidal seaways in the world when they could nip over to, say, Czechoslovakia, buy a bunch of black-market Semtex and just drive it here in the back of a van? Semtex is more powerful than TNT, a lot more stable and far easier to handle. Plus, if you can get your hands on some from the early production runs, it's also odourless and won't show up on X-ray machines. And if the bad guys, for some reason, can't source a bunch of plastic, they can turn diesel oil and fertilizer into a bloody efficient IED. Just look at the damage to the Murrah Federal Building in Oklahoma.'

'OK, Richter, you've made your point. I'll note that you don't believe Inspector Mason's idea has too much merit.'

'What did Five think of it?'

'Pretty much the same as you, actually. The officer he spoke to earlier thinks Mason's probably using this theory to wrap up the unsolved murder of the tramp in Sheerness.'

'I think he's got a lot more work to do, then. He can't just claim "Some unidentified terrorists killed the guy" and hope that's the end of it.'

'Noted.' Simpson passed the file folder across his desk. 'As you're now more or less in charge of this case, you can hang on to this.'

'Thanks. Anything else?'

'Not really. Five sent out a nationwide alert yesterday to all ports and airports, and all the other usual warnings, but nothing's come in so far. I'll let you know.'

Calais, France

Hans Morschel had experienced no difficulties in leaving Germany and driving across north-east France in the four-year-old Mercedes 300 saloon with Munich plates. His only minor discomfort was the unusual thickness of the carpet, which meant the position of his feet on the pedals was slightly raised.

In fact, it wasn't the carpet itself that was causing the problem: the entire floorpan beneath it, the underlay having been removed, was covered in a one-inch thick layer of Semtex. That was the maximum Morschel believed they could hide using that method. The plastic explosive was arranged in individual packs, specially flattened to fit into the available space, and altogether it weighed around 85 kilos.

Early that afternoon, just outside Calais, as Morschel had begun looking out for signs for the car ferry port, the driver of the Renault Laguna saloon behind him had flashed his headlights once, then overtaken. Morschel raised a hand in acknowledgement as the other car sped past, carrying a second load of Semtex hidden under the carpet in precisely the same fashion. As a basic precaution, the Laguna would be taking the Channel Tunnel train. Neither Morschel nor his associate, Ernst Hagen, thought there was even the remotest chance of either of them being stopped, but taking separate routes to their destination seemed a wise move.

Just as happens at Dover, every vehicle that leaves France through Calais is subject to surveillance. Pictures are taken, by fixed cameras, of both the driver's face and the vehicle's number plate while it is stopped at the ferry check-in booth. Every passport is inspected by immigration officers, both French and British, and those that are machine-readable are run through a scanner. There are also large inspection sheds where vehicles that look suspicious, for whatever reason, can be inspected by French customs officers, and, if necessary, be reduced to their component parts.

As a frequent border-crosser, Morschel was well aware of this routine and anticipated little trouble in passing through. He wasn't concerned that the Mercedes's registration plate would be recorded, because he already had a solution for that, and the same applied to his identification document.

Exactly as expected, Morschel's perfectly genuine German passport was accepted by both French and British immigration officers. A few weeks earlier, one of his associates had found a drug addict who bore a slight resemblance to Morschel, and the man had taken little persuasion to hand over his passport in exchange for enough cash to feed his habit for a couple of months. Thirty minutes after arriving at the ferry port itself, Morschel drove the Mercedes onto the vessel, parked it as instructed and then found a seat in the restaurant to enjoy a leisurely meal during the crossing.

He expected to reach his ultimate destination by mid-afternoon and, as long as none of his men had encountered any difficulties en route, they should be ready to move in another couple of days. That timescale was slightly longer than he'd originally planned but, for their own safety and satisfaction, he and Ahmed bin Salalah had another matter to resolve before they ordered the endgame to begin.

Two and a half hours after Morschel had driven onto the ferry, Helmut Kleber steered a hired Peugeot saloon on French plates towards the same port. He had no hidden explosives in the vehicle, but there were several items of hardware that he had no wish for anyone to find, and these were well hidden in the rear of the vehicle. He, too, had no fears that he would be stopped, because the passport he was using was absolutely genuine, even though the name inside it wasn't 'Helmut Kleber', or anything like it.

But even if he was stopped for any reason, unlike Hans Morschel, Kleber possessed a guaranteed 'get-out-of-jail-free' card. The trouble was that, once he used it, he'd blow the entire operation, so it really was a genuine last resort.

Hammersmith, London

'What is it?' Simpson asked as Richter entered.

'I've just taken a call from Karl Wolff, who's given me an update on what the BGS have found out so far from examining that property in Stuttgart.'

Simpson closed the file he had been reading and leant back in his swivel chair. 'Go ahead.'

'As you know, the Germans recovered a couple of laptops and a handful of mobiles from the safe house and the bodies of the terrorists. Some of the phones were quite badly damaged, and one of the computers had taken a bullet, but the forensic people did quite a good job of recovering the data.

'The mobiles first. They were all cheap pay-as-you-go phones, presumably purchased for this one operation, whatever it is. According to the call lists in the phones themselves, most of the calls made were from mobile to mobile within the group, and they all had the other numbers pre-programmed into the speed-dial facility.'

'Pretty much what you'd expect,' Simpson pointed out.

'Exactly,' Richter nodded. 'But they also found four other pre-programmed numbers, both belonging to mobiles that they *didn't* find anywhere on the property. If you recall, when GSG 9 hit the building, the surveillance teams reported that there would be eight occupants, but when the shooting stopped they found only six bodies. Hans Morschel and one other man had presumably got out through their improvised escape route some time earlier, while two other bad guys were already known to be away from the property at the time of the assault. The Germans have made the obvious deduction that these four numbers belong to the phones that were carried by Morschel and the other three men unaccounted for.

'As soon as Wolff was given this information, he asked the German phone companies for a history of the mobiles' locations, and a list of the calls they made and received. As already discovered, the majority of the calls were made from one member of the cell to another, and most of the time the phones had been located either inside the building itself or within that same area of Stuttgart.'

'This is boring me, Richter. Get to the meat of it.'

'I already have. According to the phone companies, two of the mobiles that weren't discovered in the safe house had been switched off about fifteen minutes after the GSG 9 assault. One of them hasn't been used since, but the other has. The interesting thing is the call record of this phone. It was used to make a total of seven calls to another mobile number over the past five days. This morning it was switched on again and the user made one short call yet again to the same number. After that, both phones were turned off. Wolff reckons this phone was probably the one being used by Hans Morschel himself.'

'So?' Simpson still didn't seem particularly interested.

'The new number – the one that wasn't programmed into the speed-dials of the other phones found in the safe house – was tracked to a location a few miles south-west of Geneva last weekend. It was only switched on for about fifteen minutes and during that time it received a call from what Wolff believes is Morschel's mobile, which suggests the two users had some sort of communications schedule in operation. So maybe there was a direct link between the two cells, and that could mean that the phone tracked to Switzerland was being used by this mysterious Schröder character.'

'Or maybe it's just a coincidence.'

'Maybe.'

'And this information helps us how, exactly?'

'Not very much,' Richter admitted. 'Wolff thinks that the chips or even the phones themselves have been dumped already, so these numbers are probably no more use to us because they'll never be used again.'

'What about the laptops, then?'

'They were slightly more interesting. The damaged one took a bullet through the screen but the base unit was untouched. All the same, it didn't have a lot on it, apart from a collection of games and some low-quality porn. But the other one had been used on the web, and some of the sites were interesting and relevant. The two that Wolff flagged up in particular were the Channel Tunnel website and a discount car-ferry booking agency, which might suggest the bad guys are indeed planning on moving their act over here.'

'No bookings recorded, presumably?' Simpson was now suddenly alert.

'No, they obviously weren't quite that stupid. They also looked at a couple of hotel and B&B sites, checking on different accommodation in London and the south-east, but again they didn't make any bookings.'

'Anything else?'

'No, but I think that what Karl Wolff and his merry men have turned up does suggest we probably have a group of terrorists on their way over here.'

'Wrong tense, Richter,' Simpson said. 'You mean "had", not "have". The ten men in that safe house would have posed a viable threat to us but, with six of them laid out in a German mortuary, I think most of that particular threat has evaporated, don't you?'

'Not necessarily. After all, it only takes one terrorist to plant a bomb.'

'You're stating the obvious. But what I meant was that, if a group of ten men had formed a terrorist cell to carry out a bombing campaign, or whatever, presumably that means they'd decided they needed ten men to accomplish it. They wouldn't recruit any extra bodies just for the fun of it – too much of a risk. With six of them dead, my guess is that they'll need a few weeks, even months, to find replacements, if they bother at all.'

'That's a good point, but only if you also assume that *those* men were the intended perpetrators. What bothers me most about this is that we have two terrorist cells which seem to have links to a potential London bombing, but which were apparently also intending to carry out two different attacks in mainland Europe. That could mean that the London team was a separate group altogether. The worst-case scenario is that we could be looking at what was planned as a coordinated attack in three countries at more or less the same time, so the fact that two of the terrorist groups have been eliminated won't necessarily have any effect on whatever they've got planned for this side of the Channel.'

'Christ, you're full of good news today, aren't you?' Simpson muttered sourly, then swung round and stared out of the window towards the Hammersmith flyover. 'I hope you're wrong, but if we assume you're right,' he said, turning back to face Richter, 'what else can we do?'

'Not a lot. The alert's in place, so it's really just a matter of waiting for someone, somewhere, to spot something else. What I'll do now is contact Five at Thames House, tell them what Wolff discovered on the laptop's hard drive and suggest they tell the plods to concentrate their efforts primarily on London and the south-east. And at the moment, that's about all we *can* do.'

Dover, Kent

Before leaving the Port of Dover, all arriving cars and small vehicles have to pass through a narrow exit, with inspection sheds on both sides, where customs officers stand waiting, and there are cat's claw vehicle immobilizers to ensure any drivers who are requested to stop will do so.

The exit lane was Morschel's only worry, but he was still not unduly concerned. Under his jacket he was wearing a belt holster with a Glock 19 pistol tucked into it, and he was perfectly aware that the British officials would be unarmed. If by some chance the customs officers stopped him, he would answer their questions politely and, if requested, drive the Mercedes into the inspection shed. He would even get out and open the boot if they asked him to. But if they started really searching the car, he was sure that the Glock would be all the persuasion he would need to convince them to let him pass. And once out in the streets of Dover, he was aware of numerous different routes he could take to get away.

In the event, his lack of concern was entirely justified. As he drove through the exit lane, none of the customs officers did anything more than simply glance at him and also at the number plate of the Mercedes. So, fifteen minutes after the ferry had docked, Morschel was already on the A2 dual-carriageway, heading north-west towards the M2 motorway.

At the first large service area he came to, he pulled into the car park and chose a secluded corner. When he was certain that he was unobserved, with no CCTV cameras covering that section of the parking area, he got out of the Mercedes, walked round to the back and opened the boot. He lifted the carpet, reached underneath it and pulled out a flat packet a little over a foot long and about four inches wide. He opened it and extracted the two Austrian registration plates which rightfully belonged on the car. The German plates used for his journey so far had come from an identical model Mercedes that had been written off in a traffic accident. He selected a cross-head screwdriver from the tool kit and within minutes had substituted the two Austrian plates. He then pulled the oval 'D' sticker from the boot lid and replaced it with one bearing 'A' for Austria. In the same packet he'd taken from the boot was an Austrian passport, which he slipped into his jacket pocket. The photograph inside showed a man looking rather like Morschel, but clean-shaven, so that was the final thing he now needed to rectify.

Opening one of the suitcases, he removed a small leather wash-bag that he slipped into his jacket pocket, then headed over towards the service area itself. In the male toilet he first washed his hands and, at a moment when no other men were using the facilities, he opened the bag and extracted a pair of sharp scissors, a razor and some shaving cream. It was the work of only a minute to snip away most of his straggly beard and flush the hairs down the sink. Then, more relaxed, he thoroughly lathered his face and took all the time he needed with the razor, because the sight of a man shaving in a motorway service area was not at all unusual. While he was thus engaged, two men came in to use the urinals but neither so much as glanced at him.

His appearance now transformed, Morschel went and sat down in the restaurant and drank a cup of moderately bad coffee before returning to the Mercedes. The last thing he did before resuming his journey was to toss the packet now containing the original number plates and German passport into an overgrown ditch that ran between the perimeter of the service area and the uncultivated field adjacent to it. He realized it would be discovered at some point but guessed that wouldn't be any time soon.

And, even if somebody found it almost immediately, it still wouldn't really matter.

Romford, Essex

On the south-east side of the town lay a small industrial estate occupied by the usual wide range of businesses, including a discount tyre company, depots for two courier firms, a car repair specialist and a small computer software company.

On the far side of this estate stood a warehouse identical in size to the others, but without any identifying name outside it, though the mark left by the logo of the previous occupants was still visible on the front of the building. A discreet sign taped on the window right next to the door leading into the former offices bore the company name 'BB Productions'

– which was an almost entirely uninformative label – and a mobile phone number. Outside the warehouse, two nondescript saloon cars were parked in marked spaces, but otherwise there was no sign of any business activity.

Just after four that afternoon, an articulated car transporter turned into the estate, the driver slowing almost to a crawl as he searched for the building that was his destination. The vehicle stopped right beside the tyre company, and the driver climbed down to ask there for directions. A couple of minutes later he re-emerged with a youth wearing grubby overalls, who pointed further down the road. The driver nodded his thanks, climbed back into his vehicle and, with a hiss from the air brakes, moved away slowly.

Outside the unmarked warehouse he again stopped the lorry and descended from the cab. Just then, the side door of the building opened, and two men emerged and headed towards him.

'This BB Productions?' the driver asked.

One of the men nodded and turned to his companion. 'Get the main doors open,' he instructed.

The driver handed over a clipboard bearing several sheets of paper. 'Sign here, here, and here,' he requested, and watched carefully as the man complied. 'Thanks. So you want them inside the warehouse?'

'Yes. You'll find four other vans in there, but there should still be enough space in front of them. Where are the uniforms and the other stuff?'

'Inside two of the vans. You'd better check all of it before I leave here, OK?'

'You can count on it.'

The driver took back the clipboard, walked over to the cab of the lorry and placed it on the passenger seat. Then he went to the rear of the vehicle and extended wheel-ramps down from the steel framework to the road surface. Once he was satisfied that the ramps were properly positioned, he walked up the narrow gap between the side of the transporter itself and the rearmost of the four vans it was carrying.

He opened the van's door, slid into the driver's seat and started the engine. The reversing lights illuminated, and the van backed swiftly down the ramps. Once it was clear of the transporter, he drove it forward to the warehouse, where the double-width roller-shutter doors were now fully open, then steered it inside and parked it where the other man indicated. Ten minutes later, he was parking the last of the four white Ford Transit vans neatly alongside the third. All of them were fitted with roof-bar lights, and with metal grilles over their windscreens. There were 'Metropolitan Police' logos emblazoned each side, and 'Police' markings on the bonnets.

After checking their registration numbers against those listed on a sheet of paper, he announced: 'The uniforms are in this one, and the weapons in that one over there.'

He opened the rear doors of the two vehicles he'd indicated. In the back of the first were two hanging rails on which were hung twenty black uniforms, and in the second two large wooden boxes. The driver lifted one of the box lids and pointed down at the row of a dozen Heckler & Koch MP5 sub-machine guns with attached magazines, nestling neatly in racks. In the second box were twenty semi-automatic pistols, with a selection of belts, holsters, helmets and bulletproof jackets. A couple of dozen boxes of ammunition completed the inventory.

'Right,' the driver said, after the two men had finished counting all the equipment and checking it against their inventory. 'What is it you're making with this lot?' he asked.

'Buggered if I know. Some bloody cops and robbers thing for TV, I suppose. We've got nothing to do with the filming. We just deliver the hardware and make sure the actors are wearing the proper uniforms and carrying the right guns when the director shouts "Action".'

'Well, have a good one,' the transporter driver replied and turned to walk back to his vehicle.

Even as he drove away, the main doors of the warehouse slid closed, quickly hiding all the vehicles from view. As soon as they were fully lowered, the two men bolted them shut on the inside. Then they turned their attention to the weapons that the theatrical supply company had provided.

Even to an expert, the sub-machine guns and pistols would have been indistinguishable from the real thing, until you picked one up, of course. Audiences expected such weapons to look real: anything obviously fake would destroy the illusion. But although they had the look and feel of the genuine article, with bolts that opened and closed convincingly, they were all, nevertheless, just harmless replicas, and replicas weren't what these men needed.

Methodically, they collected all the MP5s from the box, carried them to the rear of the warehouse and placed them inside a crate in a store-room, then repeated the process with the pistols and ammunition.

One of the men led the way to another storeroom, the door of which was fastened with two exterior-quality Chubb locks and additionally secured with two bolts fitted with heavy-duty padlocks. He pulled a bunch of keys from his pocket and methodically undid all four locks, then pushed open the door. Inside the windowless room stood half a dozen dark green steel boxes of a distinctly military appearance.

He opened the first one and picked out another Heckler & Koch MP5 that looked virtually identical to those they'd just stored away. But these weapons were not studio props, and there were also twenty boxes of 9-millimetre ammunition, all marked 'A/P' for 'armour-piercing'.

Working quickly and efficiently, they carried the sub-machine guns, pistols and ammunition out to the 'Metropolitan Police' Ford Transits and stowed them in the purpose-built boxes bolted to the floor in the backs of the vans. Then they locked all the vehicles securely.

A few minutes later, one of the two men emerged from the building, walked over to his car and drove away. His companion would be stay-ing there in the warehouse overnight, to be relieved by another member of the team the following morning.

Every door and window in the warehouse was fitted with an alarm, and they'd converted one of the offices into sleeping quarters, equipped with a microwave oven, a small fridge, a television set and a camp-bed. As well as these home comforts, the man would also have a loaded Glock 17 and a Heckler & Koch MP5 sub-machine gun for company. Now they were so close to the start of their operation, it made sense to provide a permanent guard on such vital equipment.

Rochester, Kent

Hans Morschel pulled off the M2 at the Rochester junction and steered the Mercedes towards the centre of the town, following a set of directions he'd previously printed from an Internet site. As he approached the out-skirts, he turned aside onto a minor road and shortly afterwards stopped the car outside a line of shops. He locked it and returned twenty min-utes later after having made a number of purchases. But he was still missing one item, so he drove on, closer to the town centre, and eventu-ally found another shop selling exactly what he wanted.

Ten minutes later he parked outside a middle-sized hotel where he'd pre-booked a room. Knowing that the German police, and probably the Bundesgrenzschutz as well, were looking for him, he'd made all his bookings from a series of Internet cafés located in and around Stuttgart and felt quite certain none of the German authorities even knew he was here in Britain.

Morschel plucked his bags out of the boot of the Mercedes, carried them inside and checked in. His room was situated on the second floor, with a small en-suite bathroom. It was a little dingy, but would do well enough for the few days he intended staying in the area.

Once he'd unpacked, he glanced at his watch. He still had plenty of time before his meeting, so he checked that the door was locked, then lay down on the bed. His alarm set for six thirty, he closed his eyes and within minutes was sound asleep.

Hammersmith, London

Richter had decided he would work late at Hammersmith. His leg was stiff and ached badly, and he didn't fancy the horrors of Friday-evening rush hour on the Underground. He'd rather wait until the crowds had dispersed before making his way back to his attic apartment in Stepney. As usual, there would be nobody waiting there for him.

He decided to call Karl Wolff's mobile to check on progress at the German end of the investigation, but the Bundesgrenzschutz officer had no further information. His technical support unit was still examining the laptops and mobiles they'd recovered, but they'd found nothing else useful and, Wolff guessed, there probably wasn't anything more to extract.

'These men were obviously very careful,' he commented to Richter, shortly before ending their conversation. 'My guess is that they used these laptops solely for obtaining general information, but anything more specific or incriminating – emails, credit-card payments, that kind of thing – was carried out in cyber cafés. They hadn't even set up any email accounts on the laptops, and the browser history suggests they didn't use a web-based service either.'

'So we're still stumbling around in the dark?' Richter remarked.

'That's an appropriate way of putting it. I'll let you know if anything else turns up, but I'm not very hopeful.'

'And Hans Morschel?'

'Vanished from sight. Nobody's seen any sign of him here in Stuttgart, so by now he could be anywhere.'

'That,' Richter said, 'is exactly what's worrying us. And what about our "Superintendent Schröder"?'

Wolff laughed bitterly. 'Like a ghost in the night. When he walked out of that hospital, he simply disappeared. We've still got no idea at all who he really is, or why the hell he's involved in this. Personally, I think he's a part of the cell, maybe Morschel's number two, and he killed the last survivor just to stop him talking to us.'

'Perhaps, but there's still the phone that was traced to Onex. If that was his mobile, how could you square that with him also being a part of the Stuttgart cell?'

'In two ways, and neither is entirely convincing. Either there was some kind of rivalry between these two terrorist groups, and Schröder deliberately pointed the finger at the Swiss cell so that the police would carry out an assault, or the two cells were genuinely working together and somebody else blew the whistle. Maybe Schröder merely tried his best to warn them, but it was already too late for the terrorists to get out of the building.

'Now,' Wolff went on, 'before you pull those suggestions apart, let me save you the trouble. Terrorist groups aren't normally rivals to each other. Even if their philosophies are entirely dissimilar, they're usually fighting what they see as a common enemy, and therefore they're far more likely to cooperate with each other and share resources than to tip off a law-enforcement agency.'

'That's our thinking too,' Richter confirmed.

'Right. So that makes the "working together" hypothesis sound more likely, but what bothers me is the fact that the mobile – which I think might be Schröder's – was switched on for only such a brief period in Switzerland, and, as far as we know, he was never spotted anywhere near the target building. My understanding from the Terrorism Investigations Unit is that no unidentified people were detected entering or leaving the property. If he really was a part of that cell, why didn't he ever visit the apartment?'

'And why,' Richter interjected, 'did the warning about the raid come so late, just seconds before the Swiss police went in? Our hypothesis is a little different, or at least mine is, since my boss remains unconvinced. We believe the mystery caller *wanted* the terrorists to react the way they did, because he intended that none of them would survive that assault. That's pretty much the same as happened in Stuttgart, and Herr Schröder was waiting in the wings there to ensure that the only survivor died peacefully and harmlessly in his sleep.'

'You may be right,' Wolff replied, 'but what was his motive? Why is Schröder betraying terrorist cells? And don't forget that the Stuttgart group was detected by a German police officer, so there was no tip-off regarding their presence. How do you explain that?'

'I don't know, unless Schröder realized that the target building was already under surveillance, which meant that he didn't need to bother contacting the police himself. But you're right about motive. It really doesn't make sense.'

Fifteen minutes after he'd ended this call to Wolff, the internal line from the duty officer rang.

'Richter.'

'That's a surprise. I thought you'd be long gone. Everybody else has.'

'Obviously,' Richter said, 'since Friday is POETS Day – piss off early, tomorrow's Saturday. Did you actually want me for any reason, or were you just feeling lonely down there?'

'Not lonely enough to want to talk to you, thanks. No, I've had a call from my opposite number at Five, looking for Simpson, so I've been trying all the office phones to track him down.'

Richter glanced at the wall clock. 'It's gone six,' he pointed out, 'and you'd be lucky to find him here at this time even during the week. On a

Friday there's no bloody chance because by now he's probably half-way to Lincolnshire or wherever one of his land-owning pals has invited him this weekend. What's it about, anyway?'

'Did you know that Five has requested an analysis of all the passenger-lane camera images from Calais, Boulogne, the French Chunnel terminal and all the other ports, for the last couple of days?'

'Yes, actually it was me that asked for it.'

'Oh, right. Well, it turned up a few oddities, just as you might expect, but Five has flagged up one that might be significant, in view of Stuttgart.'

'Go on.'

'This afternoon a Mercedes on German plates was photographed at Calais waiting to board the P&O ferry to Dover. The driver was a single male, and his passport checked out as being legitimate.'

'And?'

'Five has carried out routine checks on all car registrations since the watch order was initiated. Obviously this takes time because they have to run the checks through the vehicle registration systems in the respective countries of origin. Anyway, this one came back from the Germans with a flag.'

'False plates?' Richter suggested.

'Oddly enough, no. The plates are legitimate, registered to a Hanover address, but the car they should be attached to is sitting in a wrecker's yard near Munich. It was written off in a three-vehicle crash on the autobahn about a month ago. It's the same model as the Mercedes that took the ferry, and it's even pretty much the right colour – dark grey.'

Richter felt a buzz of excitement. 'They got pictures of the driver?'

'Yes, and his passport details.'

'Fat lot of use they'll be. If the car's on false plates, the driver will have a spare identity tucked away in his pocket. Are the pictures here yet?'

'Yes. I've just put them on the system. You can access them on your PC in a couple of minutes.'

'Thanks,' Richter said, and rang off.

Three minutes later he was studying an image of the front end of a Mercedes saloon, and a few seconds after that a slightly blurred image of the driver. The nineteen-inch monitor offered pretty good reproduction, but Richter preferred to hold the pictures in his hand, so he printed out both photographs on the colour laser sitting beside his desk.

Then he took out a magnifying glass and began studying the images carefully.

Chapter Ten

Friday
Hammersmith, London

Richter took a last look through the magnifying glass at the face of the driver of the Mercedes saloon, then reached for the phone and dialled Karl Wolff's mobile in Germany.

'It's Paul Richter again. I think we might have something here.'

Quickly, he explained about the Mercedes saloon with the wrong number plates fitted. 'This could be someone completely innocent,' he added. 'Somebody who's bought a second-hand Merc from a shady source somewhere, and I don't want to generate an APB – an all-points' bulletin – here just to catch some German tourist driving around in a dodgy set of wheels. I recall you ran some kind of photo-recognition software before in order to identify Morschel. Can you do the same thing with the picture we've got here?'

'That depends on how good the image is. I'm no computer expert, but I understand the program needs to be able to identify certain key facial features to make a positive identification. If it can pick those out, it'll work; if it can't, it won't. Can you send it over immediately by email?'

'Of course. Let me have the address.'

Having jotted down what Wolff told him, Richter turned to his computer and swiftly drafted an email to which he attached the two images from the Calais port cameras. Then he picked up the phone again.

'OK, Karl, it's on the way to you right now. I've sent both pictures. Is there anyone there at the moment who can run a comparison?'

'Our office is always manned, but I'll head back there straight away, just to make sure we get an answer to you as soon as possible. Will you still be available on this number?'

'No. I'm heading home in an hour or so, but you can call my mobile.

It's an Enigma secure cellphone, so we can speak freely as long as you have compatible equipment.'

'I'm sure our technical support people can sort something out. I hope to get back to you in a couple of hours.'

Richter put the phone down and stared again at the photograph of the man in the driving seat of the Mercedes. Then he shut down his computer and locked his safe – part of the standard 'clear desk' routine FOE followed – and then took the lift down to the first floor.

'You off home at last, then?' the duty officer asked.

'Not just yet,' Richter replied. 'Listen, regarding those pictures you got from Five. I've asked the German BGS to run a photo-comparison analysis, and they'll call me with the result later this evening. If it is Morschel, I'll want the watch order modified to start looking for him and his car specifically, and that will include motorway CCTV cameras and anything else the plods have got that might show where he went after he left Dover. You can handle that, through Five, on my authority?'

'Yes, of course. I'll have to inform Simpson, but I think that can wait till Monday.'

'Right, I'll call you later this evening whatever the result. And while I'm here, I'd better sign the authorization chit for the watch order.'

Dover, Kent

Helmut Kleber drove without a pause through the exit lane at the ferry port, and then took the A20 southern coast road, heading for London. He knew Morschel would be staying somewhere in Rochester, but himself had already booked a room in a hotel in Maidstone, a few miles south.

There were two simple reasons for his choice. The first was that he didn't like or trust Morschel and had no wish to be anywhere near him if he could avoid it. But the second reason was more pragmatic, as the headquarters of the Kent Constabulary were located in Maidstone, and Kleber considered that was the most obvious place to make his first move.

He knew he would have to meet Morschel the following day, not least because they had now entered the final phase of the operation, and both of them would have a lot of tasks – though entirely dissimilar – to complete over the weekend.

As he picked up speed and joined the M20, Kleber pondered exactly what his next move should be. He knew what he had to achieve, and he was well acquainted with the different sections of the British law-enforcement organization and the way they worked. Ideally, he knew he ought to find the answers to a number of questions before he did anything further, but he was afraid there simply wasn't time, and time was now becoming his major concern.

No, Kleber rationalized, he had to act sooner rather than later. In fact, he decided he ought to start that same evening, after he'd checked into the hotel, just to ensure that he got the wheels turning in time. That must be his first priority, he decided. If he delayed until tomorrow, it might be too late.

Hammersmith, London

The call from Wolff came just thirty minutes later, while Richter was still in his office.

'Wolff,' the German identified himself. 'This is a secure line, which you can consider the good news. The bad news is that we've run the checks, and the best I can give you is what the Americans might call a definite maybe. The picture was, as you warned, slightly blurred, and that's the main reason why we can't be too specific here. The section of the image you asked us to analyse is quite small, which means the points we need to use for comparison are very tiny, so the results can't be absolute. As you'll appreciate, an error of even one or two pixels in the base data can dramatically alter the result of the analysis. I'm sorry.'

In truth, that was more or less what Richter had expected. He'd tried to study the image of the driver's face through a magnifying glass, and even then the features were relatively indistinct.

'Thanks anyway, Karl. Look, I won't hold you to this, but in percentage terms how likely is it that the man in the picture is Hans Morschel?'

'You want my best guess?'

'Yes.'

Wolff paused for a few seconds before he replied. 'If you'd only shown me the picture and hadn't explained the circumstances, I'd probably have said around fifty-fifty. But there are three other relevant factors to consider. First, he's driving either a stolen car or at least one that's running on false plates. Second, we've had two independent tip-offs that some kind of terrorist attack is planned for Britain, and this man you're investigating was waiting to board the ferry to Dover. Third, as you requested, I asked the regular police to run a check on the individual whose passport this man used at Calais. As you know, the document itself was completely genuine, but we now know that the man to whom it was issued is still in Germany. To be exact, right now he's in a cell in a Munich police station and pretty soon he's going to have to find convincing answers to a number of awkward questions.'

'And who is he?' Richter asked.

'At the moment, we don't know much except his name, Anton Berg, and that he's a junkie. The police were lucky to find him so quickly, but he's still completely incoherent. His passport could easily have been lost or stolen without him knowing about it, just because of his lifestyle, such as it is, but he's certainly never reported that happening. You'll be aware that there's a huge black-market trade in EU passports, so he might have simply applied for one and then sold it on, so it's quite possible that he might have nothing at all to do with Morschel directly. Or he could even be one of his friends or acquaintances, or maybe a relative. Don't worry, we'll find out.'

'I'm sure you will. The real question is how long it'll take to break him.'

'I think once he comes down from his present fix he'll start talking, but whether he actually knows anything is another matter. But to answer your original question, my guess is that the man caught by the cameras *was* indeed Hans Morschel. How certain am I? Sixty, maybe seventy, per cent.'

'That's good enough for me, Karl,' Richter said. 'Just to keep you in the loop, I'll be sending out a revised watch order tonight, for both the man and the car. I'll let you know immediately if we get any results.'

As soon as he'd finished the call, Richter dialled the duty officer's direct line.

'This is Richter,' he said. 'I've just heard from Germany and the photo analysis was inconclusive, but the man in that car looks enough like Morschel for us to move. Contact Five and initiate a revised watch order immediately. I want all roads in southern England watched for that Mercedes and the man in it. Ensure that all police forces get details of the registration plate and also a description of the driver. And make sure they understand it's a *watch order*. Under no circumstances are they to attempt to intercept or detain the driver. We just want to know where he is and what he's doing. Nothing else.'

Maidstone, Kent

'Can I help you, sir?' the desk sergeant asked.

'I hope so,' the heavily built man standing in front of him replied. 'I need to get an urgent message to your Security Service, MI5.'

The sergeant had seen and heard it all before. 'And why is that, sir?'

Kleber didn't reply for a few moments but simply reached into his pocket and produced two objects which he then placed on the desk. The first was a slip of paper on which were written a six-digit number and a single word, and the second was a golf-ball sized lump of what looked like plasticine.

'Could you please pass on *that* word and *that* number to the Security Service duty officer,' he said. 'And that' – he pointed at the round lump – 'is sufficient plastic explosive to destroy a car.'

The sergeant took a couple of steps backwards and as he did so pressed a bell-push below the desk.

'You needn't worry.' Kleber smiled. 'Semtex is completely inert unless you stick a blasting cap in it to trigger it. But I need to talk to MI5 soon, because I know a man who's got about 300 pounds of plastic. I think I know what he's going to do with it, and he could be starting as soon as tonight.'

Two burly constables had by now appeared in answer to the sergeant's silent summons and seized Kleber's arms, immobilizing him. He didn't resist, because this reaction was exactly what he had expected.

Five minutes later, having been searched thoroughly – to reveal absolutely nothing because he had left everything in either his car boot or his hotel room – Kleber was sitting in an interview room looking sceptically at a mug of dark brown liquid he had been told was tea, while being watched over by two large, but slightly apprehensive, uniformed constables. It isn't every day that a man walks into a police station carrying plastic explosive and Kleber was still the object of considerable suspicion.

The sergeant had talked to the duty inspector and then contacted Thames House on the open-line number, passing on the word and the string of numbers. The MI5 duty officer had promised to look into it.

'And that,' the desk sergeant remarked as he ended the call, 'could mean any bloody thing.'

Hammersmith, London

'You're still there, then?' the duty officer asked when Richter answered his call.

'Obviously. What do you want this time? I was about to head off home.'

'Just an oddity – well, two actually. We've just received a parcel here, addressed to you personally from somebody named Wilhelm Schneider with an address in Switzerland. We've run it through the scanner and there don't seem to be any nasties inside it. Do you want to risk opening it, or what?'

'I know Schneider, so I'll risk it. What was the second thing?'

'Five has just sent out a Flash "anything known" round robin. Apparently about twenty minutes ago some guy walked into a Kent police station and handed over what he claimed was a lump of Semtex.'

'Really? And is it?'

'No idea. Could be just plasticine, or even ear-wax, for all I know. He said he knew where there was another 300 pounds of the stuff, and that he believed the man who's got it could be planning on using it soon.'

'How soon?'

'Maybe even tonight, but that's not what they're asking about. This man also gave them a slip of paper with just a word and a number written on it. It doesn't mean anything to the people at Thames House, or at least to my opposite number, who claims he's about the only one left in the building. That's why he's asking around. The thing is, the single word is "Onex", the place you went in Switzerland and had that spot of bother.'

For a moment or two Richter was puzzled, then made an intuitive leap.

'Hang on a second,' he said, and accessed one of the files on his desktop computer. 'Let me read a number to you.'

He flicked through the report he'd written for Simpson after his return from Switzerland, found the six digits he was looking for and read them out to the duty officer.

'Is that the same number this man gave the police?'

'Yes. How the fuck did you know that?'

'It doesn't matter, but I need to go and see him right now,' Richter said. 'Which police station is he being held at? And what cars are available at the moment?'

'Just a sec . . . Right, he's at Maidstone nick, and they're not likely to let him go in a hurry.' He paused. 'According to the list there are four cars in the garage – the two Fiestas, the Mondeo and the Jaguar.'

'I'll take the XJ6.'

'Simpson won't like that.'

'He isn't here to argue about it, and I don't have time to hang about. Plus the Jag's got satnav, and I barely even know where Maidstone is, far less the cop shop. Give the woodentops a bell and tell them I'm on my way down there. Tell Five the same. What's the precise address of the station?'

'Sutton Road – the Kent Police headquarters.'

'Right, got that. One last thing – tell the duty driver to get the XJ6 out of the garage and into the street, then give its number to the Met and the Kent Police. Tell them the approximate route I'll be taking, because I won't have the time or the inclination to argue with a car full of Black Rats trying to pull me for speeding. If possible, try and get me an escort.'

South-east England

Before he finally left the office, Richter used his computer to check conditions on the roads in south London, and decided his best bet was to rely on the Jaguar's speed and take the M4 and then drive all the way round London on the M25, where the traffic was unusually free-flowing for a Friday evening. It would almost double the distance he had to drive, but he still reckoned that would be quicker than trying to fight his way through Richmond or Croydon or some other clutch of suburbs.

As soon as he picked up the M25 he switched on the headlights, eased over into the outside lane and wound the Jag up to a touch over 110. Three sets of speed cameras had flashed him before he reached the M23/Gatwick junction, but he saw no police cars until he peeled off the M25 and joined the M26 near Sevenoaks.

Then, coming up fast behind him, he saw a typical 'jam sandwich' – a Volvo estate car with the usual high-visibility paint job, blue lights flashing behind the front grille and its roof bar pulsing like a disco light show, the whole effect augmented by the two-tone wail of the siren. For a few seconds, Richter debated about simply accelerating away: he knew that the Jaguar could lose the Volvo without any particular difficulty, but it would mean winding the car up to over double the legal speed limit. On the other hand, the police could be on their way to an accident somewhere, so he eased over to the centre lane.

The Volvo pulled alongside him and matched his speed, but the officer in the passenger seat simply pointed ahead and nodded, then the car accelerated away. Richter nodded in turn, and fell in behind the estate car, the Jaguar easily matching its speed. The two cars powered along the M26, swept on to the M20 near Borough Green, and continued east at well over a hundred miles an hour. When they reached junction six, Richter had expected the Volvo to turn south towards Maidstone – which the satnav suggested was the most direct route – but the police car continued on to junction seven.

Richter glanced at the satnav, though the navigation system was virtually redundant as long as he had the Volvo in sight, and guessed they'd chosen that route to avoid driving through Maidstone town centre.

Less than five minutes later, the patrol car turned right into the first of the two entrances to the police station, and Richter swung the Jaguar across the road right behind it. The station was enormous, more like a vast sprawling country house than a normal cop shop, but at least there was plenty of parking. He found a vacant space, slid the car into it, switched off the engine and climbed out. The two officers stepped away from their Volvo, which they'd stopped close to his Jaguar, and one pointed towards the doors at the front of the station.

'Thanks, guys,' Richter called out as he walked across to the building.

As he stepped inside, a uniformed sergeant approached him. 'You the bloke from MI5?'

'More or less,' Richter admitted.

'Can I see some identification, please?'

Richter proffered a small leather wallet. The sergeant studied it, nodded and handed it back. 'You got here quickly,' he said.

'I had help. Now, where's this man with the lump of Semtex?'

Rochester, Kent

Just after seven that evening, Hans Morschel locked the door of his hotel room, followed the corridor to the main staircase and descended to the ground floor. He entered the fairly empty bar and ordered a beer, speaking in fluent but heavily accented English. The barman didn't seem disposed to make small talk, which suited the German just fine. He signed the chit for his drink, picked up the beer and a newspaper and took a seat at a small table in the corner.

He'd been sitting there about twenty minutes when another man walked in, and Morschel raised his hand in greeting. Ernst Hagen nodded in recognition, bought himself a drink, then walked over to the table and sat down.

'Any problems?' Morschel asked, in German, and Hagen shook his head.

'None at all. I came straight through. And you?'

'The same. Where's the car?'

Hagen gestured towards the windows overlooking the car park. 'Outside, right behind yours, in fact.'

Before they left Stuttgart, they'd discussed the best method for liaising with each other and had decided that the easiest way was to simply act like tourists. With the notorious reluctance of the British to speak any language but their own, Morschel had reckoned that the chances of anyone understanding what they were saying were slim. Even so, they would take care to keep their conversation non-specific and avoid any detailed discussion of the operation unless they were absolutely certain nobody could overhear them.

'Where's Helmut right now?' Hagen asked.

'I've not heard from him since just before I left Stuttgart. But don't worry, he'll get here. Did you get yourself a new mobile number?'

Hagen nodded, fished in his jacket pocket and passed a slip of paper across to Morschel, who glanced at it before tucking it away in his wallet. Then he repeated Hagen's actions and gave him a card with his own mobile number scribbled on it.

'What about the others?' he asked.

Hagen glanced around before replying, but there was nobody anywhere near them. 'As you know, the recce group arrived here three weeks ago and they had no problems getting everything sorted. The vehicles are in position in long-term car parks, all fully fuelled and checked. They hired the warehouse and bought a front company and once they'd done that they closed the bank accounts they'd been using, to stop any tracing action. They researched the areas you'd already nominated and then selected the most suitable of them. We have four stolen vans to use as delivery vehicles.'

Morschel smiled slightly at Hagen's choice of words.

'They've changed the plates and loaded the devices, so the vehicles are ready to go right now. The other vans arrived today,' he continued, in a low voice, 'and all the equipment you requested for phase one is in place and ready. So that just leaves the boat to collect and prepare.'

'We can do that tomorrow morning, as originally planned. Now, bin Salalah's already booked into a hotel in central London. He flew straight into Heathrow, as usual.'

'Of course he did,' Hagen muttered. 'The playboy terrorist. He's probably getting comprehensively laid right now.'

'Jealous?' Morschel asked.

'Obviously.'

'It's the best possible disguise,' Morschel pointed out. 'With his lifestyle, who would suspect what he's really doing here in Britain? But I happen to know he's not in bed with a magnum of champagne and a couple of high-class whores right now. He called me just before I came down from my room to tell me he's hired a car and he'll arrive here in a couple of hours.'

'Here? What's he coming here for? I thought we'd only see him and his man when we started the final phase.'

'He's coming because there's one other thing we have to do before we start this operation.'

'What's that?' Hagen asked, so Morschel told him.

After he'd finished, Hagen sat back in his seat. 'Are you sure?' he asked doubtfully.

'No, I'm not,' Morschel said, 'but I'm not prepared to take the risk, and nor is bin Salalah. There are too many questions about this business for my liking, and before I finally commit us I want some real answers. I'm not prepared to even start this unless I'm pretty certain we can walk away from it. Right, let's go and have dinner now. We can talk while we eat.'

He stood up and led the way out of the bar and into the dining room.

Maidstone, Kent

Richter stood in the darkness of the observation room, peering through a two-way mirror into the brightly lit interview room. Sitting at the table, looking entirely relaxed and composed, was a heavily built man, an empty mug and plate in front of him. He was flicking through a copy of the local paper somebody had presumably given him.

'Have you talked to him yet?' Richter asked. 'I mean, in any detail?'

The sergeant shook his head. 'This is the middle of Kent. Normally, we deal with road accidents, or stack lorries every time the bloody French block the Channel ports. Foreigners carrying handfuls of Semtex are a bit out of our league. The inspector said we should just hold him here and wait for the cavalry to arrive. And you're it, I suppose,' he added doubtfully.

'Yeah,' Richter replied. 'I left my horse tied up outside. OK, let's get started.'

'How do you want to play this? Go in by yourself, or pretend to be a police officer working with one of our detectives?'

'I don't think we've got time to fanny around, so I'll go in there alone. Get some more tea or coffee sent in, please. And there are security implications in this, so I want the constables out of the interview room, no tapes running, and nobody sitting here listening and watching through this mirror. That means you put the lights on so I can see exactly who's here in this room.'

'That's not normal procedure,' the sergeant objected.

'This isn't a normal situation,' Richter snapped. 'If you've got a problem with that I can make a couple of calls and turn it into an order.'

'No, you can play it your way. I'm just pointing out what we normally do. Follow me.'

The sergeant led the way to the door of the interview room, knocked twice and opened it. He gestured to the two uniformed constables, who left their posts by the wall and stepped outside.

Richter walked in, shut the door behind him and sat down. Then he stretched out his hand and popped the eject buttons on the two fixed tape recorders. He removed the cassettes and placed them on the table.

The man opposite looked at him appraisingly and opened his mouth to speak, but Richter held up his hand, looking pointedly across the room at the two-way mirror. After a few seconds, a fluorescent light flickered into life behind the glass, and he could see the dim shape of the observation room, which was obviously empty.

Kleber turned round, following Richter's gaze, and nodded. 'You're not a policeman,' he said, a statement rather than a question. 'So who exactly are you?'

'My name's Richter. More importantly, who are *you*?' Richter countered. 'Am I talking to Rolf Hermann – or rather his doppelgänger?'

Kleber inclined his head. 'You recognized the significance of the number I gave to the police?'

'Yes. You provided the Swiss police with the same information – the serial number of a stolen Kalashnikov AK47 – and that was why they mounted the assault on that apartment in Onex.'

'I had to give them something I knew they could check.'

'Four Swiss police officers died during that assault. Did you consider that possibility when you walked into the Onex police station?'

'I told them the residents of the apartment were armed. I expected the assault to be conducted in a competent manner.'

There was a knock on the door and a uniformed constable entered with a tray with two plain mugs on it. He put it on the table between them, picked up the plate and empty mug and left.

'So why did you tip off the bad guys just before the police went in?' Richter asked, reaching for one of the mugs. 'That more or less guaranteed a bloodbath. Or was that your intention?'

'You work it out,' Kleber said.

'Oh, I think we already have. You were involved with the Onex group as well as the terrorists in Stuttgart and you really couldn't afford to leave any of them alive and in police custody to identify you as the man who telephoned that last-minute warning. That's why you finished off the only survivor in the Stuttgart hospital. That *was* you, wasn't it?'

'It might have been,' Kleber said, 'but you'll never hear me admit it, with or without tapes in these machines. This whole room could be wired for sound, for all I know.'

'I'm not interested in the murder of a piece of shit like him. I'd have done the job myself, given the opportunity. Now, I know you're not Rolf Hermann, because he's a rickety old fart currently trying to sue the Swiss government for damages, so give me a name I can use. Who the hell are you?'

'My German passport says Helmut Kleber.'

'I don't believe that, obviously, because your accent is American, but we'll use it for the moment. OK, Helmut, who are you working for? The CIA? FBI? DEA? NSA? Or some other three-digit secret squirrel outfit in the States?'

Kleber shook his head. 'Why do you think I'm working *for* anyone?'

'This time, *you* work it out.'

'The AK47 serial number?'

'That's one point. Knowledge of something like the serial number of a stolen assault rifle more or less guarantees you have access to government data, because you won't be able to find that information anywhere else. Nor was it the number of any of the weapons the Swiss police found in the apartment they raided. That all suggests you do work for a government agency, probably American. And as you've left a trail of blood and bodies half-way across Europe, my guess is you were given your orders not too far from Langley, Virginia.

'The other factor to consider is the incidents you've been involved in. If you were just an undercover cop, it's possible you might have been part of the Onex cell – but not the one in Stuttgart as well. But if the CIA had sent you undercover to burrow deep into a Europe-based terrorist organization, you could well have links to both. Or that's the way we're looking at it, anyway.'

'OK, Mr Richter, you're not too far from the truth, though I don't actually work for the CIA. On the other hand,' Kleber added, with a slight smile, 'even if I did, I probably wouldn't tell you, would I? Now, cards on the table. I *am* an undercover agent and I *am* working for a particular government – though you'd already guessed that – and I *was* trying to infiltrate this terrorist group. In fact, I have infiltrated it and I've been supplying money and logistical support for the last few months.'

'What was your brief, then?'

Kleber shook his head. 'I can't tell you my real name and I also can't tell you that. Even if I could, you simply wouldn't believe it. The orders I've been following, frankly, amount to a suicide mission, but the money was very good, and I've been real careful along the way. Now, I've been trying hard to ensure that the group's attacks have either been foiled completely – as in Switzerland and Germany – or at least resulted in minimum casualties.'

'So you've been helping to fund a terrorist group and supplying – what? – weapons or explosives or something, and encouraging them to attack civilian targets. But at the same time you've been tipping off the authorities ahead of those same attacks. That's either wildly schizophrenic or quite simply insane. Which is it?'

Kleber smiled. 'It's neither, actually, but I agree it doesn't make obvious sense. At least, not without a knowledge of the briefing I was given.'

'Which you won't tell me,' Richter pointed out.

'No,' Kleber said, and changed the subject. 'Maybe you heard about two earlier terrorist attacks, the bombings in France and Italy? They were both linked to bank robberies that took place nearby.'

Richter nodded. 'In both cases the police received warnings and managed to clear most of the civilians out of the way, but we understood they were tip-offs from members of the public reacting to something suspicious. Did you make those calls as well?'

'Yes.'

'Well, I suppose we should thank you for that, at least.'

'The thing is, those early attacks were just the preamble, as it were. How much do you know about what's happened so far?'

'As much as anyone else,' Richter said. 'I was on the ground at Onex and Stuttgart, and I also know about Hans Morschel.'

'Do you?' Kleber raised his eyebrows. 'How?'

'He paid a visit to the building in Stuttgart where the bad guys were holed up, and the BGS got a couple of pictures of him. But he wasn't inside when the troops went in.'

'He wouldn't have been,' Kleber concurred. 'Morschel is really cautious and thoroughly nasty – a right bastard, in fact. He tends to set things up and then watch from a safe distance how they pan out. And he almost always makes his attacks self-financing. Whenever his men detonate a bomb, another group almost always hits a nearby bank at about the same time. In fact, it's a bit of a moot point whether he's a genuine terrorist or just a particularly violent bank robber.'

'What's his agenda? Why's he doing this?'

'I didn't hear this from Morschel himself, but a couple of the other gang members claimed that he's working with a radical Islamic group – for money, obviously. The story was that, since 9/11, Arab terrorists have found it increasingly difficult to mount successful attacks, simply because they *are* Arabs, so they've started recruiting non-Arabs to do their dirty work. Obviously they're not likely to find many suicide bombers among European terrorists, but that doesn't mean their recruits can't operate successfully. But I've no idea if there's any truth in the story.'

'How many people in his group?'

'He seems to have a hard core of about a couple of dozen, but he uses a lot of extra foot-soldiers for each operation. In Switzerland, for example, three of the terrorists that died – interestingly, one of them was an Arab – had been recruited from Morschel's underworld contacts and paid lavishly to join. A fee up front, plus a bonus after the job's over.'

'How many attacks had he planned, exactly?'

'Five. The four in Europe, plus the big one, the one that Morschel had really been concentrating on, which will be in London.'

'We guessed as much from some of the conversations taped by the BGS in Germany. And we think he's now here in Britain. We've had an unconfirmed sighting of him coming through Dover this afternoon, driving a Mercedes on dodgy plates.'

'Could be,' Kleber said. 'He was running around Stuttgart in a Merc with a Hanover registration. I can even give you the number if it's any help.'

'Thanks for the offer, but it won't be. Morschel will know those plates would have been photographed and fed into the system when he came through the ferry port, so he'll have had another set ready to replace them. We've got CCTV cameras set up on just about every street corner in Britain, so there's a good chance we'll pick him up somewhere. I'm more interested in this so-called 'big one'. And, while we're on the subject, why you are sitting here talking to me.'

'Those two questions are linked,' Kleber replied. 'Although it wasn't really his idea, I know that the culmination of the campaign Morschel's been running is intended to be what he calls "The London Event". The problem is, that's about all I do know. With those attacks in Europe I knew dates, times, places, targets and even which of his men were going to carry out the bombing or whatever. But for this London operation I've been kept right out of the loop. And I'm sitting here talking to you because whatever he's planning is devastating – I've gathered that much – and pretty damned imminent. Days, maybe even only hours, away.'

'Why is this London attack the biggest?'

'I don't think that was originally Morschel's idea. I believe he was told to do something impressive by his Arab paymasters, assuming what I'm told was correct. The rationale was that, because Britain is undoubtedly America's most important ally in the war on terror, it's become one of the principal targets of radical Islam, and so al Qaeda would love to visit something like 9/11 on this country. What I do know is on his return from Britain six weeks ago he was very excited about something. About a month ago he sent three of his men over here to start making preparations, and Morschel himself was back here again at the beginning of this week, just for a couple of days, I think.

'The other reason I'm here,' Kleber went on, pushing away his empty mug, 'is that I think Morschel's now getting suspicious of me, which is why I've been told so little about this latest attack, and I don't yet know what he's going to do about it. So I'm giving you as much warning as I can, despite the lack of hard evidence to back up what I'm saying.'

'And you expect us to do what?'

'I don't know.' Kleber spread his hands in a gesture of helplessness. 'I had no clue whether the British intelligence services were involved in investigating these attacks, but I now feel better knowing that MI5 has been taking part. You *are* a Security Service officer, I presume?'

'Sort of,' Richter admitted. 'So what now? You've given us almost nothing to go on, and your immediate problem is that the local plods have every intention of keeping you locked up here because of the Semtex.'

'What Semtex is that, then?' Kleber asked innocently. 'I didn't actually say the stuff I put on his desk *was* plastic explosive. All I told the sergeant was that a piece that size was sufficient to destroy a car. That lump was just plasticine.'

Richter grinned. 'It was quite an attention-getter,' he said, 'and it certainly got me down here bloody fast. OK, so what are you going to do now?'

'Go back to my hotel, turn my phone on and wait for Morschel to contact me. If you give me your mobile number, I'll pass on any information I get.'

Richter took a card out of his wallet, wrote a number on the back and passed it over.

'That's switched on twenty-four hours a day. Oh, one last thing. When you tipped off the Onex police, you claimed to have seen something on a laptop computer about "FRB London". Was that true, or did you just make it up as *another* attention-grabber?'

'No, that was true,' Kleber said, taking the card, 'but it was something I overheard a few times, not saw on a laptop screen. The "shopping list" I claimed to have seen was entirely fictitious, just to get the Swiss moving before those bastards tried to blow a hole in the middle of Geneva.'

'Any idea what this "FRB" refers to?'

'No, but knowing Morschel's fondness for hitting banks, I'd hazard a guess about the letter "B". So if I were you I'd start looking at places in the City of London, maybe a merchant bank or somewhere like that. But it's also worth mentioning that Morschel is paranoid about security and often gives code words to his operations. So the "FRB" might mean something completely different.'

'Thanks,' Richter said, with mild sarcasm. 'That's been a big help.'

Rochester, Kent

Morschel took a brief call on his mobile as their coffee arrived and then he immediately asked for the bill. When he'd signed it, he stood up and led the way outside to the car park.

'That was Ahmed,' he explained, as they moved away from the hotel. 'He'll be here in a couple of minutes.'

They walked over towards their vehicles, the Mercedes and Renault, on the far side of the hotel's private car park, and stood waiting. In well under the promised two minutes, a dark blue BMW pulled in and stopped close by. Bin Salalah climbed out of the vehicle and walked across to them.

'Any problems?' he asked.

'No, none,' Morschel replied.

'Good. We'll do it right now, then. Just get it over with.'

'OK, I'll call him.'

Morschel took out his mobile and dialled a number from memory.

'It's me. Where are you?' he said. 'Which hotel?' He listened for a few seconds. 'Good, I'll see you tomorrow.

'He's in his room at the hotel,' he told the other two men.

Maidstone, Kent

Thirty minutes later, Morschel braked the Mercedes to a halt in a side street just around the corner from another hotel on the outskirts of Maidstone. Bin Salalah remained in the car, in case he had to move it in a hurry. The other two men got out and walked over to the edge of the hotel's open parking area, looking across at the dozens of vehicles occupying its bays.

'There it is.' Morschel pointed to a Peugeot saloon parked about fifty yards away.

'Are you going to call him first?' Hagen asked, 'or just go straight up to his room?'

'We'll ring his mobile and ask him to come down,' Morshel replied. 'We definitely don't want any of the hotel staff seeing our faces. You call him. Tell him there's a problem. In fact, tell him my car has broken down and that he'll have to help shift the plastic out of it before it goes to a garage. Tell him that we need him right now in Rochester and we'll meet him on one of the main roads close to the junction with the M2, say.'

'OK.' Hagen pulled out his mobile phone.

'Helmut, we've got a problem,' he said, as soon as his call was answered. 'The Mercedes has broken down out on the road. You know what's inside it, so before we can let any garage people near it, we have to empty it. The only place we can put that stuff is inside another car – yours, to be exact. Can you get over to Rochester right away?'

Hagen listened for a few seconds, then snapped the phone closed. 'He's on his way down,' he said.

Up in his hotel room, which he'd only reached a few minutes earlier after leaving the Sutton Road police station, Kleber looked thoughtfully at the telephone. Hagen might just be telling the truth. Mechanical problems could occur in any car, and if Morschel's Merc did need garage attention they'd obviously have to shift all the Semtex before letting some grubby-fingered mechanic loose on it. On the other hand . . .

Kleber picked up his mobile again, pulled a card from his pocket and dialled Richter's number.

M25 motorway

When it rang, Richter was proceeding at a steady, and entirely legal, sixty-five clockwise around the M25. He picked up the mobile, recognized the number and immediately pulled over to the hard shoulder. He switched on his hazard flashers before answering the call.

'Richter.'

'Kleber. I don't know if it's significant, but I've just had a call from Ernst Hagen, who's Morschel's number two. He claims the Mercedes has broken down somewhere on the road and they need to shift the Semtex into my car. They want me to drive over to Rochester right now.'

'And will you?'

'I don't have a lot of choice. If I don't go, Morschel will realize something's wrong, and anyway Hagen could well be telling the truth. We still have no idea what they've got planned, so clearly I do need to keep in with them.'

'Your decision,' Richter said. 'Are you armed?'

'Always – except, of course, when I'm sitting in one of your police stations.'

'OK, tell me exactly where you're heading in Rochester and I'll get over there myself. But I'm not carrying, so if this does turn into a shooting match, I'm gone.'

Two minutes later, Richter punched the details he had been given into the satnav and started the Jaguar's engine. He swung back out onto the motorway, took the next exit and pushed the big car as hard as it could go.

TIMEBOMB

Maidstone, Kent

Morschel and Hagen were standing behind a Renault people carrier, parked just a few yards from Kleber's Peugeot, and both were carefully watching the hotel entrance.

'Here he comes now,' Hagen murmured.

Both men ducked out of sight, relying primarily on their hearing to track Kleber's progress across the crowded car park. When they guessed he was quite near the Peugeot, Hagen eased his head around the front of the Espace, at the same time pulling a cosh from his pocket.

Though he was walking quickly, Kleber was obviously cautious, his glance flicking from side to side. His most vulnerable moment would be as he opened the door to get into the car and that, predictably enough, was when Hagen struck. He covered the few feet between the parked Renault and the Peugeot in under a second, and before Kleber had time to do more than turn his head towards the sound of the approaching footsteps, Hagen smashed the cosh down on the side of his head. Morschel watched with quiet satisfaction as the big man grunted just once, then tumbled senseless to the ground. Hagen replaced the cosh in his pocket and looked round. There was nobody else in the car park, and nobody driving past on the nearby road. It was now the work of just a few moments to pick up the unconscious man and dump him in the boot of the Peugeot.

Before Hagen closed the lid, Morschel reached down and, with some difficulty, removed the two weapons Kleber was carrying, also his mobile and his wallet. He lashed the unconscious man's wrists and ankles together with plastic cable ties, so as to completely immobilize him, and tied a rudimentary gag around his mouth.

Then he picked up the set of car keys that had fallen from Kleber's hand.

'Here.' He handed them to Hagen. 'You drive his car and follow us.'

Morschel hurried out of the car park, climbed into the Mercedes and pulled away from the kerb, Hagen following a few yards behind in the Peugeot. Within seconds, both cars had vanished from sight.

North Downs, Kent

None of them had any very clear idea where they were, but that didn't matter. They'd left the Mercedes in a public car park outside Sitting-bourne, and then Hagen had driven the Peugeot along a series of increasingly narrow country lanes and eventually taken a winding track that led up into the hills lying south of the town. From their present location they could see the lights of vehicles driving along the M2 motorway, but as far as they could tell there were no houses nearby.

And that was exactly what Morschel and bin Salalah wanted.

Hagen drove the Peugeot off the track, stopping it at the edge of a small wood, where there was a large area of flattened earth, and switched off the engine. He guessed the site was probably used by courting couples, or maybe it was where hunters left their vehicles before going after pigeons or rabbits in the woodland.

'This will do,' Morschel announced.

'Are you certain we need to do this?' Hagen asked, his face troubled.

It was bin Salalah who replied. 'No, but it's the only way to make absolutely sure, and we have to be *absolutely* sure. So open the boot and get him out.'

Kleber was still unconscious, but showing the first signs of recovery. Hagen was a big man and hoisted him across his shoulders without much difficulty.

'Where do you want him?' he asked.

'Over here.' Morschel opened the rear door of the Peugeot and pulled out a couple of plastic carrier bags, one of which clattered slightly as he moved it. He led the way to the trees at the very edge of the wood, took a torch from his pocket and shone the beam up at the overhanging branches.

'That one,' he decided, focusing the torch beam on a substantial oak with a thick branch projecting almost at a right angle from the trunk, about ten feet above the ground. He opened one of the carrier bags, took out a length of rope and tossed one end of it over the branch.

'Strip him first,' Morschel ordered.

Hagen carried the unconscious Kleber across the clearing and dumped him under the projecting branch, removed his clothes and then busied himself tying the end of the rope firmly around his wrists. Once he was happy with the knots, he nodded to Morschel, and together they began hauling on the other end of the rope. In a couple of minutes, Kleber was swinging gently, suspended by his wrists.

But if Kleber was who Morschel now suspected he might be, they would be wise to immobilize his feet as well. The German shone the torch around again till he spotted a large broken branch lying on the ground a few feet away. Together, the pair dragged it over, and Hagen tied another piece of rope to Kleber's ankles and its other end around the middle of the branch. Even Houdini, Morschel thought, looking at their handiwork, would have found getting out of that a challenge.

'Now what?' Hagen asked.

'Take off his gag,' Morschel replied, directing the beam of the torch at Kleber's face.

Once Hagen had removed it, Morschel switched off the torch and leant back against a tree trunk. 'Now we wait till he wakes up,' he said. 'Then we'll see if Ahmed can persuade our friend to answer a few simple questions.'

Ten minutes later, they heard groaning sounds as Kleber slowly regained consciousness, but Morschel left it another five minutes before he spoke. It was very dark there in the wood, and he deliberately kept the torch switched off to further disorient his captive.

'Helmut?' he began quietly.

'What? Morschel? Is that you? What the fuck's going on here? Cut me down, you bastard.'

'Not yet, Helmut.' Morschel kept his tone low and reasonable. 'First I think we need to have a little talk.'

The German settled himself more comfortably and paused a few seconds before continuing. 'We have a bit of a problem, Helmut, and I believe you can help me solve it. If you recall, you approached me a few months ago with a rather ambitious plan. You had the money and the military sources, and I had the contacts, and to begin with everything seemed to be working out well. But in the last week certain things have gone badly wrong.'

He paused and waited.

'I don't know what you're talking about.' Kleber's voice was harsh and strained.

'Not the most original response,' Morschel said, and picked up the torch, 'but I haven't asked you anything yet. This little question-and-answer session will proceed much more satisfactorily if you remember to speak only when I ask you something.'

He switched on the torch and aimed it directly into Kleber's face, effectively blinding their captive. 'Ahmed,' he called.

Out of sight of the bound man, bin Salalah – now wearing latex gloves and a one-piece set of overalls – picked up a length of heavy-duty electric flex and swung it with all his strength at Kleber. The crack as the flex bit deeply into the flesh of the bound man's back was drowned immediately by his howl of pain.

Morschel switched off the torch. 'That, Helmut, was just a taster. Now, as I was saying, some things have gone badly wrong this week. First, despite taking every precaution to avoid detection, my colleagues in Onex were wiped out by a surprise raid by the Swiss cops. That could have just been unfortunate, like some other resident seeing something suspicious, but when almost exactly the same thing then happened in Stuttgart . . . Well, I've never believed much in coincidence – do you?'

Kleber said nothing.

'You can speak now, Helmut,' Morschel said. 'In fact, you'd be wise to.'

'I had nothing to do with those raids,' Kleber gasped. 'I knew nothing about them until afterwards. You have to believe me.'

'Actually,' Morschel said, 'I don't have to believe you. And in fact I *don't* believe you. You see, ever since that incident in Germany, I've been thinking hard about what happened. And the only common links between Onex and Stuttgart were you and me. We two were liaising with both cells simultaneously, and I certainly know *I* didn't tell anyone else about them. *You* were the one to choose the targets. And in Onex you even rented their apartment. Now to me,' Morschel continued in the same conversational tone, 'that means the only one who could have betrayed both cells to the authorities was you. What I don't know for sure is whether you were just incredibly careless, or whether betrayal was your plan all along. And that, my friend, is what we're here to find out.'

Morschel again shone the torch into Kleber's face, and again the flex cracked across his back – once, twice, three times. Then the torch went out, and the only sounds in the all-enveloping darkness were the loud moans of pain.

'Now that the preliminaries are over,' Morschel growled, 'let's see if we can get some honest answers. We'll start with a really simple question. Who the fuck are you? What's your *real* name?'

Forty minutes later, Morschel, bin Salalah and Hagen headed back to the Peugeot. Hagen was carrying a bulging black rubbish bag containing the overalls, now heavily bloodstained, the latex gloves, a bundle of tools and a small plastic carrier bag, securely knotted. He opened the boot, put the bag inside, then climbed into the back seat. Morschel slid behind the steering wheel, bin Salalah beside him, started the engine and eased the car back onto the track.

'We'll dump all that stuff when we're well clear of the area,' Morschel decided.

'What about this car, though?' Hagen asked.

'We'll swap it with the Mercedes once we get to Sittingbourne, and this one can stay there in the car park. We'll wipe it clean and walk away.'

'Somebody's bound to notice it eventually.'

'That doesn't matter. We got what we wanted, and there's nothing to link us to him. The treacherous fucking bastard – it's a shame we didn't have more time. I'd have liked to make him really suffer.'

'Oh, he suffered,' bin Salalah murmured. 'There's a limit to what pain a human body can tolerate before it simply shuts down, and Kleber reached that stage at least three times tonight. Anything more would probably have been pointless.'

There was silence in the car before Hagen asked the obvious question. 'Do we still go ahead?'

Morschel nodded as he turned off the track and onto a tarmac road, heading in more or less the direction they wanted to go.

'Yes,' he said, 'because he didn't know enough yet to betray this operation. We can still see it through exactly as we'd planned. That's the best possible way to avenge our comrades in Stuttgart and Onex. And,' he added with a slight smile, 'to strike a blow at London that will take the British decades to recover from.'

Rochester, Kent

Richter had been waiting futilely in the Jaguar for over an hour, watching the location where Kleber was supposed to meet Morschel. He'd even called the mobile number Kleber had given him, as soon as he'd checked the road and seen no sign of a broken-down Mercedes. That had convinced him Kleber was walking into a trap, but then, as on his subsequent four attempts, the phone system reported the mobile as unavailable, presumably switched off.

There was nothing Richter could do except hope Kleber had sufficient wits about him to avoid whatever nasty little plan Hans Morschel had hatched. But with the evidence now available to him, that looked like a fairly forlorn hope.

Chapter Eleven

Saturday
North Downs, Kent

'So who discovered the body?' Dick Clark was staring with a kind of horrified fascination at the small woodland clearing in front of him.

After receiving the call at home – where he'd actually still been asleep and technically off duty – he had picked up DI Mason on his way out towards Sittingbourne. They'd arrived about a quarter of an hour after the pathologist and the SOCOs, and by now there were some twenty people milling around at the edge of the woodland.

Like every crime scene the detective sergeant had ever been summoned to, it had a somewhat surreal appearance, made even more so by the poor light. The day was dull and overcast, and the tall trees surrounding the clearing ensured that it was perpetually gloomy. The purposeful movements of the pathologist and white-suited officers were illuminated by portable floodlights and given grim emphasis by the pulsating blue and red lights of the roof bars on the patrol cars and intermittent flashes from still cameras wielded by SOCOs as they recorded every detail that was visible. This crime scene, he knew, would stay embedded in his memory for a long time.

The naked body of a strongly built man was suspended by a rope from the bough of an oak tree, his feet lashed to a weighty branch on the ground below, which was quite literally covered in blood. The pathologist had already confirmed that the man was dead, and the main task of the SOCOs now was to find whatever evidence they could before they cut the body down and had to trample all over the crime scene to do so.

'The farmer who owns this wood found him,' a police constable informed Clark. 'He was driving up here in his jeep – that vehicle over there,' he added, pointing to a dirty green short-wheelbase Land Rover standing at one side of the lane. 'He was intending to shoot a few wood pigeons, so he parked and walked over here. Once he got to the edge of the wood, he saw this.'

'Nice, first thing in the morning,' Mason remarked.

'Yes,' the uniformed constable agreed. 'He lost his breakfast a few seconds later.'

A lean, cadaverous figure wearing a white one-piece disposable suit approached them. The Ghoul was looking even more corpse-like than ever, his grey features having little more colour than what he was wearing.

'Good morning, doc,' Mason said, his voice determinedly cheerful.

'Is it?' The Ghoul responded.

'Any idea of the cause of death?' Clark asked. 'And maybe the time as well?'

'He died in the early hours of this morning. Based on the body itself and ambient temperature, probably not before midnight, and I doubt if it was any later than three. As for the cause of death, take your pick. He was badly beaten with some kind of a whip, but he looks as if he was a strong man, so I doubt that was enough to kill him. Then somebody started using a blowtorch on him. There are burn marks all over his body, especially around the groin, and both his eyes have been burnt out. He's severely bruised almost everywhere, which suggests an attack with fists or maybe clubs. But that lot probably still didn't kill him, so then he was disembowelled and just left hanging there to die slowly.'

The Ghoul turned back to look again at the body, then swung round to face Mason and Clark. 'This attack was medieval in its sheer ferocity, inspector. I've been a police pathologist for almost all my career and I've never seen anything like this before. Whoever did this is little better than an animal.'

As the pathologist turned to go, Mason stopped him. 'This isn't a question I normally ask, doc, but what's your off-the-record opinion about this killing? I mean, does it look like a gangland execution, something like that?'

For a second time, The Ghoul gazed back at the clearing and the horrendous object suspended there. Then he shook his head. 'A gang execution? I doubt it. Why would they bother torturing their victim? A bullet in the back of the head is much more likely. No, this looks to me like an interrogation. They started by simply beating him, and I presume that didn't work so they moved on to more sophisticated methods. And it was definitely planned. This was no off-the-cuff job. Whoever did this came up here with all the equipment they needed.'

'They?' Mason asked.

'At least two people. The victim was simply too heavy for one man to pull him up like that, unless the killer was unusually powerful. And they clearly hated him. After they'd finished questioning him, they could have just shot him, or strangled him, or even cut his throat. To disembowel their victim and leave him to die slowly like that suggests a level of hatred that I've never seen before.'

'Any idea who he might be?' Clark asked. 'Did you find anything on the body?'

'He's got short hair, not quite a crew-cut, which might suggest he's in the military, or maybe an American. But for a positive identification we're going to have to rely on his dental work, and that's always a slow job.'

'We could try his fingerprints,' Mason suggested, but The Ghoul shook his head.

'He hasn't got any. Someone's removed the top joint of each finger and thumb, probably with a pair of heavy pliers or bolt-croppers. They're not anywhere here, as far as I can see, so presumably his killers took them away with them to dump elsewhere and that way make identifying him as difficult as possible. And, judging by the bleeding, the victim was still alive when they did that to him.'

'Jesus.'

'As for other means of identification, there's a pile of clothes over at the far edge of the clearing. There was no wallet or anything like that in the pockets, but I recovered this from the trousers.' The Ghoul proffered a clear plastic evidence bag in which was what looked like a credit card, its magnetic stripe visible.

'What is it, exactly?'

'I don't recognize the logo, but I'm fairly certain you'll find it's a smart card for a hotel room. A lot of hotels use these now instead of a key, because it doesn't matter if they get lost. They just change the room access code and then issue a new card to the next guests.'

Rochester, Kent

Hans Morschel had got back to the hotel in the early hours of the morning, but was up and in the hotel dining room in time for a late breakfast.

When he'd finished eating, he walked through into the deserted lounge with a cup of coffee and flicked through a couple of newspapers. Then he pulled out his mobile phone, checked Hagen's new number and dialled it.

'Half an hour?' he suggested, when Hagen responded.

'Fine. At the hotel, you mean?'

'Yes. We need to go in one car. Make sure you've transferred the stuff to a bag before you get here.'

'I've already done it,' Hagen replied and rang off.

Hammersmith, London

'Nothing at all?' Richter asked grimly.

The duty officer shook his head. 'The cameras at Dover recorded the car as it left the port, and one of the traffic cameras on the M2 motorway possibly also detected it.'

'Possibly?'

'The cameras are designed to monitor traffic flow, spot any accidents, that kind of thing, not to read car number plates. All the plods are prepared to admit is that a left-hand-drive Mercedes was seen heading west along the M2. It was a 300, so it's the right model and more or less the correct colour.'

'Where, exactly? And how many people in it?'

'That camera was positioned just a few miles outside Dover, which isn't much help, and it looked like a single occupant. Anyway, since then, nothing further.'

'I'm not too surprised,' Richter said. 'Almost certainly he'll have changed the plates by now. You'd better widen the watch order to include *any* left-hand-drive Mercedes 300-series with a single occupant. That probably won't do any good, because there'll be thousands of them over here at this time of year, but let's make the effort anyway.'

As Richter stood up and turned to leave the room, the parcel Wilhelm Schneider had sent him tucked safely under his arm, the duty officer stopped him in his tracks.

'Hang on a minute,' he said, staring at one of his monitor screens. 'Five seems to think of this as *your* operation and they've just flagged up an incident they reckon might fall under the general heading of terrorism. It might also relate to your session last night in Maidstone nick.'

'What is it?'

'The Kent police have found a body in a wood outside Sittingbourne.'

'Oh, shit. Who was it?'

'Just a sec.' The duty officer was busy scanning the lines of text on his screen. 'The victim was a middle-aged male, carrying no identification, and apparently he was tortured to death, very messily.'

'This isn't good news. It could be the same man I met. Anything else? Did the Kent plods say why they thought it might be terrorist-related?'

'No, unless it was just the way he died, combined with the fact that he wasn't carrying any ID. Anyway, Five want us to send someone down there to liaise. You up for it?'

'Yes,' Richter said. 'Give me the details and I'll drive down straight away.'

The Medway, Kent

The Blue Skies Marina was only a few miles south-west of the centre of the cathedral city of Rochester, but it was on the other side of the River Medway, so the actual distance they had to drive was more like five miles. That wasn't a problem, and Morschel was able to use the time to run over their plan one more time with Hagen, checking for any possible hitches.

After they arrived at the marina, Morschel parked the Mercedes just inside the gates and strode across to the office.

Inside, a swarthy, middle-aged man was sitting behind a desk, a telephone clamped to his left ear while he made notes on a large pad with the stub of a pencil. Noticing the car stop outside, he wrapped up his conversation quickly, replaced the receiver and stood up.

'Mr Heinrich?' he enquired.

Morschel nodded and shook his hand. 'Is it ready?'

'Of course. As you requested, we gave it a full service and filled up the tank.'

'And it's in the water?'

'Yes, for a couple of days now. How will you be paying for the boat?'

'Cash, if that's acceptable to you.' Morschel wanted neither delays nor complications, and paying cash was the obvious and easiest method of avoiding both. Besides, it wasn't a large enough transaction to raise any suspicions.

A few minutes later, he followed the boatyard manager out of the office and across to a pontoon, where about half a dozen boats were moored.

'Here she is.' The manager indicated the one on the end, a small fibreglass powerboat about seventeen feet long, with a dark blue hull and white superstructure. A large Evinrude outboard motor was strapped to the transom and connected to a set of remote controls – wheel, throttle and ignition switch – located at the rear of the cabin.

They climbed aboard, and Morschel listened attentively as the manager explained the boat's operation. The German was very experienced in boat-handling, but he was aware that every vessel had its own foibles and he had no time to discover them for himself.

'If you're ready, Mr Heinrich, let's take her out, just in case you find anything you're not happy about.'

'Good idea,' Morschel replied, and he cast off the bowline as the other man started the engine.

They took the boat about a quarter of a mile down-river, then the manager handed over the controls to Morschel, who steered the vessel back to the boatyard and brought it expertly alongside the pontoon. Once the line was attached, he switched off the engine and they stepped out of the boat.

'A pleasure doing business with you, Mr Heinrich,' the manager said. 'Will you be taking the boat away now?'

'Yes. I've got a berth organized for it down-river.'

'Fine. But if you need a boat-trailer, or anything else, just let me know. You've got my card.'

Once he'd returned to his office, Morschel and Hagen hauled four large black leather bags from the boot of the car and stowed them in the cabin of the powerboat. Then Morschel started the engine and swung the boat round to point down-river towards Rochester. As he steered the craft out into the river, Hagen drove away in the Mercedes.

About half an hour later Morschel was mooring the vessel at a marina located between Rochester and the M2 motorway, where he'd earlier booked a berth for a week. He'd just finished securing the ropes when Hagen walked along the pontoon and stepped on board. The berth Morschel had selected was well away from the centre of the marina and there was nobody else in evidence, either on the neighbouring pontoons or any of the boats at nearby moorings.

The two men moved inside the small cabin and began to open the four bags they'd carried from the Mercedes. They took out wires, detonators, batteries and a selection of tools from one, and dozens of packets of Semtex from the other three. As in many boats of its type, the cabin floor comprised a horizontal platform of wooden planks, specially shaped to lie on the interior of the hull. Under the floor, therefore, was quite a large space and, once Hagen had used a screwdriver to lift a couple of the planks to expose the void, they carefully stacked all the plastic explosive inside it, along with the detonators and wiring. When they'd finished replacing the planks, everything they'd brought aboard the boat was completely hidden.

'We'll finish this tomorrow,' Morschel decided. 'I've got to study the GPS and autopilot installation manuals, and that could take me some time.'

Ten minutes later the pair emerged from the cabin, locked the door behind them and carefully checked the security of the mooring lines. They then headed towards to the car park where Hagen had left the Mercedes.

North Downs, Kent

'And you are who, exactly?' DI Mason asked.

Richter had arrived a couple of minutes earlier and parked the Jaguar in the lane next to the farmer's Land Rover. One of the constables had stopped him before he reached the edge of the wood and refused to let him go further without the DI's approval.

Richter reached into his jacket pocket, pulled out a small leather wallet and showed Mason the identification card it contained. The DI peered at it and then studied Richter's face.

'It's not much of a likeness,' he pointed out.

'Tell me about it,' Richter said. 'The photographers we use are no better than those idiots on the high street doing passport piccies.'

'So your name's Paul Richter, OK, but I don't understand the rest of what's on this card. Who exactly do you represent?'

'At the moment,' Richter said, 'mainly the Security Service, I suppose. You received instructions last night to institute a watch order, looking out for a Mercedes saloon on German plates?'

'We did. But how did you know about that?'

'I know about it because it was my idea – requested by my section through Thames House.'

'So you're a spook?' Mason handed back the leather folder.

'More or less, yes.'

'OK, I'm satisfied. I'm DI Paul Mason and this' – he turned and indicated another man standing a few feet away – 'is DS Clark. Dick,' he called out, 'come and meet a real live secret squirrel.'

Richter shook hands with both men. 'Right,' he said, 'what can you tell me about this business? You've found a murder victim and you think his death might be related to terrorism?'

'It might be,' Mason conceded, 'just because of the way this man was killed.' He explained the injuries the pathologist had found on the corpse.

'Where's the body?' Richter enquired.

Mason glanced at his watch. 'By now, it should have reached the mortuary. We're still processing the crime scene here, but in a few minutes we'll go down there and see what else the pathologist can tell us about the victim.'

'I gather this man wasn't carrying any identification?'

'Only this.' Mason showed Richter the card The Ghoul had found in the dead man's pocket.

'It looks like a hotel room key card.'

'That's what we think, too,' Mason agreed.

'If you need any help tracing it, let me know, and I can send a request through Five for an expedited search. Do you mind if I tag along with you to the mortuary?'

'I don't suppose I really have a choice here, so be my guest.'

Forty minutes later, Richter was standing in the mortuary beside Mason, looking down at the mutilated corpse of the man he'd known only as Helmut Kleber, now lying naked on a dissection table. The Ghoul hadn't yet started the full post-mortem, but he had completed the external examination.

'Jesus Christ,' Richter muttered. 'What the hell did they use on him – a hedge-trimmer?'

'At the moment, I don't know,' the pathologist replied, 'but my guess is some kind of short-bladed knife, very sharp. Now, it looks pretty much as I suggested to you at the scene,' he went on, turning to Mason. 'This man's been whipped, beaten and burnt, probably in that order, and finally disembowelled. The implement used to beat him was unusual in one respect. Most whips taper, but this one appeared to have the same thickness throughout, which probably means it wasn't actually a whip as such.'

'You mean like a length of steel cable?' Mason asked.

'Yes, but probably not exactly that, because there's no evidence of striations or marks within the wounds, which you'd expect from a metal cable. A steel bar is a possibility, though that too would probably have done more damage. My guess is some kind of plastic-covered heavy-duty electric flex, something like that.'

'And all the other injuries?' Richter asked. 'Anything special about them?'

'Apart from the savagery involved, no. The other bruising was probably caused by fists or feet, or both, and the burning with a regular commercial blowtorch, the kind a chef would use in a kitchen or a handy-man in his workshop. You can easily pick one up in any hardware store. The fingertips, as I mentioned, were severed with something like a bolt-cropper. Two blades, cutting from either side of the digit.'

'So it looks as if whoever did this probably bought the tools in advance, and then drove the victim up to the wood under restraint to do the job. And you're right,' Richter added. 'This was most likely an inter-rogation, with one guy asking him questions while the other supplied the persuasion. And afterwards they did their best to make the identifi-cation of the victim nearly impossible.'

'What do you reckon, then?' Mason asked him. 'Is it possible this could be terrorist-related?'

'Definitely,' Richter said, staring at the terribly mutilated corpse in front of them and wondering how much – or how little – he should be telling Mason about the dead man. 'Let me have the results of the autopsy once it's finished.' He handed Mason a card with his mobile number written on it. 'Please keep me posted about that key card. I'd like to be there when you search his hotel room. You could also,' he sug-gested, 'keep your eyes open for an abandoned car. If he took a hotel room, he might also have hired a vehicle. If you can, I'd suggest getting a picture of his face out to your local police stations for circulation to all vehicle hire companies, that kind of thing.'

'That *was* my plan, actually,' Mason replied in a world-weary tone, 'once the doc's cleaned him up a bit.'

Richter decided to add something. 'When you start canvassing hotels, you'll probably find he was registered under the name "Helmut Kleber".'

'How the hell do you know that?'

'I know,' Richter said, 'because I spent a couple of hours last night talk-ing to him in Maidstone nick. This is the guy who walked in yesterday, claiming he was carrying a lump of Semtex.'

'Shit,' the inspector muttered. 'I heard about that. And you've no idea who did this to him, I suppose?'

'None at all,' Richter said, though in truth he knew exactly who was responsible, and why. 'One last thing. There are international security implications in this matter. I realize a large number of people will now know you've found a dead body in the woods, but can you please ensure that's all the information that's released? No further speculation about his identity, or the way he was killed. If pushed, you can suggest that his death might be gangland-related.'

'Why the caution, exactly?'

'Because there are two different people I now want to track down. One is the man who physically did this to him, but the other is the guy who issued the orders – and right now I've no idea who they are. What I do know is that, if Kleber's boss finds out he's dead, I'll probably never be able to identify him.'

Rochester, Kent

Morschel had bought the combined GPS navigator and linked universal autopilot system in Germany, because he had needed an outfit equipped with two particular features, and he was unsure if he'd be able to find a suitable unit in Britain.

Once he'd checked that he had all the components locked in his car, Morschel called Hagen on the mobile and told him to meet at the marina, and to buy a heavy-duty 12-volt battery and a mains-powered battery charger on his way there. They would have to spend the rest of the afternoon installing the system on the boat, and then making sure that it worked properly. If they found any serious problems with it, they might have to postpone the start of the operation, and Morschel really didn't want to have to do that. Everything was now prepared for Monday afternoon, and if they couldn't make that deadline they would be obliged to wait for the next high tide. It would still work, he knew, but there was a very good reason why next Monday was the optimum date.

Maidstone, Kent

Richter had stopped for lunch at a pub just off the A2, and his mobile rang as he was finishing a plate of fairly average steak and chips.

'This is DI Mason,' the caller said. 'We think we've traced the hotel.

One of my men recognized the logo, and we've contacted the head office of that particular hotel chain. Though they use the same format of card for all their establishments, they're colour-coded for different towns. The card we found was dark blue, which means Maidstone. The manager's expecting us shortly. And you're right: they did have a guest who checked in under the name "Helmut Kleber".'

'Give me the address,' Richter requested. 'I'll be there as quickly as I can.'

Twenty-five minutes later he pulled the Jaguar to a stop in a hotel car park on the northern outskirts of Maidstone. A police patrol car was stationed outside the main entrance, plus a white van and an unmarked Ford with two men sitting inside it. As Richter approached, the doors of the Ford opened and Mason and Clark climbed out.

'We've been waiting for you,' Clark said.

'Good,' Richter replied, which probably wasn't the answer the DS had been expecting. 'Let's go.'

The manager was sitting in readiness behind the reception desk, obviously waiting for them. He stood up as they approached.

'Good afternoon, sir. I'm Detective Inspector Mason of the Kent police and this is Detective Sergeant Clark.'

The manager glanced briefly at their proffered warrant cards then looked enquiringly at Richter, who volunteered nothing.

'Do you recognize this man?' Mason continued, passing a photograph across the desk.

The manager stared at the picture intently. The face it showed looked dead to Richter, even upside-down, but after a few seconds the manager nodded.

'Yes, I think I do,' he said. 'It looks like Mr Kleber. But he looks rather ill? This photograph . . .?' His voice trailed away into an expectant silence.

'I'm afraid this man is dead, sir,' Mason replied. 'Can you be sure it is Mr Kleber? He would almost certainly have been a single guest.'

'Let me just check that in the register.'

A few moments later he looked up at Mason. 'We have several men staying in single rooms here at the moment, but none of the others look like this. I'm reasonably certain it's him.'

'Then we'd like to inspect his room, please.'

'This way,' the manager beckoned and led the way across the lobby to the lifts. The four men ascended to the fourth floor and headed down a carpeted corridor. 'This is his room,' he said and knocked briskly on the door, but inevitably there was no response from inside.

A tiny red light glowed beside the handle, directly below a card slot on the lock. 'Do you have the key card?'

'We have, sir,' Mason confirmed, 'but not with us, of course, because it's still being subjected to forensic tests. Please use your master key.'

'Very well.' The manager extracted a card from his pocket, slid it into the slot and waited for the red light to change to green. Then he turned the handle and pushed the door open. 'Mr Kleber,' he called out clearly, but again without response. Finally he pushed the door fully open, flicked on the lights and stood to one side.

Mason and Clark both pulled on latex gloves before even crossing the threshold. The DI looked pointedly at Richter. 'I'm sure I don't have to remind you to touch nothing.' He then turned to the manager. 'Our forensic specialists will be coming up soon, sir. Please wait out here for them, but don't come in yourself.'

It was a standard hotel room, boring and anonymous. Its walls were decorated in restful pastel shades, the curtains were pleasantly neutral, and the double bed – which had clearly not been slept in since last being made – was covered in a light grey counterpane. Clark walked straight across the room to a wheeled suitcase that rested on a wooden luggage frame, flipped back the cover and began looking through the contents. Meanwhile Mason slid open the wardrobe doors and rummaged round amongst the clothes hanging up inside it. Richter himself remained near the centre of the room and just looked around.

Almost at once, Clark let out a low whistle and reached inside the suitcase to pull out a small cardboard box. Richter recognized its distinctive shape immediately. '9-millimetre Parabellum?' he asked.

Clark nodded, as he opened the box and looked inside. 'There are about twenty rounds left.'

'Right,' Mason said, 'that lifts this case into a different league, I think. We're now looking at either a serious criminal or a terrorist here, so I'm glad you're along, Richter.'

'The victim had no weapons on him when he died, obviously, and I presume your men did a thorough search of the wood?'

'Yes, they did,' Mason said. 'There was no weapon anywhere there, unless it was extremely well hidden. Right, let's get those forensic guys in here right now.'

Outside the room, the DI briefed the SOCOs and the team who were already waiting in the corridor with their equipment.

'We'll wait out here,' he decided. 'I need to call the DCI and brief him.' He glanced at Richter. 'And no doubt you'll have to tell your people about that ammunition?'

'I'll see you downstairs.' Richter turned away, heading for the lifts.

In the residents' lounge, he ordered a pot of coffee and, while waiting for it, called up the duty officer using his Enigma mobile to ensure his call was securely encrypted. He explained where he was and what had happened. 'This looks like being a long job,' Richter concluded. 'The SOCOs are taking the room to pieces right now, and we've no idea what else they'll find, so I'm going to hang on here until they've finished. I might even have to spend the night down here.'

'Anything you want me to do at this end?'

'Yes,' Richter reflected. 'The fact that we've found a half-empty box of nine-mil suggests that Kleber's killer – who's almost certainly Hans Morschel – is now running around the Home Counties carrying a pistol or maybe even a sub-machine gun, plus whatever weapons he had with him here already. In view of that, call Simpson and tell him I'll be drawing a personal weapon. If he wants to argue about it, he can call me direct on the Enigma.'

'But he's away for the weekend.'

'Exactly. Unless he's taken a secure mobile with him, he'll probably have to come back to London to do so, and I don't suppose he'll bother. If I decide to stay down here, I might ask you to rustle up one of our couriers to deliver the weapon to me, but I'll let you know later.'

Richter had just poured his first cup of coffee when Mason appeared in the lounge, carrying a sheet of paper inside a clear plastic evidence bag.

'What's that you've got?'

'I have no idea,' Mason replied. 'We found it folded up in a sort of secret pocket under the base of the case Clark examined. It looks like gib-berish to me, but I was rather hoping you might have a clue.'

Richter took the evidence bag and stared at the single sheet, which was covered with typed groups of five letters arranged in ten vertical columns. 'Interesting,' he remarked.

'What?'

'As I thought when I met the man, our deceased friend was an Amer-ican.'

'How the hell can you tell that?' Mason demanded.

'Simple. This isn't our normal A4 paper. It's an American size – letter, I think it's called.'

'But what is it exactly? What does the typing mean?'

Richter shook his head. 'I don't know what it means,' he said, 'but I can tell you what it is. This is an encrypted message or more likely a data-set. It could be anything from a set of instructions to a list of contact details for the dead man's associates. The five-letter groups are a give-away.'

'Can you decode it?'

'Me, personally, not a chance. But if we send it to the boffins at the Doughnut out at Cheltenham, and they feed it through one of their Cray super-computers, there's a fair chance they might crack it, but probably not quickly. There was nothing else along with this?' he asked.

'Nothing else that we've found so far. Why?'

'Well, I don't know too much about codes, but one of the commonest methods of creating one is to use what's called a transposition cipher. To encrypt or decrypt a message, you need one key word for single-transposition, or two words for a double-transposition cipher. Typically you pick words of ten or twelve letters that are easy to remember. A pro-fessional would never, ever, write down the key words, but it's always worth looking.'

'So that's what you think he was? A professional terrorist?'

'Maybe, but I'm not yet aware of any groups that use this method. They're more likely to use simple verbal codes that are essentially mean-ingless to anyone outside their group. For example, Mohammed Atta, the lead 9/11 terrorist, contacted his al Qaeda controller a few days before the attacks on the World Trade Center took place to tell him the exact date it was going to happen. The FBI monitored the call, but what he said meant absolutely nothing to them at the time. During the conversation, Atta used the expression "plate with one stick, two sticks down". It was only after the event that the FBI realized the phrase decoded easily enough as a verbal description of a figure nine followed by an eleven.'

'So any thoughts about who this man Kleber was?'

'I don't know exactly,' Richter said, 'but he told me he was an undercover agent of some kind and he dropped hints that he was working for Washington.'

'But they've got no jurisdiction over here.'

'That's what I meant by "undercover". He'd successfully infiltrated a gang of terrorists, but because of what happened to him, they almost certainly guessed who he was.'

'So what do we do now?'

'If he was working over here officially, somebody should have known about him, probably someone in Five. I'll run his picture through Thames House and see if it jogs any memories. I'll also request details of any infiltration operation they knew was being run by the Americans, or anyone else. I know you could do that, too, but I promise we'll get the results quicker if I request it.'

'Right,' Mason said. 'One other snippet, though. The hotel manager reappeared on the fourth floor to give me all the details of his late guest's registration. The man offered a passport in the name of "Helmut Kleber", but unfortunately the reception staff can't remember the country of issue, and he was paying his bill by a credit card in the same name. Obviously we'll run a check on the card because the hotel insisted on taking the number when he originally made the booking, and we can presumably check with the Germans to see if the passport's valid.'

'Good luck,' Richter said. 'But without a passport number that's going to take quite a while.'

Mason smiled at him, and Richter guessed the DI had already found a short-cut.

'The manager also remembered that this man Kleber – or whatever his real name was – arrived by car. They always get guests to supply the vehicle details when they check in, so they know which cars should be taking up space in the car park. This man arrived in a French-plated grey Peugeot, though the hotel staff didn't bother taking down its registration number, because it was the only non-British car here. That vehicle's not in the parking area now, but I've put out an APB for all the Kent forces to watch out for it. But the point is, he must have crossed the Channel by ferry or through the Tunnel, and that means the port authorities should be able to marry the car to the passport of the man who was driving it.'

'Good thinking,' Richter said. 'Make sure you let me know the result, please.' He handed back the evidence bag. 'If you can photocopy that sheet of paper for me, I'll get Cheltenham to take a look at it, but I'm not too hopeful. If it's a single-transposition, they might crack it fairly quickly, but anyone who's gone to the trouble of preparing this will almost certainly have used a double. If so, Cheltenham will have to get both words correct, and that means the possible permutations are almost infinite.'

'OK,' Mason said, 'I'll make you a copy right now. I'm sure the reception desk will oblige.'

Ten minutes later, Richter was in the Jaguar and heading back to Hammersmith. The sooner he got the encrypted data to GCHQ at Cheltenham the better, but to transmit it he was going to have to use a secure communications system. And the closest place where he could do that was almost certainly the building in which he worked.

Chapter Twelve

An hour after arriving at the marina, Hans Morschel could survey their handiwork with some satisfaction. The wooden floorboards inside the cabin were now properly fitted back in place, while below them, between the repositioned boards and the inside of the fibreglass hull, lay a total of 170 kilos of Semtex. All the explosive was completely invisible, and absolutely the only indication that there was anything unusual about the cabin was a pair of thin wires that emerged from below the floorboards in one corner. Any casual observer might assume they were simply attached to some piece of electrical equipment.

'OK to drill here?' Ernst Hagen asked, pointing to the rear corner of the cabin. He knew that on the other side of the bulkhead were the wheel, throttle control and ignition switch.

'Let me just check you're not going to hit anything vital.' Morschel stepped out into the cockpit and checked the bulkhead. 'OK,' he told Hagen, 'keep the drill low, and that should be fine.'

Hagen carefully positioned the bit of the battery-powered drill and in under a minute had driven a small hole, about a quarter of an inch in diameter, through the fibreglass bulkhead. Then he threaded the two wires through it and coiled them on the floor of the cockpit. Connecting them to the battery and the autopilot system would be almost the last thing they did.

There were several other preparations to make, but for Morschel the most vital job was installing the autopilot, which would be the most complicated operation of them all. As Hagen sorted through various boxes and laid out the components on the floor of the cockpit, Morschel flicked

open the manual and again read carefully through the installation instructions.

Hammersmith, London

Richter turned up at Hammersmith very early that morning, because
he guessed that matters were now coming to a head. Almost the first
thing he did was take the lift down to the basement and collect a 9-
millimetre Browning Hi-Power, a shoulder holster, two spare magazines and a box of fifty Parabellum rounds from the duty armourer.
He normally preferred to carry a revolver, but he had a feeling that in
the current situation speed of fire might be more important than pure
accuracy.

Then he returned to his own office and called the duty officer for an
update on overnight events. He wasn't surprised to hear there really
weren't any, because he realized it would take GCHQ some time to make
any sense of that enciphered data, if they ever managed to crack it. Nor
had he expected the autopsy on the murdered man to produce any startling new information. But it was time he started shaking the trees at
Thames House and probably at Langley as well.

Richter had a few good contacts within the Security Service. So the
previous evening he'd rung Thames House, spoken to a desk officer he
knew slightly and flagged up his belief that the dead man was an undercover agent, probably working for some arm of the US government. The
MI5 officer had stoutly claimed he had no knowledge of any American
infiltration operation currently running in Europe or Britain, and Richter
was inclined to believe him. That didn't, of course, mean that there was
no such operation running, just that his contact himself hadn't been
briefed on one. After all, like every other intelligence agency, the Security Service operated a strict need-to-know policy. But once Richter had
explained the sequence of recent events, his contact promised to raise the
matter with his superiors and so obtain as near a definitive answer as it
was ever possible to extract from MI5. In addition, he had promised
Richter he would go to the office on Sunday, just to ensure there was
some kind of continuity with the enquiry.

Richter now sat at his desk and dialled the same colleague's number at Thames House, using secure communications. The call was answered almost immediately.

'I guessed it would be you, Paul, and I wish I had something useful to tell you.'

'Nothing yet?'

'Nothing at all. I've sanitized the enquiry and run it through all the desks here, and nobody will admit to knowing anything about it. I specifically didn't ask for any operational details, just a straight "Anything known?" request.'

'What's your view, then?' Richter asked.

'I'm pretty satisfied nobody here knows anything about any current foreign-service undercover infiltration operation, and we certainly aren't running anything like that ourselves. If you're right, and this Kleber *was* an American agent, he was *deep* undercover, and totally unacknowledged by us. Have you tried Vauxhall Cross? They just might have something of their own running, despite the rules.'

The Secret Intelligence Service has a remit to operate only outside the United Kingdom, but on occasion has been known to trespass on the turf officially occupied by the Security Service. The rules are simple enough: the Security Service, MI5, is Britain's counter-espionage agency, and its operational area is restricted to the United Kingdom. SIS, the Secret Intelligence Service, is the country's espionage arm and should always work outside Britain. But there are, inevitably, grey areas and situations where a certain amount of ambiguity arises.

'I haven't talked to them yet, but I will. OK, thanks for that anyway. I'll keep you posted.'

But before Richter could connect to SIS headquarters at Vauxhall Cross, the duty officer called him on the internal phone.

'I've got some egghead on the line from Cheltenham, wanting to talk to you about that page of coded data you sent over there yesterday.'

'Good, put him through, please.'

There were a couple of clicks, and then a new voice, slightly high-pitched and obviously cultured – a kind of 'double first at Oxford' voice.

'Am I talking to Mr Richter?'

'Yes.'

'The same officer who sent us that sheet of forty-eight five-digit groups yesterday evening?'

'Have you got anywhere with it?'

'I would hardly be calling you if we hadn't, would I? Right, we assumed that the encryption used a standard double-transposition cipher and we programmed one of the computers to run first with all possible eight-letter words, then all nine-letter words and so on. That was a quick and dirty attempt to crack it, though we were, frankly, not particularly hopeful of it producing a solution.'

'And did it?' Richter prompted. He was now worried that this man from Cheltenham was warming up to give him a lengthy lecture on decryption techniques and just now he had better things to do with his time.

'Er, yes, it did indeed, about twenty minutes ago. The two key words were "NOTATIONAL" and "OVERWHELMS", in that order. Both are composed of ten letters, as you can see. Do you want us to fax you the decrypted text, or would you rather do the decode yourself?'

That, Richter thought, was arguably one of the stupidest questions aimed at him to date. He'd been taught a bit about ciphers on a course he'd attended a couple of years earlier, and the best way to describe the encryption and decoding process was tortuous and tiresome.

'No, just send me the text, please. And thanks for such prompt service.'

'It's not us really, old chap,' the specialist murmured, and then added a somewhat surprising postscript: 'These computers are fucking marvellous.'

'Well, thanks anyway.'

Richter picked up the phone again and pressed the button for the duty officer.

'It's Richter. There'll be a page or two coming through on the secure fax shortly from Cheltenham. Give me a call when it arrives, please.'

Five minutes later, Richter collected two sheets of paper from him and took them back up to his own office. Laying them side by side on his desk, he studied the decoded text carefully. At first sight, the data looked innocuous enough, but after a few moments Richter realized exactly what he had in front of him. The two sheets contained a long list of names and telephone numbers, including the international dialling codes which identified each country, and two phrases assigned to each name. Richter guessed that the phones themselves were probably disposable mobiles, and the phrases were simple, easily remembered English expressions clearly intended as challenge and response codes. There were two names listed for virtually every country in Western Europe, from Spain in the south right up to Norway.

At the bottom of the sheet were several other pieces of data, which it took him a few minutes to recognize.

These two pages basically comprised a spy's entire support mechanism, confirming what Richter already knew about the man now lying dead in the Maidstone mortuary. Whoever he was working for, he was clearly part of a very large and well-funded operation, as was confirmed by the sheer number of support agents he could call on. That immediately suggested that he had been a CIA operative, despite Kleber's outright denial when Richter had questioned him. This deduction was supported by two other facts: by the size of paper the codes had been printed on and by one of the French support agents' challenge and response codes. The first of these read 'I love the color of the sky in the morning', for which the response was 'My uncle Jacques often paints the dawn'. *Color*, Richter had instantly noted, the American spelling, not *colour*.

Just then his internal phone rang again.

'Our esteemed leader would like a word with you,' the duty officer began. 'He's on a secure line, so I presume he must be using communications from some military base in Lincolnshire.'

Seconds later, Richard Simpson's unmistakable voice sounded in his ear. 'This is a secure line, Richter,' he confirmed.

'I know.'

'Right, what's going on? I gather you've drawn a pistol without consulting me. Have you shot anyone?'

'Not yet,' Richter admitted.

'Good. Let's try and keep it that way, shall we?'

Richter outlined to him the discovery of the dead man near Sittingbourne, and also what they'd found among his belongings.

'So who was he, do you think?'

'Based on a couple of pointers, I'd say he got his orders in Langley, though he told me categorically he didn't work for the CIA.'

'And you believed him, I suppose? Get real, Richter. But if he *was* a Company man, this a serious breach of etiquette. The Yanks know bloody well they're not supposed to play around in our backyard without giving us a heads-up first. You don't think this was a freelance op?'

'Not with the level of support this man could command. And there's one other thing: the manager of the hotel remembered him driving a French-plated car. I think that struck him as odd because "Helmut Kleber" is a German name. I'm just waiting for the Kent plods or Immigration to match the number plate to his passport, and then we'll try to find his car. The name in his passport was probably false, and obviously—'

'Yes,' Simpson interrupted. 'If he was previously in France, maybe the DST or DGSE might have known about him. Maybe he wasn't actually up to anything over here but just ran for the ferry to get away from some French hoods who'd unmasked him. Give the Frogs a tug and see if they know anything.'

'Your phraseology does occasionally leave something to be desired, Simpson.'

'Just do it, OK? Brief Five and Six about the contact data you found on that sheet of paper and tell them to start running down those support agents. A word or two with them might be very instructive. And remember to keep me in the loop.'

'And you'll be where?'

'On my way back to London in about two hours. That means about three hours on the road, depending on the number of idiots cluttering up the motorway in front of me. I'll come straight to the office, so if you have to shoot off somewhere, make sure the duty officer's fully up to speed. Oh, and whether or not the French knew about this guy, contact Langley and express to them our extreme displeasure over this incident.'

Rochester, Kent

The installation of the autopilot had taken a considerable time, but that was mainly because they were both determined there should be no mistakes.

The mechanism itself was simple enough. It consisted of an electric motor and linkage to turn the wheel, and another, much less powerful, motor driving a rod attached to the throttle. Both were connected to a 'black box' that delivered current to each motor as required, and was itself attached to the GPS unit. These two electronic devices essentially comprised the brains of the system. Power was supplied by the heavy-duty battery that Hagen had bought on Morschel's instructions, and that he had charged fully overnight in his hotel room.

'That's it, I think,' Hagen said, inspecting the connections once more.

'We still need to give it a trial run. Go get the ropes.'

Morschel himself stood behind the wheel and started the engine. He waited while Hagen released the fore and aft mooring ropes, then turned the wheel and increased the throttle setting to move the boat away from the pontoon. Carefully, he navigated the craft well clear of the marina and then out into the open waters of the Medway.

'Right,' he said, 'give me a position from the chart.'

Hagen picked a location some distance up-river and read out the coordinates while Morschel fed them into the GPS unit. Then he flicked a switch on the autopilot control box, stood back and watched what happened. For a few seconds, nothing did, presumably as the GPS worked out the most direct route from the boat's present position to its programmed destination, then the throttle opened slightly and the wheel swung round to point the bow in the desired direction.

'Looks good,' Hagen said.

'So far, yes,' Morschel agreed. 'But let's see what happens when it reaches the position I set.'

Just over ten minutes later, the throttle began easing back, and then the motor reduced to a gentle idle.

'This is the interesting bit,' Morschel announced, watching carefully.

The tide was running, and in just a few seconds the boat had been carried away from the position he'd programmed. Almost immediately, the wheel swung round and the engine revolutions increased to drive the boat back to the correct location. Three times this happened before Morschel declared himself satisfied.

'That'll do,' he said, switched off the autopilot and took the wheel himself for the run back down-river to the marina.

'What time tomorrow?' Hagen asked.

'High tide's at three thirty-six,' Morschel replied, 'so that's when we should hit the button, plus or minus about twenty minutes, since it's not that critical. The distance the boat has to cover is about twenty miles, so we'll need to have it out of the marina no later than one thirty. I reckon it'll take us at least an hour to connect everything up and install the anti-handling devices. Then add thirty minutes for other contingencies, so we need to be down here by twelve, latest. I'll pass that on to Ahmed, because his man needs to be here by then as well. And that'll give you plenty of time to pick out another boat for the transfer and to hot-wire it.'

'The other guys. What time for them?'

'I'll check the vehicles and equipment this afternoon, and we'll have a final briefing for everyone tomorrow morning, just to go over every-thing one more time. I've programmed their last withdrawal' – Hagen smiled slightly at the word – 'for one thirty, because they have to be clear and complete no later than three.'

Hammersmith, London

Richter's internal phone buzzed with a call from the Duty Office, which he answered immediately.

'I've got a DI Mason on the line for you, from the Kent Constabulary. How did he get this number?'

'He got it because I gave it to him. So put him through.'

'Good afternoon, Mr Richter,' Mason began.

'Hi. Any news?'

'Of a sort, yes. We've now heard from Immigration, but the results are a bit odd. We sent them a photo of the dead man which we took in the mortuary, mentioned the name "Helmut Kleber" and requested that they match the passport with the car. It should have been a mere formality to just check the passport records and the vehicle-lane cameras and tie the two bits of information together.'

'Let me guess,' Richter said. 'Nobody with that name has entered Britain in the last couple of weeks?'

'Actually, no. In fact, three men called "Helmut Kleber" arrived here, but all three came by air, and our initial checks suggest they're alive and well and busy trying to sell us whatever their respective companies manufacture. Because the Maidstone hotel manager remembers Kleber arriving in a car with French plates, but called to make his reservation from Germany last week, we've presumed he crossed the Channel either by ferry or through the Tunnel, which means he must have used a different passport.'

'How did the manager know Kleber was originally calling from Germany?'

'They have automatic caller identification software on the hotel switchboard, and he even printed out the records to show me. Most of their clientele is British, so the call struck him at the time as fairly unusual.'

'OK, what else?'

'We went back to Immigration and asked them to check their camera images over the last two weeks, looking for *any* French-plated cars – just in case the manager got it wrong and it wasn't a Peugeot saloon – with a male driver and no passengers. That produced over 2,000 possibilities from all the ferry ports, but they could filter out most of them quite quickly, simply because the drivers looked nothing like Kleber, or else they were driving the wrong kind of vehicle – meaning a sports car or a jeep or an MPV, that kind of thing. Anyway, the short version is that they sent us details of thirty-two potential matches, and we now think we've got him. I'm currently looking at a picture of a French-plated Peugeot saloon, and I reckon the man in the driving seat looks pretty much like "Helmut Kleber". I've shown this photograph to the hotel manager and some staff and they all agree.'

'And the passport?'

'I was saving the best bit for last. The passport presented by the man in the Peugeot was perfectly genuine and had been issued by the US Department of State about two years ago. It looks as if our "Helmut Kleber" was really an American citizen named Gregory Stevens.'

'I knew it,' Richter muttered.

'Anyway,' Mason finished, 'the Immigration people have told us he entered the country at Dover on Friday afternoon. We've already checked the hotel car park and all the streets in the vicinity, and there's absolutely no sign of the Peugeot. We've widened the search, and I'll let you know as soon as we hear anything. Oh, by the way, any progress with that sheet of paper we found?'

Richter deliberated for a few moments, trying to decide what he could – or should – disclose. Then he mentally shrugged, and decided they were both on the same side.

'Yes. Fortunately, GCHQ at Cheltenham cracked the cipher,' he said, and explained what the decoded page contained.

As soon as Mason rang off, Richter dialled his Thames House contact to pass on this new information, then telephoned the SIS duty officer at Vauxhall Cross to do the same. Entirely unsurprisingly, neither organization would admit to having any knowledge of a 'Gregory Stevens' operating undercover in Europe.

Although Richard Simpson had instructed him to contact the two French security organizations, the DST and the DGSE, about 'Helmut Kleber', the fact that he now knew the dead man had been carrying a genuine American passport obviously changed the focus of the investigation. Richter doubted very much if the French would have anything useful to tell him, simply because, whatever Stevens had been up to in Europe, the dead man's briefing had almost certainly been delivered to him somewhere in Virginia. It was time, instead, to see what the CIA had to tell him.

Romford, Essex

Ernst Hagen braked the Mercedes to a halt outside BB Productions' small warehouse on the industrial estate. He and Morschel climbed out and headed round to the side door of the unprepossessing building, which swung open just as they reached it. The man inside nodded to them as they walked past into the premises, then locked the door behind them.

Morschel stood in the large open space that comprised most of the interior and stared at the four vans sign-written 'Metropolitan Police'.

'From the outside, they're completely indistinguishable from the real thing,' Hagen assured him. 'Unless he ran a check on their registrations or the numbers painted on the roofs, not even a police officer could tell the difference.'

'Good. Now show me the uniforms,' Morschel instructed, and the two men proceeded through to one of the storerooms at the rear.

'Again, they're just like the genuine article,' Hagen commented, 'and they probably even came from the same supplier. They've got personal radios, too – inoperable, of course, but they look right – and I doubt these bulletproof waistcoats would stop anything more dangerous than a wasp sting. The helmets are pretty tough, though.'

Morschel turned to the man who was acting as a guard over the building. 'You've already swapped the weapons?' He was pointing down at a collection of sub-machine guns and semi-automatic pistols stashed in a crate on the floor in front of him. 'So these are the props?'

The man nodded. 'That was the first thing we did once the vans were delivered. The real weapons are already stored inside the security box in the back of each vehicle, along with the magazines and ammunition.'

'Good,' Morschel nodded, and walked back into the centre of the warehouse. He glanced again at each of the 'police' vehicles, checking that everything was ready. Finally, he inspected the rear compartments of the other four vans parked at the rear of the warehouse. Each of these was carrying a very special and sensitive cargo, and he was careful not to disturb their contents.

'Right, we're ready,' Morschel said. 'Ernst and I will handle the next phase of the operation and we'll be back here tomorrow morning at eight thirty. Make sure everyone's here by then, and that everything's ready to go. That means a thorough check of each vehicle, and to make sure the tanks are full of fuel. Then we'll have a final briefing, and we can get the ball rolling.'

Hammersmith, London

Richter had known John Westwood ever since he'd first begun working for Richard Simpson and had the American's home number in his organizer. This was just as well, because he had no illusions about the potential difficulties in trying to extract information about any covert CIA operation out of an uninterested weekend desk officer at Langley, and especially over a transatlantic telephone line.

'Hi, Paul. It's been, what, six months?'

'Probably, but far too long anyway. How're you keeping?'

Westwood chuckled. 'I know you, Paul. You haven't dragged me out of bed at eight on a Sunday morning – you *do* know there's a time difference, don't you? – just to check on me and my beloved family. You obviously want something, so why not get to the point? What's the story this time?'

'OK, John. Does the name Gregory Stevens mean anything to you?'

There was a short pause while Westwood considered the question. 'Not that I can recall, no. Is he a Company man? Or is that what you're trying to find out?'

'More or less, yes. Briefly, we have a dead body over here, very messily murdered. He was going by the name of Helmut Kleber, and aged about forty to forty-five years of age. What's interesting is that he used a genuine US passport, in the name of Stevens, to get himself into Britain a couple of days ago. That suggests either he genuinely *was* Gregory Stevens, or his name really was Kleber and he somehow got hold of the Stevens passport. Whatever the truth, we have a couple of concerns. First, when we searched his hotel room, we found a half-empty box of 9-millimetre ammunition. Second, in the same place we found a typed sheet of coded five-letter groups and, when our computer wizards at GCHQ ran them through a Cray, they came up with the decryption keys. It used a standard double-transposition cipher with two ten-digit key words. The sheet listed names, mobile phone numbers and challenge and response codes for a bunch of people we assume are support agents based in almost every country in Western Europe. MI5 and SIS have been running checks on them through the phone numbers, but most they've tried so far are no longer on the system, so we guess this Stevens character has already made use of their services and now they've ditched the chips or even the phones. That would be standard procedure for us.'

'For us, too,' Westwood agreed.

'The US passport, the spelling of one word in the encrypted data and the size of the paper itself all suggest an American connection, and we're assuming that this Kleber, Stevens, or whatever he's really called, was part of an undercover operation being run on our side of the pond. And don't the words "undercover" and "CIA" just seem to fit together naturally?'

'Yeah,' Westwood agreed, 'usually with the words "incompetent" and "turned to rat-shit" tucked in there somewhere as well. So that's why you've called me?'

'Yes. Naturally, my boss is steaming slightly about this, because, if the Company *was* running some kind of covert op, you should have advised us about it. The other possibility is that he was actually working somewhere on the continent and fled here because he was worried about being unmasked by the group he'd targeted.'

'It all sounds a bit vague, Paul.'

'Well, the body's real enough, and there have been a handful of unusual terrorist-related incidents in Europe over the last two or three weeks. I actually interviewed this man Stevens, and he claimed he was responsible for tipping off the authorities in two of them, and there's evidence to support that. He also claimed to have done the same in a couple of earlier terrorist incidents. Anyway, I reckon this falls more or less within your terms of reference, so can you have a scout around tomorrow and see what you can find out?'

'I'll check, yes, but this really doesn't sound like Company business. I mean, if we *had* mounted some kind of undercover operation in Europe we would, at the very least, have given your SIS and the French and German security forces a heads-up on it. Apart from anything else, we'd have preferred to use official resources rather than a network of probably part-time, perhaps amateur, support agents. This sounds to me more like a freelance operation, maybe with just a measure of official support.'

'Now,' Westwood said, 'if that's the case, this man Gregory Stevens won't be a current Company agent and may not even a past employee. He could be an ex almost anything: DEA, FBI, ATF or any of the other three-digit agencies that seem to infest the Land of the Free. Or even a cop, I suppose. Anyway, give me his passport number, and I'll check it out.'

Richter read out the number he'd been given by Mason.

'OK,' Westwood said, after he'd read the number back as a check, 'and can you send us his dabs as well, for a positive ID?'

'I wish I could, but the guys who killed this man took the trouble to remove his fingerprints permanently, using pliers. I've got post-mortem mug-shots of the victim, and I'll be getting X-rays of his dental work, but that's about all we have to go on.'

'Nasty,' Westwood remarked. 'OK, I'll call you, but unless you're giving this a real high priority, it'll probably be tomorrow before you hear from me.'

'Thanks, John. You've got my numbers.'

Central Intelligence Agency Headquarters, Langley, Virginia

In fact, John Westwood decided not to wait till the next day. There was, he rationalized, a positive advantage in going to Langley that evening to run the search routines on the massive CIA computer system, known to Agency insiders as 'The Walnut'. With few other staff in the building on a Sunday, the response speed should be a lot faster than usual, so hopefully he could find an answer to Richter's question fairly quickly. Besides, his diary the next day was already pretty full.

Westwood drove to Langley from his home in Haywood, Virginia, and entered his office at just after seven thirty that evening. He powered up his desktop PC and logged on to the system. As head of the Foreign Intelligence (Espionage) Staff, a position he had held for a little over four years, he was allowed virtually unrestricted access to all sections of the CIA's database.

Running a search for the name 'Gregory Stevens' in the register of current employees, he found it appeared three times but, on checking the employment details for each of these men, he found that none of them fitted Richter's criteria. Two of them were approaching retirement age, and the third was a young man currently recovering at home after a recent operation to remove his diseased appendix.

Next, Westwood expanded his search to include all agents who had retired or resigned from the Agency, and that produced a single match for 'Gregory Stevens'. The man in question had been employed in the Clandestine Services section, which would certainly mean he possessed the right background. But it seemed he had retired on grounds of ill-health and had died about a year later. So that, too, was literally a dead end.

Westwood nodded thoughtfully. It looked as if Richter's 'Stevens' was nothing to do with the Agency, but then he decided to try one other route. The CIA had links to numerous other databases, including that of the Department of State. He opened an online enquiry form, typed in the passport number Richter had given him and waited for the result. What appeared next was unexpected. A message inside a red dialogue box popped up in the middle of the screen to inform him that all details of this passport holder were 'reserved'.

'Oh, shit,' Westwood murmured, knowing exactly what that meant. To avoid personal details of CIA agents and certain other US government officials being disclosed, access to passport details and other identifying data held on official websites was severely restricted, even to other branches of government.

Richter had told him the passport had been read electronically, and the name 'Gregory Stevens' displayed, and this quite probably meant that the former Clandestine Services' agent of that name wasn't anything like as dead as the CIA personnel database claimed. Or, rather, he probably really was dead now but he'd been working undercover ever since his supposed retirement on grounds of ill-health.

Westwood went back to the 'deceased' agent's personal records and checked the section on identifying marks. There were no tattoos or convenient birthmarks that might confirm the man's identity with certainty, but there were a couple of other things that would at least help with identification.

He checked his watch, working out the current time in Britain, then shrugged, reached for the phone and dialled one of Richter's various London numbers.

Just over half an hour after Westwood climbed back into his car to return home to Haywood, the duty computer system manager at Langley returned to his desk after taking a meal break. As he switched the computer screen back on, the first thing he noticed was a flashing dialogue box containing a message that he'd never seen before. It wasn't indicating a system fault, just an urgent instruction to locate a particular senior CIA officer and pass him a brief and very specific short message.

The manager attempted a couple of calls, but as soon as he realized where the officer was, and the local time there, he decided not to call him but to pass on the message using an encrypted email, for his eyes only.

Fifteen minutes later, he had sent the email and returned to his normal duties. Thirty seconds after the message had been sent, it arrived in an in-box at the US Embassy in Grosvenor Square in London, where it would remain until the addressee opened it.

The message read simply: 'Tripwire one: Stevens.'

Chapter Thirteen

Monday
Maidstone, Kent

Richter braked the Jaguar to a halt outside the police station, grabbed the file sitting on the seat beside him and marched inside the building, where DI Mason was waiting for him.

'Early start for you, isn't it?' the officer demanded, as they shook hands.

'Yes,' Richter admitted, 'and I didn't get a lot of sleep last night. I took a call at just after three thirty, and that's the reason I'm down here now instead of napping at my desk.'

'You said you had some information? And wanted another look at the body?'

Richter nodded. 'That call was from my contact in Langley. He reckons that "Helmut Kleber" might be a former CIA agent named "Gregory Stevens", based on the name in the passport he used at Calais. I just need to see the body one more time to check a couple of things that might confirm this identification.'

'OK,' Mason agreed. 'We'll take my car.'

Fifteen minutes later they were standing side-by-side in the mortuary, gazing down at the mutilated naked body. After the post-mortem, the torso looked slightly less like raw meat than it had before. The jagged incision running from the breastbone almost down to the pubis was now held roughly closed by large stitches made with strong and coarse thread, while above the breastbone the V-shaped cut made by the pathologist looked neat by comparison.

'The Ghoul, the local pathologist, now thinks the wound was probably made by something like a Stanley knife, and his attackers had to make multiple cuts just to get through the skin and subcutaneous fat.

Obviously the victim would have been struggling violently, hence the jagged edge of the knife wound.'

'That's a hard way to go,' Richter muttered.

'You're not wrong. Now, you had something?'

'Yes.' Richter opened the file folder he was carrying and extracted a single sheet of paper, with a couple of scribbled paragraphs at the top and a very rough diagram of a human body below them.

Mason looked at the page with interest. 'Is that some kind of arcane coding system that's impossible to decipher?'

'No,' Richter replied, 'it's my personal scribble, and it's just what my writing looks like when I'm woken up in the middle of the night and asked to take notes. Now, according to my source at Langley, about ten years ago Gregory Stevens had a minor operation to remove an infected cyst from his left forearm, so there should be a small scar there.'

Mason leant forward and peered at the corpse's arm. 'There's something here,' he said. 'An old scar about two inches long. Is that about right?'

'Yes, that looks like it,' Richter agreed. 'The second is a bullet wound – just a graze, really – on the inside of his right calf.'

Again, the DI looked at the corpse. 'Yes. Just here, there's a ragged scar running across the muscle, maybe three inches long and about half an inch wide. It looks like the kind of wound a bullet would make.'

'OK,' Richter said, stepping back from the corpse and closing the folder. 'Obviously those checks aren't conclusive, but they're certainly indicative. To be certain we'll need to send off his dental chart to Langley, but I'm now reasonably certain this man *was* indeed Gregory Stevens, and that raises a whole bunch of new questions.'

'What questions, exactly? We've got a tentative identification, so that's a step forward, surely.'

'Yes, and no. The most interesting aspect of this situation is that, as far as my contact at the CIA has been able to find out, this man was retired from the Agency some eight years ago on grounds of ill-health.'

'So? He might have since recovered from whatever illness he had.'

'He might,' Richter admitted, 'but the Agency records don't agree. They show that he died within a year.'

'What? He died twice?' Mason stared down at the body.

'Only James Bond lived twice.' Richter smiled. 'No, it's a lot simpler than that. Occasionally, when the Agency wants somebody to go *deep* undercover, they "kill" them, so that any checks come up against a literal dead end, and anyone investigating will know there's no point in chasing a dead man. But they still always provide their undercover agents with genuine passports, to facilitate border crossings and so on, and often they have a kind of emergency pack if they get really stuck – something that will guarantee assistance from any friendly government or agency.'

'So this guy *was* a CIA agent?'

'Not exactly,' Richter said. 'I suppose the best description of him would be a contract agent. That means he would be employed as a totally deniable asset by an agency – and not necessarily the CIA – to undertake a specific task.'

'What task do you mean?'

'That,' Richter said, 'is now the big question. I told you about the two anti-terrorist operations in Europe and how somebody tipped off the bad guys just before the police kicked down the doors. When I interviewed this man a couple of days ago, he claimed he was at the other end of the phone each time. But if he was, that raises a couple of obvious questions. If the CIA or some other agency was running an operation to infiltrate terrorist groups in Europe, why didn't they liaise with us – with MI5 or the SIS – before doing so? We could have easily provided back-up and support, as well as current intelligence. And, just as important, why would they be using a contract agent instead of a regular agent? That very fact implies that the task was something more than just infiltration.'

Richter paused and looked down again at the corpse.

'Anyway, I think we now know who this man was. What we need to do next is find out just what the hell he was doing over here. I'll talk to my man in Langley and let him know we've made a tentative identification. Once you've got his dental chart, I'll send it across the pond to get definitive confirmation of his identity.'

'No problem. It's already being organized.'

As they left the mortuary, Mason's mobile rang, and he stopped just outside the building to answer it. A few seconds later he snapped the phone shut and turned to Richter.

'We've found the Peugeot,' he said. 'It's sitting in a public car park on the outskirts of Sittingbourne.'

Romford, Essex

In addition to Morschel and Hagen, there were sixteen men, all bulky and fit-looking, standing in the limited area of open space between the two lines of vans occupying the warehouse. Each was holding a couple of sheets of paper that Morschel had printed from his laptop computer earlier that morning. Facing this group, next to Hagen, was a large whiteboard on which a list of times and actions had been clearly written, and beside that was an expanded map of central London.

'We've rehearsed this often enough,' Morschel said, as a kind of introduction, 'so by now you should all know precisely what you're supposed to be doing. This board here, and the timetable you're each holding, should serve merely as reminders of what we've planned, nothing more. But I'll go through everything one last time, in case we notice any last-minute problems.

'I've given each of you two sheets of paper, the first of which is the timetable, and I'll get to that in a moment. The second one is just as important, as it lists all your first names and your mobile numbers. Remember, our mobiles are our lifelines. Once you've completed a specified action, you must tell me. More importantly, if anything goes wrong, I need to know immediately. If I don't know, I can't help you. So check right now that your name appears on that page, and that the mobile number listed beside it is correct.'

Morschel looked round, but all the men just nodded.

'Good,' he said. 'It's obvious, but you must make sure that your mobile is switched on and fully charged before you leave here. There are power points all over this building, and plenty of socket adaptors in the office at the rear.

'Now, the timetable. We've worked backwards from the big one, and I've allowed forty minutes between each of our operations. That will give the Metropolitan Police just enough time to respond, and to concentrate their resources in exactly the wrong place each time.'

Several of the men smiled grimly at his words.

'The first detonation is timed for precisely eleven o'clock, here at Greenford.' Morschel picked up a ruler and pointed to a red mark on the map, then he cross-referred to the timetable on the board. Then he moved his makeshift pointer to three other locations in turn, all situated north of the Thames, at each one running through the exact sequence of actions necessary for the operation.

'The final attack will occur at one thirty this afternoon,' he finished. 'You already know your escape routes, and you've all reconnoitred your targets so you know exactly where to position the vehicles. Now, are there any questions?'

Again, nobody responded.

'Right,' Morschel continued. 'Hagen and I will go and get ready for our own part in this. The rest of you can relax until you need to get suited up ready to leave. To ensure you're in position on time, each team should be leaving here about ninety minutes before its allotted time for action. Better to be waiting somewhere close to your target than trying to hack your way through traffic and then running late.'

Morschel looked around the group one last time. 'Finally, don't forget about weapons safety. I'm not interested in how many civilians get shot, because they're expendable, but we can't afford any accidents with our own team. So those of you carrying MP5s should remember that until you actually get out of the vehicle you keep the bolt open and your finger off the trigger. Right, good luck, all of you. We'll meet up back in Germany next week.'

American Embassy, Grosvenor Square, London

Carlin F. Johnson was in a foul mood, but that wasn't unusual. He'd spent most of his long and highly successful career with the CIA in a bad temper. Currently, his mood was caused by two factors, neither of which he had the slightest control over. This, for him, was an additional annoyance.

First, he hated the British weather: the almost perpetual drizzle that had characterized this alleged summer in London. Every morning, it seemed, he had looked out of the Embassy window at grey skies leaden with rain clouds. That was irritation enough.

His second gripe was more immediate. When he'd first conceived VIPER, he'd realized that Gregory Stevens would need to go deep undercover, and that he simply wouldn't be able to establish any kind of a regular communications schedule. Reports from him had been very erratic ever since the operation started, and even more so over the last month, with the result that Johnson literally had no idea what stage Stevens had reached, where he now was, or even if he was still alive.

When Johnson checked his emails that morning and read the one sent from Langley the previous evening, he spent almost two minutes cursing under his breath. Somebody else must have become alerted to the operation – the fact that the agent's name had been entered in the database search field showed that clearly enough.

What he had to decide was whether to try and identify who had initiated the search, or just sit back and wait. But if any of the other tripwires he'd placed in the computer system were triggered over the next few days, he knew he would have to do something, and quickly.

Sittingbourne, Kent

The Peugeot was located in a bay in a corner of the car park. By the time Richter and Mason arrived the surrounding area had already been taped off, and a forensic team was poring over the vehicle itself.

DS Clark was standing nearby, having a conversation on his mobile phone, but as the two men approached he ended the call and turned to face his superior.

'That was Canterbury,' he explained to Mason, 'and we've already had a confirmation from Hertz.' The DI eyed him enquiringly. 'There's a bar-code sticker in the rear-side window,' Clark pointed, 'and the hire documents are there in the glove-box. This car was picked up by a man calling himself Helmut Kleber at Toulouse airport about ten days ago. He showed them a German passport and driving licence and paid with a Visa card in the same name. I've got Canterbury checking the provenance of those documents right now.'

'The Visa card will probably come back verified,' Richter said. 'That's just one of the things a good support agent would arrange. He would use his own contacts to set up a bank account and organize credit cards for the undercover agent he was assisting. But the driving licence and passport will most likely be faked.'

'Driving licences I can understand,' Clark said, 'but passports? You mean one of these support agent people you're talking about can get forgeries of them?'

'They're not that difficult to fake,' Richter said, 'not even the new biometric versions. Any competent forger can knock one up in a couple of hours. And don't forget they normally only have to satisfy a deputy hotel manager or maybe some girl behind the counter at a car hire company. These passports won't normally be shown to an immigration officer or anyone who would know exactly what to look for, or who has ready access to a database that can immediately identify a forgery. For that, the agent will be carrying the real thing, in a different name and probably issued by his own government. That's why our dead man used the genuine "Gregory Stevens" passport when he crossed the Channel. He couldn't afford to risk showing a faked document – not even a really good forgery.'

'Are you carrying a weapon?' Clark asked, as Richter's jacket swung open to show part of his shoulder holster.

'Yes,' Richter replied shortly. 'And I'd suggest you don't start fannying around with checking my carry permit.'

'So what now?' Mason asked.

'As I said before, even if this man was working deep undercover, he would probably have kept some kind of an emergency pack with him, something that he could produce as a last resort to the security and police forces of whatever country he was working in. That might then blow his mission completely, but it would allow him to get immediate help, and could even save his life if whatever he was doing suddenly turned to ratshit. You didn't find anything like that in his hotel room, so my guess is it's hidden somewhere in the car.

'Finding that would be a big help, because it might identify whatever agency he was working for, and knowing exactly who he was would then provide me with a big stick to hit the Yanks over the head with. And that might mean we could find out just what the hell he was really doing over here.'

Fifteen minutes later, one of the white-clad figures summoned Mason over to the rear of the car. By that stage they'd removed almost everything from the Peugeot's boot and had found nothing of interest, but once this man lifted out the spare wheel, he saw a small, flat packet taped to its underside.

Clark and Mason pulled on latex gloves and leant forward to scrutinize the object. 'There won't be a booby-trap or anything in it, will there?' Clark asked.

'Most unlikely,' Richter muttered, also peering closely at the packet. 'An explosive charge would destroy whatever documents are in it, and that's the last thing he would want. And it really isn't big enough to hold some kind of anti-handling device. I think it's just a normal pouch holding documents.'

'OK,' Clark said, uncertainly.

'Cut the tape,' Mason ordered, 'and give me the packet.'

The white-clad officer reached into a tool box beside him and selected a Stanley knife. Extending the blade, he bent forward and carefully cut straight across the black insulating tape that secured the packet to the wheel. Then he picked it up gingerly and handed it to Mason.

Despite Richter's reassurance, the DI took it with obvious trepidation and studied it closely. It was a plain black leather pouch, and the first thing he took out was an American passport. Richter pulled on the rubber gloves Clark handed him and accepted the passport from Mason. He opened it, flicked to the page with the photograph and examined the information it contained. The photograph was instantly recognizable, and the name of the holder was given as 'Gregory Stevens'.

'If we can scan this somewhere here,' Richter said, 'I'll email it over to Langley, see if the picture rings any bells with them. Anything else in there?'

'Just a bit of paper.' Mason handed it over.

Richter carefully unfolded the sheet and looked at it. The data on this one was handwritten rather than encoded, perhaps because there was hardly any information on it, yet what there was didn't make obvious sense. There were only seven lines of text, all written in block capitals:

1/8
KELLERMAN
5412
SM/VIPER
TS – SCI DINGO
NOTATIONAL – OVERWHELMS
6/30

'That mean anything to you?' Mason asked, staring over Richter's shoulder.

'Some of it, yes,' Richter admitted, 'and I don't like the look of this at all.'

'Why not?'

'Because this is beginning to look more and more as if it's a CIA operation. The Company is very predictable and, like any bureaucracy, it follows certain rules. One of them is the way it designates the geographical area in which an operation will be carried out. "SM" stands for the United Kingdom, so this' – he pointed to the fourth line – 'means that there *is* a CIA operation called "VIPER" currently being run in Britain. And it's obviously highly classified. The letters "TS" in the fifth line probably mean "top secret".'

'What about "SCI Dingo"?'

'One of the problems with the higher-security classifications – and there are about thirty grades higher than top secret – is that they're very general. I've got a "cosmic top secret" clearance, which means I can legally have sight of all CTS documents, and obviously anything with a lower classification than that. But often such documents contain information that is extremely sensitive and therefore have a very limited distribution, and that's why the SCI system was first introduced. SCI stands for Special Compartmentalized Intelligence, and it's a code word clearance system only applicable to documents classified at top secret level and above. Basically, applying SCI to a document or operation means that knowledge of it can be restricted to a very small group of people. So with a CTS clearance I can get to see a top secret document, but unless I also had, in this case, "Dingo" clearance, I couldn't see whatever else this is referring to.'

'A dingo's a kind of wild dog, isn't it?' Mason asked, frowning.

'The word chosen doesn't mean anything at all. Most operation names and SCI code words are generated at random by a computer, and that's the whole point. If you have a secret operation running, it doesn't make a lot of sense if the name you choose has some clear connection to it. That would be an obvious breach of security, hence the names being randomly assigned.'

'That makes sense, I suppose. And what about the rest of it?'

'The two words "notational" and "overwhelms" I already knew,' Richter said. 'They were the decryption key words for the double-transposition cipher on that other paper you found. The first and last lines look like dates, and "Kellerman" is obviously a personal name. But I have no clue what "5412" means. I'm going to have to talk to my Langley contact to try and make some sense of this.'

Romford, Essex

A little after nine thirty, the big roller-shutter doors at the front of the warehouse slid up fully and a man wearing blue overalls emerged. He gestured, and one of the 'Metropolitan Police' vans backed out, two shadowy uniformed figures just visible inside the cab behind the wire-mesh guard over the windscreen. The van reversed out, swung round and then drove off down the road.

It was followed shortly afterwards by another van, but this was one of those that had been parked at the rear of the warehouse and was entirely unmarked. Again, two men sat in the cab, and a keen observer might have noted that the rear doors were secured by two external hasps, each fitted with a heavy-duty padlock.

Maidstone, Kent

Mason led Richter through into a rear office of the police station, equipped with two fax machines and a photocopier. Prior to making his call to Westwood, Richter made copies of both the 'Gregory Stevens' passport and the sheet of paper they'd found in the boot of the Peugeot, before handing the originals back to the DI.

'Stay if you want,' he suggested. 'This is an open line, so I won't be saying anything that's classified.'

'Who are you calling?' Mason asked.

'He's a senior CIA agent. I've known him for a few years, and we've worked together a couple of times in the past.'

'You do know it's about four in the morning over on the East Coast?' Mason warned.

'I do, but I think this is too important to wait for the normal start of business. And anyway, knowing John, he won't mind.'

Richter pulled out his mobile and found Westwood's home number.

'You could use one of the landlines here if you like.'

Richter shook his head. 'No thanks. My friend's very particular about who knows his name and home number, so I'd best use my mobile.'

He heard the ringing tone, then Westwood's slightly sleepy voice. 'Good morning, Paul.'

'How did you know it was me?' Richter asked.

'Paul, it's four o'clock in the morning here and I'm still in bed. I've left standing orders back at Langley for them to call me at home only if World War Three has started and the enemy troops have already reached Washington. So who else could it be?'

'Point taken, John. Right, this is an open line, so no specifics, please. Regarding the matter we discussed yesterday and earlier today, we've recovered a passport that seems to confirm the man's identity, and it is precisely who we thought it was.'

'OK. I can't say I'm that surprised. Anything else?'

'Yes,' Richter said, picking up the photocopy of the document they'd found in the car. 'We also recovered some notes our man had made. Most of them I can't relay over an open line, but there is what looks like a code name that seems to suggest a Company operation over here where I live. Do you follow me?'

'Yes. You're talking about a Sierra Mike op?'

'Exactly. The other thing I *can* say is just four numbers. They mean nothing to me, but maybe they do to you.'

'Go ahead.'

'The numbers are five, four, one, two.'

For a few seconds Westwood didn't respond. 'No,' he said slowly, 'That doesn't mean anything to . . . Hang on, are you sure? Five, four, one, two? Yes?'

'Confirmed. So what is it?'

'If that means what I think it does, you're not looking at a Company op, or not in the sense you're looking at it. It's something much more serious. We need to discuss this over a secure link, Paul, and *quickly*.'

'Understood. Look, do you have a fax machine there? I can squirt this stuff over to you and I'll call you from the office as soon as I get back there. That should be safe enough.'

'No, Paul, not even a fax, please. I'm heading for the office as soon as I can. Call me when you get back to Hammersmith, and then we'll discuss it properly. Don't talk to anyone else about this.'

'You got it,' Richter said, and ended the call.

'So what does he think?' Mason asked.

'I don't know. But it sounds like those four numbers have got him really worried. So worried, in fact, that he won't even let me fax that sheet of paper. I've got to get back to London and call him on a secure line just so I can find out what the hell this is all about.'

Greenford, London

The unmarked white van turned into a side street about half a mile from its objective. There was a small area of rough ground at one end of the street, just big enough to allow the driver to manoeuvre the vehicle round to face the way it had come. He stopped the van on a set of double yellow lines, partially blocking the pavement, then wound down his window. He lit a cigarette and glanced across at his companion, who was doing likewise.

'We're well ahead of schedule,' the driver remarked, checking his watch against the digital display on the dashboard. 'I'd better check in with Hans.'

He pulled out the ashtray, carefully placed his cigarette on it, took a mobile phone from his pocket and dialled a number from memory.

'This is Alpha Two,' he said, once his call was answered. 'We're in a holding position about half a mile out.'

'Good,' Morschel replied. 'Alpha One's already checked in and they're parked, too. Once you've moved into your final position, they'll get mobile.'

Hammersmith, London

'Those two pages are on their way to you right now,' Richter confirmed. 'So, tell me. What's with those four numbers, John?'

'Hang on, I'm just reading the fax . . . OK. Now, 5412. It's a long story. Ever since the end of the Second World War, the Agency's had access to a top-secret slush fund, a pile of money that even Congress knows absolutely nothing about, and for which the director is directly, solely and personally accountable to the president himself. During Eisenhower's time in the White House, the National Security Council issued a paper recommending the creation of a top-secret group to advise the CIA on the best way to spend this cash.

'That paper's number was 5412, and the group born out of that recommendation was called simply the 5412 Committee. It's always been the single most secret organization in the States, and it still exists today, though it's gone through a succession of different and obscure designations. It's been called "The 303" and "The 40 Committee" and a number of other innocuous names, but most people in the know just refer to it as "The Special Group".

'That group's purpose today is the same as it was back in Ike's day. Every covert, illegal or simply potentially embarrassing operation the Agency wants to undertake is first approved by The Special Group, before the president gets to hear about it, so that our chief executive can then quite truthfully deny all knowledge of it if the shit hits the fan. In fact, not even the National Security Council is told about its activities, and the president's approval is only ever given verbally – nothing is ever written or signed.'

'I have heard of The Special Group,' Richter reflected, 'but I didn't know much about it, and I certainly didn't know about the identifying numbers. Who's actually part of it?'

'There are usually only four members. It's normally headed by the National Security Advisor, and the other three are the Secretary of State, the Secretary of Defense and, of course, the Director of National Intelligence ever since that post replaced that of the Director of Central Intelligence. Most of the covert stuff you probably already know about – the building of the U-2, the assassination of Salvador Allende in Chile and Iran–Contra – were all clandestine CIA projects approved by The Special Group.'

'So what's the story now? Are you saying this guy Stevens was running an operation over here on behalf of this crowd?'

'Maybe. But if he was, I've no idea of the objective, and you'll appreciate that there's no easy way I can find out. Membership of The Special Group is way above my pay scale, and for obvious reasons I can't just buttonhole the Secretary of Defense, or one of the others, to ask him about this covert op he's got running in London.'

'Is there *anything* you can do?'

'I can run a search through the computer system and see if there's any mention of SM slash VIPER, but if the operation was carried out with the sole approval of The Special Group, it almost certainly never made it as far as the database we've got here. We're probably looking at a totally deniable op, with verbal briefings, absolutely nothing in writing, and just a tiny number of people who've even heard of it.'

'Understood, John. You're probably right, but could you check anyway? Oh, and run a check on the name "Kellerman" as well, just in case that helps.'

'Will do. I'll call you back.'

It didn't take Westwood long to respond. Less than ten minutes later, Richter's secure phone rang.

'Right, Paul. First, there's no mention of an operation codenamed SM slash VIPER on the database here, so that looks like a dead end. But I have found something else that's a little odd. On the sheet of paper you faxed, the first line could be a date – 1/8 – which I assume means the eighth of January. If that was this year, there's a possible link to the name

"Kellerman". On that afternoon, the body of a junior CIA officer named Richard Kellerman was found in the north Chinatown area of Washington. He'd been shot once in the chest with a 9-millimetre pistol. The slug was pretty badly chewed up, but from the rifling marks it looked like it had been fired from a Browning. His wallet and watch were missing, too, and his empty briefcase was dumped beside him. The police investigation didn't turn up any suspects, so the killing was written off as just another mugging that went wrong.'

'And obviously that's exactly what it might have been,' Richter suggested.

'I quite agree, but there are a couple of oddities. I've looked at Kellerman's duty roster. He was supposed to be at Langley all that day and so he shouldn't have been anywhere near Washington. That's the first thing. Second, late that afternoon he was recorded as a passenger in one of our limos that was driven to an unspecified destination. He left Langley in that car, but the vehicle came back empty. At the internal inquiry that followed, the chauffeur claimed he dropped Kellerman in central Washington but refused to explain why the CIA officer had been in the car at all, where else he'd driven him or whether there had been anybody else in the vehicle.'

'Surely the inquiry could have compelled him to answer?'

'The board tried hard, but he claimed he was acting under the direct orders of a senior CIA officer, and unless that officer specifically instructed him to explain his actions, he wouldn't do so. And, obviously, he wouldn't reveal the name of the officer either. He was disciplined, and that was all they could do, because there was no suggestion of any direct connection between the journey in the limo, the chauffeur himself and Kellerman's death. But the fact that the dead agent's name and the date of his death have now turned up written on a piece of paper obviously puts a different slant on those events of last January.'

'Absolutely,' Richter agreed. 'Perhaps the two men met in Washington, and Stevens then killed Kellerman. That might explain the date and the name, but I doubt if Stevens would ever write down anything that could link him to a killing. I think it's more likely that Kellerman was Gregory Stevens's briefing officer, and that explains what he was doing in Washington.'

'Maybe, yes. And if he was, then we need to work out if he really was killed by a mugger or if somebody ordered him to be eliminated after he'd delivered the briefing.'

'Are you serious? The Company doesn't kill briefing officers – at least, I sure as hell hope you don't.'

Westwood laughed shortly. 'No, we don't. If the CIA assassinated every officer once he'd delivered a briefing, there wouldn't be enough people left at Langley to sweep the floors. I've never heard of it happening before. But it worries me that Kellerman was killed on the very date that was written on the paper, and that means it's at least possible we're looking at something more than a random mugging.'

'Let me just get this straight. You think there's a real possibility that Gregory Stevens was tasked with some mission by Kellerman, and somebody at Langley then had Kellerman assassinated? But why?'

'Look, I still think that's a very unlikely scenario, but if Stevens's mission was extremely sensitive, there's at least a *possibility* that the guy running it might have decided to tie up one loose end for the sake of operational security. It's also worth pointing out that Kellerman was a very junior officer. Knowing the way the Agency works, I would have expected a middle-ranking agent to be given the job of briefing someone like Stevens, so that's a slight anomaly in itself.'

'You mean that a more senior officer would possibly have smelt a rat, and killing a mid-rank agent would have generated a more thorough investigation?'

'You said it,' Westwood confirmed.

'I think we're building castles in the sand here, John. But if we *are* right, what mission could Stevens have been given that would justify killing the guy who had tasked him with it?'

'I have absolutely no idea,' Westwood admitted.

American Embassy, Grosvenor Square, London

Carlin F. Johnson stared at the computer screen in front of him as he read the email for the third time.

Now there was no doubt at all. When he'd initiated VIPER, he'd set up four principal tripwires to alert him to anyone searching the Langley database for details of this operation. The first had been obvious – any mention of Gregory Stevens, the name of the agent tasked with the op. The second two were 'SM/VIPER' and 'Kellerman', respectively. The encrypted email he'd just opened had revealed that somebody had carried out searches for both within the last twenty-four hours. The good news was that Johnson knew there were no references to VIPER anywhere in the database, and 'Kellerman' was a dead end – he'd seen to that back in January. It was a pity he hadn't been able to delete all references to the junior officer from the database, but the computer's auditing system had prevented him doing that.

However, the fourth tripwire hadn't yet been triggered, which was good news. If it had been, Johnson would now be thinking very seriously of taking an unplanned and extended holiday somewhere, because signs of anyone searching for those words would mean that the operation was as good as blown, and he had no illusions about the fate awaiting him if that occurred. The fact that he'd been implementing a specific directive from The Special Group would do nothing to protect him, and he would be lucky to escape with his life.

His problem now was deciding what to do next. If Stevens was still out there, and sticking to the timetable, he should by now be somewhere in the south-east of England, and Johnson would prefer to remain here on the spot as he waited for the endgame. That was, after all, the reason he'd manipulated the system to get himself sent over to London in the first place. Once the final phase of the operation was concluded, Stevens himself would become a total liability and would then have to be silenced – permanently. Johnson had already decided to carry out that task himself, which meant he had to stay on in England.

But he was also seriously worried about the searches being carried out back at Langley on the database. He had no idea who was behind them, and that was something he really needed to rectify. If he knew who was trying to trace the operation, it might be possible to dissuade him – somehow – from continuing the search. He sat in deep thought for a few moments, then composed a message of his own, which he encrypted and marked as priority one and 'eyes only' for the addressee.

TIMEBOMB

Greenford, London

'It's time,' muttered the man in the driving seat of the white van.

His companion, slumped beside him with a baseball cap pulled low over his face, immediately sat up straight, glanced at his watch and nodded agreement. He picked up the *London A–Z* from the seat beside him and opened it to the page he'd already marked. The driver took out his mobile, consulted a crumpled sheet of paper and dialled a number.

'This is Alpha Two,' he said. 'We're getting mobile now, and estimate we'll be in position at minute fifty-five.'

Then he switched on the ignition, waited a moment for the diesel heater light on the dashboard to go out, then turned the key. The engine started and soon settled down to a steady rumble. The driver engaged first and pulled away, the Transit bouncing over the kerb as he steered the vehicle down the street.

'Turn left onto the main road at the end here,' his passenger instructed, 'then right at the second set of traffic lights.'

Ten minutes later, having caught both lights at red, the driver turned the van into a side street and pulled it to a halt almost directly outside an imposing building, again stopping on a double yellow line. He switched off the engine, and both men climbed out, the driver carefully locking the doors of the cab. They walked round to the back of the vehicle, unlocked and removed both padlocks from the two additional hasps. Opening the rear door, the passenger climbed into the van and pulled the door closed behind him. A couple of minutes later he emerged, jumped down to the ground and slammed the door closed again.

'Done?' the driver asked.

'It's done,' the other confirmed.

They replaced the padlocks, made a final check that all the doors were securely fastened, then headed away towards the main road beyond. Just as they turned out of the side street, the driver made another call using his mobile.

'Alpha Two is in position. Now on foot for the rendezvous.'

'Roger. Alpha One is mobile. Rendezvous in three minutes.'

In fact, it was nearer five minutes before the white 'Metropolitan Police' van nosed its way down a narrow street and stopped outside a row of terraced houses where the two men from the first vehicle were waiting.

The moment the Transit stopped, the rear door swung open and they quickly climbed inside. Without a word, they stripped off their blue overalls to reveal the white shirts and black trousers they were wearing underneath. In a couple of minutes they were clad in police uniforms identical to those worn by the two men already in the cab.

From the box bolted to the floor, they each took a Heckler & Koch MP5 sub-machine gun and four loaded magazines. One went into the weapon, the other three into custom-designed loops on their body armour. Then they picked up semi-automatic pistols, loaded them and secured them in their belt holsters.

All they had to do now was wait.

Chapter Fourteen

Monday
South-east London

Hans Morschel was getting increasingly fed up with London traffic. Every time he got into a car, it seemed, he found himself staring at traffic lights – almost invariably red – roadworks of some sort or an unmoving line of other vehicles.

'I won't be sorry to get out of here,' he muttered to Hagen as they sat in the Mercedes behind a heavily laden articulated lorry belching diesel fumes into the surrounding air.

'Relax,' his companion muttered, glancing at his watch. 'We've got plenty of time.'

'I know. I'm just pissed off with this place. It's worse than Munich, and that's saying something. How long now?' he asked.

Hagen studied his watch again. 'Maybe ten minutes,' he said, 'depending on the accuracy of the timer.'

Greenford, London

The white van illegally parked in Greenford had not so far attracted any official attention. No traffic wardens or police officers had noticed it, and those Londoners who had to travel down the same street, on foot or by car, simply muttered unfriendly epithets about 'white van man' as they squeezed past. The vehicle looked as if it was used primarily for deliveries, and in a sense this was true. In the locked rear compartment was a 50-gallon oil drum containing a carefully calculated mixture of diesel oil and fertilizer: a lethally explosive combination when in the right proportions, and Morschel had made absolutely sure that it *was* in the right proportions. Taped to the side of the drum was a simple trigger.

They'd considered detonating the charge using a mobile phone, but Morschel had finally decided that was too much of a risk. If the police somehow guessed that there might be a series of explosions triggered by cellphones, there was a good chance they would shut down the networks to prevent any further devices from functioning. Instead, they'd chosen to use one of the simplest and most effective of detonators: a small charge of Semtex fitted with a blasting cap, a battery and simple timer, which was then attached to the drum. There was enough plastic explosive in the detonator to wreck the van, but it would be the fertilizer bomb that would do the real damage.

As the two men had left the vehicle, they had set the timer for a period of fifteen minutes, but in fact the battery connections closed in a little over thirteen minutes and twenty seconds. Not that anyone was counting. The Semtex fired less than a tenth of a second later, and around half a second after that the fertilizer bomb detonated. The result was immediate and devastating. There was an enormous blast, and the Transit van simply ceased to exist. Metal panels and engine components flew in all directions like shrapnel. A boiling cloud of dust and particles from the explosion rose above the street itself. The ground floor of the adjacent building was pulverized, bricks and timbers and glass crushed into oblivion. Its structural integrity was fatally compromised, and seconds later part of the first floor gave way and tumbled into the void already created by the explosion.

Five people walking down the street were killed instantly, two of them so terribly mutilated that they would eventually only be identified by DNA evidence.

Up and down the same street, car and building alarms howled into life, in a sudden discordant cacophony.

The real target wasn't the building outside which the vehicle was parked, but in fact the one opposite, a medium-sized bank. The damage to this structure was markedly less, because the building had to be left safe for his men to enter, and Morshel had carefully calculated that the detonation would just blow in the windows and shatter the automatic glass doors. There would probably be numerous casualties inside, caused by flying glass and other debris, but Morschel had never been concerned about collateral damage.

Over the atonic wailing of the alarms, the sound of an approaching siren gradually became audible, and a minute or so later a police van screeched to a halt in the street immediately outside the bank. Pedestrians were still milling about in shock, many bleeding profusely from severe head wounds, others with merely superficial cuts. Other survivors of the blast lay on the pavements or in the roadway, most moaning and screaming, but some ominously still.

The rear doors of the van opened, and three men jumped out. They were wearing Metropolitan Police uniforms, and all carrying MP5 submachine guns and, incongruously, large black nylon holdalls and with flesh-coloured masks obscuring the faces under their helmets. They ignored everyone – dead, wounded, and those shocked but fortunately uninjured – and raced straight into the bank. The moment the last of them had vanished inside the building, the driver swung the van into an expert three-point turn that left it facing the main road, and their pre-planned escape route.

In the bank itself, the scene was chaotic. Glass splinters carpeted the floor, and advertising placards and bits of paper were scattered everywhere. Customers and clerks were wandering about in a daze but, as the three men entered, most turned to them with expressions of shocked relief. But these men had no intention of helping anyone there – they were simply going to help themselves. They moved swiftly into the positions and roles that were now so familiar to them.

In a line down the left-hand side of the bank there were half a dozen teller positions, each protected by a shatterproof glass screen, and these, though damaged, were mostly still intact. At one end was a solid door that led behind the counter, a keypad beside it, and that was their first target. Most of the lights had blown out, though the power was still on, and the keypad and electric lock were still functioning.

The leading 'officer' stepped up to the door, levelled his MP5 at the lock and fired a couple of short bursts. Wood splinters flew like confetti as the armour-piercing 9-millimetre rounds slammed into the door and the frame directly beside it, the yammer of the automatic weapon a further assault on everyone's ears after the explosion of the bomb.

They'd assumed that the frame would have a steel insert and the door itself a metal lining and, as the wood flew off in chunks, it was immediately obvious that this was correct. But that level of security was intended to protect the bank's assets against blaggers wielding sledgehammers and crowbars; against the rapid-fire assault by the armour-piercing rounds it stood no chance.

The German stepped back from the door and kicked out hard with the sole of his boot, aimed directly against the remains of the lock. The door flew open, and the man raced inside. He was joined behind the counter a couple of seconds later by one of his companions, carrying two holdalls. The third member of the team remained on the other side of the counter, his MP5 trained on the dazed and injured customers and staff, in case of any sign of resistance.

One of the intruders pushed the dazed tellers aside, forced open all the cash drawers one by one and began scooping handfuls of notes into his holdall, his MP5 now slung over his shoulder. The other crashed through to the manager's office, the door to which was already standing open. The room was empty, so he swung round, reached down and grabbed a male clerk who was cowering under the counter. He pulled the young man to his feet, slammed him back against the wall and rammed the muzzle of his MP5 into his stomach.

'Where's the fucking manager?' he snapped, his voice harsh, the guttural accent clearly German.

The clerk just stared at him, whether in shock or incomprehension. The German lifted the Heckler & Koch, slammed the butt against the side of the man's head and sent him tumbling senseless to the floor.

The terrorist strode across to a woman cashier and repeated the question. She took one look at his masked face and pointed silently at a middle-aged man crawling away on his hands and knees, his face streaming blood from a gash on the temple.

The German seized the older man's collar and pulled him to his feet. 'The safe,' he snapped. 'Open the safe.'

The manager shook his head. 'There's a time lock,' he stammered. 'I can only open it when—'

He got no further. The terrorist swung round, aimed his MP5 directly at one of the few tellers still standing and fired a three-round burst. The man tumbled backwards, the front of his shirt suddenly sporting three crimson circles as the slugs smashed into his chest at point-blank range, and slammed him into the wall. As his lifeless body slid down to the floor, the massive exit wounds left a gory vertical streak on the light-coloured paintwork.

'Now open the fucking safe.'

'Yes, yes. Just don't shoot, please.'

The manager led the way along a short corridor and into a small room, where he stopped in front of a solid steel door with a keyhole and combination lock fitted. He took a key from his jacket pocket and slid it into the lock. With hands trembling from shock and outrage, he began turning the dial. The first time, he missed one of the numbers, either deliberately or by accident, and the German grunted in annoyance.

'Last chance,' he growled. 'Get it wrong next time and we're out of here. But you won't be because you'll be dead. Just think about that.'

The manager hastily wiped the sweat from his hands on his trousers, and started again. As the lock clicked on the final number, this time he was able to turn the key. He then seized the handle and pulled the door open, swinging easily on its massive hinges.

It wasn't a particularly big safe, because it wasn't a particularly big bank – Morschel had chosen his targets carefully, avoiding the larger branches likely to be equipped with better security systems or safes that would be more difficult to crack. Inside there were piles of banknotes in multiple currencies waiting invitingly on the shelves, and the German could see dollars and euros as well as pounds.

'Fill them,' he ordered, tossing the two nylon holdalls to the manager, then stepped back to the door and glanced along the corridor to check that his men were still in control. The terrorist emptying the tills was now standing beside the counter, the bulging holdall at his feet. He nodded to signal that he was finished.

As the manager finished stuffing money into the holdalls he stepped back, trembling, clearly wondering if he was going to survive this encounter. The German slung his weapon, plucked both bags from the ground, turned and left the room without a word. As he ran towards the main door, his two companions followed him.

Outside, the fake 'police' van was waiting, blue lights flashing and the rear doors wide open. The three terrorists jumped in and slammed the doors shut. Immediately, the driver gunned the engine and accelerated hard down the street, the siren blaring to clear a path.

In the back, the leader pulled off his mask and looked at his watch. The entire raid had taken under four and a half minutes, thirty seconds less than Morschel had planned.

As the van screamed down the centre of the road, drivers pulling their vehicles over to allow it to pass, he took out his mobile phone, dialled a number and waited for the call to be answered. When it was, he said simply, 'Alpha is complete.'

Hammersmith, London

Richter pushed open the door of Simpson's office. The call from his superior had been brief, peremptory and almost entirely uninformative.

Simpson had the phone to his ear and silently pointed to the chair in front of his desk.

'How many dead?' he asked and jotted something on the pad in front of him, as Richter sat down.

A few seconds later he ended the call and gazed across the desk. 'Now we know what Morschel and his merry men were talking about. An IED has just been exploded outside a bank in Greenford. What appeared to be a Metropolitan Police van arrived on the scene a few minutes later. Three men got out and robbed the bank, killing one of the staff members in the process. It's still very confused over there, but the initial reports suggest maybe half a dozen people were killed, about thirty injured, one building was totally wrecked, and the robbery netted perhaps three or four hundred thousand pounds.'

Richter digested that for a few seconds, then shook his head. 'I doubt it,' he said.

'What the fuck's that supposed to mean? I've just come off the line to the Five duty officer, who was briefed five minutes ago by the Met. This has all just happened, so what exactly don't you understand?'

'I don't mean about the robbery. I mean that if this *is* connected to

Morschel, it's not what he would consider a major terrorist attack. The conversation recorded by the German police in Stuttgart mentioned the "big one" in London. But to me, this incident sounds like the Germans just picking up some loose change to fund their operation.'

'Six people are dead, Richter. Don't forget that.'

'I'm not. I just don't think this is all that German bastard has got planned.'

'So what, then, do you think *would* count as the "big one"? Doing a Guy Fawkes job at Westminster? Something like that?'

'Maybe. Something impressive, that's for sure, and knocking over a high street bank doesn't count, in my opinion. Half the appeal for the terrorist mind-set is the shock factor, like knocking over the Twin Towers while most of the world sat and watched it on satellite television.' Richter paused for a second or two, thinking. 'How big a bank was it?' he asked, finally.

'What do you mean?'

'I don't know how they classify banks – branches, sub-branches or whatever. What I'm interested in is the size of the bank, and the sort of money it was likely to hold. In other words, was this a major bank raid that went wrong, with the result that they walked out with less than half a million? Or did they deliberately pick a small bank and get away with most of what was there?'

'I see where you're going with that,' Simpson said. 'I don't know, but I'll find out.' He picked up the phone, to ask Thames House a couple of questions.

'Right,' he said eventually, replacing the receiver, 'basically Five don't know for certain because the Met haven't told them – information's still coming in, obviously – but they think it was just a small local bank, and the take was probably most of what was currently in the safe.' Simpson eyed Richter questioningly. 'You think this is just a diversionary tactic, that Morschel's got something else up his sleeve?'

'Makes sense to me. And while half the Met descends on Greenford looking for clues that they probably won't find, I wouldn't mind betting Morschel's out there right now organizing another withdrawal somewhere else in London.'

'You could be right,' Simpson said. 'I'll pass that suggestion on to the Met through Five.'

'It won't help. There are probably thousands of banks in the Greater London area, and these bastards could be planning to hit almost any one of them. They have the element of surprise, and there's nothing we can do about that. What are the plods up to now?'

'They're instituting checks at all exit points from the UK, working on the assumption that these guys are German and so they'll want to get back to the continent with their ill-gotten gains.'

'That's probably a waste of time, seeing how leaky the Channel ports are.'

'Agreed. Apart from that, they're probably chasing down the only actual lead they've got so far.'

'The fake police van?'

'Exactly. The witnesses aren't going to be a lot of help, since most of them would still be in shock after the explosion, and I doubt anyone would have noticed a little detail like the van's number plate. But it's possible we might get something useful from the CCTV cameras in the area.'

'And don't forget that van had to have come from somewhere. My guess is they stole it and faked the markings themselves, but there's a possibility they hired it from one of those companies that supply film props. Somebody's chasing that down already, I hope?'

'If they aren't, they will be as soon as I've briefed Five,' Simpson said.

'And the same applies to the gear these guys were wearing. I presume they were all dressed as policemen?'

'So I've been told.'

'OK, what do you want me to do?'

Simpson looked surprised. 'Get yourself over to Greenford, of course. It's only just up the road. Five want a liaison officer there, as usual. More importantly, you know about Morschel, and the plods don't, so you might come across something that's significant. You're still armed, presumably?'

Richter eased open the left side of his jacket and nodded. 'Right, then,' he said, standing up. 'I'd better get going.'

A2, south-east London

The Mercedes finally reached the dual-carriageway section of the A2, and Morschel began to accelerate, though checking his speed and watching out for cameras.

His mobile rang as they passed Bexley, and Hagen picked it up to answer it. The conversation was brief, just a few words.

'The second group's in position, and both vehicles have reported ready,' he announced, but almost immediately the phone rang again. This time the conversation took longer, and when Hagen ended this call he was smiling.

'Alpha is clear and complete,' he said. 'They've ditched the police van and everything except the weapons, and they're now in their getaway cars and heading for the Channel ports. They've split the take between them, and a rough count gives us just over four-hundred-thousand pounds' worth of mixed currencies in total.'

'Good. If the other groups are as successful, we'll have sufficient funds to last us for quite a while. And as long as this last phase works as we've planned, we've got the final payment from our Islamic colleagues to look forward to as well.'

Hagen looked at the dashboard clock, then down at the road map on his lap. 'We'll reach the marina in about ten minutes, so we're pretty much on time.'

American Embassy, Grosvenor Square, London

News of the bank raid had reached Grosvenor Square at about the same time as the Security Service duty officer at Thames House had been notified, and the information, although sketchy, was flashed to every computer within the building as a ticker running across the bottom of the screen. When Carlin Johnson saw it, he knew exactly what it meant. VIPER had to be running, and Stevens must still be out there, somewhere. He also knew it was time he left the building.

As he stood up, his computer emitted a soft tone indicating receipt of an email, so he sat down again and clicked the mouse to open it. It originated from Langley, encrypted and designated for his eyes only. Johnson ran the decryption routine and studied the text. Then he sat back in his chair and muttered a single expletive. All his contact back at Langley had been able to find out so far was that the person who had run the searches on Walnut was John Westwood, and that wasn't good news. Westwood was a Langley wheel, not some inquisitive junior officer who could be easily warned off. But, Johnson now reasoned, if Stevens was still out there directing VIPER, the endgame was now so close – a matter of hours, rather than days – that it might not matter. Once the final phase was complete, he could locate Stevens – not difficult, because the man had been given an emergency contact routine – and eliminate him.

That would neatly tie up the sole remaining loose end, and none of the other four people indoctrinated into the operation would be able to say a word about it, *ever*, because the whole plan was their idea, and admitting to any part of it would be tantamount to signing their own death warrants. And VIPER had been specifically designed to point the finger of suspicion in a direction well away from Langley, Virginia, so once the job was finished and Stevens was dead, that would be the end of it. Whatever trail there might be would stop right there.

Greenford, London

Finding the scene of the bombing wasn't difficult. Richter just followed a couple of speeding police cars and an ambulance, then stopped the pool Ford, half on the pavement, just short of the location and walked the rest of the way.

The street was a scene of devastation. On one side of the road and across half of the pavement was the floor-pan and a scattering of other mechanical components that had previously comprised a medium-sized van. Twisted, burnt and blackened bits of the bodywork were strewn around the scene, some of them dozens of yards from the epicentre of the explosion. Brick rubble, broken glass and pieces of shattered timber from the partially destroyed building added to the mass of debris.

The street was still chaotic, with police officers, firemen and ambulance crews running in all directions, trying to help the injured, or putting out the handful of fires that had started and generally trying to restore some kind of order. The flashing blue and red lights of the parked vehicles provided a kind of surreal additional illumination, and shouted orders and cries of agony from the wounded victims combined to create a continual torrent of noise. Lying close to the remains of the van, half a dozen motionless shapes testified to the horrendous effectiveness of the attack.

Richter was aware that he was essentially a spectator, and that there was almost nothing he could do to assist either the police or the casualties. And, frankly, he wasn't convinced that there was any point in him being there at all. Any clues left in the bomb vehicle would no longer exist, unless some forensic genius with a microscope managed to pick something out of the total wreckage. The bank raid, too, had been fast, brutal and extremely efficient, and he doubted very much if the bad guys were incompetent enough to leave behind anything that might help identify them.

He watched the activity from the end of the street, taking in the scene and snapping a series of pictures with a small digital camera. The images might help him reconstruct the sequence of events when he got back to Hammersmith. Or not, as the case might be. He really didn't know, and didn't particularly care. The bomb had exploded, the bank had been robbed, and there was nothing that anybody could now do about either event apart from clear up the mess. In his opinion, the most important thing was to try to deduce where the next raid would take place.

And that, as Richter had already pointed out to Simpson, was going to be sodding difficult, given the number of banks scattered across London. And it wasn't just banks: there were also building societies, jewellery shops and a host of other potentially attractive and high-value targets in the city. Assuming the gang was planning another hit – and that was still Richter's best guess – they could next strike absolutely anywhere.

The bank itself was fairly small, with houses on one side and shops on the other, and faced a short parade of businesses on the opposite pavement, where the van had been parked. There was nothing about the street, or the bank, or anything else that Richter could see that struck him as being even slightly unusual. It was an entirely typical London thoroughfare. Without looking at the street names or consulting a map, there would be no way of telling exactly where it was located.

That started a new train of thought. Richter took a few last pictures, trying to get a panorama of the scene in front of him, then walked back to his car and rummaged around in the glove-box. He pulled out a *London and Home Counties A–Z* road map that showed the entire city and a good portion of south-east England, opened it up and studied it for a few minutes.

Then he started the Fiesta's engine, put the car into gear and performed an illegal U-turn before heading back towards Hammersmith. On the way, he pulled out his mobile and told the duty officer what he thought he might have discovered.

Chapter Fifteen

Monday
Hammersmith, London

'This is bloody thin, Richter,' Simpson snapped. They were again meeting in his office, the Home Counties map lying open on the desk between them.

'I know it is, but you told me to visit the scene of the Greenford bombing, and this is the only useful conclusion I reached.'

'Useful? That's not what I'd call it. Is this really all you could come up with?'

'Simpson, a fucking *bomb* had gone off. What did you expect me to find – a trail of fingerprints? Maybe a picture of one of the bad guys lighting the fuse? The whole street's like a war zone, plods and medics running in all directions, blood, bodies and bits of debris all over the place. This was the only thing that struck me while I was there and, yes, I might be completely wrong.'

'I don't think "might" is the correct word, Richter. You really think the terrorists chose that bank in that street simply because it would be easy for them to get to the motorway after they'd done the job? Give me a break.'

'I didn't actually say that. What I suggested was that the proximity of the A40 and the M4, two major roads heading directly out of London, might have been a contributing factor in their choice. That's all. Obviously they would also have had to scout the area, select their target and probably go inside the bank a few times to check the layout. But if they do another one, as I believe they will, I'll bet it's also close to a major arterial road. Look, these guys are probably German, so they won't know London well, and the last thing they'd want to do is get stuck somewhere in the backstreets, trying to find a way out. This isn't some real-life rerun of *The Italian Job*.'

'I'm not convinced by any of this, Richter. I still think we may have already witnessed Hans Morschel's "big one".'

'Not a chance.' Richter shook his head firmly. 'I reckon this is something his group's organized just to get us looking the wrong way and put some extra funds in his pocket. I'm convinced he's got something else in mind. And another thing. That first bomb blast was in north-west London, so if there's another IED somewhere in the city, my bet is it will also be north of the river.'

'Why?'

'Because I think Morschel is deliberately trying to get us to concentrate our resources in the wrong area. Most of the Met's mobile patrol officers are now probably in the Greenford area, leaving the way clear for another attack somewhere else. Once that happens, there'll be two serious crime scenes in London, and they'll become the total focus of all police activity. So if Morschel has got something much bigger planned here, it will almost certainly involve a target south of the river.'

'Like what?'

'Take your pick. There are plenty of possibilities, but my guess is that he'll be aiming to hit something instantly recognizable, like the Royal Festival Hall, the London Eye or maybe even Vauxhall Cross. Don't forget, the IRA did a fair bit of damage there with their home-made mortar.'

'Yes, but Legoland's pretty well protected these days. I doubt if even a suicide bomber could get close enough to do much damage, and I don't think Morschel's men are likely to have embraced radical Islam.'

'It's well protected on the south side, from the road, but what about from the Thames? Suppose Morschel is planning something with a stolen boat or a barge? Remember that sodding great fertilizer bomb the IRA detonated in the City? That was just a truck bomb, so think how much more explosive they could pack into a barge. And, come to think of it, the Palace of Westminster is another obvious target in the area.'

At that moment, Simpson's direct line to the duty office buzzed, and he reached over to answer it. 'Where?' he asked, after just a few seconds. 'Right, got it,' he said.

'Another one?' Richter asked.

'At a fairly small bank branch over in Barnet,' Simpson confirmed.

'And the same MO, presumably.'

'Exactly. An IED in a parked van, and then three men wearing police uniforms hit the bank. It looks like about the same number dead, but fewer serious injuries. The haul from this bank's estimated at around three hundred grand.'

Richter stood up and pointed silently to the location of Barnet on the open map.

'I know, I know,' Simpson said, glancing down. 'It's nice and close to the M1, or the M25 if they felt like a challenge. So you might be right after all. But even if you are, what can we do about it?'

'Bugger all, as far as I can see. Virtually every district in Greater London has access to either a motorway or a major feeder route. The only thing I'd suggest is that the plods should concentrate their searches on the outer suburbs, because I don't think these comedians are going to try hitting a bank in the centre. The problem is that London's full of white vans driven by barely competent idiots who park illegally as a matter of routine, so spotting the one that's got a bomb ticking away in the back is going to be virtually impossible.'

'Right,' Simpson said. 'I'll pass your thoughts on to Five. If you've any other bright ideas, this would be a good time to share them. You've still no clue what Morschel's real target could be?'

'None at all. There's a huge choice of buildings and landmarks he could hit, but whatever he's picked will be deliberately spectacular.'

Romford, London

Close to a bank in Romford, two men climbed out of a white van and headed off to their pre-briefed rendezvous position. Twelve and a half minutes later, the IED in the back of the vehicle detonated, and a mere eight minutes after that, four men wearing Metropolitan Police uniforms were driving away from the scene at high speed, nylon holdalls packed with cash lying on the floor of the van between them.

Once clear of Romford, and about to join the M25 motorway, one of the men sitting in the rear of the Transit made a brief call on his mobile to report that Charlie group's operation had been completely successful.

Hammersmith, London

Richter's internal phone rang just after three.

'There's been another one,' Simpson reported grimly. 'A bank in Romford. Same MO, same sort of casualties. These guys really are pissing all over us.' His voice sounded old and tired.

Richter scanned the large-scale London map displayed on the wall of his office. 'Easy access to three main roads,' he pointed out. 'From there, they've got a choice of the A12, A127 or even the M25.'

'Don't rub it in, Richter. Is that the last strike, do you think?'

'No idea, but they've been going in a more or less clockwise direction around north London, and this one is the closest to the Thames and the river crossings, so it might be their final shot. On the other hand, that's probably too simplistic, so I think there'll probably be another one or two.'

'This is turning out to be a very bad day, Richter.'

'I wouldn't disagree with that. I'd also suggest you don't nip out to Barclays until we know this really is over.'

'Don't be flippant.'

Richter had barely replaced the phone when it rang again.

'Any news?' John Westwood asked, speaking from Langley.

'Plenty,' Richter said, 'but I've no idea if any of it relates to Gregory Stevens.' Quickly, he explained about the three incidents in London.

'That doesn't sound at all like anything Stevens would have been tasked with,' Westwood commented finally. 'I realize he was an ex-CIA covert agent and so not subject to the usual rules, but I still don't think he would have gotten himself involved with a group of bombers, and certainly not with a gang of bank robbers. Is it possible these events are entirely separate? Are you looking at some terrorist group that's self-funding – like you told me Morschel's "Stammheim" is – and whoever killed Stevens is someone completely different?'

'Maybe. I really don't know, but we think – or, rather, I think – there's something else going on here behind the scenes, something we know nothing about yet. My worry is that it *is* in fact Stammheim that's doing these bank jobs, but they're intended just as a diversion to get us all looking the wrong way. My guess is that Morschel's real target is a key structure somewhere in London, maybe one of the Thames bridges or even a tunnel, and that—' Richter broke off suddenly as another thought struck him. 'John, sorry, I'll have to call you back.'

Richter opened his web browser and input a search into Google, typing the three letters 'FRB', but that only produced a number of links directing him to various Federal Reserve Banks throughout America. But if the 'B' didn't refer to some bank, what about a bridge? He thought for a few seconds, checked his London map and then input 'F R Bridge'. The only thing that came up that seemed in any way relevant was 'Fulham Railway Bridge', and that, he realized, could easily be the target Morschel was after. A small barge, loaded with explosives and detonated under the bridge as a District Line underground train was passing over it would kill or injure hundreds of passengers, not to mention the months of disruption to the underground system and the millions of pounds it would cost to rebuild it. OK, it wouldn't be as big a bang as the Twin Towers going down, but it would still qualify as 'the big one', and it would hit London hard.

For a few seconds he just sat there thinking, then stood up and walked across to the wall opposite, where a large-scale map of the British Isles was pinned. He first searched the entire area around London, then tapped his finger on a spot near Stowmarket in Suffolk.

'That'll do,' he muttered, stepping back to his desk to access his contacts database on the computer.

He dialled a number, and his call was answered almost immediately.

'This is a Military Flash call,' he announced. 'Twenty-two Squadron, please. Duty pilot.'

Having explained what he wanted, Richter ended the call less than a minute later, then rang the armourer in the basement to issue crisp instructions, before checking his database once again and dialling Karl Wolff's office.

A voice answered in German, and for several frustrating seconds Richter tried explaining what he wanted, before realizing that the man at the other end spoke very little English. He then found Wolff's mobile number and tried that, too. The German police officer answered almost immediately.

'Karl, it's Paul Richter in London. We have a problem here. I urgently need some information about Hans Morschel.'

'We've heard about these bombings and the robberies,' Wolff grunted. 'Do you reckon he's responsible?'

'Yes, probably, but that's not why I'm calling. When you briefed me about Stammheim during the operation in Stuttgart, I think you said Morschel might have had a military background. If so, any idea which branch he was in?'

'Frankly, no. It's just that his operations always run with such military precision. He seems able to decide what he wants, set out a timetable, and then brief his men thoroughly to achieve it. Why do you ask?'

'Because I've suddenly realized what's been staring me in the face for the last few days, and it's finally starting to make sense. I think he's planned a massive explosion here in London and I'm trying to work out what his target might be. So I wondered if you knew whether he was competent at handling boats.'

'Sorry, I've no idea. How big an explosion?'

'Big enough, Karl. Sorry, I'll have to call you later.'

Rochester, Kent

Locking the Mercedes, Morschel followed Hagen along the pontoon to where they'd moored the boat.

As they stepped on board, Morschel glanced at his watch. 'We've got two hours left before we have to leave the marina,' he said. 'That should be plenty of time.'

Hagen nodded. 'But even then, it's not that critical. I mean, fifteen or twenty minutes either side wouldn't make too much difference?'

'No, but ideally I'd like this finished before the tide turns this afternoon. That's the optimum time.'

The two men set to work. The autopilot was working properly, and they'd already tested it, so all Morschel had to do was enter into the GPS the exact coordinates of the boat's destination – a point it would reach long after they had left the area. He entered the figures, and then he and Hagen both checked them twice. Then they consulted an Admiralty chart and carefully entered the waypoints they needed, because they would be abandoning the boat once they reached the open water that lay beyond Lower Upnor, and the most direct route from that point to the vessel's destination was overland, which clearly wouldn't work. The waypoints would ensure that the boat stayed in the open channels and, as far as possible, kept clear of all obstructions.

They did have a back-up option in mind but, until Ahmed bin Salalah arrived at the marina, they had no idea of how comprehensive it would be, and Morschel was determined that the boat's navigation system would still do the job even if the Arab failed to turn up.

The next part of their preparations was fairly complex. The GPS/autopilot unit Morschel had bought included a warning system – a low-voltage electric bell that would ring once a particular destination or waypoint had been reached – and this was one of the two features that had been the major selling points for him. The idea of this device was that, in open-water navigation, where there was little danger of collision, a single-handed sailor could set the GPS to wake him up when the boat reached a specific location. He could then check his radar and do a visual sweep to ensure that no other vessels were nearby, then grab another hour in his bunk.

Morschel had no use for the bell, of course, but he did have a very good one for the electric current that powered it. The two wires Hagen had routed from the cache of plastic explosive concealed beneath the floorboards terminated in dozens of electric detonators, commonly known as blasting caps, wired in parallel and each pushed deep into one of the packets of Semtex. Any one of them could trigger the entire mass of explosive, but redundancy was always a good idea.

Hagen had already threaded the wires through the small hole he'd drilled in the bulkhead between cabin and cockpit, and they were still lying coiled up on the floor below the wheel. Morschel watched closely as Hagen attached one of these wires to the end of the bell wire from the GPS unit and carefully taped the ends together. The last thing they would do before they left the boat would be to attach the second wire to it in the same way. Once they'd done that, the activation of the bell circuit once the GPS unit had successfully navigated the boat to its destination would send a current down to the electric detonators, and that would trigger the explosive.

It was a simple enough plan, and Morschel reckoned there wasn't a great deal that could go wrong with it. He would have preferred to trigger the device himself, using a mobile phone, but that was now impossible because of the target. If he was close enough to check the boat's position, he'd be unlikely to survive the subsequent detonation. Nor could he use a standard timer, as his men had been doing in London, because for the plan to work the explosive had to fire only when the boat reached the precise location of the target, and that would obviously depend upon the currents and tides. But he did incorporate one device, as a last-ditch back-up, set to detonate the explosive fifteen minutes after the latest possible estimated time of the boat reaching its destination. One way or the other, those charges were going to blow.

With the first stage of the wiring now completed, both men turned their attention to installing comprehensive anti-tamper devices. These were small charges of Semtex with the usual electric detonators, and Hagen and Morschel spent some forty minutes connecting them to the obvious weak points of the system – the door into the cabin, the wiring that led from the GPS/autopilot unit, the engine and steering controls, and so on.

When they finished, the cockpit had become a maze of wires and junctions, enough to confuse anyone. Once they'd made the final two connections, just before abandoning the vessel, anyone attempting to remove the autopilot linkages, or disable the engine, or simply open the cabin door, would be blown to pieces. The explosion of one of these devices, Morschel realized, would probably also destroy the GPS unit and almost certainly trigger the main explosion, but there wasn't anything he could do about that. All he could hope was that nobody would guess what was happening until it was too late to stop it.

TIMEBOMB

Hammersmith, London

'It's Richter, and I'm on the way up to see you. And before you wonder what all the noise is, I've just whistled up a SAR chopper from Wattisham. It should be landing on the roof helipad in about twenty minutes.'

Before Simpson could do more than splutter the beginnings of a question, Richter had replaced the telephone and was on his way out of the door.

'What the hell are you dressed like that for?' Simpson demanded, as soon as his subordinate entered. Richter was wearing jeans, trainers and a leather biker's jacket, a Kevlar waistcoat, shoulder holster and the Browning just visible beneath it, and carrying a SPAS-12 combat shotgun and a Heckler & Koch MP5 sub-machine gun. 'What's with the weapons?' Simpson pointed. 'And why do you need a helicopter?'

'I have a horrible feeling I know what Morschel is planning. That's why I need the chopper, because I've got to get to Fulham pretty damn quick. And I need the weapons because no doubt Morschel and his men will be heavily armed.'

'Fulham? It's just down the road. You can drive there in fifteen minutes. What the hell do you need a helicopter for?'

'According to our late friend Stevens, Morschel's biggest target is right here in London, and he overheard some of the terrorists talking about "FRB". The only London district lying south of the river I can think of that begins with "F" is Fulham, and the most obvious target there is the railway bridge, hence "R B".'

Simpson swung round to look at the map on the wall behind him. 'You're still convinced the attack will be south of the river, then?'

'Yes, because all of the car-bombs have been to the north.'

'So . . .' Simpson broke off as his phone suddenly rang. A minute later he replaced the receiver. 'There's been another bombing,' he said, 'this time at Wanstead. And, to save you checking, it was nice and handy for the M11 and A12. That's four so far.' He returned his gaze to the map. 'But you've forgotten Falconwood.'

'What?'

'Falconwood. It's south-east, out by Eltham. And, actually, you do know that Fulham is *north* of the Thames?'

'Yes, but if I'm right, the target is actually on the river itself. And I've never even heard of Falconwood.'

'No,' Simpson agreed, 'frankly, nor had I until I looked at this map, but maybe you should still check it before you swoop out of the sky on Fulham with all guns blazing.'

'That wasn't exactly what I'd planned. I was going to check all the boats and barges heading towards the bridge there, and I'll only start shooting at them if they fire at me first.'

Simpson looked doubtful. 'You think they're planning their big attack so soon?' he asked.

'Yes, obviously. They'll want to take full advantage of all the confusion caused by those car-bombs. My guess is that whatever vessel they're using to deliver their device must already be fairly close to the Fulham Railway Bridge. That's why I whistled up the chopper.'

'So what about Falconwood?'

At that moment the throbbing of rotor blades became clearly audible even through the bulletproof glass of Simpson's office windows. Then the noise died away as the aircraft landed on the reinforced flat roof.

'If you're bothered, check it out yourself. I don't have the time. What you can do, though, is call the Met and suggest they get some ARVs and snipers down to Fulham straight away.'

SAR Sea King helicopter, callsign 'Rescue 24'

'Who are you exactly, and where are we going?' the RAF pilot demanded as Richter strapped in and pulled on a headset.

'Let's get airborne first, and I'll fill you in on the way. Head for Fulham, and get down low over the Thames. And put your foot down – I'm in a hurry.'

'Fulham? Christ, you could have walked there in the time it took us to fly here from Wattisham.'

'I know,' Richter snapped, 'but just do it now, will you?'

'Right. Going off intercom to get clearance,' the pilot said.

A few seconds later, the noise of the two jet engines rose to a scream, and the big helicopter rose into the air, adopting a nose-down attitude as the pilot swung the aircraft around to the east and accelerated.

'Now who are you, then?' the pilot demanded again.

'My name's Paul Richter, and I suppose you could say I'm a civil servant.'

'A fucking well-armed civil servant,' the aircrewman contributed. 'Boss, this guy's carrying a sub-machine gun, a combat shotgun, even a pistol under his arm.'

'I do like to be prepared,' Richter said.

'OK, Mr Richter, we're on the way. Now answer my question: what are we supposed to be doing down in Fulham? In case you hadn't noticed, this is a military rescue helicopter, not a taxi service. If you just needed to get there in a hurry, you could have whistled up a civilian Jet Ranger or something.'

'I was aware of that, thank you,' Richter replied. 'I called you because Wattisham is pretty close to London, and I know you've got a maximum response time of fifteen minutes in daylight hours. That was one thing but, more important, this chopper has a winch and a guy in the back who knows how to use it. Your average Jet Ranger doesn't possess either.'

'So this *is* a rescue, then?' the pilot asked.

'In a manner of speaking, yes. I'm looking for some kind of river vessel loaded with explosives that a bunch of German terrorists is intending to blow up under Fulham Railway Bridge, most likely when an underground train is crossing it.'

'Are you sure?' the pilot asked doubtfully.

'Right now,' Richter said, 'we're not sure of anything, but that seems the most logical deduction. Why?'

'It's just that a railway bridge is a really hard target. I mean, it's designed to take the weight of a train, so it's incredibly strong, all reinforced concrete piers and massive steel girders. Even demolition teams find them difficult to destroy by using shaped charges and drilling holes into the concrete for the explosives. I'm not sure that even a barge full of Semtex would be enough to bring one down.'

'Are you an explosives expert, or what?'

'No,' the pilot replied, 'but I did watch a programme about bridge demolition on the Discovery Channel a few weeks ago. It was really interesting.'

'I'm sure it was,' Richter muttered, as the helicopter dropped down over Putney Bridge. The railway bridge was right in front of them, and the helicopter banked as it overflew the structure.

Looking down at the massive reinforced concrete piers and monumental steelwork, Richter had to concede that the pilot had made a good point. Blowing a hole in something constructed like that wouldn't be easy, and he experienced a sudden hollow feeling in his stomach. Suppose he'd completely misread Morschel's intentions? What if the German had a completely different target in mind?

And as he stared up and down the river, and saw nothing looking even remotely like a vessel carrying an improvised bomb, these doubts were reinforced.

'Just take a quick flip half a mile down-river,' Richter instructed, 'then do the same upstream, and keep your eyes peeled for anything suspicious.'

Ten minutes later, they gave up. All the river traffic they'd overflown seemed depressingly normal and legitimate.

'What's the terrorists' objective?' the pilot asked, as he turned the helicopter back towards Fulham.

'A big bang,' Richter replied, 'and the bigger the better. Somewhere in the London area.'

'Well, if I was him, I know exactly where I'd go to set off my load of plastic explosive.'

'Where?' Richter asked, sharply.

So the pilot told him.

Rochester, Kent

The two Germans double-checked all the connections they'd made to the wiring, making sure that everything was absolutely correct and secure, because the small vessel had quite a long way to go to reach its objective and probably would have to travel over fairly rough water. Though the marina itself was sheltered, there was quite a stiff wind blowing, and they knew that once the boat left the River Medway, the sea would become quite choppy. The last thing they wanted was for the weapon to detonate prematurely or, worse, for a connection to come loose and prevent the explosion from occurring at all.

They'd just completed their final checks when Hagen spotted two figures heading along the pontoon towards them. He nudged Morschel, and they both climbed out of the boat to meet the new arrivals.

The Saudi looked as immaculate as ever, and he was accompanied by another man, almost as big as bin Salalah. Probably in his late twenties and wearing casual clothes, his features were regular, his face tanned, but what the two Germans noticed straightaway was that his eyes shone with a strange fervour.

'This is Badri,' bin Salalah said. 'He's one of my cousins and has volunteered to accompany the two of you on this vital mission.'

'Your cousin?' Morschel asked.

'Yes.' Bin Salalah looked slightly surprised at such a question. 'I'd always rather offer this kind of opportunity to a member of my family if possible.'

'Opportunity?' Morschel thought and realized in a single moment of crystal-clear revelation that he would never, ever, begin to understand the Arab mind.

'He *does* know the schedule?' Hagen asked.

'Oh, yes,' Badri replied firmly, his English fluent but heavily accented. 'I also know you will both be leaving the boat well before it reaches its target. When Ahmed suggested I consider joining this mission, that was one of my first concerns. No offence to either of you, but I have no wish to share my moment of glory with a couple of infidels.'

'Jesus,' Morschel muttered. 'OK, can you handle the boat if something goes wrong en route?'

'I have sailed several times,' Badri said, with a trace of pride, 'but I had understood the boat would be automatically guided to its destination.'

'It certainly should be.' Morschel nodded. 'We've fitted a GPS and linked it to an autopilot. It was just in case something went wrong out in the estuary. Are you competent enough to take over if the GPS fails, say?'

'If you mark the precise position on a chart, and there's a compass on board, yes.'

Which was exactly the right answer, of course, though Morschel doubted if anything really would fail. The GPS and autopilot combination had been designed to be robust enough for trans-ocean sailing, which was one reason it had been so expensive, and it now only had to hang together for a couple of hours at the most.

'OK, Badri, welcome to the team.' Morschel turned to bin Salalah and glanced at his watch. 'Now we need to hot-wire one of these other boats.'

Hagen nodded. 'There's a twenty-footer at the other end of this pontoon. Judging by the state of it, it's not been used recently, and I don't think there's even an alarm fitted. That should do us.'

'OK, we'll get it now, then, just in case there's any problem. Badri, please just hang on here for a few minutes, then we'll talk you through the controls and other stuff.'

'No problem,' bin Salalah said. 'That will give us time to take the photographs.'

As the two Germans walked away down the pontoon, Badri stepped aboard the boat, stood in the cockpit and raised a copy of the Koran above his head. Bin Salalah removed a digital camera from his jacket pocket and took a series of photographs of the *shahid*, pictures that he would post on the Internet and release to the news media once this operation was completed. Following bin Salalah's explicit directions, Badri had already made a video explaining his motivation for choosing martyrdom. That, too, bin Salalah would be releasing in a day or two. It was essential for radical Islam that, not only was this attack successful, but the reasons behind it were clearly explained.

At the far end of the pontoon was moored a slightly grubby-looking craft, a little larger than the one Morschel had bought, with a blue hull and white superstructure, the cockpit currently hidden by a light blue cover that was torn in a couple of places. And Hagen was right: it didn't look as if anyone had been anywhere near it for weeks.

'There's no power line,' Morschel observed, 'so even if there's an alarm fitted, the battery will probably be flat by now. As long as the engine works, it should be fine.'

They glanced round but could see the entire marina was virtually deserted, and there was nobody anywhere near the pontoon they were standing on. Hagen bent down and released the eyelet securing one corner of the cover, then swiftly unhitched half a dozen more. He lifted the edge of the cover, peered into the cockpit, then stepped on board. He unclipped the rest of the eyelets, pulled off the cover entirely and folded it.

The boat had a cabin just forward of the cockpit, the door secured with a small padlock that yielded without any particular difficulty to the screwdriver Hagen carried in his pocket. He tossed the cover inside the cabin and turned his attention to the control panel, while Morschel checked the fuel level.

'We've got about three-quarters of a tank,' he announced. 'That should be more than enough.'

The boat had a good-sized outboard motor, with all the controls, including the ignition system, slaved to the control panel. Hagen unscrewed a small inspection hatch on one side of it and peered inside. The terminals of the ignition switch were clearly visible. He clipped two leads to a couple of the wires he could see and touched the bare ends together. Nothing happened: no spark, and no lights illuminated.

'Either the battery's been disconnected or it's totally flat,' he said. 'If it's got no charge left at all, we might have to pick another boat.'

Below the control panel was a small square box, the lid again secured with a padlock. As with the cabin door, a few tugs from Hagen's screwdriver freed the lock. He opened the lid and looked inside. There was a heavy-duty 12-volt battery, both terminals connected, and with an isolator switch screwed to the side of the box. Hagen looked at the switch, then reached down and rotated it. Immediately an alarm began shrilling, and he turned it off again.

'It's here,' Morschel said, pointing at a small speaker attached to the bulkhead above the wheel. He took a pair of pliers from his pocket and snipped through the wires leading to the speaker, then nodded to Hagen to try again.

This time, no alarm sounded, and when he touched his two wires together, the ignition warning light illuminated brightly.

'Looks like a go,' Morschel said, and waited while Hagen connected yet another wire, this one to the starter circuit. The outboard engine turned over but didn't start.

'Just a minute. I'll prime it.' Morschel walked to the stern of the boat, squeezed a small bulb in the fuel line a few times, then nodded to Hagen. 'Try it now.'

The motor span, coughed twice, then caught and settled down to a comforting growl.

'I'll get the ropes,' Morschel said, hopped out onto the pontoon and quickly removed the bow and stern lines. 'Take it round to the other end,' he ordered, before walking back to the innocent-looking floating bomb they'd constructed earlier.

A couple of minutes later, Hagen expertly manoeuvred the stolen boat alongside the pontoon and held it in position while Morschel and Badri – who clearly knew at least something about boats – secured its lines to the mooring posts of the vacant berth just behind.

In reality, there wasn't a lot they had to explain to Badri, since the detonation sequence would be automatic once the vessel reached its target, but Morschel showed him how the GPS worked, which he'd already set to use English, as Badri spoke no German.

'That is important for me,' Badri said, 'because I'll need to know exactly when the explosion will occur. I have prayers to say just before that happens.'

'Right,' Morschel murmured, somewhat at a loss as to what else he could say.

He went on to show Badri how he could short out the wires and initiate the explosion manually if necessary. The anti-tamper devices were still unarmed, and with Badri on board there was probably no need for them to be activated, but Morschel would connect them before he left the boat, just in case.

Together, Morschel and Hagen carried out a final comprehensive check of everything they had done, concentrating on the boat carrying the bomb itself, but also making sure that the second vessel was ready for their escape trip. Only when both of them were completely satisfied did Morschel give the order to start the engines. Then he, Hagen and Badri climbed out of the boats and all three walked over to where Ahmed bin Salalah stood watching.

'We'll see you back in Germany, Ahmed,' Morschel said and shook hands with him. Hagen replicated his action, and both Germans stepped back and turned again towards the boats, as the tall Arab embraced his cousin for what they both knew would be the last time.

Moments later, Badri trotted across the pontoon, released the mooring lines on Hagen's hijacked boat, repeated the action on the bomb vessel and nimbly jumped aboard to join Morschel. On the pontoon, bin Salalah waved briefly, then turned back towards the car park.

It was just after one fifteen when the two small vessels headed away from the marina and out into the slightly choppy waters of the Medway.

Chapter Sixteen

Monday
Hammersmith, London

The big Sikorsky settled on the landing pad atop the FOE building, and the aircrewman slid open the side door.

'Just wait here,' Richter instructed. 'I'll be as quick as I can.'

Thirty seconds later he entered his office, sat down and powered up his desktop. While he waited for the computer to boot up, he made a brief call using an outside line. Then he opened his web browser and carried out a short but very specific search. He printed off a couple of sheets of paper through his laser, then shut down the PC and left the office at a run.

SAR Sea King helicopter, callsign 'Rescue 24'

Back on the roof, Richter strapped himself back into the seat in the Sikorsky, before instructing the pilot to head this time to a completely different destination.

'You were right,' he said grimly. 'Sheppey, as quick as you can.'

'You got it,' the pilot replied, and almost immediately the big helicopter lifted off the helipad and turned due east.

'Have you got a second radio I can use? Preferably one I can link to a landline? I need to brief my own people on what we've worked out and if I try using my mobile, nobody will hear a word I say in here.'

'Yes, hang on and I'll try and patch you into the system through one of the Coastguard frequencies. What number did you want?'

Richter gave him the open-line number for FOE and waited. After about two minutes he heard a ringing tone in his earpiece, and the duty officer answered moments later.

'It's Richter. Patch me through to Simpson, please.'

'There is a procedure for this kind of thing, you know.'

'Screw the procedure. Just plug me in.'

'OK, OK. Hang on.'

Simpson's voice was unmistakable, and unmistakably irritated.

'Richter? I've got armed officers from the Met swarming around Fulham Railway Bridge, but they're reporting no activity whatsoever, and your helicopter has apparently vanished. Where the hell are you?'

Richter looked out of the door windows. 'Over central London, just passing the Gherkin, en route to the Isle of Sheppey.'

'What the hell are you going there for?'

'Because that's where our German friend is holding his party. I was wrong about Fulham, and it took an RAF pilot to put me right – which is embarrassing enough for an ex-Navy officer. We need armed support on Sheppey and the surrounding area as quickly as possible.'

'No way, Richter. I'm going to have a hell of a job explaining Fulham, as it is. I'm not doing anything else until you tell me exactly what's going on.'

'OK.' Richter paused for a second or two, marshalling his arguments. 'If I'm right, it's been staring us in the face ever since I got back from Germany. You remember that old tramp who had his throat cut, the one whose body fetched up down the coast at Reculver?'

'Yes,' Simpson replied. 'What about him? You mean he's linked to this somehow?'

'Only indirectly. According to the forensic evidence, he was actually killed at Sheerness, and I think he died because of what he witnessed that night.'

'Which was?'

'I don't know exactly, but almost certainly a diver checking on the wreck of a ship.'

'So?' Simpson still sounded unconvinced, but Richter forged on.

'Just off Sheerness lies what's left of the *Richard Montgomery*, the Liberty ship that sank during the Second World War. That Kent detective, Mason, came up with a theory about terrorists taking explosives out of the wreck, but we wrote off that suggestion, because we didn't consider it feasible. But the wreck itself is real enough.

'Gregory Stevens overheard some members of the group discussing the London event, and they used the initials "FRB". Those three letters could stand for "Fulham Railway Bridge", but now I'm convinced that they don't. Stevens told me that Morschel often used code words to identify his targets, and I think that's exactly what he's done here. In fact, it's a kind of double-bluff.

'In one sense, "FRB" *does* mean the bridge at Fulham, but that's only the shorthand code he'd decided to use for convenience. The important thing wasn't the bridge itself, but its geographical location. The Ordnance Survey National Grid identifier for Fulham Railway Bridge is TQ 243756.'

'Richter, you're talking in riddles. Get to the point.'

'That *is* the point. Forget the "TQ" part – 243756 was the official ship number of the SS *Richard Montgomery*. That's been their target all along.'

'So you mean terrorists *are* busy taking stuff out of the wreck, and that's what the old tramp saw?'

'No,' Richter said. 'It's a lot simpler than that. Morschel isn't planning on taking stuff *out* of the wreck. Instead, he's intending to blow it up, which would create the world's biggest ever non-nuclear explosion. There are 3,500 tons of highly unstable munitions in that wreck, about half of that weight being the explosive, and they've been lying there for the last half-century. It's assessed as being so dangerous that there's a permanent exclusion zone around it, and the area is under constant radar surveillance. No vessels are allowed within 500 feet of it, just in case one hits the wreck by accident and it blows.'

'Why the hell wasn't that cargo cleared during the last war, or just after it?'

'Probably because Sheppey is a long way from Westminster. I can guarantee that if this ship had sunk right outside the Houses of Parliament, they'd have shifted it in a couple of weeks. It wasn't a high priority then, so they just left it where it was, and now it's too dangerous to even try moving it. It's inspected every year by highly experienced divers, but that, and imposing the exclusion zone, is about all that's been done about it.'

'What sort of explosives are we talking about?'

'The details of the original manifest are well established, but what's not quite so clear is exactly what was removed from the wreck immediately after it was stranded. There are several different assessments of what's left inside her, but it's generally believed that the contents of holds one, two and three were hardly touched. That means mainly bombs between 250 and 2,000 pounds which are filled with TNT – which is unaffected by immersion in sea water – plus phosphorous smoke bombs. The biggest danger is that around 175 tons of fragmentation cluster bombs were stored on the deck immediately above the holds. If the deck plating gives way and they fall on the rest of the cargo, you can almost guarantee the whole lot will blow.'

'It's that unstable?' Simpson didn't sound entirely convinced.

'Absolutely. In 1967 preliminary work was being done on a Polish ship named the *Kielce* that sank off Folkestone in 1946, with about the same tonnage of munitions on board. The salvage company fired three small cutting charges to start clearing collapsed hull plating. The first two didn't do anything except cut steel, but the third caused the cargo itself to explode. It detonated with a force equivalent to an earthquake measuring 4.5 on the Richter scale and caused a seismic shockwave that was detectable about five thousand miles away. But that wreck was lying in ninety feet of water, and so most of the energy of the detonation was directed downwards, into the seabed. The situation with the *Richard Montgomery* is entirely different, because it's lying in shallow water.

'So if Morschel can get most of the cargo to cook off, that could equate to about a one and a half kiloton blast. To put this into perspective, the Hiroshima nuclear weapon's yield has been calculated at around fifteen kilotons, so we're looking at an explosion equivalent to one tenth of that, or about the same as a low-yield tactical nuclear weapon. Such a detonation would flatten most of Sheppey and the Isle of Grain – including the power station, the container port and the natural-gas import facility – but that would only be the start. The most significant destruction would be caused by the Thames itself, because water's incompressible.

'Look at the damage the Asian tsunami did a few years ago. A one and a half kiloton blast on the seabed off Sheppey would cause a tidal wave that would sweep across the Thames Estuary and do significant damage to the south coast of Essex, and especially to Southend and Canvey Island. The towns of Rochester and Gillingham would suffer as well but, because the entrance to the River Medway between Sheppey and the Isle of Grain is comparatively narrow, there'd be a lot less damage.

'But our real problem would be London. The Thames is shaped like a funnel that narrows significantly when it reaches the centre of the city. A four-to-six-feet wave out in the estuary by Sheppey – and that's the sort of height this explosion could easily cause – could reach twenty or thirty feet or even more by the time it gets to Gravesend, where the Thames narrows and the banks force the water even higher, and at the same time make it move quicker. We could then have a twenty-foot-high wall of water surging up the river at thirty miles an hour, getting higher and faster as it nears central London. And it's worth saying that one calculation has suggested the explosion could create a column of water and debris over a thousand feet wide that would reach about ten thousand feet into the air and cause a wave over fifteen feet high, off Sheppey. If that's accurate, we could have a forty-foot-high tsunami running right through the centre of London.'

'What about the Thames Barrier?' Simpson asked.

'A complete waste of time,' Richter said. 'The Barrier's intended to cope with spring tides, not something on this scale.'

'But won't most of the force of the explosion be dissipated in the open water lying to the east of Sheppey?'

'Yes, but that wouldn't help. The explosion would cause a wave that would radiate in all directions more or less equally, so there'd still be a massive wall of water heading up the Thames.'

'Have you worked all this out for yourself, Richter, or have you spoken to somebody who actually knows what they're talking about?'

'It's not just my take on it. I spent an interesting few minutes on the phone to a hydrodynamicist from London University. The figures – or rather the guesses – I've given you are his, not mine. And there's a refinement that I only just found out about from this same scientist, who's now probably packing his bags and heading for higher ground. Have you noticed the moon?'

'What?' The apparent non-sequitur obviously threw Simpson. 'The moon? What about it?'

'It's a new moon, and that's important. About once every eighteen months, there's a phenomenon known as the Proxigean Spring Tide. It occurs when the moon is at its closest point to the earth, its perigee or proxigee, and is directly between us and the sun. That gives rise to unusually high tides and—'

'Don't tell me. It's today.'

'Got it in one,' Richter confirmed. 'I think Morschel must have carefully planned this some time ago, and if he succeeds it will devastate London. The underground networks and all the tunnels under the Thames will be flooded. Certainly the City, the East End and most of the rest of London will suffer massive flooding. The sewers will be flushed out, filling the streets with excrement and God knows what else. The water supplies will break down. Electricity sub-stations will flood, too, and power will fail over almost the whole city.

'We're talking national catastrophe here, Simpson, not just a few days paddling around in green wellies. The total bill for repairing the damage could run into billions of pounds, maybe even tens of billions, and if we don't do something the loss of life that's forecast will reach over a hundred thousand. That's a conservative estimate and depends on exactly when the wave hits. In all, this would make 9/11 look like a minor traffic accident.'

'Oh, shit,' Simpson muttered.

'That's a fair summary,' Richter agreed.

'But what does this fucking German want? What's his motivation? Just blackmail?'

'He's already got the money he wants from the bank raids, and if it was blackmail, he'd have issued some demand by now, and then we'd know exactly what he was threatening. No, this is a simple plan with a simple objective. From what Karl Wolff told me over in Germany, Hans Morschel is a pure terrorist, a straight-line descendant of Andreas Baader. He's even named his gang after the prison in Stuttgart where Baader and the other members of the Red Army Faction were held – which was also where they died. Morschel is only interested in destruction, I think. He organized these robberies to get some walking-around money and also as a diversion to attract the woodentops and get them well out of his way while he attacked his real target.'

'So what can we do? Start an evacuation?'

'Evacuate Greater London? At this time in the afternoon and at about an hour's notice? Good luck with it. Considering the time we've got left I doubt if we could even evacuate Sheerness. If you agree with the logic, I suggest you pass on my suspicions immediately to Five and the Met. Dump it on them – it's really not our problem. Oh, and I suppose they could close the Thames Barrier as a precaution, not that it'll do much good.'

'While you do what?'

Richter glanced at his watch before replying. 'High tide's in just over an hour so, assuming I'm right, by then Morschel or whoever's triggering this thing will have to get a boat full of explosives either on or near the wreck of the *Richard Montgomery*. I'm going to find them, and do my best to stop them. Could you tell Five to bell the Kent police and ask them to start an immediate search for Hans Morschel. He's got to have either bought or stolen a boat of some sort, so if they could check the boatyards and marinas on Sheppey and in the Medway area, they might just trace him. They'll need firearms officers and ARVs on hand, because he'll certainly be carrying a weapon.'

'Anything else?'

'Yes, the obvious. Alert the coastguards to what we think is happening. And if there are any Royal Navy ships in the area, make sure they get Flash signals from CINCFLEET at Northwood so they're in the loop. If any of them have choppers on board, getting them airborne wouldn't do any harm as extra sets of eyes in the sky, that kind of thing. But unless they can reach Sheppey within about half an hour, it'll probably be too late. If you need to get a message to me, contact 22 Squadron at RAF Wattisham. They'll either be able to call the chopper directly or relay it through local ATC.'

'What about kicking the SAS into gear?'

'Good idea,' Richter said. 'We might well need them to help track these guys down, but the first thing is to stop that bomb going off, and they won't get there in time to do anything about that.'

'Richter,' Simpson said, after a pause, 'one point. If you do find this fucking German, don't bother bringing him back. Just take care of everything out there, OK?'

'I hadn't planned on him ever enjoying the privilege of standing trial,' Richter replied, and broke the connection.

Back in Hammersmith, Simpson stretched out a hand for the telephone.

Medway, Kent

When Morschel had originally devised the plan that they were now implementing, he'd spent considerable time studying maps and charts of the area. He'd realized immediately that to get his boat laden with explosives from any of the Medway marinas out into the Thames Estuary, he couldn't rely totally on an automatic pilot and GPS navigation system. There were just too many other boats and too many obstructions, including shallow water and several small islands. That was why he and Hagen were now steering their two vessels around the last section of the S-shaped bends in the River Medway, between the motorway bridge south-west of Rochester and Lower Upnor. At that point, the river widened dramatically and would offer them a more or less straight run out to Sheppey and the estuary beyond.

The first of the waypoints Morschel had put into the GPS was a spot in the open water just north of Darnet Fort. From there, the boat would be able to steer almost due east for some two miles before turning north-east for the actual mouth of the Medway. But before they reached that point, once they were over Hoo Flats, lying north of Hoo Fort, with plenty of water under their keels on the flood tide, and no other boats anywhere near them, Morschel signalled to Hagen and throttled back, keeping the boat's bow pointing east and maintaining just enough throttle to hold the craft in position.

Hagen expertly brought the stolen boat alongside, only a few metres clear, and kept pace with Morschel's vessel as his fellow German prepared to abandon ship.

'Watch this carefully, Badri,' Morschel instructed. 'These are the connections for the main detonator and the anti-tamper charges.' He swiftly completed all the necessary connections. 'Right, now it's all up to you,' he said. 'You're happy with the controls?'

In fact, Badri had been at the wheel of the boat virtually since it had nosed out of the riverside marina, and the German was quite satisfied that this young man could handle the vessel competently.

'Yes, no problem.'

'And you know the exact coordinates of the target? And how to disarm the anti-handling devices if you need to?'

Badri nodded. 'I know precisely where to go, and I'm now perfectly familiar with all the connections onboard. Don't worry, Mr Morschel, I know exactly what I'm doing.'

'I'm just checking, that's all.' Morschel bent down to unzip a bag on the floor of the cockpit. 'Now, have you ever used one of these before?'

He reached inside the bag and pulled out a Heckler & Koch MP5.

'No,' Badri admitted, 'but I have used a Kalashnikov.'

'In Pakistan?' Morschel asked.

'Afghanistan, actually, a couple of years ago.'

'Well, this is similar. It's smaller, lighter and more accurate than the AK47, but it works the same way.'

'Point it and pull the trigger?' Badri suggested.

'Exactly. You shouldn't have to use it, but it's there, just in case, with a few spare magazines. Anything else?'

'No, nothing. Mr Morschel, now you should leave.'

'Right. Once I'm aboard the other boat, press this' – Morschel pointed to a button on the box he'd clipped to the control panel – 'to engage the autopilot and then don't touch anything else. The whole route is pre-planned from here on, and all the controls are fitted with anti-tampering devices. If you even touch them, the charges attached to the controls will blow up. If the autopilot fails, or you have to take manual control for some other reason, you'll have to undo all the connections you just saw me complete. OK, now we'll follow you a short distance out towards the estuary, just to check everything's working properly.'

He straightened up and gestured to Hagen, who immediately closed the gap between the two vessels long enough for Morschel to step across between them.

'Back to the marina?' Hagen asked.

Morschel shook his head. 'Not yet. This is a one-shot operation. We'll follow the boat for a few minutes, just to make sure that the GPS is doing its stuff properly.'

As they watched, Badri pressed the button as instructed and sat back, waiting. After a few seconds, the GPS obviously completed its calculations because the autopilot smoothly opened the throttle on the other boat, and the vessel began to increase speed. Hagen then accelerated to match its speed, but deliberately dropped back about fifty metres.

'How far do you want us to follow?' Hagen asked. 'The first waypoint?'

'That should do,' Morschel agreed.

About five minutes later, they watched the wheel on the smaller boat make about half a turn clockwise, and the direction in which the vessel was travelling changed slightly. Hagen copied the turn, and watched the small compass mounted above the wheel settle onto a new heading.

'Due east,' he confirmed. 'Looks OK to me.'

'Me too,' Morschel agreed. 'Close up on him again.'

Hagen accelerated until the craft was alongside Badri's. The young Arab turned to them, smiled and waved.

'Right, there's nothing else we can do,' Morschel said. 'Let's get out of here, Ernst.'

SAR Sea King helicopter, callsign 'Rescue 24'

'So what are we looking for?' the pilot asked.

'I really don't know, but anything suspicious in the vicinity of that wreck. How long before we get there?'

'About fifteen minutes.'

'Right,' Richter said. 'When we reach Sheppey, head to the wreck's location. You've got the coordinates?'

'Yes. They're marked on all the maritime charts. But then what? I mean, are we looking for divers, or what?'

'A boat's much more likely. The wreck's nearly two miles off Sheerness, and that would be a hell of a long swim for somebody in a wetsuit lugging several kilos of plastic. And then there would be problems detonating it. With Semtex, the normal method is a blasting cap, actuated by a battery or a dynamo. I don't think these terrorists could have run a cable out to the foreshore somewhere on Sheppey, intending to use a hand-cranked dynamo or something. But they might have left a charge with a timer on the wreck itself. If they have, there's nothing much we can do about it now. There's certainly not enough time left to get a diver down to the wreck, locate the device and disarm it. But my guess is that they didn't do that either. The wreck's heavily silted after sitting there for half a century, and they'd need to get quite a lot of explosive out there and on board to guarantee it would blow. It would mean a lot of physical effort in very difficult diving conditions, and they couldn't use a normal dive boat because of the permanent radar surveillance of the site.'

He paused to think for a few moments. 'No, if *I* wanted to get that wreck to blow, I'd pack a small boat with plastic explosive, moor it directly over the *Richard Montgomery*, set the timer and retire to a very safe distance, which in this case would probably mean somewhere in France.'

Chapter Seventeen

Monday
Canterbury, Kent

Detective Inspector Paul Mason hurried out of the police station, wrenched open the door of the unmarked police car, sat down and clipped on his seat belt. DS Clark already had the engine running and, the moment the inspector's door was closed, he accelerated away from the kerb, switching on the flashing blue lights behind the front grille as he did so.

'Rochester,' Mason snapped. 'And quick as you can.'

He leant forward and started up the siren to move a line of cars out of their way as Clark headed out of Canterbury towards Harbledown and the A2, the shortest route to get them to junction seven of the M2 motorway.

'What's going on, boss?' Clark asked, turning off the siren once the road ahead was clear.

'I've just taken a call from the spooks at Thames House. If you believe what they're saying, it looks as if some of these recent incidents are related – the death of the old tramp, the body in the woods up on the North Downs and those four bombings this afternoon in London. Apparently it all comes down to a potential terrorist attack.'

'So what the hell are we supposed to be doing at Rochester?'

'Checking out the local marinas. The theory is that some German terrorist might be using a boat to try to get a load of explosives out to the *Richard Montgomery*. I've already got people back at Canterbury telephoning all the marinas and boatyards in the Medway area, and we've got uniformed officers heading for Sheppey, just in case there are any boats missing out there. There are six ARVs cruising the area in case of any contact.'

'Fuck,' Clark growled. 'If the *Richard Montgomery* blows, we're all in the shit. If that load of bombs goes off, it could wipe out most of Sheppey. So apart from us going around politely asking marina owners if they've mislaid any boats recently, is anything being done to stop this German bastard actually lighting the fuse or whatever?'

'I don't know, but I'd be amazed if an SAS team or somebody wasn't already out hunting this guy down.'

SAR Sea King helicopter, callsign 'Rescue 24'

In fact, the 'hunting' at that stage consisted only of Richter and three RAF aircrew in a bright yellow Sea King helicopter.

'So that's what we're looking for?' the pilot asked. 'A small boat?'

'Any boat, in fact,' Richter said, 'and it could be heading towards the wreck from almost any direction. That means from somewhere on Sheppey itself, or out of the Medway, or even directly across the Thames Estuary from Southend. That's why we need to start searching at the wreck's location and work outwards from there.'

'And we'll need to check every boat we see?'

'Not quite. We can ignore sailing yachts, but every powerboat we see that's heading in the right direction, yes. Those we'll have to take a look at. In fact, unless they've already managed to moor a vessel near the wreck, we're probably looking for two boats – one stuffed full of Semtex or C4, and the other to take the pilot of the first one to safety after he's positioned his floating bomb.'

Richter looked out of the window on the sliding side door of the Sea King. They had just passed the Dartford Crossing: the huge span of the Queen Elizabeth Bridge carrying southbound traffic on the M25 was an absolutely unmistakable landmark.

'So what's your plan once we get there?' the pilot asked. 'You'll want lowering down by winch onto every boat you need to check?'

'That depends on how many of them there are. Time's of the essence here, so we'll have to identify the target vessel as quickly as possible. If there are a lot of boats, we'll just have to check them visually from the air. Whether you winch me down or whether I do something else will depend on who or what's on board.'

'By "something else", I presume you mean shoot the occupants with one of your nice little selection of weapons?'

'If it comes to that, yes,' Richter snapped. 'Don't forget what these people are up to. If the only way to stop them is to blow them away, that's exactly what I'll do. But if the boat with the explosives is empty, meaning rigged up with an automatic pilot and navigation system, then I will want winching aboard.'

'Right. My aircrewman, Dave here, will give you a briefing.'

'That's probably not necessary. I used to fly Kings and Harriers for the Queen, so I've been dangled from a winch before.'

'My aircraft, my rules, Mr Richter. I don't care about your previous experience. Just listen to the briefing.'

'Fine.'

The aircrewman gestured to the rear of the aircraft. 'There's an immersion suit back there, as you requested. Put that on first, then I'll run you through the safety rules and signals.'

Richter removed his leather jacket and shoulder holster, then unfolded the heavy rubberized suit and climbed into it. The garment was secured by a long, waterproof zip that ran diagonally from one hip to the opposite shoulder, but he left that open for the moment. He knew from previous experience that once the zip was secured, the suit would get very hot, very quickly.

Next, the aircrewman briefed him on the hand signals he would use and the procedures they'd follow, which were very much as Richter remembered from his time in the Royal Navy.

'Personal radio?' Richter asked.

'Right here.' The aircrewman handed over a small black box that Richter clipped to the immersion suit. 'You've used one before?'

'Yes. The press to transmit switch is here' – pointing at a button on one side of the unit – 'and I'll have to put the earpiece in before I leave the chopper.'

'We're less than five minutes from Sheppey,' the pilot said, 'and I've just had a message relayed to me through base ops. There are no Royal Navy vessels anywhere in the area, and no other helicopters able to get to the scene within the timescale you specified. Does that make sense?'

'Yes, unfortunately.'

'OK. Are you ready back there?'

'Affirmative.'

Richter zipped up the immersion suit, settled the earpiece as comfortably as he could in his left ear, and pulled the headphones on over the top of it. Then he secured a harness around his torso and clipped it to a safety line inside the cabin, while the aircrewman slid back the door and peered out.

Richter stood up and joined him. Directly in front of him, probably four or five miles away, was the open expanse of the River Medway, and he was surprised at how many small boats were out on the water, which obviously wouldn't make detecting the target vessel any easier. Ahead, he could see the Isle of Sheppey, with its principal town, Sheerness, lying directly in front of the helicopter.

'Are there many vessels north of Sheerness?' Richter asked. 'Out in the main estuary itself?'

'A handful, yes, but most of them look like bigger stuff. Any chance this German terrorist has taken over a coaster or something?'

'I doubt it, because that would involve a lot more manpower, and they'd have problems getting a vessel that size close enough to the wreck to ensure it would blow. Not to mention the difficulty he'd have in persuading some of his gang that staying on the ship and detonating a 3,000-ton bomb underneath it was a good thing. Morschel and his men may be a lot of things, but suicide bombers they're not – at least as far as we know.'

'Could they have recruited some ragheads to press the button for them?'

'Our intelligence hasn't confirmed a link between his group and any radical Islamic sect,' Richter said. 'On the other hand, we don't actually know a hell of a lot about these guys. Our assessment is that they're more likely to have acquired a smaller craft to use as the trigger. That way, they can get close to the wreck, probably right on top of it, and, with enough explosive packed into it, they can pretty much guarantee the sunken ship's cargo will explode.'

'A surface explosion could do that?'

Richter nodded – a pointless gesture, as neither pilot could see him. 'Almost certainly. They'll probably be using Semtex or C4, and that's a serious explosive, twice as powerful as TNT. Three pounds of Semtex can destroy a two-storey building, and my guess is that Morschel will have packed his trigger vessel with at least ten times that amount. OK, a lot of the blast will be directed upwards and outwards, but water's incompressible, and the shock-wave will send a hammer-blow straight down to the wreck below.

'The most dangerous munitions left on board the *Richard Montgomery* are the cluster bombs stored on the deck above the main holds. They're very fragile, and a good hard blow could fire them, so they're likely to detonate as soon as the blast wave hits them. But even if *they* don't explode, the metal plates of the decking are rusted and crumbling, and the surface blast will probably finish the job. As the deck gives way, the cluster bombs will drop onto the heavyweight munitions stacked in the remains of the holds, and then they'll most certainly blow. And that, I can pretty much guarantee, will cook off the rest of the explosives.'

Medway, Kent

The two Germans looked up as the bright yellow Sea King helicopter passed to the north of them, on an easterly heading.

'What's that doing?' Hagen asked.

'Probably nothing. It's a military rescue chopper heading out into the estuary, maybe on a training exercise.'

'You don't think somebody's guessed what we're up to?'

'I doubt it. But even if someone has worked it out, it's too late to do anything about it now. There are dozens of craft on the estuary, and checking them all will take a while. Even if they manage to identify the boat, they've got to get past Badri's MP5 and the anti-handling devices we've rigged. Either one should stop them disarming the bomb in time.'

SAR Sea King helicopter, callsign 'Rescue 24'

In the Sea King above the estuary, Richter was faced with exactly that difficulty. There appeared to be literally dozens of small craft ploughing the choppy grey waters of the Medway, and the only good news was that none was particularly close to the wreck of the *Richard Montgomery*, the tops of the masts of which were still just visible even at the present high tide.

'So now what?' the pilot asked.

'Now we start checking each boat,' Richter said grimly.

'And how will we know when we find the right one?'

'We'll know,' Richter replied, 'because they'll probably start shooting at us.'

Rochester, Kent

Mason slipped the mobile phone back into his pocket and turned to Clark. 'Right, get us north of the River Medway. We might have a hit there.'

Clark nodded, dropped a gear and accelerated away, switching on the siren and the flashing blue lights. They'd been cruising around on the outskirts of Rochester, waiting to hear of any possible sightings of Morschel or news about boats.

'What's the address?' Clark asked.

'The Blue Skies Marina,' Mason replied, inputting the postcode he'd just been given into the satnav.

'Bloody silly name that, considering it's in England,' Clark muttered, pulling out to overtake a line of cars that had eased over to the side of the road on hearing the siren. 'So what's the lead?'

'The marina's owner thinks it might be this guy Morschel who bought a boat from him a few days ago. But we've already had quite a few false starts this afternoon, so this could easily be another case of mistaken identity.'

Fifteen minutes later, Clark pulled their unmarked police car to a halt outside the marina, and both men hurried towards the office. But before they even reached it, the door swung open and a middle-aged man peered out at them anxiously.

Mason pulled out his warrant card, but the man hardly glanced at it. 'Come in,' he said. 'I've been expecting you. My name's Tom Collinwood, and I've already dug out the paperwork.'

'What did they tell you on the phone, sir?' Mason asked, as Clark began scanning the documents the boatyard manager had produced.

'The officer asked me to check all sales and leases for the past month, apart from those involving boats smaller than twelve feet, and I don't handle any of those. He was only interested in boats that were still out there.'

'And I gather you sold a boat to a German customer?'

'Yes, a few days ago.'

'And what made you think this might be the sale we're trying to check on?'

Collinwood sat down behind his desk, motioning the two detectives to a couple of guest chairs. 'Several things, really. The officer from Canterbury said you were looking for a boat arranged for a German gentleman driving a Mercedes, and especially in a cash transaction. Well, I sold a boat to a German with a Mercedes, and he paid cash for it.'

Clark glanced up sharply but didn't interrupt.

'His name was Heinrich, and he first contacted me by email several weeks ago.'

'What did he say he was looking for?' Mason asked.

'His requirements seemed simple enough, just a boat that would take four to six people, and that was seaworthy enough to handle the waters out in the Thames Estuary. He claimed that he intended to visit various coastal areas of Kent and Essex, and maybe do a bit of sea fishing as well.'

'And you had one suitable?'

'Yes, in fact, we had several. Eventually Mr Heinrich decided on a seventeen-footer fitted with a fairly big Evinrude outboard.'

Clark opened the folder he'd kept tucked under his left arm. Besides several sheets of paper, it contained a photograph that showed a single figure sitting in a German-plated Mercedes waiting stationary at some kind of booth. This he placed on the desk in front of Collinwood.

'This was taken at Calais, shortly before this man boarded a ferry to Dover. Does he look familiar?'

Collinwood peered closely at the picture, then looked up after a few seconds.

'I'm not sure,' he said, 'it could be him, but he didn't arrive in *this* car. The Mercedes that arrived here had Austrian plates.'

Clark asked the obvious question. 'Did you make a note of the registration number?'

Collinwood shook his head. 'No, once Heinrich introduced himself, I completely lost interest in whatever car he'd arrived in. All I remember for sure is that the plates were Austrian. They're quite distinctive.'

'Anything else you can remember about him?'

'No, not really. And I never got a decent look at his passenger.'

'His passenger?' Mason queried.

'There was another man in the car with him, a big guy, very bulky. Anyway, the second man stayed in the car almost the whole time and drove off in the car after Heinrich took the boat away.'

'Do you know where this Heinrich was heading when he left here?' Clark asked.

Collinwood shook his head. 'No, he just said he'd got a berth in a marina somewhere down-river.'

'Anything else relevant?'

'Well, one thing did seem odd. After we'd concluded the deal, he and the second man carried four large heavy-looking bags from the boot of his car and put them on board the boat. That's not usual, unless he was planning a trip somewhere immediately. Even then, most people can pack enough stuff for a long weekend into a couple of carrier bags. I didn't think that was anything sinister, just unusual.'

'OK,' Mason said, 'that's very helpful, Mr Collinwood. One last thing. The boat – can you describe it for us?'

'I can do better than that,' the manager replied, 'I've got some photographs here.'

He opened a file on his desk and handed over about half a dozen eight-by-ten colour pictures of a fairly undistinguished blue and white craft.

Mason studied these for a few seconds, then pulled a mobile phone from his pocket and punched in the open-line number for FOE at Hammersmith.

'This is Detective Inspector Mason of the Kent Constabulary,' he announced as his call was answered. 'I need to speak to Paul Richter, please. It's urgent.'

'He's not in the building.'

'I guessed that. Can you patch me through to wherever he is? Or give me another number or something?'

'Wait.'

There was silence for a few seconds, then Mason heard a few clicks and beeps and then, with no ringing tone or anything else, Richter's voice was loud in his ear, albeit against a loud throbbing noise in the background.

'This is DI Mason. Where are you?'

'In an Air Force chopper over Sheppey right now, and we're fairly busy. Is this important?'

'It might be. We've been running checks on the Medway boatyards and we might have a hit. A German named Heinrich bought a boat for cash from a local marina. I'm looking at pictures of it right now.'

'I'm listening,' Richter said. 'Give me the description.'

'It's blue and white, seventeen feet long with a small cabin and it's powered by a hefty outboard motor. Does that help?'

'It might,' Richter said. 'We're starting our search just north of Sheppey right now, so thanks for that.'

'Right,' Mason said, 'and it's probably a bit late now, but this man Morschel has probably fitted Austrian plates on the Mercedes.'

'OK. I'll amend the watch order for him – that's if we ever manage to find this fucking boat.'

SAR Sea King helicopter, callsign 'Rescue 24'

Richter glanced at his watch. If the hydrodynamicist had got it right, the optimum time for the explosion to be triggered was either at, or very shortly before, high tide, when the natural flow of water up the Thames Estuary towards London would assist the progress of the tsunami it created. And high tide was in just under thirty minutes.

The description of the boat forwarded by Mason was proving less useful than Richter had hoped, because blue and white now appeared to be the commonest colours boat manufacturers used. Almost every vessel they'd spotted so far had that kind of colour scheme, though in varying shades of blue, which might be one good reason Morschel had picked it.

And what they'd all failed to spot so far were two boats obviously proceeding in close company, or even a pair heading in roughly the same direction. That suggested either his theory was completely wrong, and that Morschel had found some other way of triggering the detonation, or they might be looking at a suicide mission with a single volunteer prepared to stay on the boat all the way to oblivion.

'Right, there's nothing vaguely close to the wreck right now,' the pilot announced, 'but we can see about a dozen small boats heading out of the mouth of the Medway.'

'All of them blue and white, I suppose?' Richter asked irritably.

'Not *all* of them, no. There are a few other colours, but blue and white does seem to be this season's favourite combination.'

'I guess we could apply a bit of filtering here. We can probably eliminate all those obviously carrying family parties, unless they're being held at gunpoint – which is an unlikely scenario in my opinion. So keep your eyes open for those boats with only a single person in the cockpit. And if you see a boat with *nobody* in the cockpit, that's the one.'

'Copied. OK, we're in the drop now. I'll fly alongside each boat as close as I can without the risk of swamping them, which means holding about fifty yards off. I'll manoeuvre the aircraft to the left of each vessel, so you'll have the best possible view of it, and I'll hold it there for about five seconds, unless you instruct me otherwise. Would that be satisfactory?'

'Excellent, thanks.'

As the Sea King descended towards the grey and hostile-looking waters of the entrance to the Medway, Richter checked the SPAS-12 and the MP5 one last time.

Medway, Kent

Badri hadn't been lying about his previous boating experience but he had, to borrow the phrase made famous by a senior British politician, been economical with the truth. He had indeed handled small craft on numerous occasions, but almost always in rivers or lakes. His few experiences of open-water sailing had been notably unpleasant because he found himself suffering from chronic sea-sickness and, within minutes of Morschel leaving the boat, he'd already begun to feel nauseous.

As the boat, still navigated and controlled by the GPS and automatic pilot, reached the much rougher waters at the mouth of the Medway, Badri's head was pounding, and he felt ready to vomit. He huddled miserably on the curved bench that ran around the stern of the boat, fixing his eyes on the far horizon and trying to control the turmoil in his stomach. The boat kept bouncing quite violently as it butted through the waves at the mouth of the Medway, the pitching and twisting motion exacerbated by the lack of a helmsman able to anticipate the incoming waves.

At least, Badri reflected, his torment would be over within a few minutes. The fact of the sea getting rougher meant the boat was leaving the shelter of the river, and that must mean the wreck should be almost in sight. That was his hope, at least, but right then he felt too ill to stand up and take a look out of the cockpit to check.

For some time he'd been aware of the noise of an aircraft. A large yellow-painted helicopter had been flying around the area, obviously searching for something, but Badri hadn't been able to pay it much attention. But now he noticed it descending close to sea level, approaching a small powerboat about half a mile in front of him. Perhaps somebody on board was ill and the chopper had been sent to rescue them.

Despite his nausea, Badri stood up and staggered to the control panel, seizing one of the grab-bars beside the wheel – Morschel had strongly warned him against touching the wheel itself – so he could get a better view.

Whatever was happening, he soon realized it wasn't a rescue, simply because the aircraft wasn't getting close enough to the powerboat to winch anybody off. Even as he watched, he saw the helicopter lift away from the hover and begin to accelerate.

But then he saw the aircraft repeat this action, descending to a hover close to another vessel, and there was only one conclusion he could draw. They were systematically checking the boats, looking for something – or perhaps for someone. For a few seconds Badri just stood there, his seasickness rapidly diminishing in importance as he guessed exactly what the men in the helicopter were searching for. He bent down, picked up the MP5 and first made sure that the magazine was firmly home and then checked that the other magazines were fully loaded and ready to hand.

There was a good chance that he'd be able to get pretty close to the wreck before the search team in the helicopter realized he was their quarry. And, even if they did close up on his boat to check him out, the Heckler & Koch should be all he needed to persuade them to back off. One of the things Badri had always found baffling about both the British police and their security services was that, although battling criminals who carried arms as a matter of course, their own personnel were almost invariably unarmed. Whoever was in the helicopter, he guessed they might have a couple of pistols between them at most.

He now remained standing by the wheel, watching the helicopter's activities carefully. The search routine its crew was employing seemed simple enough, and fortunately the aircraft seemed to be gradually moving further away from him. Badri checked the display on the GPS unit and noted with satisfaction that he only had about another three miles to go. Within a matter of minutes, neither the searching helicopter nor anything else was going to matter.

SAR Sea King helicopter, callsign 'Rescue 24'

'Talk about finding a needle in a sodding haystack,' Richter muttered, standing by the open side door of the Sea King and staring at yet another blue and white powerboat hammering through the waves a safe fifty metres away. The couple in the cockpit stood waving and grinning like idiots.

'I've got a suggestion,' the pilot said.

'I'll listen to anything constructive.'

'If you're right, and somewhere among this lot is a boat with a bomb on board, finding it this way is a bit hit-and-miss. Almost any of the boats heading out of the Medway could be the one we're looking for, and just because there are several people in the cockpit waving at us doesn't mean they aren't the bombers.'

'Agreed, though I think that's less likely. So?'

'If this plan is going to work, the vessel's going to have to get pretty close to the wreck before the perpetrators fire the IED. So instead of chasing round here looking at boats in the Medway, why don't we wait out in the estuary itself, near the wreck, and intercept any vessel trying to get anywhere near it?'

'Yeah,' Richter said, 'that sounds more sensible than poncing about here. Let's do one more quick sweep round the Medway, just in case we spot anything interesting, then head out to the *Richard Montgomery*. You're still watching the site on radar?'

'Yes. There are no vessels within about half a mile of the exclusion zone, and no sign of anything heading towards it.'

Medway, Kent

Something had changed, Badri realized. The helicopter had climbed out of the hover, but instead of again descending to sea level, it had continued up to about 500 feet and then swung right in a long sweeping turn. Perhaps it was leaving the area altogether, Badri wondered, still watching it carefully. But his hopes were dashed when the pilot continued the turn until the aircraft was heading in more or less the same direction as he was, and out into the estuary.

And then he saw it start descending, apparently aiming for a position somewhere near his boat.

SAR Sea King helicopter, callsign 'Rescue 24'

'Take us down,' Richter said, peering through his binoculars. 'The blue and white boat that's almost dead ahead.'

'What is it?'

'Just one thing – there's a lone male in the cockpit, but it looks to me as if he's holding onto a grab handle, not the wheel.'

'He could be using an autopilot.'

'Exactly, but why? In these choppy conditions, every other skipper we've seen has been driving the boat himself, trying to minimize the effect of the waves. And why would he need to use an autopilot here, virtually at the mouth of the Medway, where he'd have to keep making course changes to avoid other boats and keep clear of navigation hazards?'

'Granted. And there's something else. The other boats have all been avoiding the exclusion zone by a significant distance, yet this guy's just altered course slightly so he's now heading straight for the edge of the zone.'

'Right, that's got to be him, then.'

As the Sea King began to lose height, Richter picked up the MP5 and checked it once again, an automatic reaction.

'How do you want to play this?' the pilot asked.

'By ear, I suppose.'

'You were once a pilot, so I don't need to remind you that a helicopter is a delicate piece of kit. If bullets start flying around, we're out of here.'

Richter looked through his binoculars again at the boat, now probably only a couple of hundred yards in front of the Sea King. He was increasingly certain that the man in the cockpit was simply standing by the controls, touching none of them, yet the wheel was moving back and forth to maintain the correct heading, so obviously some kind of autopilot was in use. His gut feeling was that they'd found the right boat, but what the pilot had just said was true – helicopters *were* fragile machines – and Richter was concerned that the man in the boat might well open up with a Kalashnikov or some other automatic weapon. If the boat was stuffed with Semtex, he'd be very surprised if there weren't one or two assault rifles on board as well. If their suspect got lucky and hit something vital on the King, that might be the end of the matter.

There had to be another way.

Richter carefully studied the layout of the boat through his binoculars. The open cockpit was positioned at the stern, and directly in front was the small cabin. Beyond that, at the bow, was a small area of flat decking surrounded by a low guard rail. As far as he could see, the foredeck was invisible from the cockpit unless the skipper leant out on one side or the other and peered around the structure of the cabin. That had to be the optimum approach, therefore, and from the starboard side of the boat, too, as the controls in the cockpit were located on the port side, where the man was now standing.

Richter glanced around the rear of the helicopter and spotted what he needed lying at the back. 'Change of plan,' he said quickly. 'Ignore the boat. Just fly past it and come to a hover about a quarter of a mile in front, over open water.'

'What are you intending to do?'

'I'm going to try and sneak up on him,' Richter said, then explained exactly what he had in mind.

'That's madness,' the pilot protested.

'Not necessarily, and the only alternative is to end up with a shooting match out here on the Medway, with bullets flying in all directions. Anyway, it has to be my decision, so let's do it. Just remember to pick me up afterwards.'

With the help of the aircrewman, Richter swiftly pulled off the immersion suit and stripped down to his underwear, then pulled on the wetsuit he'd noticed at the rear. It was a little tight, but that wouldn't matter, and there was a waterproof pouch attached to the back of the weight-belt which was just big enough to hold the Browning. The shotgun and MP5 were useless for what he planned, and would stay in the helicopter. Fins, mask and diving knife completed the outfit.

'You ready back there?' the pilot asked.

But Richter was already off intercom, waiting by the door and staring at the uninviting grey sea below.

The aircrewman tapped him on the shoulder, and received a thumbs-up in return. 'We're ready,' he announced.

'Roger. We have to get the timing right, so make sure Richter's ready the moment I give the word.'

The Sea King descended to a low hover, turned so that its port side faced the suspect boat, still some 500 yards away, then dipped even lower, holding a mere four or five feet above the surface, and began moving forward slowly, the left-hand-seat man watching the boat very carefully.

The downwash from the massive rotors churned the surface of the water and, more importantly for Richter, it was also throwing up a fine mist of spray that surrounded the aircraft and the sea directly below it. It was a mist almost impossible to see through.

'Nearly there. Fifty yards . . . Thirty . . . Twenty.'

'Ten seconds. Get ready there in the back, Dave.'

'On the bow now, now, *now*.'

'Dave, go.'

In the rear compartment, the aircrewman slapped Richter on the back, and he instantly stepped out of the starboard-side door, his legs held together, and plummeted straight down into the water.

'He's gone, boss,' the aircrewman reported.

'Roger,' the pilot acknowledged, and he immediately broke the aircraft out of the low hover and climbed away.

Medway, Kent

Badri was now beginning to breathe a little easier. The helicopter had shot past him, the crew clearly taking no interest in him whatsoever. The chopper had merely dropped down almost to the surface about 500 yards ahead, and then climbed away almost immediately. Maybe the crew weren't searching for him, and were perhaps on some kind of training exercise.

As the aircraft circled round to the east of his vessel, Badri continued to watch it because there was nothing much else *to* watch. There were no other boats near him, now that he was well clear of the coast. The Sea King flew almost a complete circle around him, and then came to a hover a couple of hundred yards off his port beam. As he watched, an orange harness was lowered slowly towards the water on a winch cable, then equally slowly raised. The helicopter moved forward about fifty yards and the manoeuvre was repeated. Quite clearly the crew were just carrying out some very basic rescue exercises, and the route his boat was taking simply gave him a ringside view.

And that was actually the intention. The winching exercises were being performed for one purpose only: to keep his attention on the helicopter and avoid him looking directly ahead. And the reason for that was now in the dark water only a hundred yards or so in front of him.

As Richter hit the water, the cold made him gasp in shock, but the wetsuit trapped a thin layer of water that his body heat would quickly warm up, so he knew his discomfort was only going to be temporary.

The Sea King climbed out of the hover with an increased roar from the jet engines and a thudding sound as the massive rotor blades clawed the air, the downwash churning the water into a maelstrom all around him. In seconds, the helicopter was moving away, and Richter looked cautiously back towards the boat he'd identified shortly before. There were no other vessels particularly close, and he could see it quite clearly, the white 'dog's bone' of the bow-wave getting more obvious as it headed straight towards him.

The strategy he'd decided on was risky, without question, and one-shot. If this failed, the only alternative was to get back into the Sea King and then try to take out the boat's skipper using the Heckler & Koch. He had no illusions about how difficult that might be, firing a sub-machine gun from an unstable airborne platform against a small boat bouncing around in a choppy sea. Add the ever-present risk of a stray slug detonating whatever explosives were stashed on the boat, and the near-certainty that the man onboard would be firing back at him with an automatic weapon, and that definitely made it the less attractive of the two options.

Not that his present plan was risk-free – far from it. If the boat changed course more than a few degrees, or even accelerated significantly, he'd never be able to catch up with it. Success or failure hinged on the fact that, if the boat's route out towards the wreck of the *Richard Montgomery* had been programmed into the automatic pilot, it would probably consist of a series of straight lines linking way-points. They'd already noticed a slight course change from the helicopter, and Richter was gambling on the likelihood that the next alteration would be the final one, and thereafter the boat would head straight for the wreck from the edge of the exclusion zone. Until that point, he hoped, the boat would continue directly towards him.

Despite the wetsuit, the water was biting cold, and already his fingers were feeling numb. Treading water, and keeping his head as low as possible to avoid being seen, he began flexing them to restore the blood flow. But all the time he kept his eyes fixed firmly on the approaching craft.

Richter's assumption was right. Morschel had indeed programmed the automatic pilot to follow a series of way-points linked by straight lines, but he'd included more way-points than he needed, so as to keep the boat moving in the right direction, but not holding any single course for too long. Most small-boat skippers were not that competent, and so, for the sake of appearances, having a five- or ten-degree change of course every now and again seemed a good idea.

The GPS unit interrogated eleven satellites to confirm the unit's precise position on the surface of the globe and then noted that it had just reached another way-point. Accordingly, it immediately sent a new instruction to the autopilot, which responded by turning the wheel anti-clockwise. Within a few seconds, the boat's course had veered about five degrees to port.

Chapter Eighteen

Monday
Rochester, Kent

Hans Morschel steered the stolen powerboat back through the marina entrance, and both men scanned the pontoons, looking for trouble, but saw nothing to give them cause for concern. A couple of men were standing on their boats, tinkering with various bits of equipment, and another two were busy cleaning the decks of other vessels. Nothing in the marina looked out of place.

'OK, Ernst, I think we're clear. Get ready with the ropes.'

Hagen climbed out of the cockpit, stepped forward to the bow, picked up a rope and stood waiting.

Morschel brought the boat alongside the pontoon opposite its original berth, turned it through 180 degrees and used the engine and rudder to expertly manoeuvre the vessel. A couple of minutes later, Hagen stepped onto the pontoon, looped the mooring rope over a small bollard, then jogged towards the stern of the boat and repeated the operation.

Morschel removed the wires from the inspection hatch on the side of the control panel and the engine spluttered into silence. He replaced the metal plate, handed Hagen the zipped bag holding their personal weapons, quickly checked that they'd left nothing behind in the cockpit and then himself climbed out of the cockpit. Together, Hagen and Morschel replaced the cover on the boat, then headed swiftly back towards the car park where they'd left the Mercedes.

They were still walking along the pontoon when a Kent Police car swung through the gates of the marina and braked to a stop in front of its small office building. Two uniformed officers emerged from the vehicle, their heavy black waistcoats festooned with equipment. They glanced briefly around them, then knocked on the office door and entered.

Medway, Kent

'Oh, shit,' Richter muttered, as he saw the bow of the target vessel moving gently away from him. Immediately, he started swimming as hard as he could, digging the fins powerfully into the water, ignoring the increasing pain from his injured thigh and tracking through the waves at right angles to the course the boat was taking.

He was on the starboard side of the vessel, which at least made him virtually invisible to the man in the cockpit, and was probably seventy yards away from it when he started swimming. The fact that he was comparatively close to the boat meant he didn't have to cover much distance to again position himself on its course, but even swimming the thirty yards that was necessary proved very hard work. In the calm of a swimming pool it would have been an easy task, but it was a different story in the open sea. When he finally stopped, he was panting from the effort.

He spun round in the water to face the approaching craft. Fortunately, he seemed to be more or less right in front of its bow again.

When he estimated his distance from the boat was around twenty-five yards, Richter again turned round in the water and began swimming in the same direction the craft was heading, matching its course and picking the optimum method of getting on board. There were fenders along both sides, but no mooring ropes were visible, so the fenders would just have to do.

The boat was now close enough for the noise of its engine to be clearly audible, and its course appeared unaltered. Richter speeded up and then, as the bow passed him, reached up and grabbed one of the fenders, wrapping his fingers around the rope that secured it to the deck cleat.

The instant his fingers clamped around the rope, it felt like his arm was being pulled out of its socket. The strain on his muscles was immense, and he knew he would have to get on board as quickly as possible. With his other hand, he reached down to his feet and released the fins, because they would be of no more use to him, then dropped his mask. Holding firmly onto the fender rope with his right hand, he reached up with his left and seized one of the safety rail stanchions. Twice his fingers, numb with cold, slipped off the stainless steel, and all the time the strain on his right arm increased horrendously. He tried once again and this time managed to get a firm grip on the rail. He released the rope, reached up and grabbed another stanchion. Then he began to ease himself on board, under the lowest guard rail, keeping absolutely flat on the foredeck.

For a few seconds, Richter lay still, recovering his breath. Then he moved.

SAR Sea King helicopter, callsign 'Rescue 24'

'Boss, he's on the boat now. On the foredeck, starboard side, as planned.'

'Roger that,' the pilot replied. 'Time for our little show.'

He pulled the Sea King up into a hard turn, heading directly towards the boat, then continued to turn away, passing within about twenty yards of the vessel before opening to the south.

Rochester, Kent

Hagen stopped in mid-stride and half-turned away, but Morschel shook his head in warning and carried on walking. Half-way along the pontoon was a bench seat, and the two Germans stopped beside it. Morschel unzipped the bag he was carrying and reached inside it. Keeping his hands hidden in the bag, he checked that the two MP5s were resting on top of the ammunition and other stuff, then nodded to Hagen.

'Only if we have to,' he muttered, and then they walked on.

Medway, Kent

With the various manoeuvres the helicopter had been performing, Badri would have been less than human if he hadn't turned round in the cockpit to watch it depart from the area. But as he turned back to the control panel a movement caught his eye, one that didn't make immediate sense.

Then he realized exactly what was happening, grabbed the Heckler & Koch from the bag beside him and swung it up. How the black-clad figure had managed to get on board he had no idea, but it would take him just seconds to eliminate the problem.

Richter had briefly considered simply shooting the man with his Browning, but decided against it on the slim chance that he'd picked the wrong boat and the occupant of the cockpit was an innocent holidaymaker. So, instead, he'd decided to tackle him face-to-face. But the moment he pulled himself over the top of the cabin and dropped into the cockpit, he realized that was a mistake. The man reacted immediately, grabbing for something hidden in the open bag lying at his feet.

Richter threw himself across the cockpit and slammed his left shoulder into the other man's chest just as he raised the weapon, which Richter immediately recognized as a Heckler & Koch sub-machine gun. That told him all he needed to know about the man he was now facing, and he also knew he had to get the gun away from him. At that close range, one burst from the MP5 would turn Richter into chopped liver.

The force of his impact had forced Badri back against the stern rail, but he managed to keep his grip on the MP5. He swung the weapon round in a vicious arc that connected with the side of Richter's head.

For a second or two, he saw stars. Badri was big and strong and, if it hadn't been for the thick neoprene hood Richter was wearing, that might have been the end of the fight. He shook his head to clear it, dashed aside Badri's right arm with his left and slammed his right fist into the man's solar plexus. Badri grunted and then swung his head sharply forward, aiming to smash his forehead directly into Richter's face. But the Englishman drew back just in time.

As he moved away, Badri swung again with the Heckler & Koch, and the butt of the weapon connected sharply with Richter's ribs. He ignored the sudden pain and delivered another punch to his opponent's torso, then saw the Arab turning the MP5's barrel towards him.

Richter grabbed his opponent's arm just above the wrist, stopping the upward movement of the sub-machine gun, took a step forward and instantly turned so as to place his back to Badri's chest. He altered his grip on the Arab's right arm and pulled it forwards and downwards, simultaneously bending at the waist. The man flew over Richter's bent back and crashed down onto the floor of the cockpit, driving the breath from his body. As he landed, Richter stepped forward and kicked out hard, catching Badri's right arm about midway between wrist and elbow. With a howl of pain, the big man dropped the MP5 and clutched at his forearm. Richter jumped over him, scooped up the weapon and quickly reversed it to aim at the recumbent figure.

'The game's over,' Richter snapped.

'It's not a game,' Badri panted, 'and it's not over.'

He staggered to his feet, glanced across the cockpit at Richter and then made a dash for the control panel.

'It is now,' Richter said grimly. He fired a three-round burst that tore into the Arab's chest and smashed his body against the side of the cockpit. Then, for good measure, he fired a second burst into him.

He put the weapon down on one of the seats, dragged Badri's body over to one side and stepped across to the control panel. As he'd guessed, there was a GPS unit attached to the top of it, linked to an automatic pilot. That should be simple enough to deal with, but what worried him was what else he could see. It looked to him as if the cabin door was fitted with an anti-handling device, and there was a veritable maze of wires running around the cockpit, some vanishing through holes into the cabin itself.

Given time, he could probably have worked out which wires did what, and disarmed or disabled the explosive charges, but time was one thing he hadn't got. Richter peered over the cabin roof and in the distance he could already see the tops of the masts of the *Richard Montgomery*. As if to reinforce the fact of this proximity, the wheel suddenly turned as the autopilot made its final heading correction and the bow of the boat swung round to point directly towards the masts.

Richter studied the GPS unit. The distance still to go registered as a little over a mile and a half, and he was by no means convinced that the people who had wired this boat so comprehensively would have entrusted the detonation solely to the man now lying dead on the floor. There might well be a manual switch somewhere, but the primary ignition system would definitely use some kind of an automated trigger, probably based on the GPS.

But there was no time to find it. The boat was travelling at around eight knots, he estimated, which meant that it would cover the remaining distance in about six minutes, maybe less if whoever had programmed the GPS hadn't got the wreck's position absolutely right.

Somehow, he had to slow down the craft while he figured out the wiring. Richter instinctively reached out to grab the throttle but immediately changed his mind. That, like all the other controls, was clearly protected by an explosive charge. If he tried to alter the setting, he would no doubt lose his hands. And he simply hadn't anything like enough time to start dismantling the anti-handling devices. So that was a non-starter.

He checked the GPS again. Just over a mile – and maybe five minutes – to go. If he couldn't slow the vessel, the only alternative was somehow to steer it away from the wreck. But he couldn't turn the wheel because it, too, was wired with explosive charges. Richter was standing helplessly in a boat full of Semtex, a boat that he could neither turn nor slow down, and that was fitted with an electronic trigger which might detonate the plastic explosive at almost any moment.

Rochester, Kent

Hagen and Morschel had just reached the end of the pontoon and were heading over towards the car park when the office door swung open. A tall, thin man wearing dark blue trousers and a blue sweater stepped out, the two police officers following him. He pointed down towards the pontoon while he explained something.

The two Germans ignored the three men, not even giving them a glance, and continued walking. But then they heard a shout from behind.

Morschel looked back to see the two policemen jogging towards them and, he noted immediately that each man was carrying not only a holstered pistol at his hip, but a Heckler & Koch MP5 slung across his chest, his right hand already cradling the pistol grip. Clearly the British authorities had managed to find out something of their intentions and had successfully tracked them down.

Morschel dodged quickly behind the first vehicle in the car park, dropped the bag and grabbed for one of the weapons it contained. Beside him, Hagen did exactly the same. The two men spun round, using the line of cars as cover, brought their sub-machine guns up to waist height and opened fire.

The two police officers were highly trained in the use of firearms, had excellent scores on the training ranges and could field-strip and rebuild any of the weapons they were qualified to use well within the specified time. Unfortunately, the one area in which they'd never received any instruction was in street-fighting, whereas Morschel and Hagen, in contrast, were experts.

The first bullets were screaming towards the two officers before they'd even properly aimed their weapons, and before either one of them had opened his mouth to issue the official challenge that the rule book required them to utter before opening fire.

The MP5 is an assault weapon, and on all such arms speed of fire and reliability count for more than accuracy, but at that range – less than thirty yards – even the most incompetent of shooters can expect to hit a man-sized target. And Morschel and Hagen were far from incompetent. They fired off tightly aimed bursts of three rounds, and almost half their bullets found their mark.

The two police officers staggered to a halt as the 9-millimetre slugs tore into them, then they fell backwards almost simultaneously. Their Kevlar jackets protected their torsos, but one took a round in the shoulder and the other was hit twice in the thigh. It was all over in less than three seconds.

As their weapons fell silent, Morschel and Hagen stood upright, looking across at the two fallen men, and then jogged the rest of the way to the Mercedes. Hagen tossed the weapons and the bag on the back seat as Morschel started the engine, and with a sudden spurt of gravel the car powered out of the marina.

Behind them, the silence was broken by the moans of pain of the two wounded men, then a series of high-pitched screams erupted from the office as one of the female secretaries rushed to the window to peer out.

Medway, Kent

For several seconds, Richter stood motionless in the cockpit, staring with increasing desperation at the rigged controls. As far as he could see, about his only option was to blow one of the anti-handling devices. With any luck, that would disrupt the firing circuit and prevent the main explosive charge from blowing. Or maybe it would blow the main charge, but still far enough away from the wreck that the half-century old munitions wouldn't detonate. Unfortunately, in either case, he himself would be unlikely to survive.

He was actually on the point of touching the charge fixed on the autopilot when he happened to glance again at the GPS. That was it, he suddenly realized. That was the only weak point in the system – the only component that Morschel hadn't been able to safeguard with explosives. The Semtex that he was certain was somewhere in the boat itself would blow when the vessel's location matched the coordinates stored in the GPS program. All he had to do was change that program, add a way-point that would force the autopilot to take the boat a long way round. A very long way round indeed.

'Got you, you bastard,' Richter muttered.

He pressed the GPS menu button and a list of choices popped up on the screen. The third one was 'Add way-point'. He tapped the screen and in that instant realized that Hans Morschel was both smarter and more thorough than he'd expected. As the screen cleared, a new dialogue box had appeared. In English, the text read: 'Route protected. To alter destination or set a new way-point, insert password.' Below that was a password-entry box, four blank spaces waiting to be filled.

But Richter hadn't got the slightest idea what the password might be.

SAR Sea King helicopter, callsign 'Rescue 24'

After overflying the target boat, the pilot had taken the helicopter up to about a thousand feet and begun to follow it at a distance, the crew watching intently what happened below.

'Why the hell doesn't he turn the boat round, or slow it down?' the pilot muttered. 'The fucking thing's nearly on top of the wreck.'

'Maybe he can't. Maybe the controls are locked, or something.'

'If it's going to blow, we need to get out of here, or at least grab some height. Take us up to two and a half, and then move over Sheppey itself.'

Medway, Kent

For a couple of seconds, Richter just stared at the screen of the GPS unit.

'Fuck,' he murmured, and stepped back from the control panel, rapidly assessing his options. He couldn't slow the boat down or turn it. He couldn't alter any of the controls, and even obvious weak points like the fuel supply and the engine mounts themselves had been protected by explosive charges. And the boat was getting closer to the wreck of the *Richard Montgomery* with every second that passed. He reckoned he now had maybe two minutes to do something before the main charge blew.

Then a thought struck him. He couldn't stop or turn the boat, but maybe he could sink it. Or at least slow it down.

He grabbed the Heckler & Koch, stepped across to the right-hand side of the cockpit and leant out as far as he could. Then he squeezed the trigger and sent a three-second burst of 9-millimetre shells smashing into the side of the fibreglass hull. That, he knew, wouldn't be enough to actually sink it – boats of that type were stuffed full of buoyancy tanks and were virtually unsinkable – but if he could open up a hole in the side of the vessel it would start taking in water and veering to starboard.

The fibreglass disintegrated under this sledge-hammer assault and a ragged-edged gash, about a foot across, appeared in the hull of the boat right at the waterline. Grey-brown water began pouring in, and Richter could feel the boat start tipping slightly to starboard and lurching in the same direction under the increased drag from that side of the craft.

He leant over the rail again and repeated the assault with the MP5, about a metre behind the first hole.

He glanced back across the cockpit. The automatic pilot was already beginning to compensate, the wheel turning anti-clockwise to swing the boat back on course, but Richter could tell that the vessel had slowed perceptibly. Yet he also knew that he was only delaying the inevitable. The damage he'd inflicted on the hull of the craft had given it a pronounced list to starboard, and severely affected its ability to steer a straight course, but unless he could do more – a lot more – the autopilot would eventually succeed in manoeuvring the boat to its planned destination.

He had to do something else, something a lot more dramatic. He pointed the Heckler & Koch straight down and pulled the trigger again, repeating the punishing treatment on the floor of the cockpit. Wood splinters flew in all directions as the 9-millimetre rounds smashed through the duckboards, and only moments later water began flooding in. But the boat still wasn't going to sink, and Richter knew that.

He had, he realized, only two options left. Either he blew one of the anti-tamper charges, which would probably disrupt the main explosive charges and wreck the boat – blowing him to pieces in the process – or find a way of sinking it and himself staying in one piece.

And he could only think of one way to achieve that. He stood up and looked around, searching for the helicopter. As soon as he saw it, he began waving both arms frantically.

SAR Sea King helicopter, callsign 'Rescue 24'

The Sea King was still holding over Sheppey, basically circling Sheerness at a couple of thousand feet, the eyes of the crew fixed on the silently unfolding drama being played out a mile and a half offshore from the town's sea front.

'It's turning away from the wreck, but really slowly. Wait one – he must have sorted it out. He's waving for a pick-up.'

'Right,' the pilot said. 'Dave, get ready with the winch.'

The pilot eased the control column forward, turning onto an intercept course, and began to rapidly descend the aircraft back towards the sea.

Medway, Kent

Richter bent over the Arab's body and searched it. He wasn't surprised to find no wallet or any form of identification, but in one pocket of the man's jacket he discovered a well-used copy of the Koran. That, also, was no surprise. He left the book where it was and looked around for the chopper.

The helicopter was now about a mile behind the boat, but in a steep descent, so Richter guessed it should be above him in about thirty seconds. He just hoped that would be enough time. He checked the cleats and rails around the cockpit and on top of the cabin and then selected the grab-bar that ran along the port side of the cabin roof. That should be strong enough.

The boat was heading broadly north-east, away from Sheppey, and bouncing fairly violently in the waves. And, now that it was clear of the island and the sheltering effect of its landmass, the stiff breeze was very noticeable, the vessel was surrounded by white horses. The water it had already shipped, and the three holes blown through the hull, had markedly altered its handling characteristics, and the boat was lurching violently from side to side.

The helicopter came to a hover just off the port side of the bouncing craft, the winch cable and lifting strap already dangling below it. In the back of the Sea King, Richter could see the aircrewman guiding the cable down towards him. The end of the cable dipped into the water and then skimmed across the surface towards him and, as soon as the lifting strap reached the side of the boat, he reached out and grabbed it.

But instead of dropping the strap around his own body, Richter unclipped one end of it, slipped it under the cabin grab-bar and re-attached it to the clip on the end of the winch cable.

SAR Sea King helicopter, callsign 'Rescue 24'

'What the fuck?' the aircrewman protested on the intercom. 'Boss, that fucking idiot's just attached the lifting strap to one of the stanchions on the boat.'

'He's done what? Jesus. Has he got a radio?'

'No. He ditched it when he put on the wetsuit.'

'Watch him, then. What the hell's he trying to do? And keep your hand on the cable-cutter, just in case.'

Medway, Kent

Richter looked up at the yellow bulk of the Sea King hovering above him, the massive down-wash from its rotor blades combining with the pitching and bucking of the boat to make it difficult for him to keep on his feet. Without a radio, he couldn't explain what he was trying to achieve, so he'd have to rely on hand-signals and just hope the crew grasped his intentions.

Richter leant back against the rear of the cockpit and braced his legs. He extended his right arm horizontally, pointing out to starboard, and brought his left arm up in an arc over his head to point in the same direction. It was a standard signal used by a marshaller to indicate that a hovering helicopter should move over to starboard. Richter repeated it twice more.

SAR Sea King helicopter, callsign 'Rescue 24'

'He wants you to move to starboard, boss,' the aircrewman said. 'OK. I think I see what he's trying to do. He's blown holes in the hull, so the boat's shipping water on its right-hand side and he's attached the winch cable to the left side of the cabin roof. He must be trying to capsize the boat.'

'Why the hell doesn't he just cut the engine or something? This is too fucking risky by far.'

'I don't think he can. That cockpit's a mess of wires, so I think it's probably got booby-traps all over it. This might be all he's got left.'

'This is never going to fucking well work,' the pilot muttered, but he eased the control column gently to the right.

Medway, Kent

Richter watched as the Sea King began moving slowly to his right, while descending slightly, the winch cable hanging loose. He stepped forward a couple of paces and checked the GPS readout. The boat was less than half a mile from the wreck itself.

The helicopter was still moving slowly to his right, but then suddenly stopped, maintaining its position just on the starboard side of the boat.

Richter looked up, wondering what had changed.

SAR Sea King helicopter, callsign 'Rescue 24'

'Dave, watch the cable. Any problems, you cut it and we're out of here.'

'What's wrong, boss?'

'In this position I can't see the boat, that's what's wrong. If this is going to work, I'm going to have to turn us round.'

Medway, Kent

Richter stared upwards, then suddenly guessed what the pilot intended to do.

Above him, the Sea King turned in its own length – in the strong prevailing wind, an impressive piece of flying in itself – and then began matching the boat's sluggish forward speed, which meant the helicopter was flying backwards.

Richter could see the aircrewman begin tensioning the winch cable, the right-hand seat man looking down and obviously calling distances and angles.

The boat suddenly pitched bow-down. The winch cable snapped taut and Richter could feel the lurch as the turning force exerted by the cable started lifting the port side of the craft. The cockpit was now awash to a depth of about a foot, and the vessel had about a twenty-degree list to starboard, caused by the flooding of the buoyancy tanks on the right-hand side of the hull. It shouldn't, he hoped, take too much to capsize it altogether.

SAR Sea King helicopter, callsign 'Rescue 24'

'Keep your eyes on that cable, Dave. I'm moving away now.'

'Roger, boss.'

The pilot began easing the control column slightly to the left, away from the bouncing boat, trying to keep the winch cable reasonably taut and waiting for the right moment. He watched the waves, seeing how the seventeen-footer below rose and fell. He waited until a large swell passed under the boat, so that it began to roll even further over to starboard as the wave lifted its port side. That was the optimum moment.

He increased power slightly and moved the control column a little further to the left.

Medway, Kent

Richter felt the port side of the boat lift, and he moved over to the right-hand side of the cockpit, grasping a stanchion with both hands. Even as he did so, the combined effect of the damage he'd already caused, the wave passing under the boat and the lifting effect supplied by the helicopter achieved the result he'd been hoping for. With a suddenness that almost took him by surprise, the boat flipped, and his world instantly turned black as the craft rolled over on top of him.

SAR Sea King helicopter, callsign 'Rescue 24'

'It's gone, boss,' the aircrewman called out, simultaneously releasing the winch cable so that it hung slackly beneath the helicopter.

'Roger that,' the pilot replied, moving the Sea King back and to the right, until it was almost directly over the upturned boat.

'Where the hell's Richter?'

'He went over with it.'

Medway, Kent

Richter had taken a deep breath as the boat rolled over, just before he sank beneath the waves, and he was now struggling under the craft, trying to find the end of the winch cable in the darkness. And he *had* to find it, because without the cable he had no way of getting back into the Sea King.

A heavy object struck him in the face, and he realized he was wrestling with the body of the dead Arab. He pushed the arm of the corpse aside and again began groping around in the dark. But the cable remained elusive.

He surfaced briefly in the upturned cockpit, where a pocket of air was trapped in one corner, breathed out, gulped in another lungful, then ducked under the surface again, feeling for the rail running along the top of the cabin. This time he found it and in the gloom he could just detect the yellowish shape of the lifting strap.

Richter grabbed it, ran his hand along it until he found the catch, then pressed it open. He released one of the ends of the strap, and pulled on the other. At first it came freely, then it stopped, jammed somewhere.

Conscious of his increasingly urgent need to breathe, Richter slid his hand down the length of the strap, feeling for the obstruction. Then he found it. The ring at the end of the strap had jammed vertically under the stanchion atop the cabin, but a quick tug freed it.

Keeping tight hold of the strap, Richter pushed himself down and away from the cockpit. Kicking out powerfully with his legs, he clawed his way to the surface.

SAR Sea King helicopter, callsign 'Rescue 24'

'There he is. About ten feet west of the hull. And he's got hold of the cable. I can see the lifting strap.'

'Roger. Get him inside as soon as you can.'

Medway, Kent

At the surface, Richter just trod water for a few seconds, getting his breath back. Then he clicked the loose end of the lifting strap onto the hook at the end of the winch cable and dropped the strap over his shoulders, settling it under his arms.

He looked up, checked all around him to ensure that the lifting cable hadn't snagged on anything, gave a thumbs-up gesture then forced his arms down by his sides. The cable tightened almost immediately, and a moment later he was ten feet above the surface of the water and rising steadily.

As he began his ascent towards the hovering Sea King, the timer Hans Morschel had wired into the detonator circuit as a fail-safe had less than three minutes to run. And, battery-powered like the plastic explosive to which it was connected, its immersion in sea water would have no effect on it at all.

SAR Sea King helicopter, callsign 'Rescue 24'

'He's safely in the aircraft, boss,' the aircrewman reported on the intercom as he slid the side door closed and watched Richter walk across the rear section of the aircraft and peel off the wetsuit hood.

'Roger that. Get a headset on him as soon as possible, will you?'

'Any second now.'

Richter grabbed a towel, quickly dried his face and hair, then pulled on a headset.

'Richter.'

'Right, we're heading back up the Medway. Who do you want to talk to, and do you want me to pass on any messages for you?'

'Yes, just while I get dressed, could you contact the Coastguard and give them the approximate course that overturned boat's following. Warn them it's loaded with explosives, and that they might find one dead body in the cockpit – unless it's floated away by now.'

'Who was he?'

'No idea. He looked Middle Eastern, and the Koran in his pocket probably means these German terrorists did have a connection to al Qaeda after all. The boat will need specialist examination when they recover it, because the terrorists stuffed it with booby-traps as well. They'll also have to—'

Richter broke off as a huge explosion rocked the Sea King.

'What the fuck was that?' he demanded. 'Was that the boat?'

'Wait.'

Richter braced himself against the side of the fuselage as the helicopter swept round in a hard starboard turn.

'That,' the pilot announced, once he'd stabilized the aircraft on a north-easterly heading, '*was* your boat, with the emphasis on the past tense. Something made the explosives on board detonate.'

'Let me see,' Richter muttered and threaded his way through to the back of the cockpit. Peering between the two pilots, he could see a huge circular area of disturbed water, small pieces of debris barely visible, and an expanding surface wave. Above the site of the explosion, an enormous spray of both smoke and water was slowly dispersing.

'Could that cause the munitions on the *Richard Montgomery* to explode?'

'I don't know,' Richter muttered. 'It's quite a long way from the wreck, so I hope not. But we'll find out in just a few seconds.'

The pilot turned the Sea King again, back towards Sheppey, but kept it well clear of the wreck site. They watched as the wave created by the explosion washed over the half-submerged masts of the remains of the Liberty Ship. They were involuntarily holding their breath, but nothing further happened.

'Good,' Richter breathed. 'I guess the detonation needed to be right on top of the wreck for this plan to work. There must have been a timer in the circuit as well as the GPS-triggered detonation system.' Richter glanced at both pilots in turn. 'I'm fucking glad you picked me up so quickly, otherwise I'd now be discussing my entry criteria with St Peter, and probably not doing all that well at it. Thanks, guys. I mean it.'

'No problem. All part of the service. I'll update that message to the Coastguards, then?'

'Yes, please. Right, I'd better get dressed. Can you now head back towards London?'

'You got it.'

Rochester, Kent

Both police officers were still alive but bleeding profusely from their wounds. Within seconds of the fire-fight finishing, one of them had gasped an urgent call for assistance into his personal radio. This roughly coincided with two panicky '999' calls from marina staff – the manager using his mobile, and one of the secretaries on an office phone.

The marina staff did as much as they could, wrapping towels and anything else suitable they could find around the officers' wounds to try to staunch the bleeding. The first two police cars arrived within twelve minutes, and the ambulance three minutes after that. Within half an hour the car park and lane outside were virtually full of official vehicles of various types, and for nearly twenty minutes now six officers had been gathered inside the office building taking statements from the handful of witnesses.

Their questioning had resulted in the release of an APB for a grey Mercedes on Austrian registration plates, with the caveat that the occupants were well armed and certainly dangerous.

SAR Sea King helicopter, callsign 'Rescue 24'

'There's been a shooting,' the pilot reported on the intercom. 'At a marina just outside Rochester. Two police officers have been seriously injured, and the cops are searching for a grey Mercedes saloon, two up.'

'I know who the bad guys are, or who one of them is, anyway. Right, can you patch me through to the Kent Police control room?'

'Yes, we should be able to.'

'And I don't know exactly where we are now, but can you get us over to the Rochester area ASAP?'

'No problem. We should be over the town itself in about three minutes.'

Thirty seconds later, Richter was talking on the phone to a constable at the Maidstone headquarters of the Kent Police Force.

'And you are who, exactly?' the officer asked.

'I'm an armed intelligence officer overhead Rochester in a Royal Air Force helicopter and I want to be patched through to Detective Inspector Mason.'

'I'm not sure that's permitted.'

'I'm not interested in what the rules and regulations say. Just do it.

Bugger me about, constable, and I can make sure you end up pounding the beat for the rest of what passes for your career.'

'Is that a threat, sir?'

'More of a promise, really, so just get on with it.'

'I'll be reporting this to my superiors.'

'Be my guest, but just get a fucking move on.'

Ten seconds later, Richter heard Mason's voice in his headset.

'This is Richter,' he said. 'Give me a SITREP, please.'

'Right, we've got two officers down, badly wounded but both should survive, thanks to their vests. They were running a check at a marina just outside Rochester, and two men were just leaving one of the pontoons. The officers called out for them to stop so they could question them, but instead the men opened up with sub-machine guns. Then they drove off in a grey Mercedes. We're assuming one of them must have been Hans Morschel.'

'Certainly makes sense,' Richter said. 'Which way did they go? I'm in a chopper right now, so give me a direction, and we'll run a search.'

'We've no idea, because nobody saw which way they turned. There are two motorways and a couple of trunk roads nearby, so they could be heading in almost any direction except north, because that's a dead end. My guess is that they'll either try to lose themselves in London or blast straight down to Dover or one of the other Channel ports. We're trying to cover everything now.'

'Morschel's not stupid, and he'll have an escape route already planned. My guess is he'll either have a clean car stashed somewhere, or maybe even another boat, so there's a good chance we won't find him. It'll probably be a complete waste of time, but we'll check the coast-bound motorways and see if we can spot him.'

'Thanks. We'll keep this line open, just in case.'

Chapter Nineteen

Monday
SAR Sea King helicopter, callsign 'Rescue 24'

'Sorry, but that's about it. Our fuel state means we've got to cut this off now, unless you want to come back to Wattisham with us.'

'An attractive offer, but no thanks,' Richter said. 'On the way, can you take me back to Hammersmith?'

'Yes, I was already factoring that into the calculations. Same place, I suppose?'

'Please.'

The chopper had systematically flown up and down the coast-bound roads, its crew searching for a grey Mercedes on Austrian plates, but without result.

'Hang on a minute,' Richter said, as the Sea King began a long turn to starboard. 'I think we're missing something here. We know what Morschel looks like, so whatever car he's driving now there's a good chance he'll be recognized at whatever ferry port he chooses. I somehow don't think he'd take the risk.'

'What about a boat, then?' the pilot suggested. 'There are dozens of places where he could pick one up in Kent.'

'Agreed, but my guess is that he'll want to get out of here as quickly as possible. Don't forget, he's left about twenty dead bodies behind him in London. In fact, I think he'll want to fly out.'

'You could be right, but which airport?'

'How many are there in this area?'

'Several, that's the problem.'

'OK,' Richter said, 'let's try and narrow it down a bit. He won't be flying commercial, so that eliminates places like London City and Gatwick, but wherever he's chosen will most likely have a proper runway, not just a grass strip, because he couldn't have been certain about the state of the weather. And it will be fairly close to Rochester, as he wouldn't want to drive far with most of the Kent Constabulary out looking for him. You know the area better than I do, so what would be your choice?'

'The closest is obviously Rochester itself, but that's fairly busy – lots of microlights and stuff – so I'd guess Biggin Hill, or maybe Headcorn. Plus there's Lydd, but that's a bit too far away, right down by New Romney.'

'Right, thanks. Don't leave the area, though. If necessary, get some fuel at London City or Manston.'

Richter changed channels and opened the line to Mason again. 'Richter. I'm only guessing, but I think Morschel will want to get out of here as quickly as possible. Can you check with the airfields at Biggin Hill, Headcorn, Rochester and Lydd and see if any of their aircraft are flight-planned for departure to France today, or specifically if any two men have booked a flight together, with or without a pilot.'

'Got it,' Mason replied. 'Anything else?'

'No. That's about the only idea I've had. Any progress on the ground?'

'Nothing yet. And, realistically, they could be almost anywhere by now. We'll keep looking, obviously, but I'm not hopeful.'

Kent

Morschel wasn't heading for either London or the Channel ports: he had a very different destination in mind. He'd steered the Mercedes south down the A229 as far as Maidstone, then pulled the car into a multi-storey park on the northern outskirts of the town. He took a ticket at the entrance, waited for the barrier to lift, then drove up to the fourth-floor level. In one corner stood a dark-blue Jaguar on British plates, and Morschel slotted the Mercedes into an empty bay a few yards away.

He climbed out, retrieving the ticket, waited for Hagen to pluck their bag of weapons off the back seat, then locked the car and pocketed the keys. Then Morschel took another set of keys from his jacket and aimed the remote control at the Jaguar. Hagen deposited the bag on the floor right in front of the back seat, where it would be easily accessible if necessary, though neither man really expected to need the weapons again.

Morschel backed the Jaguar – purchased by one of his men almost a month earlier and parked here waiting for this moment – out of its space and drove it down the ramps towards the exit. He stopped on the second floor and fed the ticket into a machine, paid the modest charge – having been in the car park only about eight minutes – then drove on down to the exit. The automatic barrier lifted as soon as he inserted the ticket in the slot, and he turned the Jaguar out of the car park and onto the street.

'We need the southbound A229,' he instructed Hagen, who was studying a map of Kent. 'Keep your eyes open.'

Because of the traffic flow, and the sheer volume of vehicles on the road, they had little option but to drive through the centre of the town, but that wasn't a problem. They now had plenty of time in hand.

'OK,' Hagen said, 'straight on here, and just follow the signs for Staplehurst. When we get to Shepway, look out for the left turn towards Tenterden. That's the A274.'

'Got it. Make the call now and tell them we're about ten minutes away.'

Hagen pulled the mobile from his pocket and dialled a Kent number. 'This is Mr Williams,' he announced, in fluent and unaccented English, once his call was answered, 'just advising you we'll be with you in about ten minutes. We're running a bit late, so if you could be ready as soon as we get there, that would be much appreciated.'

He listened for a few seconds, then ended the call.

'They'll be waiting for us,' he confirmed.

SAR Sea King helicopter, callsign 'Rescue 24'

Mason was back on the line in under four minutes.

'All the airfields have flights booked that fit your criteria – lots of training trips, first-time experience flights and PPL lessons, but only Lydd and Headcorn have bookings for flights to France. There are three from Lydd and a couple from the other airfield. In all cases the passengers are a couple of males.'

'Thanks. We're guessing that Headcorn's the most likely, because it's closer to Rochester. Thanks for that. We'll take it from here.'

Richter got back on the intercom. 'Headcorn,' he instructed the pilot.

Headcorn, Kent

Just eight minutes after leaving the outskirts of Maidstone, Hans Morschel was driving over the bridge at the southern end of Headcorn village on the Biddenden Road. Almost immediately beyond, he pointed to the left.

'There it is,' he said.

Hagen nodded and replaced the map in the glove-box.

A few seconds later, the Jaguar turned left off the main road into Burnt-house Lane, and then swung left again, taking the second entrance into Headcorn aerodrome.

'The weapons?' Hagen gestured to the bag stashed behind the front seats, as soon as Morschel had pulled the car to a stop.

'We'd better take them, just in case.'

Each man was wearing a modified shoulder holster designed to carry the MP5 with the stock folded. Within a few seconds they'd pulled the sub-machine guns from the bag, checked that each magazine held a full load and carefully tucked the weapons out of sight. The two men left the main parking area and headed for the terminal buildings, but almost the first thing they saw when the runway came in sight was a large yellow Sea King helicopter, emblazoned with RAF roundels, sitting on a hardstanding.

Hans Morschel had survived as long as he had through possessing a highly developed sense of danger and the moment he spotted the chop-per he stopped dead.

'We saw one just like that over the Medway,' Hagen remarked anxiously.

'Exactly,' Morschel replied, his glance flicking left and right, searching for any signs of a police presence. But he saw nothing to give him cause for concern and then began to relax as Hagen pointed out a bowser approaching along the taxiway and coming to a halt beside the Sea King.

'It must have just come here to refuel,' Hagen said.

'Maybe,' Morschel responded. 'Or maybe not. Let's assume it didn't, so keep your eyes open, just in case.'

Then they carried on towards the building housing the air charter company they'd booked with.

'Is that them?' asked Richter, staring through the window at the two approaching men, both carrying large holdalls.

'Could be,' said the young pilot standing beside him, 'but don't forget I've never laid eyes on this man Williams. The booking was done over the phone, and he's supposed to be paying cash, so I've no confirmation that's even his real name. The timing's about right, though.'

He glanced at the combat shotgun Richter had stashed behind the office door. 'What are you going to do now? Arrest them?'

'Probably shoot them,' Richter confessed, 'once I know for sure they're the two men I'm looking for.'

'Jesus,' the pilot muttered. 'They don't look much like terrorists.'

'If we knew what terrorists actually looked like, identifying them would be a whole lot easier. Right, give me your name tag and then thin out. I'll take it from here.'

The pilot handed over a plastic clip-on identification badge that bore a set of stylized wings and the name 'Peter Hughes'. He then disappeared through a door at the rear of the office.

Richter clipped the name tag to the lapel of his leather jacket, which he had to keep on to conceal the shoulder holster he was wearing, picked up the SPAS-12 and carried it behind the counter that ran along the back of the room.

Moments later, the office door opened, and the two men he'd been watching from the window walked in. The moment Richter saw the thin-faced man clearly, and from a distance of no more than fifteen feet, he was ninety per cent sure he was looking at Hans Morschel. The image Karl Wolff had originally shown him was indelibly imprinted on his mind.

'Good afternoon,' Richter began, in his best corporate voice. 'Can I help you?'

'Yes.' Hagen placed his bag on the floor and stepped towards the counter. 'You've a reservation for Williams plus one, for a flight to France?'

For a bare half-second, Richter glanced down at the booking ledger lying open in front of him, then looked up with a smile. 'Dinner in Le Touquet, I gather, gentlemen.'

'Actually, we've got business there this evening,' Hagen said, 'and we decided to spend the night.'

'Good decision. Le Touquet airfield closes at eighteen hundred UTC, so you probably wouldn't be able to get back tonight anyway. And what about tomorrow? Do you want to book an aircraft for your return journey?'

'No, thanks,' Hagen said. 'We might decide to stay on for a day or two. We'll let you know later.'

'No problem,' Richter said. 'We'll be taking the Piper PA28 Cherokee that's parked just outside.'

He pointed to a red and white aircraft visible through one of the office windows and, inevitably, both men glanced in that direction. As they did so, Richter dropped his gaze from their faces and looked at their chests or, more accurately, their jackets, and could see the distinct bulges under their left armpits. OK, that was far from conclusive – they could just have very fat wallets – but it suggested they were armed, and that was almost enough for him. But there was still the faint possibility that he was mistaken and he needed to be absolutely sure before he acted.

As the two men returned their attention to him, Richter stared at Morschel. 'I'm sure I know you from somewhere,' he said. 'Have you flown with us before?'

The German shook his head firmly. 'Definitely not.'

'Oh,' Richter said, reaching down behind the counter and seizing the pistol grip of the SPAS-12. 'Then it must have been over in Germany, just before GSG 9 hit your base in Stuttgart.'

For an instant, neither man moved, then almost simultaneously they stepped apart, moving sideways to present separate targets as they reached inside their jackets, their movements very smooth and well practised.

Although Richter was expecting them to do exactly that, the two

Germans moved much more quickly than he had anticipated. Before he could bring the shotgun to bear, Hagen squeezed the trigger of his MP5, and Richter had to dive for what little cover the counter offered him.

A stream of 9-millimetre bullets tore through the thin wood that formed the base of the structure, smashing into the wall behind as they sought out their target. He popped up for an instant, squeezed off one round at Hagen from the combat shotgun, then ducked back down and rolled the other way.

Both MP5s opened up on him, their staccato yammering deafening in that confined space, and Richter knew he had to finish this, and quickly, or else they'd finish him. If the two Germans reached the opposite ends of the counter while he was still behind it, he'd be caught in a crossfire, and seconds later he'd be dead. He poked the muzzle of the shotgun over the top of the counter, fired blind, then ducked back again, dodging sideways.

Richter heard guttural shouts in German and, from their voices, guessed where the two terrorists had to be standing. He jumped up, finding Hagen right in front of him, sighted instantly and fired another shell from the SPAS-12 directly towards him. Then he threw himself sideways as Morschel swung round the muzzle of his MP5.

A three-round burst from Morschel smashed through the wooden counter and into the brick wall less than three feet from where Richter was crouching. But it was, he noted, now only a single weapon firing. Hagen's MP5 had fallen silent, so maybe the last shot from the SPAS-12 had hit home.

And it actually had been the last shot, he realized. The breech of the shotgun was locked open, meaning that the magazine was now empty. Without hesitation, Richter dropped the weapon on the floor, pulled the Browning out of his shoulder holster and clicked off the safety catch. For only the briefest of instants he debated which way to go, then the sound of Morschel's footsteps made the decision for him.

As the German stepped over to one end of the counter, Richter scuttled to the other, leapt out from behind it and turned instantly, the Browning held at arm's length, his left hand bracing his right, the weapon aimed steadily at Morschel.

The German was caught totally wrong-footed, his sub-machine gun pointing downwards and in the wrong direction. Immediately he swung around, bringing the MP5 up to the aim. But it was never going to be fast enough. Richter pulled the Browning's trigger once, then a second time. Morschel tumbled backwards, his shirt suddenly turning deep red as the two bullets struck him, the Heckler & Koch falling from his grasp.

Richter took a quick glance to his left, where the second German lay motionless. The 3-inch magnum round from the SPAS-12 had blown a 6-inch wide hole in the middle of his chest, and he was very obviously dead. But Morschel wasn't, as Richter realized when he took a couple of steps towards him.

He was lying flat on his back at one end of the ruined counter, his left hand pressed against the sodden front of his shirt. It looked as if Richter's bullets had both hit close to his right shoulder. He was cursing fluently in German and using his feet to try to reach the MP5 he'd dropped. Richter stepped around him and kicked the weapon out of reach.

Morschel glared up at him, and switched to English.

'Get me to a fucking hospital, you bastard.'

For a few seconds, Richter just stared down at him, then he shook his head. 'Sorry, my friend, but I've had explicit orders about you. You died in the fire-fight when I tried to arrest you. Just like your friend over there.'

'You can't do that,' Morschel snarled. 'That's murder.'

'Tell me about it – you're the expert, aren't you? No, my boss told me he doesn't want the expense and inconvenience of a trial, but even if he did, I'd kill you anyway. And this has nothing to do with the bank jobs your men pulled up in London today, or your failed attempt to blow up the *Richard Montgomery*.'

'So why, then?' Morschel spluttered.

'Because I met Helmut Kleber, or rather Gregory Stevens, on the last night of his life. And then I saw what you did to him. For me, that's reason enough.'

Richter aimed his pistol at Morschel's head.

'Wait, wait,' the German screamed. 'That wasn't me.'

'Maybe not, but you organized it, and that's the same thing, in my book.'

'No, it isn't. I'll trade you. Get me to a hospital and I'll tell you who killed Stevens. And who decided to try to blow up the munitions on that wreck.'

'OK, I'm listening.' Richter lowered the pistol.

'We were working with al Qaeda, and the man I dealt with was named Ahmed bin Salalah, and he's their front man in Europe. He came up with the idea for hitting that ship – and he killed Stevens.'

'Who was the man on the boat, then? I presume he was a member of al Qaeda?'

'He was just someone called Badri, and he was bin Salalah's cousin. I don't know if he was a member of the group or just recruited for that one job. Now I've told you, so call me a fucking ambulance.'

'I don't think so. That information's helpful, but not helpful enough for me to change my mind.'

'You promised, you bastard.'

'I lied,' Richter said, and pulled the trigger.

Hammersmith, London

Richter leant both the SPAS-12 and the MP5 against the wall in one corner of Simpson's office and then dropped an overnight bag beside them.

'What's in that?' Simpson pointed.

'Hans Morschel and his boyfriend had a pair of MP5s. I brought their weapons along with me.'

'Just make sure they get into the armoury, Richter. I don't want to find you've stashed them away somewhere else. Right, so what exactly happened?'

Richter explained the sequence of events to him.

'So it definitely *was* an attempt to blow up those munitions on the *Richard Montgomery*?'

'Absolutely.'

'And you couldn't have stopped it any other way? By cutting the fuel line or something?'

Richter shook his head. 'Just about every control and connection was fitted with an anti-tamper charge. The man who prepared that craft knew exactly what he was doing.'

'And that wasn't the Arab, whoever he was, sitting in the cockpit?'

'No. According to Morschel, he was only there as a bodyguard to repel boarders, and as a final way of detonating the explosive if everything else failed. The whole thing was automated, and he was pretty much just along for the ride.'

'Did you have to kill him? He might have told us something useful.'

Richter nodded. 'I had no choice. It was either him or me. He made a dive for the controls and I reckon he was going to try to fire the main explosive charge right then.'

'No idea who he was?'

'Apparently his name was Badri and he was a cousin of Ahmed bin Salalah. I think he was just a *shahid* recruited for the operation, but we'll never know now, as he's busy feeding the aquatic livestock off Sheerness. If you fancy a fish supper, Kent and Essex might be good places to avoid for the next few weeks.'

'Don't be disgusting, Richter. Now, back to Morschel. I know I told you I didn't want that German thug to stand trial,' Simpson had a sour expression on his face, 'but what you did was an execution, pure and simple. Not exactly what I had in mind.'

'It doesn't matter, one way or the other. He forfeited his right to live because of what he did to Gregory Stevens. The last thing we needed was a trial with some whingeing liberal defence lawyer explaining to the jury about Morschel's deprived childhood and all that bollocks. You have a boil, you lance it, and that's exactly what I did. End of story. If the woodentops do come chasing after me, I'm quite sure you can arrange me a water-tight alibi. Perhaps a dinner in Yorkshire with a couple of the more pliable Members of Parliament who owe you favours, that kind of thing.'

'Probably,' Simpson nodded curtly.

'Any sign of the money Morschel's men took from those banks?'

'Not yet. The Met have discovered that the fake vans were hired from a television prop supply company. They'd apparently been booked by an outfit named "BB Productions", with an address on a trading estate in Romford. The plods have raided the premises and found nothing there apart from the replica weapons and blank ammunition supplied as part of the package, so that trail's gone cold. All the bank accounts used to buy the company, pay the rent, hire charges and all the rest have been closed. We could try back-checking all the documentation these guys used to open those accounts, but my guess is it'll prove to be another dead end. Two of the police vans were also found, both cleaned out. No fingerprints or trace evidence in either of them, or at least nothing the Met's admitted to yet. No sign of the uniforms, weapons or the money, obviously. But I suppose something may still turn up.'

'I wouldn't hold your breath waiting. This wasn't just a bunch of hoods with shooters and a getaway car hitting a couple of banks. This was a very slick operation, carried out by a gang of ruthless thugs who knew exactly what they were doing. Look at the planning that was involved. They set up bank accounts, created a front company, hired premises and all the rest. You've almost got to admire the sheer professionalism of it. And I don't believe that a bunch of people taking that kind of trouble wouldn't have worked out a way to get themselves and their loot out of the country. We've no clue who they are, apart from Hans Morschel himself, so there's no way of identifying and then stopping them.'

'And the money?'

'If they haven't organized a container or something to hide it in and then ship it over to Germany, they've probably just tucked it away in suitcases lying in the backs of their cars, or stuffed it under the seats. It's amazing how much cash you can hide inside the spare wheel well. With the amount of vehicular traffic using Dover, there's no way every car, or even every hundredth car, can be searched, so they've got a very good chance of not being stopped.'

'The Customs people will be targeting German cars,' Simpson pointed out.

'Good plan. Unfortunately, we've no idea if Morschel's men will be driving German vehicles. He arrived in a car on German plates, but the vehicle itself was probably registered in Austria. Remember how Stevens was driving a French-registered hire car, so these people probably hired cars from a bunch of different locations in Western Europe – France, Belgium, Holland, Italy, Spain or wherever – and we can't hope to stop *every* non-British-plated vehicle. And there's nothing to say, either, that they didn't fly to Britain and hire cars here to drive back to Germany. No, I don't think we're going to recover any of that money, and I very much doubt if we'll see any of those guys standing in the dock.'

'In short, we've been comprehensively pissed on,' Simpson said acidly.

'In a nutshell, yes. But we did get Morschel and the man I presume was his number two, which should please the German authorities, and we stopped them detonating London's permanent timebomb in the Thames Estuary, so in that sense you could say we lost the battle but won the war.'

'Good cliché.'

'Good and, like most clichés, also true. But this isn't quite over yet.'

'You think you can find this bin Salalah?' Simpson's surprise was obvious.

Richter shook his head. 'Not any time soon, and I wasn't actually thinking about him. I meant Gregory Stevens. I know he's dead, but I've been going over what he told me – or rather didn't tell me. We know he was a former CIA officer who 'died' shortly after retirement from the agency so that he could operate undercover more easily. When I talked to him down at Maidstone, he made a remark that didn't make much sense at the time. We were discussing this bombing campaign, and Stevens said something like 'It wasn't really Morschel's idea.' I meant to ask him what he meant by that, but I forgot.

'Now, put that together with what I learnt from John Westwood at Langley, that something called The Special Group was probably involved with this operation, and I'm wondering if the prime mover in this plan was actually Stevens himself or, in fact, the man he was report-ing to. In short, I think it's possible that Morschel's bombing campaign was orchestrated, or at the very least suggested, by somebody in Wash-ington.'

'Are you serious? Why the hell would the Yanks want to do that? Aren't we *supposed* to be their staunchest allies?'

'Right now, I've no idea. But Stevens did tell me that I wouldn't have believed his briefing.'

'So what are you going to do about it? Do you actually know who briefed him?'

'He may have been a CIA officer named Richard Kellerman, but he's dead too.'

Richter told Simpson what Westwood had discovered about Kellerman's murder in Washington, and his possible link to Stevens.

'But if Stevens and Kellerman are both dead, that's the end of the trail, isn't it?'

'Not necessarily. If John Westwood's right, Kellerman was just an expendable junior officer instructed to deliver a briefing, who was then killed simply to tie up a loose end. If so, I need to talk to the man who ordered his assassination, because he was ultimately the brains behind whatever this plan was about.'

'And how, pray, can you do that?'

'There might be a way.' Richter then explained what he'd found on the sheet of coded groups that Cheltenham had decrypted for him.

'OK,' Simpson said, when he'd finished, 'so now you'll want to head across the pond, I suppose?'

'Probably not, in fact. My guess is that this mystery man would have wanted to be in at the kill, so to speak, and I think he's probably already over here. Once the bombing campaign finished, he would want to ensure Gregory Stevens wouldn't be able to tell anyone what he'd been up to, because he really was the last loose end. I suspect he's still here, waiting for Stevens to show himself, and then he'll try and kill him.'

'But Stevens is already dead.'

'*We* know that, but I specifically asked the Kent woodentops to keep it quiet as long as possible, so most likely this guy *won't* be aware of it. I hope. So I'm going to use Stevens's emergency exfiltration code and see what that produces.'

Simpson mulled that over for a few moments, then nodded agreement. 'Approved. Do you need any back-up?'

'Yes, but I'll arrange it myself, thanks. I think this operation has been very tightly controlled, and the last thing this man will want is a lot more people getting involved, especially if they might become witnesses to a killing. My guess is, if he responds at all, he'll be acting by himself, or maybe just with one or two accomplices. But I've no doubt they'll be bristling with weapons.'

'Right. Just make sure you extract whatever information he's got before you blow him away. No doubt that's your intention?'

'Oh, yes. This man may personally have clean hands, but he's indirectly responsible for dozens of deaths. If I've got anything to do with it, he'll be heading back to the States in a pine box.'

American Embassy, Grosvenor Square, London

Carlin F. Johnson had two mobile phones, only one of which was registered to him. The second one contained a pay-as-you-go chip, and he only switched it on for three one-hour periods every day. Since the operation began, it had never rung once, but that evening, at exactly seven twenty-nine, it did.

Johnson made no attempt to answer it, just checked the caller's identity, which was predictably unhelpful, as the phone simply reported a 'private number'. He looked at his watch and began counting. It rang three times, then stopped. Two minutes later, it rang again and this time stopped after precisely nine rings. After that, it remained silent, but the mobile had conveyed all the information he needed. Stevens had completed his assignment, even though Johnson was somewhat disappointed with the result, and the code '3, 9' meant he should 'meet at the emergency rendezvous tomorrow morning at ten twenty'.

And that meant he had plenty of time to make all the preparations necessary.

Chapter Twenty

Tuesday
Dungeness, Kent

It was almost, Richter thought, like a moonscape: bleak and with a peculiar other-world feel to it. Dungeness was, without question, one of the strangest places he'd ever visited. The beach, if one could call it that, was shingle and almost completely flat, with metalled roads meandering through it, an expanse dotted with what looked like large beach huts, but which on closer examination were more like small weekend cottages. In total contrast, the western edge of the promontory was dominated by the distant hulking shape of the Dungeness nuclear power station.

He'd checked the location very carefully the previous evening. The sheet of paper the Kent detectives had found in Stevens's hotel room, and that GCHQ had subsequently decrypted, had specified the exact geographical coordinates of this emergency rendezvous, and also a simple date and time code to be conveyed by ringing a particular mobile phone number.

Richter had arrived there at a quarter to ten and parked the Jaguar – claiming to Simpson that he needed the car's built-in satnav to make sure he found the place in time – at the precise location, which was simply an unmarked concrete slab just off the single-track road. In his shoulder holster he had the Browning, and resting on the passenger seat was the fully loaded SPAS-12, the best close-quarter weapon he'd ever used.

He glanced at his watch. Ten zero five. If the man was going to turn up at all, he should arrive in about fifteen minutes. But even as that uncertain thought crossed his mind, he saw two black American Ford saloon cars approaching, the vehicles bouncing on their soft springs as they lurched over the uneven surface.

Richter left the shotgun on the passenger seat, but pulled out the

Browning and checked it yet again. Then he replaced it in the holster and waited, watching the approaching vehicles carefully.

One Ford stopped about twenty feet away, on the other side of the concrete slab, and the second on the road just behind it. The windows and windscreens of both vehicles were heavily tinted, and all Richter could see were a couple of vague shapes in each.

Then a man climbed out of the driver's side of the car nearest to him. The moment Richter saw him move, he did the same. He picked up the SPAS-12, stepped out of the Jaguar and walked round the car to lean against the passenger door. The figure who had emerged from the Ford looked American – dark suit, loafers, a light tan and dark hair cropped short – and he stared across at Richter with a sour expression. The MAC-10 sub-machine gun he was holding also looked American. The weapon, Richter saw immediately, was fitted with a bulky suppressor, which was hardly good news, and the man looked as if he knew exactly how to use it.

To his left, Richter heard the sound of car doors closing and glanced round. Two other men – virtual clones of the first one – had emerged from the second car and immediately moved apart. He noted, without surprise, that each was also holding a MAC-10, and that the muzzles of the sub-machine guns were pointing directly at him.

He was instantly outgunned and guessed that, if he raised the shot-gun, now hanging loosely from his right hand, he'd be dead in seconds. But he didn't even attempt to move because, apart from the SPAS-12, he had two aces up his sleeve.

'Figures,' the man opposite him muttered and slapped the roof of his car. Immediately, the passenger door opened. Yet another man stepped out and glared over at Richter.

'Who the fuck are you?' he demanded. 'And where's Stevens?'

'Stevens didn't make it,' Richter said. 'But we thought you'd want to know what happened to him.'

'How did you know our emergency rendezvous routine?'

'We decrypted the data sheet you supplied him, or maybe that was Kellerman.'

'How the hell do you know about Kellerman? And who are you?' he repeated.

'My name's Richter, and I work for the British government,' Richter responded, 'and we've been tracking your man Stevens for a while.' A lie, but it could easily have been the truth. 'What's *your* name?'

'It's Johnson, not that you're going to live long enough to use that information.'

'We'll see about that,' Richter replied. 'We know that when Agent Kellerman was shot in Washington it wasn't just a random mugging. Who did you order to do it, then? The chauffeur? That was Roy Craven, wasn't it?'

'Jesus, what the hell else do you know?'

'Almost everything.'

'So why are you here?'

'I'm here because about the only thing we don't know about this business is why. Why did you order this operation? Oh, and we don't know who you really are either, but actually we don't care. We just assumed you were another expendable asset recruited by The Special Group to do their dirty work.'

The American was clearly growing more angry by the second, and Richter guessed he'd like nothing better than to order the three bodyguards, who'd barely moved a muscle since they'd climbed out of the Fords, to kill him and end this.

'OK, wise guy. I don't give a flying fuck who you are, who you work for, or what you know. This operation is over. Give me one good reason why I shouldn't shoot you right now.'

'I can give you two, actually,' Richter said. 'This beach may look pretty deserted, but it's not. There are two SAS snipers with rifles trained on you right now.'

The American glanced round uncertainly, then swung back to face Richter.

'You're bluffing.'

'Am I?' Richter asked. 'Left-hand rear,' he murmured.

There was an almost instant bang from the back of the car next to the Jaguar, and the left-hand rear tyre of the Ford blew, the sound followed a split second later by the flat crack of a rifle shot.

'I hope you remembered to bring the spare wheel and a jack,' Richter said, almost conversationally. 'Now,' he continued, 'what I'd like is for your three goons to drop those ugly little MAC-10s right now and then climb back into their cars and shut the doors.'

'There are four of us, and one of you, plus the guys you've got staking out this place. Suppose I just tell my guys to open up?'

'You're welcome to try, obviously. You can probably see a small black object here on my lapel. That's a microphone, and on my belt there's a radio transmitter. Every word you or I say is being listened to by the snipers. The moment you try anything, two of your three men will be taken out. The good news is, they won't feel anything. Then it'll just be two of you looking down the barrel of this combat shotgun. So it's up to you.'

Riyadh, Saudi Arabia

Ahmed bin Salalah paid the driver and stepped out of the air-conditioned cab on the outskirts of the city. He waited on the pavement until the vehicle was out of sight, then made his way swiftly down a succession of side streets, getting further and further away from the main road. He stopped at an unmarked door set in a whitewashed wall and knocked three times. After a few moments a narrow horizontal slit was opened from the inside and he found himself staring into a pair of hostile dark-brown, almost black, eyes. The slit slammed shut, and bin Salalah heard the sound of keys rotating in locks and bolts sliding back. The handle turned, and he stepped through into a narrow hallway. Two heavily built Arabs holding Kalashnikovs nodded a greeting to him and gestured for him to advance. Three doors opened off the hall, two of them closed and one open. Bin Salalah paused at the open doorway and gazed into the room beyond.

Inside, three men sat on large cushions arranged more or less in a circle, a brass tray in the middle of the floor, coffee pots, tiny cups and plates of sweetmeats arranged on it. Leaning against the walls behind them were several assault rifles and two RPG launchers. The men stood up as bin Salalah entered and greeted him warmly. Then they sat down again and all four ate and drank while discussing everything except the immediate reason for bin Salalah's presence. Only when they'd finished and the tray had been removed did they finally turn to the business at hand.

'So, Ahmed,' the oldest man began, 'tell us what went wrong.'

Dungeness, Kent

Johnson stared at Richter, then glanced in the direction from which he thought the shot had probably come – a wide and featureless area of the beach – and then nodded to the three armed men standing nearby. Reluctantly, they lowered their sub-machine guns and placed them on the ground, then walked slowly back to their cars and got inside them.

'So what now?'

'I'd like some answers,' Richter said, 'otherwise the next bullet from the sniper will be aimed straight at you. Now, what was the purpose of this operation? Why exactly did you order Stevens to orchestrate a bombing campaign in Europe and then tell him to ensure the casualties were minimized?'

'Is that what he told you?' The American laughed shortly. 'It was nothing like that. He was just meant to infiltrate a terrorist network, nothing more.'

'Now why don't I believe you?' Richter asked. 'Oh, yes, it's because I talked to Stevens myself, and what he told me is rather different. Last chance, and your choice. I say one word and you'll die right here, right now. Or you tell me what the hell's been going on and then, if I believe you, you might still be able to walk away.'

'Oh, shit,' the man muttered, looking at Richter and clearly not liking what he saw. 'OK, I'll tell you, but just remember I've got diplomatic immunity. If you kill me, or my men, you'll be in a world of trouble.'

'I'll take my chances. Go on, tell me.'

'Look, originally it wasn't my plan, but you're right about The Special Group. That was where the idea came from. I was just tasked with its implementation. You have to understand the atmosphere in Washington. The President was getting worried about America's place in the world. In the first Gulf War, we had the approval of almost every nation on earth. In the second, our only real ally was Britain and the President was concerned even then that British support was starting to slip away. He saw the anti-war protests in Britain and he knew your government is basically weak and too much swayed by public opinion, and he was worried that the "Special Relationship" was starting to unravel.'

'So what did he do?'

'He tasked The Special Group with concocting a scheme that would ensure Britain stayed firmly on-side.'

'How?'

'They looked at the aftermath of the 9/11 atrocity back home, and the way the American people reacted to it. There was a lot of anger and a lot of blame directed at the intelligence community for not preventing it from happening, but the country basically closed ranks against al Qaeda and against radical Islam. Then they studied the July 7th bombings in London and saw that there was almost the same result. A lot of questions were asked about intelligence failures and why that group of men had decided to carry out the attacks, but there was no question of changes in policy or initiating a dialogue with the terrorists.

'The Special Group reported these findings to the President, but he wasn't convinced. He thought the next time America needed public support to take on one of those countries designated as part of the "Axis of Evil", Britain might not be willing to step up to the plate. It wasn't military support he was worried about – America can handle that, no problem – but world opinion is important. What the US can't do is be seen to be acting all alone. We absolutely need at least one other nation to support us, and the only one that's ever done that consistently is Britain. If Britain were to refuse, that would be a serious blow to us.'

'I think I can see where this is going, unfortunately, but carry on.'

'OK. The Special Group came up with a plan. They decided that the easiest way to keep Britain firmly supporting American foreign policy was to launch a series of bombings in Europe, ending with a major attack on London. If it could be established that all these atrocities were the work of radical Islam, The Special Group believed that some other European nations might also decide to support America, which would be a bonus, but a serious assault on London – something like 9/11 – would definitely make Britain join forces with us against al Qaeda and radical Islam, and that was our primary concern.'

'Unbelievable,' Richter muttered.

'That was the briefing Stevens was given. We believed he was the ideal man to handle it, because he had the language skills to pass as either a Frenchman or a German, besides having the right background in Agency work.'

'You mean his career in Clandestine Services?'

'OK, I can see you've done your homework. But I guess you can also see why we mounted this operation, though with hindsight it looks like Stevens wasn't the best choice for the job. How was he minimizing casualties? By calling the authorities before each attack occurred, I suppose?'

'Exactly.'

'It looks like he fucked up in London, because what happened there wasn't exactly what we had in mind. A series of glorified bank robberies isn't really in the same league as the Twin Towers.'

Richter shook his head. 'Those bank jobs were just intended to raise some cash for a German terrorist group and to cause a certain amount of confusion. The real target was a sunken ship in the Thames Estuary, stuffed full of explosives. If that had gone off, we'd have had our very own 9/11 right here in London, thanks to your foul little scheme.'

For a moment the American looked almost pleased. 'So Stevens was on track after all,' he muttered.

Richter shook his head. 'No, not really. That plan was the brainchild of a German named Hans Morschel, and the target was suggested to him by an al Qaeda front man.'

Johnson hesitated. 'So if it had worked, it really would have been down to radical Islam?'

'Yes, oddly enough. But didn't you ever wonder, you Yankee fuckwit, how *we* might react if we discovered that our capital city had been devastated by some crazy plan cooked up by the bloody CIA and The Special Group, on the instigation of the President of the United States?'

'Obviously we considered that, but we decided that the chances of exposure were sufficiently small that it was worth taking the risk.'

'Did you, now?'

'Stevens was a highly experienced agent, very familiar with this kind of operation. We reckoned he had the ability to handle this and keep our involvement secret.'

'And now? Now that we know exactly what you planned and why?'

'It's unfortunate, is all.' The American shrugged. 'I suppose the bomb or whatever this guy Morschel planted didn't go off?'

'It went off all right,' Richter said, 'just not in exactly the right place.'

'And Morschel?'

'He's no longer with us.' Richter paused for a few seconds. 'Do you have any idea how many other people died in this little operation of yours?' he asked.

Johnson shrugged again. 'I've no idea. Quite a few, probably. But they're just collateral damage. You're bound to have casualties in ops of this sort. Eggs and omelettes, that kind of thing.'

'I don't have all the figures myself,' Richter said, in a voice that was low and dangerous, 'but in Onex in Switzerland four police officers died, and the same number in Stuttgart. Then, here in London, Morschel's men slaughtered probably a couple of dozen in all, just ordinary men and women going about their normal business. So that's over thirty people massacred, and you're telling me the reason is just to let the fucking President of the United States of America retain some political credibility.' His voice rose almost to a shout at the end of the sentence.

Johnson grinned at him. 'Politics is a dirty game, and you British need to grow up and recognize that, if you're going to play with us big boys. While you' – he jabbed a finger towards Richter – 'you need a reality check. You might not like it, but we've all got diplomatic immunity, and that means we're untouchable. We're leaving here, and you won't dare try and stop us. Both these cars are armoured, so screw your snipers. My men are aiming their pistols at you right now, so drop the shotgun and back off.'

Richter glanced to his left. In the Ford parked about twenty feet away, both side windows were now open, and in each a figure was clearly visible, a handgun pointing in his direction.

Johnson was absolutely right, and Richter knew he had no real choice. He was probably already in trouble for blowing the tyre on the American's car. You didn't mess with people who had diplomatic immunity. But then he thought about all the people who been blown to pieces by Morschel's truck bombs in London, bombs that had been placed by the German terrorist group, but essentially working to Johnson's plan. And then he thought about the way Stevens had been butchered, and he realized that there really was only one choice he could make.

'Fuck you, Johnson,' he said and tilted his head forward, his mouth close to his lapel microphone. 'Take him out,' he snapped.

Johnson's face turned suddenly grey as he heard these words, and then his body jerked sideways as the sniper's bullet took him in the chest.

And then the three bodyguards in the parked Fords opened up, and before he could bring his SPAS-12 up to the aim, Richter felt three solid punches in his chest as he tumbled backwards, collapsing to the ground beside the parked Jaguar.

Riyadh, Saudi Arabia

'I genuinely do not know.' Bin Salalah spread his hands in a helpless gesture. 'Badri was there on the boat and had full instructions on how to detonate the explosives should the automatic system fail. I know that our objective wasn't achieved, but my understanding is that the explosives on the boat *did* detonate. That suggests that either the explosion didn't provide a high enough yield to cause the sympathetic detonation we expected . . . or something else went wrong. Perhaps the autopilot failed to navigate the boat to the optimum position, or Badri himself became confused and triggered the explosion prematurely.'

'Or perhaps some third party intervened and managed to detonate the explosives well away from the wreck.'

Bin Salalah inclined his head. 'There is also that possibility,' he agreed.

'What of the other incidents in London?'

'I gather those worked exactly as our German colleague anticipated. His men completed their tasks as planned, and as far as I know not one of them was apprehended. And, of course, we are not in any way implicated in these somewhat sordid crimes.'

'I'm pleased that something worked as planned,' the elderly cleric murmured. 'So there really is nothing we can salvage from this?'

'At this stage, no,' bin Salalah replied, 'but I have another suggestion you might like to consider. Not as spectacular a result as this operation would have achieved, but financially almost as destructive to the British – and also with a significant death toll.'

'And just as complicated, I presume?'

'No, much simpler. It will require two vehicles, two controllers, four *shuhada* and approximately half a metric tonne of plastic explosive. And I do not see how it could be detected or prevented.'

The old cleric leant forward, his eyes shining. 'Tell us,' he instructed.

Dungeness, Kent

'How is it, then?' Colin Redmond Decker asked, as he eased Richter into a sitting position against the passenger door of the Jaguar.

'I feel numb, mostly,' Richter said, his breath coming in short and painful gasps.

'I'm not surprised. One of those guys was using a 44 Magnum. That's bound to sting a bit, even with what you're wearing. And where the hell did you get that body armour? We've only just started testing it at Hereford.'

'It was a gift from a friend in Switzerland,' Richter said, glancing down at the Dragon's Skin vest Schneider had sent him and trying a smile for size.

He looked around at the carnage on the pebble beach. One of the Fords – the one that still had all four tyres intact – had gone, powering away from the scene seconds after Johnson's body had hit the ground, and the snipers had made no move to stop it. But when the third body-guard had aimed his pistol from the disabled car at the crumpled shape lying beside the Jaguar, Dekker and the second sniper, also from 22 SAS, had opened up immediately.

Johnson had been right in claiming that the Ford was armoured, but vehicle armour is intended to defend against small-arms fire and will only normally cope with rounds fired by pistols, assault rifles or sub-machine guns. Dekker, however, was using a Barrett, a lethally accurate ultra-long-range sniper rifle that fired a half-inch round, and against that the car's armour had proved completely ineffective. The first round had smashed through the rear window and ploughed on through the rest of the vehicle, virtually cutting the bodyguard in half on its way. The following half-dozen rounds essentially reduced the Ford to scrap metal.

'You're lucky they didn't try for a head shot,' Dekker said.

'It was a gamble,' Richter admitted, 'but American basic combat training always recommends aiming at the centre of the body mass. Particularly with a pistol, which was all those guys had. A head shot is just too difficult: it's far too easy to miss.'

'Right, are you OK to drive now? Or do you fancy nipping over to the Britannia Inn for fish and chips?'

'Another time, Colin. Once I get in the driving seat I should be fine,' Richter said, struggling to his feet. 'But I'll be bruised for bloody weeks.'

'What do you want us to do about this mess? I mean, do you want me to call it in, or just get the hell out of here before the plods arrive and start asking awkward questions?'

'Collect the weapons and any ID these two guys are carrying, then let's get out of here. I'm sure you can play with the MAC-10s up at Hereford. You could make an anonymous triple-nine call from a phone box somewhere near here to get things moving, and I'll call the Kent woodentops once I get back to London and steer them in the right – or rather the wrong – direction. I've got a contact I was working with earlier on during this op and I'm sure I can use him.'

'What's the story?'

'It'll be pretty close to the truth. I taped what Johnson said and I'll feed edited bits of that to Five, just enough to establish that he was the original architect of the scheme. I'll even suggest that when his masters discovered what he'd done, they ordered his termination. There'll be a lot of unanswered questions, but there's enough truth in the story to stop any serious fallout. And I know a senior guy in the Company, so I'll make sure he knows what really happened.'

'What about you?'

'What about me?'

'You ordered the assassination of two CIA officers, both with diplomatic immunity. Isn't Simpson going to want your balls on a platter or something?'

'Probably,' Richter grinned, 'but that's nothing new. In my job, I'm pretty well always in the shit – the only thing that varies is the depth. But I'll survive, I guess.'

'OK, Paul, we'll get out of here now,' Dekker said, as Richter lowered himself carefully into the driving seat of the Jaguar. 'Until next time. And there *will* be a next time, I suppose? Some other op going bad and you need the boys from Hereford to bail you out?'

'You can count on that, Colin. There'll definitely be a next time.'

Author's Note

SS *Richard Montgomery*

The SS *Richard Montgomery* was a dry cargo Liberty ship built by the St John's River Shipbuilding Company at Jacksonville, Florida, completed in July 1943 and named after an Irish soldier killed in the assault on Quebec in 1775. In August 1944 the ship embarked 6,127 tons of assorted munitions at Hog Island in Philadelphia and immediately sailed for Great Britain, arriving in the Thames Estuary in preparation for joining a convoy to Cherbourg.

Upon her arrival, Acting Lieutenant-Commander R. J. Walmsley, the King's Harbour Master, ordered the ship to anchor in a berth off the northern edge of Sheerness Middle Sand, despite the fact that at low tide the water depth there was a mere 24 feet, and only 30 feet at high water. As trimmed, the *Richard Montgomery* drew about 31 feet – 3 feet more than the 28 feet of most Liberty ships – because of the weight of her cargo. The discrepancy was quite obvious to the assistant harbour master, Roger Foley, who tried to berth the ship elsewhere, but he was overruled by Walmsley. Foley refused to carry out the original order unless it was put in writing, which Walmsley declined to do, and Foley left the office.

On 20 August, the *Richard Montgomery* began drifting towards Sheerness Middle Sand, driven by a northerly wind and buoyed by a spring tide. Despite nearby ships trying to attract the attention of her crew, nobody on board the *Richard Montgomery* did anything constructive until the ship actually ran aground, when they all took to the lifeboats. This was the worst-case scenario: the ship was heavily laden and had struck the sandbank at high water.

As the tide ebbed, the ship stuck fast, and a further problem soon became apparent. The Liberty ships were built very quickly, using a welded plate design – the record for completion of a ship from laying the keel to launching was under five *days* – and, as the *Richard Mont-gomery* settled onto the sandbank, her welded hull plates began cracking open, a noise audible over a mile away.

Salvage operations commenced almost immediately, and over the next weeks about half the cargo of munitions was successfully removed, holds numbers four and five and the mast locker being completely emptied. Four days after grounding, the hull split just forward of number three hold, flooding that hold, and numbers one and two, virtually stopping any further salvage efforts in them, and the ship broke her back early in September.

The wreck was finally abandoned on 25 September, by which date only 2,954 tons of munitions had been removed, and no subsequent salvage attempts have been made. The contents of holds one, two and three were virtually untouched, leaving nearly 3,200 tons of high explosive, mainly 250-, 500-, 1,000- and 2,000-pound bombs, white phosphorus smoke bombs and cluster fragmentation bombs in the wreck, a mere 3,000 yards from the seaside town of Sheerness.

Roger Foley was posted to another department immediately after the ship grounded, to ensure that his evidence wouldn't be heard at the subsequent Board of Inquiry. Bizarrely, despite the fact that the grounding of the vessel was entirely caused by Walmsley's gross incompetence, the ship's captain and chief officer were found guilty of placing their vessel in a hazardous position.

Since 1944, the wreck has broken into three pieces and has sunk a little way into the sand, but is still only just below the surface, the masts clearly visible. The remains are cautiously inspected by divers every year or so, and there have been representations to the British Government by everyone from the people of Sheerness, who are pretty much at ground zero, to the American Government, which still nominally owns the cargo, suggesting it might be time to either remove the explosives or make them safe. Every approach has been rejected, presumably on the grounds that the wreck isn't close enough to Westminster to be of any real concern to the politicians.

It's argued by some that the longer the wreck stays there, the safer it gets. This suggestion is somewhat naive, because the bulk of the explosive material is TNT which, just like the plastic explosives C4 and

Semtex, is largely unaffected by submersion in water. The reality is that the *Richard Montgomery*'s cargo is just about as lethal today as it was when the ship was stranded.

In 1970, the British Government produced a report which estimated that the explosion of the wrecked ship's cargo would punch a 1,000-feet-wide column of water and debris 10,000 feet into the sky and generate a wave over 15 feet high. It would be the world's largest ever non-nuclear explosion.

Sheerness and the surrounding areas – including the oil refinery on Sheppey, and the eastern end of the Isle of Grain – would suffer catastrophic damage. And the destruction wouldn't stop there. It's probable that the wave resulting from the explosion would swamp Canvey Island, South Benfleet and Southend-on-Sea on the south Essex coast. It would also sweep into the Medway and cause flooding in Rochester, Chatham and Gillingham. But possibly the most destructive effects of the wave would be felt some distance away. The narrowing Thames Estuary would have the effect of increasing the height of the wave as it approached Greater London. It would probably overwhelm the Thames Barrier and flood the lower-lying areas of the city, including much of the Underground system and the road tunnels under the river, causing considerable loss of life and widespread destruction that would take months to rectify.

The explosion would be, quite simply, the biggest economic and environmental disaster ever to strike the United Kingdom, infinitely more destructive than all the bombs and V-weapons that fell on London during the Second World War, and equivalent to the north-east corner of the Isle of Sheppey being hit by a tactical-yield 1.5 kiloton nuclear weapon.

The Special Group

The Special Group was created by President Eisenhower under the auspices of the National Security Council as a sub-cabinet level organization. Then known as the 5412 Committee, it was tasked with oversight of all the country's clandestine operations and, more importantly, of insulating the president from official knowledge of those operations. The Special Group was, and is, the most secret organization in America.

The name has been changed frequently – over the years it's been known by numerous innocuous titles such as 'The 303' and 'The 40 Committee' in a modest attempt to muddy the waters – but its concept and purpose have remained unchanged. Normally headed by the president's National Security Advisor, and including the Director of National Intelligence (formerly the Director of Central Intelligence until this post was disestablished after 9/11), the Secretary of Defense and the Secretary of State, The Special Group approves all sensitive, and especially all illegal, activities proposed by the CIA.

These 'projects' have included the various attempts to assassinate Fidel Castro; building and operating the U-2 spy plane; Iran–Contra; the murder of Salvador Allende in Chile in 1973; financing anti-government rebels in Mauritius; attempts to destabilize the Libyan regime; providing the *Mujahadin* in Afghanistan with money and weapons to counter the Russian invasion; and money-laundering plots almost without number. The latter included the smuggling of a ton of pure cocaine into the United States from Venezuela in 1990, cocaine that was later sold on the streets of America after a complex and unworkable plan to ensnare drug traffickers had failed.

Each of these ventures was, of course, approved by the then president, but never in writing. The Special Group would assess the viability and utility of each proposed operation, and brief the president verbally about it. If he agreed, also verbally, the CIA would be directed by the Group to implement the plan. If – or, more likely with many CIA operations, *when* – the operation failed or was exposed to public scrutiny, the president could legitimately disavow all knowledge of it, and the lack of any paper trail would support that denial.

As with so many political matters, what's important isn't the truth, but what somebody can *prove* to be the truth.